Immortals:
The Gathering

IMMORTALS:
THE GATHERING

JENNIFER ASHLEY

LOVE SPELL NEW YORK CITY

LOVE SPELL®

September 2007

Published by

Dorchester Publishing Co., Inc.
200 Madison Avenue
New York, NY 10016

ISBN-13: 978-0-7394-8930-7

Printed in the United States of America.

ACKNOWLEDGMENTS

I would like to again thank Joy Nash and Robin Popp for being such fabulous authors and collaborators on this series. Thanks for giving me such fun characters to play with! It was a terrific ride all the way. Also thanks to Leah Hultenschmidt at Dorchester for keeping us all sane and on track, and for the production and art departments for their hard work and wonderful covers. I must also thank Diane Stacy at Dorchester for being supportive above and beyond the call of duty.

And thanks to readers who have stayed with and enjoyed the series thus far. As always, read more about it and upcoming adventures at the series Web site: www.immortals-series.com.

Lastly, thanks to Forrest—but he already knows that.

IMMORTALS:
The Gathering

CHAPTER ONE

Hunter always hated to wake up. This time it was from a sound sleep, made sweeter by the presence of two females, one on each side of him, the three forming a warm nest on a Minnesota April night.

What . . . ?

Pain jerked him like clamps trying to tear him apart. Hunter sat up, naked and sweating, ready to blast whatever it was with his magic. But the bedroom was dark and quiet; no sign of any intruder, no sense of one. He doubled over and clutched his chest, struggling for breath. And just as suddenly as it had come upon him, the searing agony disappeared.

What the hell?

Hunter would know if anyone had entered the house. He'd put his hand to the lintel of the front door when he'd come in, marking wards to keep away both danger and inquisitive neighbors. Nothing had been disturbed that he could sense. No death magic had crossed the boundaries, no spell.

Hunter was still trying to catch his breath when the

1

cat of the house stalked by. It sank to its haunches, slitted green eyes meeting Hunter's own green eyes. It projected in the way of cats, *My bowl might be empty, maybe you should check.*

Hunter warily slid out of bed, doing his best not to wake the sleeping women. He eased a pair of jeans over his bare hips, retrieved his sword in its leather sheath he'd left leaning against the dresser, and padded barefoot to the kitchen, followed by the cat.

The house was silent. The two women lived in an ordinary neighborhood in an ordinary town in northern Minnesota and had found an ordinary method of keeping warm at night. They hadn't questioned the fact that Hunter carried around a large sword, and in fact innuendo about it in the bar tonight had led to him coming here at all.

These days most humans were afraid to walk the streets without a measure of alcohol in them to give them courage. Demon attacks had escalated of late. People hired witches to ward houses and businesses, and to provide amulets of protection, but most witches weren't strong enough to deflect demons that came en masse.

So humans stayed indoors as much as possible and drank more and laughed louder. Minnesota was farming country, but this year the ground had remained frozen too long, and Hunter heard muttering about crops not being sown on time and strange weevils infesting anything farmers managed to plant.

The two women seemed to sense that Hunter possessed incredible life magic and had purred at him until he'd given in and accompanied them home. After all, protection of humans was his Immortal warrior duty. They didn't smell of death magic; not demon-whores, but friendly young women who enjoyed men.

In the kitchen Hunter found the cat food and dispensed a measure into the almost-empty bowl. The cat twined itself around his ankles, projecting the thought that this human male was preferable to the ones who usually turned up.

Hunter suppressed amusement as he put away the bag of food. He'd figured he was the boy toy of the night, and he didn't mind at all. He made it fun and asked nothing in return. Once upon a time he'd thought of lovemaking connected with family and children and happiness, but painful experience had taught him otherwise.

He walked out of the kitchen to check the rest of the house when pain jerked him again—deep, searing magical pain that reached inside to yank him apart. Clenching his teeth, he gripped his sword and waited.

The cat lifted its head and chewed, bits of food dropping from its mouth as it mewled. With that soft sound, the comfortable kitchen suddenly shattered into large, jagged pieces, hurling Hunter away from the cat, the warm house, and the Beltane night into cold and darkness.

He saw far away a glaring light, heard voices chanting in unison. In the middle of the light stood an impossibly tall man with a hard face and coal-dark eyes. He knew the man, had last seen him seven hundred years ago in a battle in Scotland. In front of the man stood a woman in blue robes wearing a garland of flowers in her dark hair. She was chanting, chanting, chanting.

Hunter started to say, "What the f—" when the world splintered again, and he felt himself spinning and twisting uncontrollably through darkness.

He landed on something hard, the wind knocked

out of him. A warm, ocean-scented breeze wafted across his body; then someone with scalding hot breath and a face full of fur kissed him on the lips.

Leda Stowe awoke in the dawn light. The electronic clock on her bedside table told her it was a half hour before the alarm would go off. From the kitchen she heard the slow drip of the faucet that never shut off right, but other than that, her house held silence.

She lay still, stretching her witch senses to decide what had awakened her. Outside she heard the usual rush of wind in palm trees and the crash of breakers on the beach, the tide at its height. No throb of a helicopter or a motorboat, not even her animals making noises in the night. But every sense she possessed told her the wards around her island had just been breached.

In the front of her mind were the threats from the animal "collector" from whom Mukasa, the African lion in her largest enclosure, had been rescued. Diego Valdez, head of a Mexican drug cartel, had been incensed when an animal-rescue organization had liberated the abused Mukasa, and he'd vowed to get his lion back, by force if necessary. This little island of rock and beach, though technically belonging to California, lay very near the waters of Mexico.

Leda lifted the tranquilizer gun she kept next to the bed and opened the box in the bedside drawer to load it. Tranquilizer darts worked equally well on human beings as on a hurt big cat in a frenzy. The human would be out long enough for her to call the coast guard or the Drug Enforcement Administration who patrolled these waters.

She pulled on a T-shirt and khaki shorts and slipped on her sneakers. Her enclosures right now held only two animals, the lion Mukasa and a Japanese bear called Taro. Taro was waiting until facilities were ready for him in Hokkaido, where he'd be transferred back into the wild. Mukasa's fate was yet to be determined.

Valdez's threats aside, both animals were valuable to unscrupulous collectors who would sell them for untold sums, dead or alive. Leda's wards were strong, her air magic enhanced by the trade winds that blew continuously across the island. No one should have been able to breach them.

She walked onto the veranda with the rifle in one hand and her radio in the other. The radio was better than a cell phone out here, because she knew there would always be a coast guard dispatcher on the other end. She hung the radio on her belt, then reached behind the door and snapped switches that flooded the compound with light.

Taro reared up against the twelve-foot chain-link fence of his large enclosure, grunting a greeting. He was a curious animal, liking to watch everything she did, and Leda felt a measure of relief that he seemed unhurt and unbothered.

Mukasa, on the other hand, did not appear. Leda went down the wooden steps and walked quietly across the sand. She saw nothing out of the ordinary—no boat rocked next to her own sailboat, the helipad and airstrips down the beach were empty, and no lights glittered on a craft out to sea. She heard nothing but the wind in palms, the roar of waves sliding up the beach.

Something moved in Mukasa's enclosure beyond the pool of light, something upright and human that skulked in the shadows. Leda lost her temper. The threats of the drug lord enraged rather than frightened her, especially after what Valdez had done to the noble Mukasa.

She drew power from the air around her and traced a rune of protection with the toe of her sneaker, pouring her magic into it. A faint yellow glow danced from the rune, the color of air magic.

She cocked the rifle and aimed it at the gate. "I see you in there," she called. "Come out. *Now.*"

Mukasa walked into the circle of light, growling the deep, grunting growl of an irritated lion. Relief trickled through Leda that he was still alive, unhurt.

"I'm waiting," she said clearly. "I will fire this weapon, and believe me, I'm a dead shot."

She sensed the man in the enclosure homing in on her rune in the sand. What was he? Witch? Demon? But she sensed no death magic from him. Of course, a strong demon or vampire could hide its death magic—not a comforting thought.

The man walked forward and stopped behind the inner gate. Each enclosure had two gates with a small passage between—opening and closing one gate at a time ensured that the wild creature inside wouldn't charge out whenever Leda or her assistant had to enter the enclosure.

The gates were about six feet high. The man inside stood a good six inches taller, and his shoulders were nearly as wide as the gate. The lights of the compound glinted off golden highlights in his hair, but the shadows didn't let her make out his features. She sent a cautious tendril of magic toward him to learn what he was.

The blast of life magic that returned nearly knocked her over. He exuded life magic; it roared out of him to crash like the breakers on the beach. Before her startled eyes, sand rushed to fill in her rune of protection, erasing it completely.

"Come out," she repeated in a hard voice. "Leave my lion alone."

Mukasa padded over to stand beside the man. The lion, with his full mane and massive girth, came up to the man's chest. Leda watched, amazed, as Mukasa rubbed his head against the man's torso.

"Is she always like this?" the man asked her lion. His voice was deep and low, the kind that had a place in dreams of the most erotic kind. It was a voice that hinted of sultry nights and cool linen and pleasure she could scarcely imagine.

Mukasa made a faint answering noise in his throat. The man opened the gate, moved through the passage in what Leda could only describe as a saunter, and started to open the second gate.

"Close the first one behind you," she called.

"Why?"

"Because he'll get out, that's why. Mukasa is smart enough to get around you."

"He wants to come out. He wants to see what's up there." He pointed to the dark cliffs rising from the palm-lined beach. The hand that made the gesture also held something long and thick, a sword or some such weapon.

"Close that gate, or this dart goes into your chest."

The man looked back at Mukasa. "You'll have to stay behind for now, my friend."

The lion grunted, then turned and walked back into the deeper part of the enclosure.

The man closed the gate behind him and opened the second gate. He shut that one as carefully and stepped into the light.

Holy Goddess of the Moon.

Not only did his voice come from her erotic dreams, so did his body. A tall, hard body in nothing but a pair of jeans that rode low on his hips. A tattoo of some kind peeked over the waistband. He had arms thick with muscle, a chest of honed pectorals dusted with golden-brown hair, hips tight below a narrow waist, thighs outlined by denim, and strong, bare feet.

The lights of the compound accented the gold in his hair, and the eyes that studied her from an impossibly handsome face were emerald green. She could imagine those eyes half closed in seduction, fixed on her as though she were the only woman in the world.

Bedroom eyes, her mother would have called them. *Watch out for those.*

He held a sword sheathed in leather, its hilt thick and plain. A fighter's weapon.

"Put your sword on the ground," Leda commanded.

To her surprise, the man obeyed. He gently dropped the weapon and looked at her expectantly, bare toes curling in the sand. "Why did you bring me here, witch?"

"I didn't."

"To fight?" he went on as though he hadn't heard her. "Or for sex? I hear some slaves hate women summoning them for sex, but me, I'm all for it."

Slaves? Summoning? Sex?

"I didn't summon you."

He took a few steps toward her. "Do you have anything to drink? I could murder some coffee."

"Stand still and tell me who you are and why you're messing with my lion."

He didn't stop. "I'll make the coffee, I'm good at it.

Then we can talk about the summoning. Or your lion. Or sex. Whatever you want."

Was he insane? Probably. Too bad, but just because he was utterly gorgeous and exuded magic that nearly floored her didn't mean he wasn't dangerous.

He kept walking toward her, leaving footprints in the sand. His smile was lopsided, his hair mussed, sand clinging to his jeans and bare torso. He was delectable.

"Did Valdez send you?" she croaked.

"Valdez?"

She felt his magic concentrate and slide around her, and knew her own power was nothing in the face of his. His magic could make her drop the gun, fall at his feet, anything he wanted. Her island, her home, and he'd take it over with a sheathed sword and a crooked smile.

She shot him.

His green eyes narrowed, and he looked at the dart protruding from his left pectoral.

"A tranquilizer?" he said in mild surprise. "How interest . . ."

His right leg folded under him, his eyes rolled back in his head, and he toppled limply to the sand.

CHAPTER TWO

When Hunter awoke, the sun was high. He lay on a bed scented with the beautiful woman who'd shot him, a smell like the sea and lemon and fresh air.

His woman stood in the bedroom doorway speaking quietly to a man. The man was fairly tall and carried a big radio, the annoying noises of which had woken Hunter.

She looked as lovely as she had over the barrel of her shotgun. Sun-streaked brown hair was pulled back into a sloppy braid, probably to keep it tamed while she slept. Unbound, it would hang to her hips and be lush and thick as it spilled over his hands. Her eyes were deep, dark blue like the middle of the ocean on a summer day.

He imagined those eyes heavy in passion, her hair pooling on his chest as he held her in his arms, on this bed maybe. She could ride him and purr with contentment as he cradled her hips and bathed his senses in her.

She wore shorts that revealed long, strong legs. Not

slender, bikini-model legs, but tight, muscular legs tanned from the Pacific sun. She was tight all over, as though she worked out, but she retained a soft femininity that stiffened a certain part of him.

The other fact that stiffened him was that she hadn't put on a bra. Her white T-shirt clung to her chest, her pink-brown aureoles plain to see. The man with her kept trying not to look, with limited success.

Hunter yawned and stretched, liking sinking into the soft pillows of this woman's bed. "Where's that coffee?" he demanded.

The man and woman broke off their conversation and stared at him. "Who are you?" the woman asked.

"I'm Hunter. Who are you?" He swung his legs out of the bed, still dressed in his jeans, which had gotten sand all over the nice white sheets. "Just point me at the kitchen. I'll find the coffee myself."

The man blocked his way to the door, eyes narrowing. "You don't have any ID."

ID, ID, the people of the twenty-first century were obsessed with ID. Time was you could tell someone your name and they'd take you at your word. Nowadays, you had to prove it with cards and photographs. Even a letter from your parents wasn't good enough anymore. Not that his mother liked to write letters. Destroy entire cities, yes; pen correspondence, no.

"Must have left it in my other pants," Hunter said. He stretched again, loosening cramped muscles. "What was in that stuff?" he asked the woman, rubbing the back of his neck. "My head is buzzing."

The woman gave his body an appreciative glance but pretended not to. She liked what she saw—a good start.

The man looked annoyed. "You live here?" Hunter asked him.

"I'm with the Institute," the man answered, as though Hunter should know what that meant. He pulled out a leather wallet and opened it to reveal an official-looking license. A man who liked ID and lots of it. "Ronald Douglas. Give me a good reason I shouldn't call the police and have them take you in."

"Give me a reason you should." Hunter glanced from Douglas to the woman. "You two lovers?"

The woman's cheeks burned pink, but Douglas scowled. "Why aren't you carrying ID? What is your business on this island, and what were you doing in the enclosure? Hiding drugs? Or were you sent here to steal the lion?"

"Why don't you ask the lion? What did you call him—Mukasa? He likes that name, by the way."

Institute-man didn't look happy, though the woman shot him a thoughtful glance.

"I am asking *you*," Douglas snapped.

"I never carry ID," Hunter responded. "I have no business on the island, I don't know why I was in the enclosure, and I think taking drugs is the same as shoving your head in a blender. Sex is much better. Now let me ask some questions." He shifted his gaze to the woman. "What is your name, do you like chocolate, why are you alone on an island with a lion and a bear, and if you're not having sex with Douglas here, would you have it with me?"

The woman's cheeks burned scarlet. "Real subtle, aren't you?"

"People can waste so much time on subtleties. I've watched them live a lifetime believing they're sending the right signals and die before realizing they didn't. Are you going to tell me your name, or do I have to ask the lion?"

"It's Leda," she said quickly, then looked slightly surprised she'd blurted it out. "Leda Stowe."

"Leda." He rolled the name on his tongue. He wanted to lie in bed beside her and unbraid her hair and say that name. *Lee-da.* It tasted nice. "A woman so beautiful Zeus took the guise of a swan and wrapped her in his powerful wings to seduce her."

Leda continued to blush, so pretty. Douglas's frown deepened. He might not be sleeping with her, his glower said, but he hoped to, and he didn't want Hunter there.

Hunter scrubbed his hands through his hair. "I need to shower. I smell like lion." He looked around the bedroom but saw no door to a bathroom. "You do have a shower? Or do you hose off outside?" The interesting picture of Leda washing him off and he doing the same to her tightened his cock a little bit more.

"It's on the other side of the kitchen," she said.

That meant that when Leda rose in the morning, she'd walk, all mussed and sleepy-eyed, across the house to get to the shower. Any man living here, even if not sleeping in her bed, would see her drift through in robe and slippers or whatever she chose to wear. He imagined fabric clinging to her lithe body the same way the T-shirt clung to her now.

He moved to the bedroom door, but Douglas blocked his way. "Where do you think you're going?"

"I said. To take a shower."

"You aren't going anywhere near that bathroom before I search you."

Leda lost her smile and rolled her lower lip under her teeth. She didn't know what to make of Hunter, and she wasn't yet convinced he was not a criminal.

Hunter laced his hands behind his head and directed his words at Leda, his smile widening. "Fine, then, search me."

Douglas had him back up against the nearest wall and spread his legs, frisking him before Hunter could take another step. Hunter let him, though he could have blown the man out of the house with a flick of his fingers. He decided to be polite.

Douglas came up empty-handed, which of course he would. Hunter's only weapon was the sword they'd already confiscated, his drug of choice, coffee.

"Nothing," Douglas told Leda in disgust. "I do mean nothing."

Hunter hadn't bothered to put on underwear before he'd pulled on the jeans back in the house in Minnesota. "Satisfied?"

Hunter gave Douglas a grin and proceeded out the door. He found a good-sized room that had a kitchen setup on one end, living-room furniture on the other. On the wall opposite was another door, presumably to the bathroom. Once in the living room, Hunter stopped and spun around, losing his smile.

"The world isn't right," he said to Leda. "You're isolated here, but you feel it, I know you do."

Leda's lips parted in surprise. Lush red lips, and he enjoyed a nice fantasy about frisking *her* against the wall.

"You do know," he went on. "You sense the imbalance, and I'm betting it's why I'm here. Mukasa knows it."

She continued to stare at him in shock. She was a witch, of course she would have felt the draining of life magic that had become a deluge of late, and he needed to find out what she knew. After he had a shower—in her bathroom, using her towels, her soap, her shampoo.

He grinned at her one more time, then entered the bathroom, all white tiles and feminine smells. He slammed the door shut, stripped off his pants, turned on the water and plunged under its stream, whistling.

He sang in the shower. Leda brewed a pot of coffee, desperately needing caffeine after being yanked out of bed at five a.m. and confronted with an incredibly virile and handsome stranger who confused the hell out of her. Behind the bathroom door he sang in a loud, off-key baritone, anything from Irish ballads to Hank Williams, Junior.

She should be terrified of this man turning up out of the blue, and all she could speculate on was what his tall, hard body looked like wet and soapy in the shower. When he'd blatantly asked if she'd have sex with him, she'd nearly blurted out *yes*.

It had been so long since she'd even considered going to bed with a man, and here she was imagining in detail what it would be like with Hunter. She knew Ronald Douglas hoped she'd sleep with him, but they'd both recently come off bad relationships, and he was giving it time. She appreciated that. Now a stranger gave her one smile, and she was ready to rip off her clothes for him. What was the matter with her?

Ronald sat across the table from her, arms folded, while she pretended to peruse the newspaper he'd brought. Douglas worked for the Institute for the Preservation of Exotic Species, keeping watch over several projects, Leda's rescue shelter only one of them. He visited officially once a month, but they'd become friends, and he let her know he was only a radio call away if ever she needed help.

"Do you want me to have him arrested?" Douglas asked. "You have grounds; he was trespassing."

"Not yet." She felt a curious reluctance to see Hunter taken off the island with his hands manacled behind his back.

That thought catapulted her into a vision of Hunter, brawny arms pinned behind him, catching her gaze with his hot green eyes. She shivered, rubbing her arms.

Douglas watched her, waiting for her to explain, and she said quickly, "I want to talk to him."

"About what?"

"He's right about something being wrong with the world." She met Douglas's gaze. "I'm pretty remote out here, but I've been noticing bad things going on. My circles have gotten strange—I have to summon some hefty protection any time I want to do even a small spell. I've gotten nowhere near the rain I should have, and even the fish are starting to seek other waters. You know the gray whales practically live in my lagoon in January, but this year there were only a few, and no calves born. And the newspapers are full of nasty stuff."

She pointed to an article about more bad vampire attacks in the heart of Los Angeles. Usually vampires were fairly civilized and adhered to rules to feed only from the willing fools who pledged themselves as blood slaves. But suddenly gangs of vampires had gone wild, rampaging and killing with abandon. The newspaper said only the help of one of the master vampires in Los Angeles kept things from getting completely out of control.

Thank the Goddess for small favors and honest

vamps. She'd also read of demons murdering humans and life-magic creatures in places as far away as Manhattan and beyond to the U.K. and the rest of Europe.

"All of which doesn't make me want to leave this guy on the loose," Douglas said.

"He doesn't feel evil. He has so much life magic it could toss me across the room."

"Oh, good, I feel better. A complete stranger breaks into your compound, arriving God knows how—there's no boat or plane or copter anywhere—and you don't want to have him arrested because he doesn't *feel* evil."

"Something like that."

"You still don't think Valdez sent him to get the lion?"

She shook her head. "I doubt Valdez would send someone so, well, *charming*. And certainly not a man with such an amazing aura of life magic."

Demons could take the form of incredibly seductive men, she well knew, and this Hunter was certainly seductive, but no way could demons exude life magic like Hunter did. He didn't have the look of the Sidhe, but some of the half-Sidhe were very human and could be troublemakers besides. He could also be a witch, but he seemed wrong for that. The only thing she knew for sure: Hunter was *not* a normal human being.

Douglas started to answer when the water in the bathroom stopped and the singing ceased. A few seconds later, Hunter emerged, dripping wet, a towel wrapped around his waist.

Leda closed her eyes, trying to get her libido under control. If he was sexy in jeans, in nothing but a towel he was downright devastating. His hair, dark with water, was slicked back from a broad forehead, droplets from the ends beading on his shoulders. The towel revealed the tattoo that his jeans had half hidden, a pentacle—a five-pointed star surrounded by a circle. The symbol of the Goddess and the five elements: air, earth, fire, water, and the fifth, all-encompassing element of Akasha.

She'd never known a man who exuded such raw sexuality. She considered Douglas attractive, but Hunter was walking carnality. Any woman who met him would want to fling herself between the sheets with him, and she got the idea he didn't protest about that too much.

Hunter sent her a smile as he headed into the kitchen. He picked up a filter heaped with extra coffee Leda had ground and inhaled deeply, closing his eyes in reverence.

The coffeemaker beeped, its brew cycle finished. Hunter took up the pot and dispensed coffee into a mug. He leaned against the counter, set the cup to his lips, and drained the contents. His throat moved with his swallows, the stubble on his chin flashing gold in the light.

"Isn't that hot?" Douglas asked.

Hunter upended the cup and caught the dregs on his tongue. "Best way. You want some?"

He poured coffee into the mugs Leda had left on the counter and carried all three to the table. Leda switched her gaze to the newspaper, pretending not to watch him approach. He moved like a wild animal himself, in some ways like a big cat or a wolf.

Was he Were—a shape-shifting werewolf or werecat? That would account for his extreme life-magic aura plus his sexiness. Werewolves tended to draw you in with their eyes, and most had muscular good looks. Or if female, striking beauty.

No, still not right. She could tell Weres by their eyes—they had a predatory *otherness*, as though they could shift into their animal form at any moment. Hunter's eyes were clear, lucid green and regarding her with burning intensity.

Hunter took the chair next to Douglas and shoved a cup of coffee under the paper at Leda. She hastily thrust the newspaper aside and found him grinning at her, his strong fingers on the handle of her mug.

She snatched the coffee from him, trying not to touch him. "Why did you keep telling me how Mukasa feels? Are you an animal empath?"

Hunter lifted his cup and took five long swallows of coffee, then wiped his mouth and licked droplets from his fingers before he answered. "Close, but not quite."

"There are animal empaths?" Douglas asked.

Leda nodded. "I know one or two witches who can communicate with animals, not exactly telepathically, but they understand them. I'm assuming that's what you are?" Leda directed at Hunter. "A witch?"

Hunter only smiled. Mr. Cryptic. He gave Douglas a sideways glance just as Douglas's radio went off. Annoyed, Douglas rose from the table and crossed the room to have a serious conversation into his walkie-talkie.

Hunter continued to sip coffee, draining his second cup. He got up to pour another as Douglas returned.

"I have to go," Douglas said, clearly unhappy.

"Hey, don't worry about us." Hunter gestured with his cup. "We'll be fine."

"You're coming with me," Douglas informed him. "Leda is too kindhearted to want you arrested, but I want you out of here. I'll drop you off on the mainland and let you go if you promise to leave Leda alone and never come back."

"Can't do that." Hunter put down the coffeepot and took a gulp from his steaming mug. "Promise to leave Leda alone, that is. She needs protection, and I'm protecting her."

"The coast guard and DEA watch these waters pretty closely."

"Not good enough," Hunter argued. "Fine against humans, but not against the badness I can protect her from. Leda won't be safe unless I'm here."

Douglas gave him a narrow-eyed stare. "You're missing the point. I want Leda safe from *you.*"

Hunter sat back down at the table and rested one brawny arm on the top, cradling his cup. "She's plenty safe from me. I never hurt innocents." He sent Leda a wink.

She fingered her cup, trying to keep heat from flooding her body. "How do you know I'm innocent?"

"I just know," he answered softly, then turned to Douglas. "Anyone who tries to hurt her will have to deal with me. Go back to your Institute. Sounds like it's urgent."

Leda hadn't been able to decipher the blurred radio conversation, but maybe Hunter had better hearing.

"Yes," Douglas said, again unhappily. "They need me."

"Don't let us keep you. The door's that way."

"I'll be all right," Leda said to Douglas. She wasn't sure about that, but she couldn't keep him from his duties. "I can radio if I need help."

"I'll be back," Douglas promised.

After a few minutes they heard his small helicopter

warming up down the beach. It rose, the air throbbing, then faded into the distance.

"Never thought he'd leave." Hunter set down his empty mug and leaned across the table to Leda. "Want to go to bed now?"

"No," she said in a hard voice.

"You do. You just don't *want* to want to."

"Douglas isn't wrong about not trusting you." In fact, now that the neutral third person was gone, Leda felt the room warming, pheromones flying off Hunter in waves.

He gave her a smile, feral and handsome and raw. "No, he's not wrong. I am dangerous, Leda. I am the most dangerous being you'll ever meet in your life, including vampires and demons. I eat demons for breakfast. I am fantastically dangerous."

His power began to fill up the room, her own witch wards splintering and falling away in the face of his incredible magic. Then *his* magic seeped into the lines left as her wards burned out.

"What are you doing?"

"Protecting you. Darkness is moving in the world, but this place . . ." He looked around. "This place will be free of it. A haven for you. Don't leave it."

"What, not ever? That would be inconvenient."

"Why should you want to leave it? It's beautiful here. For now, you will stay here and not be hurt. When it's safe, I'll lift the wards and let you out."

Alarm came to her full blast. "Are you saying you're trapping me here?"

"For your own protection."

Leda stood up fast. She believed him. She'd never felt magic that strong from anyone alive—or undead, for that matter.

"Don't. I don't want to be trapped. I don't like . . ." Her old panic stirred. *Don't trap me, let me out.* Her mouth felt dry, her hands cold and sweaty.

"Now you know why Mukasa wants out of his enclosure," Hunter said.

"But that's different. He was hurt. It's for his protection so he won't get hurt more."

Hunter quirked his brows, and she realized her mistake.

Leda sat down again. For some reason, she was willing to accept that he knew how her lion felt, that he could trap her here, that he was a god of sexuality.

"Are you a god?" she asked on the off chance.

Hunter's cup stopped at his lips. "Not—quite."

"What, then?"

"How did Mukasa get hurt?" he countered.

Leda sighed. "A drug lord named Valdez had him tortured to entertain his guests. Chaining him first, of course, so he couldn't fight back. I'm surprised Mukasa didn't attack you. He was abused enough to fear and hate human beings, or beings who look human."

"He doesn't hate *you*."

"No?" She suddenly found herself curious about what Mukasa thought of her. "Well, I do feed him, and I haven't tried to hurt him."

Hunter set down his mug and wandered to the wide living-room window that let a semitropical breeze glide through to cool the house. His body drew her attention, especially the towel just slipping from his hips.

"Mukasa is grateful to you," Hunter said. "He was frightened when he first came here and didn't know what was happening, but he gradually understood you'd taken him from a bad place. You healed him, yes, but you also gave him back his dignity."

Leda came to stand by the open window with him. Below the veranda, black rocks gave way to beach, long stretches of golden sand that encompassed most of the island. To the west, cliffs rose, sheer black volcanic rock studded with succulents and palm trees. A mountain stream and a waterfall cascaded from its highest peak. A mini tropical rain forest all her own.

Hunter's body warmth, damp from his shower, touched her. She wanted to ask him about the tattoo on his pelvis and trace it with her fingers, wanted to see if his eyes would darken in desire as she dragged her fingertips along it.

"Tell me your story," she said. "How did you get here?"

He shrugged. "I was feeding a cat in Minnesota. Next thing I knew, I had Mukasa licking my face and you pointing a rifle at me."

"You don't know what happened?"

"Something ripped me from Minnesota and deposited me here. I figured it was you. Did you perform a Calling?"

"No. Can people Call you? Summon you, I mean?"

"Witches can. But it hasn't happened in seven hundred years. I saw a flash of one of my brothers. Maybe he was being Called too."

"Why don't you ask him and find out?"

"Because I don't know where he is. I haven't seen Adrian in, oh, seven centuries."

Leda went silent as she digested the information he'd given her. *I'm powerfully magical, but someone summoned me here. I don't look a day over thirty, but my brother and I haven't spoken in seven hundred years. I'm dangerous and I've trapped you here, but don't worry, I mean you no harm.*

"You're not a vampire, are you?" she asked suddenly. "One with a really good glamour spell?"

A vampire excellent at seduction could mask his death magic. But witches usually could see through that. Still . . .

Hunter started to laugh. He yanked open the door and sprinted outside, down the steps of the veranda and straight into the bright light of the morning.

It was the first day of May, Beltane, and the sun shone with all its might. Hunter spun around in the sand below the house and spread out his arms. "There. Believe me?"

The sun kissed his tanned and broad shoulders and sinewy arms. Wind blew his wet hair back, the sun burnishing red and gold highlights in it. He was no vampire. Even a very powerful Old One would have been a pile of dust by now.

Then before her startled eyes, Hunter whipped the towel from around his waist and tossed it onto the sand. The first thing she noticed: no tan lines. Just strong, muscular legs, taut hips, and a long, thick cock that made her wonder breathlessly how large he'd be when erect.

Right now he was laughing at her. "Nice day for a swim," he announced. "Join me, Leda."

Without waiting for her reply, he turned and jogged down the beach, giving her a full view of his tight, compact backside. He was a beautiful man, and his body in motion was incredible. So incredible she had to sit down on the nearest chair and watch him, her heart beating hard and fast.

CHAPTER THREE

Hunter knew Leda hadn't followed him. She was simply fighting feelings of *should not* that some humans had. She didn't understand the concept of *live life now,* but he could work on that. That was all an Immortal who is not allowed to make ties with anyone could do: live to suck the juice from every glorious hour.

Hunter had his own code: Don't harm innocents; do kill evil beings. An easy existence, one that let him survive and forget. Hunter needed to forget so much.

He ran out into the waves and whooped as the cold water closed over him. The tide picked him up off his feet and began to run out with him, and he let it. Inside their cages, Mukasa and Taro grunted and growled. They wanted to play in the sunshine too.

Hunter used his magic to open the cage doors. Leda was watching him, but didn't notice what he'd done until Taro came bounding down to the beach. Mukasa followed more slowly, still recovering from his wounds and not as thrilled about water as the Japanese bear.

Hunter heard Leda shriek, "Hunter, what have

you—" But her words were cut off when Taro barreled into him under the water.

He came up again to see Leda standing on the sand outside the tidal pool, barefoot but still in shorts and a T-shirt. Her hands rested on her curved hips, wind whipping her golden hair, the sun shining through her clothes. A beautiful, delectable woman.

"There are sharks out there!" she shouted.

"They won't bother us."

Mukasa lay down on the sand and proceeded to groom his huge front paws. Taro wanted to play with him. Released from confinement, the bear rediscovered his wildness along with joy that he'd found a playmate. Hunter and Taro wrestled and swam, raced and tussled until finally Hunter crawled up on the beach and flopped on his back, breathing hard.

Taro played in the water awhile longer, then trundled out of the waves and shook himself all over Hunter and Mukasa. Mukasa growled and heaved himself up, giving Taro a look of disgust. Leda had already retreated to the veranda, but Hunter heard her laugh. Sweet music.

He projected thoughts to the two animals, not words, but thoughts they'd understand. *Give us a little privacy, will you?*

Both animals retreated into their enclosures. Leda stared after them in surprise, but she made no move to lock the gates. Good for her. The creatures needed to roam, or their healing would never be complete.

Hunter retrieved the towel and used it to brush the sand from his body, then wrapped it around his shoulders and approached the veranda. Leda met him at the top of the steps with an armful of clothes, her gaze carefully avoiding the region of his lower abdomen.

"What are those?" he asked.

"Your jeans and a couple of T-shirts Douglas left behind."

Hunter lifted the plain gray T-shirts. They'd fit, but it'd be a little tight across the shoulders. "Why does he have clothes here?"

"He always brings clean ones," she said. "Taking care of the animals is messy business, and big cats like to spray."

Hunter imagined Douglas drenched in odoriferous cat fluids and chuckled. "And you're sure you and he aren't lovers?"

She regarded him in amazement. "Of course I'm sure. Why do you assume we are?"

"Why wouldn't you be? You are beautiful, the island is remote, exotic." He traced her cheek. "How could any man resist you?"

She blushed under his touch, which made her eyes starry. "They resist."

"No." He thought he understood the measure of her. "You give them no encouragement, and they are polite enough not to take what isn't offered."

She hugged the clothes to her. "You're wrong. They are not remotely interested in a divorced woman with a Ph.D. in animal behavior."

"They *are* interested. Douglas wants you, I saw it in his eyes and heard it in the way he spoke to you. He's furious that I'm here and he isn't." Hunter blew softly on her cheek. He could weave a spell to make her surrender, but that wouldn't be as satisfying as her falling on her own.

"Are you married?" she challenged. Her eyes flickered once in desire, but she held herself back.

"I used to be." He felt a prick of sadness, but he

wanted her to know. "I had a wife called Kayla and two beautiful little children, a boy and a girl. My wife came from what is now Hungary."

"And you split up?" she asked.

"They died. A demon killed them. Even my two babies."

Hunter didn't like grief, and he'd done his best to bury it deep. Everything he'd done since their deaths—every wild act, every kill, every sexual hijinks—had been to make himself forget. And here he was, sharing his pain, something he'd never done for another living being. His brothers knew what had happened, but they'd never, ever mentioned it to his face.

Leda put her hand on his cheek, which was wet with tears. "Goddess, Hunter, I'm so sorry."

He kissed her palm, tears dropping unheeded from his eyes. "It was a long time ago."

"How long?"

"Nine hundred and forty-eight years." He met her gaze, stunned to see her eyes wet as well. "I still miss them."

"You keep on missing them. Who was this demon?"

She had the look. Hunter recognized it from when he'd looked into mirrors through the centuries, from polished bronze on up through silver gilt. It was the look of vengeance, the need to right the wrong.

"Leave it alone. I'm looking for him, believe me, but I don't want him taking you away too."

"Hunter, I used to belong to a very powerful, worldwide group called the Coven of Light, which has some of the strongest witches on the planet. I quit them for personal reasons, but there are one or two I could contact and ask to help—"

"No!" Hunter growled. "This demon is an Old One who escaped eons ago, I don't know how. I fought him and lost. Lost." He stepped closer to her, needing her to understand. "Witches, even great ones, can't defeat what I can't."

"That sure of yourself, are you?"

"It's only the truth."

She stared up at him, undaunted. Hunter thought that perhaps he should go away and leave her alone, with his protection firmly covering this place, to keep her from learning more about him and his demon. He started to brush the tears from his eyes and found his arm gritty with sand.

"I need to shower again."

He walked past her into the house, and she followed on his heels. As soon as she closed the door behind them, she said, "Wait."

He turned around to find her against him. She dropped the extra clothes and put her hands on his bare chest. Her face turned up to his, her eyes dark and her invitation clear.

The lips she offered were sweet and cool. He kissed her lightly at first, wanting to get to know her. She ran her fingertips up his arms and down his back, as though she wanted to know him too.

She had the finest-smelling hair, and it was soft as gossamer. He knew part of the scent came from the shampoo he'd found in the bathroom, a spicy, not flowery, scent. He laced his fingers through her sloppy braid, loosening it.

Leda seemed fascinated by his tattoo, which he'd gotten when he'd come of age to show the world he was one of the Immortals. That was back when the world had cared. She traced it with curious fingers, which was fine with him, because it put her touch right above his rising cock.

He slid hands under her T-shirt, finding apple-firm breasts to fit his hands. Pulling the shirt off over her head allowed him to feast on her neck, lick her collarbone, kiss his way down to the aureoles, dark and tight for him.

He would get sand on her sheets, he thought as he unbuttoned her shorts and dipped his fingers inside. He found the heat between her legs, slick and hot.

But that's all right, his thoughts continued, as he and Leda drifted down to the sofa. *I'll wash them.*

She kissed him hungrily—as if she'd been wanting to kiss someone for a long time, to abandon herself to sex but feared to. She could abandon herself now, fine with him. Any frustration she needed to slake, he was here for her.

Leda made a raw noise in her throat and dug her fingers into his back. He swirled his tongue into her mouth, loving her sweet-hot taste. Not much longer now and he'd be buried inside her, ready to forget one more time. . . .

And someone touched his wards—he felt it tingle through his body. Leda sensed it too, breaking the kiss with a gasp.

The sound of a man's voice down at the water lifted to them. Hunter began to raise his head to look out the window, but Leda dragged him back down.

"What?" he whispered.

"I didn't hear a boat, and that voice is not Douglas's."

Hunter hadn't heard a boat either, no putter of an outboard engine coasting in to moor. Listening hard, he could make out a scraping sound that he knew was oars in oar locks; then came the sound of an aluminum boat scraping on sand.

Voices again. Two men spoke Spanish, one with an American accent. Hunter understood them, and Leda seemed to also. At least they weren't magical—he would've felt that.

"They've come for Mukasa," she hissed. "Bastards. Haven't they hurt him enough?"

Hunter gave her a grim nod. "I'll make them leave Mukasa alone."

He tried to get up, but Leda dug into his arms again. "Be careful, Hunter. They work for one of the nastiest drug lords in Mexico. They probably brought an arsenal with them."

"Doesn't matter."

"*Hun*ter!"

He disengaged her hands and slid from the couch to the floor. Quietly he dressed in jeans and a T-shirt and moved in a half crawl, half crouch across the room to the bathroom. The bathroom was dense with shadow— less chance of them seeing him when he looked out its tiny window.

He spotted the boat they'd rowed resting half on the sand, with a large, strong cage nestled inside it. Out to sea a yacht drifted, with several figures moving on it.

The two men who'd come ashore didn't speak much, but Hunter gleaned that they planned to drug Mukasa, dump him in the cage and chain him, row back to the yacht, and make for Valdez' compound on the Mexican coast. One man's jacket flapped open, and Hunter saw the butt of a pistol in a shoulder holster.

He left the bathroom and crawled swiftly back to

the sofa. "Two of them," he breathed. "Armed with pistols, probably automatic. They have no magic. This will be easy."

Leda had put on her T-shirt, but her shorts were still undone, showing an enticing strip of red silk panties beneath. "I've only got the tranquilizer rifle."

He grinned, his fighting instincts up. "I have my sword."

"Against two guns? Are you crazy?"

Hunter kissed her hard, enjoying the taste of adrenaline and anger. "You lie low. I'll take care of this."

Giving her one last kiss, Hunter grabbed his sword and strode out into the sunshine.

Leda saw Hunter's shadow cross the living-room window as he moved silently as a cat toward the beach. She had the radio to call Douglas, but she feared to turn it on in case the static and chatter sounded across the silence. If the men heard the noise, they might turn around and see Hunter, and she had no doubt they'd shoot him.

She slid to the floor and made her way to the bathroom so she could watch out the window. The animals at least stayed put. They distrusted humans and usually kept to the far edges of their enclosures when Douglas came around. In fact, the only human they'd responded to besides herself was Hunter.

She saw Hunter step quietly, barefoot, from the veranda to the rocks and then down to the beach. Near the house, a rivulet of water formed a stream that cut a groove through the sand. Hunter stepped over the stream and drew his sword from its leather scabbard. The blade was not straight, but squiggly, like a writhing snake.

Dropping the scabbard to the sand, Hunter hefted the sword and called out, "Hey!"

The two men whirled around, wide-eyed, but they reacted fast. Black pistols leapt into their hands, and without waiting, the men fired.

Slam, slam. Two bullets hit Hunter in the chest, right over his heart. Hunter fell back onto the sand, his eyes wide and blank, his head landing in the stream of water. Blood blossomed in ragged circles on his white T-shirt, and the ends of his hair floated in the water.

No! Leda silently screamed. *Oh, no.* Her vision blurred with hot tears. The beautiful, primal man, so alive, so quickly dead like so much meat. Hunter didn't deserve to die this way, bravely defending her and the animals.

Her throat squeezed with sobs, and she fought them back. If she ran out there swearing and shrieking as she longed to, they would shoot her too.

She had to get to the radio, no matter about the noise. Douglas was quick and resourceful—he'd have someone out here as fast as he could. Even if Valdez's men got Mukasa to the yacht, the coast guard or DEA would hunt them down and arrest them. Leda would testify that she witnessed them murder Hunter and steal Mukasa. They wouldn't get away with it.

But Hunter would still be dead.

She dashed the tears from her eyes. The radio was in the kitchen, on the table with the unwashed coffee cups. Her best opportunity for not being caught would be when they entered the enclosure to drug Mukasa and drag him out. She'd have to watch and wait.

Poor Mukasa. She hoped he'd understand. She felt momentarily surprised that Mukasa hadn't come bounding out of his open enclosure to Hunter's defense, but perhaps the lion had sensed he could do nothing.

The two men stepped over Hunter's body and retrieved a tranquilizer rifle from their boat. Leda was so intent on watching them that she missed Hunter unfolding himself and getting to his feet.

She almost screamed when she caught the movement of his arm as he brushed sand from his hair. He walked—no, he stalked—toward the men, sword hefted, blood trickling from his mouth.

"Hey!" he bellowed again.

The two men swung around, then stared, open-mouthed. Hunter swung his sword, the blade making a whistling sound.

"Now you've pissed me off," he stated.

The two men recovered from their surprise and opened fire. Hunter laughed out loud and swung the sword in a sharp arc. The air before him shimmered and the bullets struck *plink, plink, plink* against the barrier he raised, then fell harmlessly to the ground.

The men unloaded everything they had at him, shooting in blind panic until their pistols clicked on empty clips. They glanced at each other in alarm, then back at Hunter.

The glittering shield dissolved as Hunter walked through it, sword raised. He was laughing as he tossed his sword from hand to hand, sinews working.

"Let's have some fun. You want me to do this with or without the sword?"

As the two men exchanged another glance, Hunter raised his sword over his head. It burst into flames, yellow-orange fire licking up and down the blade, pale in the bright sunlight. The two men whirled and ran for the boat.

Hunter chased them. The men were in good shape—they'd have to be in their profession—but Hunter, stayed right on their heels. They reached the boat, throwing themselves against it to push it into the water.

Hunter stopped and watched them with a grin, lowering his sword and choosing to let them go.

Something glinted out on the yacht. Leda snatched up binoculars she kept hanging by the door and glared through them out to sea. Damn Valdez, he ran a high-tech business.

"Hunter!" she yelled as she ran full-tilt out the door. "They have a *grenade launcher!*"

The two men leapt into the boat, rowing frantically to get out of the line of fire. Hunter, his face streaked with blood and sand and grime, raised his fire-flickering sword over his head.

Leda felt impossible magical forces flowing from the sky and sea and island itself into the sword Hunter held high. She felt her own magic flow out to join the mix, a strange sensation of being drained and boosted at the same time.

Hunter drew in a breath and shouted one word. She didn't understand it, but out on the yacht, a man screamed loud enough to carry over the water.

Leda jammed the binocs to her eyes and saw a streak of fire go up from the grenade launcher. The man wielding it hurled it into the sea, where it exploded in a plume of spray. The yacht rocked dangerously, and she heard its motor hum to life.

Again a surge of magic, and again Hunter cried something in a strange language. The sea swelled. The rowboat shot across the water to the yacht, and then a huge wave heaved both rowboat and yacht away from the island, sending them toward the mainland—fast.

The sea roiled and bubbled in the wave's wake, then rushed back to fill in the hollow space. Inside his enclosure, Mukasa let out a growl that sounded for all the world like laughter. Taro climbed the wires of his cage, grunting his approval.

The calming sounds of the island returned—the wind in the rocks, the rustle of palm fronds, the wind chimes on the veranda, and the calls of birds in the cliffs.

Leda flung the binoculars onto a table and sprinted down the steps and across the sand where Hunter was doing a victory dance on the beach. He whooped and laughed and shouted at the fast-disappearing boats.

When she approached, he dropped the sword and caught her by the waist, whirling her off her feet and around and around.

"Woo-hoo!" he yelled. "I haven't had that much fun in a long time. I sent them straight into the arms of your DEA friends. But I can sink them if you want."

"No!" Leda wriggled out of his embrace and dragged the hair from her eyes. "You scared the shit out of me. I thought they'd killed you."

She looked at the dried blood on his chin and the burned holes in his T-shirt, and her eyes widened. She touched a bullet hole, and he winced.

"Careful, love, it's tender."

"They did hit you! Why aren't you dead? Or dying?"

His smile was dazzling. "Because I'm an Immortal, sweetheart. I meant to tell you. I thought this would be a more entertaining way to let you know."

"Entertaining? Me standing at the window thinking you were dead?" She shoved him. "You call that entertaining?"

"I didn't think you'd care whether I lived or died. I invaded your island and drank all your coffee."

"Of course I care. I was about to jump your bones. I haven't wanted to do that in a long, long time. Do you think I'd do it with someone I didn't care whether he lived or died? What is wrong with you?"

"Many things," he said, sobering suddenly. "Many things are wrong with me."

She was too impatient to reason out what he was saying. "Besides, you didn't have to let yourself get shot. You obviously can make a shield." She gestured sweepingly with her hand.

His grin burst forth again, making his green eyes dance like warm sea in the sunshine. "But my way was more fun. Did you see their faces? I thought they'd wet their pants."

"Fun for who? I was the one inside bawling for you."

He brought his fingertips up to brush her cheek. "You cried for me?"

"Yes. Why shouldn't I?"

He stared at her as though stunned. He'd been shot through the heart, had used incredible magic to defeat villains, knew the thoughts of a lion and a bear, and kissed like fire, yet the fact that she had shed tears for him seemed the most bewildering thing in the world.

He stroked the pad of his thumb across her cheek. "Why would you cry for me?"

"I don't know. Because you're . . . I don't know. So alive, I guess."

"I embody life magic."

"That's not what I mean. You're magical, yes, but

you're the most *alive* person I've ever met. Don't ask me to define it."

He gave her an odd look. "And yet I am dead inside. A thousand years ago, I died, but I can't die. So I live and live and live."

"And I've only understood about one word in six since you got here."

He traced her cheek again. "Why should you need to understand me? Why not just *be* with me?"

"I like to understand things."

"There's nothing to understand, Leda. We have the ground and the sky and the sea and each other. We need nothing more."

"Everyone needs something. Goals, dreams, other people. A purpose." She knew she was babbling, but couldn't stop herself. "Without those we aren't alive."

He went silent a moment, then lay his hand between her breasts, right over her heart. "What is your purpose, Leda Stowe? What do *you* want?"

Changing the subject, was he? "That's easy. To help animals. To stop people abusing them."

"Why?"

"Why?" She stared in surprise. "Because they don't deserve cruelty. Because I can help. Because—"

"I mean why are you *here?* Why not in some office working for a save-the-animals place? Why are you doing it yourself?"

"Because I can—"

"Everyone has reasons. What did you do that made you want to hide on an island and baby-sit lions and bears?"

Leda wet her lips. No one had ever asked her point-blank why she'd abandoned a lucrative office job to come out here and try to make up for what she'd done. Hunter was a life-magic being; she did not want to tell him the truth, not yet. She'd never get him to understand.

"It seemed like a good opportunity," she said lamely.

He laughed. "Liar, liar. Did you come here for penance?"

"Yes." The word escaped before she could stop it.

"I know all about penance." His look was strange. "Before I leave here, you will tell me everything. All about you and why you're here and why you decided to dabble in death magic."

She pushed away from him sharply. "How the hell did you know that? Wait a minute—did the Coven of Light send you? They refused to see that what I did was necessary, not that I liked doing it. There's a difference."

"I'd never heard of the Coven of Light until you mentioned it."

Her words died on her lips. He was so powerful that she'd had the wild idea that the Coven had sent him to spy on her.

"Then how did you know?" she demanded.

"It lingers on you. Very faint." His eyes darkened. "You must have been desperate."

"I was."

"Did it work? Or backfire on you?"

"It worked."

"For a price?" Hunter's eyes were sharp. "And your Coven could not stand what you did worked, that you bent it for good and were willing to pay the price?"

"Something like that. But I don't want to talk about it. I don't know you. I'm not spilling my guts to you."

He glanced at her abdomen. "No, I would not like your guts to spill out. I'd rather you stayed whole."

"How on earth do you not know that idiom?" She caught sight of his grin. "Wait, you do know; you're being a pain in the ass."

"That's what my brothers call me. 'Hunter, that crazy pain in the ass.'"

Changeable was what he was. Sweeping from sadness to the twinkling grin, to grim worry, to interrogation, back to a sexy smile that promised hours of pleasure. She'd never met anyone or any*thing* like him.

Far out over the ocean, something rumbled, and the island moved beneath her feet. "Earthquake," she gasped.

Hunter caught her against his very strong body. She again enjoyed his male scent, his strength, the feel of his hands on her back, the wild salt smell of ocean on him.

The tremor subsided as quickly as it came. Not a very big one, probably the aftershock of a larger quake somewhere out to sea. The island had tremors at least once a week, bigger ones every couple of months.

"It's nothing," she said. "You can let go of me now."

Hunter wasn't listening. He stared intently at the rocky cliffs above them, his stance and expression like some she'd seen on Mukasa. She turned to follow his gaze, but spotted nothing unusual.

Hunter released her carefully. "Leda, go inside the house."

"What is it?" she asked, but then she felt it too.

The taint of death magic, a wave of it unmistakably strong pouring toward her and the island. Gray-black clouds streamed in from the sea, north to south, riding on winds of unimaginable speed. The ocean began to boil, sudden whirlpools spouting, then dying. If she felt incredible life magic from Hunter, this was its equivalent in death magic.

"Holy Goddess, where is that coming from?" she asked. "Did I bring it here?"

"No," Hunter said quietly. "I did." His face looked strangely pale as he kissed her on the lips. "Go inside."

She wanted to argue—she was a witch, she should stay and protect her animals—but the look on his face made her stop. His eyes held a plea for her to keep safe from whatever was this menace. He needed her to. Maybe all those years ago his wife had ignored his plea and stayed to fight, dying for her bravery.

Leda knew Hunter was strong enough to shove her into the house and lock the door without her being able to stop him, but he let it be her choice. She nodded once and turned away. She could always watch from the window and throw in her magic if needed.

The animals were smart enough to hide deep inside their enclosures, and Leda saw nothing of them as she climbed the steps to the veranda. She closed the door behind her, shutting out the terrible wind.

Darkness blotted out the sun and changed the cheerful daylight into gloom. Clouds spun overhead like the eye of a hurricane, the wind picking up loose debris and flinging it across the waves. How Hunter could stop this or fight it, Leda had no idea.

She tried to tap the wind to feed her magic, except this air was fetid, and she touched something sticky and foul, with a bite of sulfur. Outside, Hunter sat cross-legged on the sand, his sword lying in front of him. He rested his hands palms up on his knees, like a yoga pose, lifted his head, and closed his eyes.

The magic that came from him was quiet and subtle, nothing like the roiling madness above them. Leda sensed his breathing, slow and steady, his mind calm in contrast to the storm. Magic flowed from him, strong like the ocean. Without fanfare, the magic doubled and tripled, growing in silent waves like a gently rippling lake on a summer day.

Leda watched the waves rise and flow like clear glass, spreading to encompass the entire island. Hunter was hiding them. Whatever entity stalked them from above would see only wave upon wave of endless ocean. She'd never felt such magic, never seen anyone use so strong a spell against something like *that*.

The darkness lasted for almost an hour. It tossed and roiled above them, fingers whirling down to create water spouts in the sea, but it never found the island. Leda waited and watched, holding her breath, while Hunter sat motionless, the magic quietly flowing out of him.

And then the blackness suddenly vanished. The sun emerged as the inky clouds dispersed, the wind dying into a peaceful breeze that kissed the island. The darkness receded to the northern horizon, then disappeared altogether.

Hunter lowered his hands and opened his eyes. Leda expected him to fall over backwards after performing magic like that, but he sprang to his feet like he had energy to spare. She left the house, and he met her, sliding his hands to her hips. Warm hands, and fire in his eyes, the remnants of magic.

"It's gone," he said. "What do you want to do now? Go to bed?"

Leda wanted to talk about his spell and how he'd conjured such magic, but his touch distracted her.

"You've been trying to get me into bed since you got here."

"You say that like it's a bad thing."

"Something's going on, Hunter," she said severely. "Something dangerous—you said so to Douglas and me. We should talk about it."

"I don't mind talking about it," he answered. "Maybe after we have sex?"

The bullet wounds behind the torn T-shirt had already closed, pink puckers where the holes had been. Her head came to his chin, and she looked up at his square, strong jaw dusted with whiskers.

"How is it possible?" She touched the warm skin of his chest. "You're healed from something that should have killed you, my lion didn't try to eat you, and that spell was bigger than anything the Coven of Light could do with all their magic combined."

"I told you. I'm an Immortal." He swept her up into his arms before she could stop him and started carrying her to the house.

"Hunter—"

"Later."

"Hunter." She said the name loudly as he kicked open the door. He needed to know. It wasn't fair to him if she didn't tell him. "I can't have sex with you."

"Yes, you can," he said. "It's easy. I'll show you."

She took a deep breath. "I have death magic inside me. Buried deep. If you touch it—Goddess knows what it would do to you."

CHAPTER FOUR

She looked up at him, eyes shining with tears. Hunter brushed one from her lashes. "Don't worry," he said. "It won't hurt me."

As she stared at him, not understanding, Hunter carried her into the house and made for the bedroom.

His body hummed with need. Adrenaline had streaked through him when he fought Valdez's men, and again when whatever evil had come rushing at the island. He'd had to draw on all his power to keep the big bad from finding them, had to connect with the bones of the island and with every bit of magic he could find in it. He'd drawn from the animals in their enclosures and the island's wild creatures, and Leda.

Touching Leda's magic had been incredible, a pure sweetness like the clean ocean air. Even so, he'd seen the taint, the darkness that stained her and tried to feed on her soul. He'd have to do something about that, but right now, his body screamed for release.

She was a soft armful, athletic Leda, her body honed from her work with the animals. The windows in the sunny bedroom were open, letting in the warm breeze and the scent of ocean. She'd painted the board walls white to capture the airiness—she would, since her magic drew its strength from the air. The bed sheets were rumpled where he'd earlier thrown them off, and he laid Leda on top of them.

He quickly stripped off his clothes, sand raining to the floor, and jumped onto the bed, landing on his side next to her. His cock was already stiff, stretched tight with wanting. She half lay, half sat against the pillows, watching him with worried eyes.

"Isn't this better?" He pushed her white T-shirt up and off over her head. "No bullies in yachts, no demons." He dipped his head and nuzzled between the perfect globes of her breasts. "You smell so damn good."

"Demons?" she asked quickly. "What demons? Did they send that darkness?"

He raised his head. Her hair straggled across her shoulders, her nipples dark against her white skin. He could feast on her.

"Hunter, what demons?"

"Only one demon, sweetheart, an Old One probably, coming to find out who used words of power out here in the middle of the ocean. I should have been more careful, but he shouldn't have been able to find me so fast. He's gone now."

Explanation done. He rolled on top of her, loving the way the points of her breasts rubbed his skin.

"Hunter."

Hands on his back, nails grazing his flesh, her body moving under his. His lips teased hers open and he slid his tongue inside, tasting her goodness and feeling something ease in his heart.

She pushed at his chest. "Hunter."

"What, sweetheart?" He nuzzled her cheek, the heat of her throat.

"You have to tell me which demon. It's very important."

"Demons are boring, love. Old Ones always go by various names, so even if I knew, the name probably wouldn't mean anything to you. They pretend to be seductive and good in bed, but it's all illusion. *This* is real."

He reached between them and unclasped her shorts. He remembered the peek of red panties beneath them, and under that he found her smooth skin, sweet softness, a swirl of wiry hair warm and quite wet. He wanted to taste her, if his needy cock would give him the time.

Leda pressed insistent hands to his shoulders. "Hunter, we have to talk."

"Why?" he asked as he worked shorts and underwear from her body. He dropped her clothes to the floor and leaned to her again. "What's to talk about?"

"You don't want to have sex with me."

"Yes, I do." He took her hand and guided it to his very stiff erection. "I really want to, can't you tell?"

Her eyes widened slightly at the feel of his huge shaft against her hand, but she shook her head. "You're beautiful, Hunter, and you saved Mukasa from being kidnapped, and you're . . ." She gulped back whatever she was going to say. "But I can't."

"I won't give you a child, if that worries you," he said. "I can choose to, or not."

"I told you, I have death magic in me."

"I remember. You said so on the porch."

Tears sprang to her blue eyes. "Why aren't you repulsed by me? You have the strongest life-magic force I've ever sensed."

She was distressed, and her distress touched him. Here he was, a big, bad Immortal warrior and she feared she would hurt *him*.

He rolled onto his back and gathered Leda against him. "Tell me about it, pet. Who were you trying to save?"

"How do you know I was trying to save someone?"

"Because I see how you take care of your animals, that you'd do anything for them. You decided to sacrifice yourself to a demon to help someone you cared about."

"Yes." She closed her eyes briefly. "I didn't know what else to do. I summoned a groth demon—they have the best healing powers, although you have to talk fast to convince them to use them for you. Mostly they heal their victims so they can torture them some more."

"I'm familiar with groth demons." He'd killed plenty of them.

"One answered me. They're hideously ugly, but he gave me the power, using me to direct the magic. Goddess, it was horrible. I felt so violated."

Demons fused with the witch who dared to summon them, melding with them psychically, rampaging through their minds all they wanted. The demon imprinted himself on the summoner, leaving a little piece of his death magic behind forever. They could make even the strongest humans seem weak and useless and dependent on further contact with them.

"So what was his price for giving you his oh-so-powerful death magic?"

She scowled at him. "What do you think?"

Hunter knew damn well what the demon had asked of beautiful Leda. He clamped down on rage that the demon would dare touch her.

"I haven't had sex with him," she said quickly.

Hunter regarded her in surprise. "He didn't ask for sex? They always ask for sex."

"He did. But not then. We made an appointment to meet later, in Los Angeles. He put a spell of compulsion on me."

"Ah," Hunter said. "They like to do that—make their victims stew about what's to come. But that's good. When's the appointment?"

"At the end of this month. Why good? I'm surprised you haven't gone off in disgust."

"And leave you?" He touched a lock of her hair, sleek and warm beneath his fingers. "I don't think so. I mean it's good because when you keep the appointment, I'll go with you and pull the demon's head off. Problem solved."

"You can't," she said in alarm. "If you kill the demon, the healing spell will reverse."

"No, it won't. I won't let it. Tell you what, we'll find my brother Tain. He's a healer—it's his special gift. He can't heal us Immortals, but he can heal anyone else. I haven't seen him in seven hundred years, but he'd be handy to have around."

"How many brothers do you have?"

She wasn't really interested, not in the front of her mind, not now, but she wanted to talk about something besides the demon.

"Four," Hunter answered. "All pains in the ass, like me. You can tell we're related by our tattoos."

He placed her hand on the tattoo on his lower abdomen, with the five-pointed star in the circle. The star represented the elements, and it also represented the five Immortals.

Her fingers lightly traced the star. "You are all tattooed—right here?"

"Tain's is on his cheek, Darius has one on the back of his neck. Kalen's is on his thigh, and Adrian, my oldest brother, has his on his butt."

She started to laugh. Good, he was easing her tension.

"I'll kill the demon for you, love," he promised. "You'll never have to touch him."

"Why would you do that for me?"

"Because I'm a sweetheart. And I like you. You should have summoned an Immortal in the first place when you wanted help—I thought you had."

"I had no idea you existed," she said. "Or how to summon you if I did."

"Someone does." He frowned, struck by a thought. "Maybe your coven of witches found the old Calling spell, and I ended up here by accident. You could ask them for me. You have e-mail?"

He said that more to prompt her to tell him why she'd left the coven at all, but she shook her head. "I don't have much contact with the mainland except through the radio. No phone lines, no cable, no Internet. I don't have the equipment to set up through satellite. Too expensive."

He slid his hand up her bare hip. "We'll call when we go back to the mainland, then."

She stared. "What do you mean, when *we* go back to the mainland?"

"To meet your demon. We'll kill him, find out what's going on, then enjoy ourselves."

"Sure," she said without conviction.

He rolled onto her, pulling her down in the bed beneath him. "I want to make love to you now," he said softly.

"You only met me this morning," she pointed out. "And I shot you with a tranquilizer."

"And I woke up in your bed, thinking how sexy you are."

She blushed. "You think I'm sexy?"

"Hell, yes."

Losing himself in a woman was a good way to let go of the world, the pain, to forget himself and not come out for a while. For a long while.

He could linger with Leda in this place away from the world, making love to her in the sunshine. He didn't mind helping her solve her demon problems in return for days of oblivion.

Her braid had come half unraveled in the wind, and he lifted the weight of it as he pressed a kiss to her throat. Another kiss in the heated space between her breasts, then to her abdomen, his tongue teasing the indentation of her navel.

"What are you doing?" Her voice was a little breathless.

"Getting to know you better."

She half laughed, half gasped as his lips traveled past her navel to her lower abdomen. She tasted like salt and spice and a special taste all her own.

"I've never done this before," she said.

"No?" He pressed a kiss to the top of her mons, where her honey-colored hair lay in a delicate whorl. "Didn't you say you were divorced? Which means you were married, and presumably had sex. Or maybe that's why you got divorced—he wouldn't give you sex. Or wasn't good at it."

"I mean I've never gone to bed with a stranger—especially only a few hours after meeting him."

"You shot me and dragged me into your house," he said between kisses. "I ran off the bad men and saved us from a demon attack. You told me about you—not everything. And I told you about me. We aren't strangers anymore."

"Did you tell me everything about you?"

"Most of it. There's not much to tell."

She shivered as his mouth came down on her. Her hips rose involuntarily, her legs parting the slightest bit.

"I have a feeling there's a lot more to you than you're letting on," she breathed.

"Not really."

He placed his hands on her thighs and dipped his tongue between them, tasting the honey that flowed with her excitement.

"Goddess," she breathed. "What are you doing to me?"

He chuckled and didn't answer. It was a rhetorical question anyway.

He could stay with her for years. And why not? If the world was going to hell, why not ride it out with her? The Immortals were forgotten, unheeded. So many people got off on letting vampires suck their blood or demons suck their souls, and they didn't want to be rescued anymore. Well, he would rescue Leda from her groth demon, and then they could retreat here and enjoy themselves.

"I'd kill every demon in the world for you," he said into her skin.

Hunter enjoyed killing demons, sometimes for fun going to a demon bar and wiping them out to the last one standing. Sure, demons had rules and codes, and there were paranormal police that made sure they followed the rules, but they were still demons. No one cried very much to find them slaughtered in the morning.

He raised his head. "But right now, I want to make you come."

"You're crazy, do you know that?"

"Yes, I do." He licked the taste of her from his lips, savoring every drop. "Leda," he said, "do you want me to show you how to get rid of the death magic inside you?"

"Is that possible?"

"Yes."

He moved his body up so they lay face-to-face, body to body, his stem sliding between them, not yet in her.

Her eyes shut him out. "I always thought that when witches dabbled in death magic, it never left them," she said. "The death magic gets inside the witch and starts to eat her soul. Before she starts, she thinks that she can handle it, but she can't."

He kissed her forehead. "That's because she doesn't have an Immortal to help her."

"Really? Sorry, that wasn't in the witches' manual."

"That's because Immortals have long been forgotten."

"I was joking."

"I wasn't," he said.

Her eyes were so sad. Leda believed it—she thought she was doomed. Witches who dabbled in death magic became more susceptible to demon attack and vampire seduction and enslavement by death-magic creatures. Death magic seduced as much as vampires did, making the witch want more and more.

Leda had known the danger, yet she had gone ahead with the ritual. The groth demon had taken advantage of her desperation, easily permeating her with his magic. For that, Hunter would kill him.

"I can take it from you," he said softly. "Will you let me show you how?"

She looked worried. "Will it hurt you? Touching the death magic?"

"Not a bit."

She gnawed on her lip, not reassured. Hunter touched her thighs, parting them.

"Let me in," he whispered, "and I'll fix everything."

CHAPTER FIVE

Leda should have known his "cure" would involve sex. Hunter had been trying to seduce her since he walked out of her lion's enclosure, and she was blithely letting him.

The weight of his body on hers, his heat blanketing her, excited her beyond belief. Ever since her divorce and the terrible events that had led to it, she'd been emotionally numb. She hadn't been able to respond to any man.

Then this stranger dropped onto her island from nowhere, and suddenly she was letting him carry her to bed, letting him undress her, letting him kiss her and taste her intimately. She felt so *needy* for him, and his tongue on her clit had sent fiery sensations through her she'd never felt before.

Only her sense of fair play had forced her to be honest with him, to warn him of her death-magic taint, though she'd feared he would run far and fast when she told him.

But he'd only shrugged and said it didn't matter. In

a few short hours this man had stripped every defense from her, every wall she'd built between herself and the world. She'd not made herself vulnerable to anyone in a long time.

She wanted Hunter, his utterly gorgeous, raw-muscled body, his green eyes framed with thick lashes, his cocky smile, his casual disregard of terrible things.

He said *Come with me, I'll make you forget,* and she held out her hand and answered, *Please.*

He slid inside her, huge and hard. She bit back a groan, lifting her hips to clasp all of him.

Hunter closed his eyes. "Goddess, you feel good."

"So do you."

She ran her fingers along his back, liking how strong and heavy he felt on top of her. He kissed her for a time, not moving, letting her get used to him inside of her.

"Do you want to get rid of the dark magic, Leda?"

"Of course I do."

"You have to want to let it go before I can show you how."

"I want to," she said sincerely.

He kissed the corner of her mouth, lips warm and heavy. "Then open yourself to me."

She couldn't help smiling; he was in her and so hard. "I thought I already had."

"With all of you. Not only your body, but your heart and your spirit."

"How?"

He touched her forehead. "You know of the chakras?"

She nodded. "The energy centers?"

"You're going to open them to me. One at a time."

"Like in tantric?"

His eyes lit in interest. "You do tantric?"

"I know the theory. Never had the pleasure," she said with faint regret.

She knew witches who used tantric to perform spells, aligning energy with their partners, then directing it in an orgasmic burst to create incredible magic. Or so she'd heard. Her husband had not been a witch himself, always hesitant about trying "that magic stuff."

"It is pleasure," Hunter said. "Believe me."

"I'm not sure what to do."

He touched the top of her head. "We'll start here, with the crown. Open that. Imagine a spinning white light."

Leda closed her eyes and pictured it, a light hovering where his fingers traced.

"Now the forehead," he said. "That one is dark blue."

She knew, having studied the chakras. The second one was what witches called the third eye, a focus of power. Hunter touched her there, above the bridge of her nose, and a blue light joined the white. She began to relax.

"The throat," Hunter went on.

A lighter blue light, moving and spinning where she felt his fingers. Then he moved his hand between her breasts, over her heart, and began the green light there.

His hand continued down to rest over her navel. He traced a pattern while she opened her fifth chakra, its light yellow.

"Open your eyes, Leda."

She opened them and gasped. What she'd pictured inside her head was real, lights white and colored hovering on her skin, bright even in the sunny room.

Hunter pressed her abdomen, just above her groin. "This one."

Orange. The glow seeped out from between their bodies, and she felt open and stretched and ready.

"Last one," he said. His cock moved inside her, touching her where his hand couldn't. "Red."

She let out a cry as she sent the red light spinning, a concentrated warmth where he penetrated.

"That's it, love," he said, voice gentle. "Open all the way to me."

Leda felt wild and strange, lying here with her legs spread, this incredible man between them. The lights warmed her, their pressing energy invigorating. She wanted to climax already, and he'd barely moved.

"My Leda," he murmured. "Zeus has nothing on me."

He slid almost all the way out of her, then in again in one slow thrust. She nearly screamed with it. She felt his magic inside her, welling into her through the energy points she'd opened.

His own chakras began to align with hers, magical energy fusing and twining together. Anyone outside the windows would see a light show, flashes of orange and red and green.

Hunter penetrated her all the way. His cock twisted and moved and she writhed against it, her body greedy for his. He fit perfectly against her, rocking his hips slightly.

How could she have believed he'd be hurt by her death magic? His strength was immense, greater than anything she'd ever experienced, not from demons, not from the most powerful witches of the Coven of Light.

He was in a class by himself. An Immortal, he called himself. A god? *Not—quite,* he'd said.

"Hunter," she said, frantic.

"Don't come yet. Hold it back." His voice was hoarse.

"I can't."

"Hold it in. Release it when I tell you."

She knew how to build energy to release into a spell, but it had never before felt like *this.* The orgasm throbbed and built inside her, its release imminent. She had to clench her fists and every muscle to keep from coming, her heels driving into the bed.

"Leda." Hunter's smile was warm and sweet, as if she were the only woman he'd ever smiled for. He placed his hand over her heart, and pulsing emerald light leaked through his fingers.

"Now!" he said.

She let go. Never in her life had she climaxed like this, and she realized dimly that she'd never truly had an orgasm. She heard screams before she knew she made them, her body undulating on waves of pleasure.

He was huge and hard, and she wanted him inside her forever. She thrust herself against him, pulling him down to touch places in her no one ever had.

Hunter lifted his hand, and she saw tendrils of black twined around his fingers like thick smoke. He was pulling it out of her heart, the death magic, and she screamed and screamed as it let her go.

As Leda's orgasm wound on, Hunter gathered the darkness into his hand. He worked his fingers, molding the death magic like it was a sticky substance, and she saw it grow smaller and smaller under his touch, its power diminishing. As more death magic streamed from her heart, the orgasm built in intensity, her own life magic rushing to heal spaces the death magic had scarred.

At last Hunter rubbed his fingertips together, smiling a little smile, and the darkness vanished.

Leda crashed against the bed, panting and spent. Hunter murmured something and drove into her, one thrust, two, three, and then he came. He shuddered as the climax ripped through him, and he collapsed onto Leda, kissing and kissing her.

What happened after that, she wasn't sure, because a wave of sleep hit her, and when she woke up, Hunter lay under the sheets beside her, head pillowed on his arm, eyes closed. She knew one thing for certain: The death magic was gone.

The darkness that had lurked inside her since she'd first summoned the demon had vanished. After the Coven of Light members told her there was no hope of saving her husband, she'd turned to death magic in desperation. She'd lost herself to it, but it had worked. The groth demon had infused her soul with his death magic, eager to taste her.

And now Hunter, with a lopsided smile and warm eyes, had taken the darkness away.

"Thank you," she whispered.

He didn't stir. He was asleep, a little snore leaking from the corner of his mouth.

Leda lay in the sunshine with him for a while, not quite believing she'd been cured. She drank in the warmth of the day, the peace of him sleeping beside her, her body relaxed in afterglow, clean once more.

She wondered if he was serious about keeping her here, protected. She had to admit she hadn't felt so safe in a long time, cocooned by his magic. He might grow bored and leave to find the next woman—she had no illusion he'd just pledged himself to her—but she would enjoy him while she had him.

She was enjoying herself so much, she almost missed the sound outside the window, the pad of feet, the strong but quiet huff of breath. Leda sat up, pushing the hair out of her eyes. Her braid was long since gone, her hair hanging in tangles. She swung her legs out of the bed, stood up, and went softly to the window. Hunter did not stir.

Leda looked out in time to see a large, tawny body turn from the house and begin loping toward the cliff path. Her eyes widened as the lion bounded from rock to rock, disappearing into the lush undergrowth.

Real life rushed back to her. She wasn't being paid by the Institute to make love all day to sexy, godlike men, but to rehabilitate animals and keep them safe.

She leaned out of the window. "Mukasa!"

If the lion heard her, he ignored the call. She saw him higher, brown body against the black rock, winding his way to the top.

Hunter's warmth closed behind her, and she jumped. "What's the matter?" he breathed into her ear.

"Mukasa's gone up the cliff path." She broke away from him, reaching for her clothes. "It's dangerous. I have to get him back."

"He's a cat. More surefooted than you or I will ever be. We'll fall off the cliff, and he'll stand there laughing at us."

"But he's hurt, and he's loose, and he's *my* responsibility. If something happens to that lion, it's my job, my grant money, my reputation—gone."

He watched, an amused look on his face, as she

scrambled around snatching up her shorts and T-shirt and searching, searching for her bra and giving up.

"You could help me," she panted, straightening up.

"He'll come back when he's ready."

"Sure, if he doesn't fall into a crevice or the lake that's up there. It's deep."

"All right, we'll go after him." Hunter cupped his hands around her face, giving her a penetrating look. "You're welcome."

She swallowed. "The death magic is gone. What did you do?"

He shrugged his powerful shoulders. "Nothing special. Once you opened up to me, I could reach in with my magic and pull the darkness out. If you had kept even one little bit closed to me, I couldn't have done it."

"You didn't tell me that."

Another shrug. "I didn't want you to worry." He released her, moving away to find his jeans, casual in his nakedness. "Let's go find Mukasa. He's waiting for us."

Hunter knew Leda was concerned about Mukasa, but her step was lighter, her magic clean and darkness-free. It had been relatively easy to strip the death magic from her, much easier than hiding the entire island from whatever demon stalked them. An Old One, something powerful, something he hadn't felt in a long, long time.

Although Leda's heart had been tainted, it had not turned her evil. She'd carry the death magic like a vessel might carry water, filled with it but unchanged itself. The relief he'd felt when he realized that had been immense. If she'd been permeated, if she had become as evil as the demon who'd used her, he would have had to kill her.

That would have been a shame. She was a beautiful woman, he thought, watching her walk ahead of him. Her body was made to be under his; he could make love to her for hours. No, days.

He'd have to build up her stamina to take him that long, and damn, he'd have fun doing it. Forget the outside world and whatever was happening. He'd keep her here with him to ride out her life, safe. The groth demon could go screw himself—Hunter could leave her long enough to find and kill him, now that Leda was free of him. Then he'd be back to stay with her as long as he could.

The sound of an engine in the clear sky made him grimace in annoyance. A twin-engine plane, not a helicopter, dropped toward the landing strip, but he assumed it was Douglas coming back to check on Leda.

Hunter contemplated shielding against the plane, letting the man circle in frustration until he had to head back to the mainland or risk running out of fuel. But Hunter saw Leda start to jog eagerly toward the airstrip down the beach, happy to see her friend, and he silently lowered the wards to let the plane land.

It touched down on the tiny runway, then turned and taxied to a stop. The props slowed, dying into a quiet whirring before halting altogether.

But it wasn't Ronald Douglas who opened the door and hopped to the ground, but a woman, lithe and slim, dark-haired and tall. Hunter felt the sticky darkness of the woman's aura, and he sucked in his breath.

"Leda, stop!"

Leda ignored him. "Samantha?" she called. "What are you doing out here?"

Hunter couldn't hear the woman's low answer. He stepped quickly back to the house, grabbed his sword and slid it from its sheath, then made for the airstrip.

He met the two women halfway back, on the pristine sands of the beach. Hunter closed the distance between them and held his sword point-first toward the dark-haired woman.

"If you get back in your plane, now," Hunter said in a clear voice, "I might let you leave without killing you."

The woman stopped, regarding him uncertainly. But she knew he meant it, her dark eyes betraying her true nature.

"Hunter, what are you doing?" Leda asked in surprise. "This is Samantha Taylor. I know her—she's with the paranormal police. We met on one of her cases a few years ago, before I quit the Coven of Light."

Hunter looked Samantha over without answering. He saw what Leda did, a young woman in her twenties with dark hair cut straight at her shoulders and a trim body. What Hunter could also see that Leda did not was the taint of death magic surrounding her, the shimmer of her form that told him she wasn't completely human.

Samantha returned his gaze defiantly, but Hunter read the fear in her eyes. She wasn't certain exactly what Hunter was, but knew he could tell what she was.

"Demon," Hunter announced.

Leda's lips parted, revealing she hadn't known. Samantha's aura was faint, likely hidden to most people, except to Hunter, who had been demon hunting most of his life. She was a lesser demon, not an Old One.

"Half-demon," Samantha answered. "My mother is as human as Leda is. I'm not sure what *you* are."

"You never mentioned this," Leda said to her.

Samantha gave her a wry look. "I thought you knew and were being discreet. Why do you think I'm so good at tracking down and arresting demons?"

Leda turned to Hunter. "It's true. The Coven helped her find a particularly nasty demon on a killing spree a few years ago. He was very strong, but we bound him. We never could have contained him without Samantha."

"What do you want here?" Hunter growled. He hadn't moved the sword. "Help binding another demon?"

"Help finding my mother." Samantha looked at Leda, her demon eyes worried. "She's disappeared. I went to the Coven of Light and told them I needed a witch who knew about wielding death magic. They sent me to you."

CHAPTER SIX

Leda saw Hunter pause, reassessing Samantha, but he didn't lower his sword. He was ready to kill her, and if he wanted to go ahead, Leda knew she couldn't stop him.

She'd only half believed Hunter when he said he was the most dangerous being she'd ever meet. With his lazy smile and wicked green eyes and the way Mukasa and Taro took to him, she could forget he was a being of overpowering magic.

He'd been incredibly gentle with her and with the animals, and he hadn't killed Valdez's men when they came for Mukasa, as nasty as they were. He'd toyed with them and sent them off to be caught, but he hadn't hurt them.

But they'd been human, she thought. She saw the cold look in his eyes now. The laughing, teasing bad boy was gone. He was the Immortal warrior, the killer, and she was about to come between him and his kill.

Taking a breath, she deliberately stepped in front

of him. "Whatever she is, she's my friend. I'll vouch for her."

"She's a demon, Leda," he said, voice quiet. "They can glam better than vampires. She wants you to feel sorry for her."

"If I wanted to cast a glam," Samantha said, "you wouldn't know I was a demon. I'd never let you see my death magic. I'm not hiding anything from you."

"Let her at least tell us what the problem is." Leda remained still, much as she would with a big cat that didn't yet trust her. "I want to hear what she has to say."

Hunter held her gaze with his for a long time, the anger she read there ancient and palpable. She also saw his effort to contain himself, to not thrust her aside and kill Samantha as he wanted to. He was stopping himself for Leda.

He lowered the sword a little. "Talk," he said to Samantha.

She swallowed. "What are you?"

"An Immortal. Created to kill things like you."

Samantha's eyes widened, black-blue and beautiful. Leda wondered if she resembled her mother, or if she'd chosen to take on the dark beauty of demons. Hunter was right about demons glamming their victims—they could appear in the guise of incredibly erotic men or women, changing gender as they liked, seducing humans with a touch or a glance. Was Samantha's demonlike beauty natural or glamour?

"Immortal?" Samantha repeated, startled. "The Coven of Light is looking for Immortals."

No interest flickered on Hunter's hard face. "How do you know that?"

"Because when I contacted them for help, they told

me to tell Leda that there's a big hunt on for what they called Immortal warriors. Leda is supposed to keep an eye out and report to them."

"Did they Call me?" Hunter asked.

"Summon you, you mean? I guess so, I didn't get all the details."

Hunter straightened, his sword loose in his big hands, and didn't answer.

Leda asked her, "Why did the Coven think I could help you with death magic? What is it you need me to do?"

Samantha dragged her gaze from Hunter and gave Leda an assessing look. "My mother is a witch. A long time ago she summoned a demon—who became my father—to tap into his death magic. He melded with her mind, became a part of her. They told me you had done the same."

Leda shuddered as she remembered what it had been like to fuse with the demon. She'd felt his death magic penetrate her, filling the private spaces of her mind, violating her. It had been akin to rape, but psychic rape, loathsome and terrifying. Leda's husband had never forgiven her for it, and she'd at last walked away from his coldness.

"I understand," Leda said softly.

"The demon did more," Samantha said. "He stayed with her and made her his slave—in all ways—and then she gave birth to me. It took her a long time to escape him, but she took me with her and raised me on her own. She set up powerful warding to keep him away from her, but I'm afraid he's found a way to come back for her."

Hunter's gaze was deadly quiet. "Why can't you track down your mother yourself? You're paranormal police, and you must have some link to this demon if he's your father."

Samantha flinched. "My demon powers aren't that well developed—one reason I can't glam you. Neither are my witch powers. It's like I inherited the only nonmagical genes my parents have. I have a little magic, but not much. A spell or two, and that's it. Not enough to find out where he's taken her, or even if she's still alive."

Her eyes filled with sudden tears, and Leda's heart softened. "I'm a damn powerful witch, even if the Coven had a backhanded way of telling you," she declared. "I can at least try a locator spell. You helped rid the world of a killer before, I can do this for you."

Samantha relaxed a little. "Thank you."

They both looked at Hunter. He said nothing, keeping his decisions to himself. At least he wasn't shoving Leda aside in order to slice Samantha in half.

Leda instinctively trusted Samantha, maybe because Samantha had been so competent on their demon hunt years ago, maybe because Leda sensed her true worry about her mother. Leda wasn't foolish enough to trust blindly, not the least because Samantha hadn't bothered to mention her half-demon nature, but Leda could give her the benefit of the doubt and be careful at the same time.

"Let me find my lion," she said. "And then we'll talk."

Samantha's eyes widened. "Your lion?"

"Didn't the Coven tell you? I work for an organization that rescues exotic animals. Except someone convinced me today that the animals needed to roam." She shot Hunter a look.

"Mukasa is fine," Hunter replied, the lines around his mouth still tight. "Of all of us, he's the safest."

"I wish I knew how you knew that."

"I just do."

"Even so, I have to get him back down here. I don't need him hurting himself."

Leda started for the cliff path as though trusting the two behind her to sort it out and help her. Hunter shouldered his sword and started walking with her.

She widened her eyes at him. "What, you decided to help?"

He didn't laugh. "It's important to you."

He waited for Samantha to catch up, making her walk ahead with Leda while he came behind. Taro came out of his enclosure and followed them to the base of the path, and prowled the rocks below while they wound their way higher, his masklike face turned upward.

"How many wild animals do you have out here?" Samantha asked, looking down the path at the bear.

"Just the two," Leda answered. "Taro and Mukasa. That I take care of, anyway. Plenty of tropical birds and snakes and insects around, too."

Samantha blanched. A city girl, Leda guessed.

Hunter said nothing. He'd sheathed his sword and slung it across his back, climbing behind the two of them in silence, his face unreadable.

About a hundred feet up, the path leveled out and wandered into a narrow valley filled with tropical plants, vibrant and blooming under the May sky. Trees lined the sides of the valley and water fell from the cliffs above, gouging a trough in the rocks and becoming a rushing stream beside the path.

They ducked under the trees, following the stream. The island had two climates tucked into one tiny space: tropical rain forest that was hot and close, and the dry beach buffeted by cool winds. Leda preferred the open air of the beach, where her magic was at its height. Her body was already covered in sweat, her T-shirt clinging to her with unpleasant stickiness.

Hunter caught up to her, not seeming to notice the heat. Except for the few beads of sweat on his upper lip, he looked utterly comfortable.

"He's close," he rumbled. He'd strapped the leather scabbard to his back for the climb, the hilt hard and dark above his shoulder. "Don't worry."

Hunter moved ahead, then stopped after a few yards and pointed through the undergrowth. Leda moved quickly and quietly to him, looking where he indicated. Samantha came behind, making too much noise, but the lion in the little clearing in front of them didn't notice.

Mukasa waited alongside the stream, which had widened here, filling a deep pool before it rushed back into the trees. The spray of another waterfall from above was cool on Leda's skin, the clearing scented with water and verdant plants.

The lion stood motionless, gazing up at a very tall woman who looked down at him. She was beautiful, her silver hair flowing from a high forehead to her feet. Her skin was silver too, almost iridescent, flashing green and gold in the bits of sunlight that filtered through the trees. The hand she held out to Mukasa showed slight webbing between her fingers, and thin webbing framed her face, slicking back to her head to become her hair.

"What is she?" Leda whispered.

Samantha, breathing hard behind her, said, "Something with strong life magic."

Hunter lifted a branch. "Undine. A spirit of the water. This is likely her territory."

Leda stared in surprise. "I've lived out here off and on for two years, and this is the first time I've seen her, or even heard of her."

Hunter shrugged. "Maybe she had no reason to show herself until now."

He stepped into the clearing. Leda expected the woman to fade back into the trees, disappearing to wherever she'd come from, but she stood and waited for Hunter to approach. Shadows rippled across her body like obscuring mist.

She doesn't have to run, Leda thought. *She can blend into the shadows whenever she wants. She could have been up here each time I came, and I'd never have known.*

"Immortal." The Undine's voice drifted across the clearing, a soft whisper like the rustle of leaves. She waited serenely for Hunter, her hand on Mukasa's shoulder.

"I'm Hunter. Who are you?"

"I am called Dyanne," she told him. Then her voice softened, and Leda could not hear what else she said.

As though frozen in her position, Leda continued to hold back the branch Hunter had ducked under. Samantha stood beside her, her slim hands pressed together, fingertips on her lips. The two of them watched, mesmerized, as Hunter and the Undine talked; then Hunter turned and reached out a hand. "Leda."

As though a force pulled her, Leda obediently left the trees and walked through the damp undergrowth to where Hunter and the woman waited. The sound of the water grew louder, and the woman shimmered as she turned to watch Leda approach.

"You are the witch." Her voice was light as gossamer, but she spoke haltingly as though she found English difficult. "You care for the creatures." She stroked Mukasa's forehead, and the lion's eyes half closed in enjoyment.

"I do," Leda answered. "Your name is Dyanne?"

Her hair shimmered as she inclined her head. "You may call me this."

Dyanne's eyes were silver. Leda looked into their depths and sensed a powerful and ancient magic.

"Her people are the water spirits of this place." Hunter spoke gently, his voice pitched low. "She has been watching you and likes your kindness."

"Oh." Leda blushed. "Thank you, I guess."

"We have lived here for . . ." Dyanne broke off as she groped for a word. "Millennia. On this island, nothing changed. Until you came and built."

"The man who donated the island to the Institute didn't know anyone lived here," Leda said quickly. He'd owned it as an investment, then donated it for the tax write-off and probably never set foot on it.

Hunter continued, "She was afraid you'd drive her people out. But they watched you and realized you weren't going to violate their territory. They approve of you."

"Good." She grew curious. "What would they have done if they hadn't approved of me?"

Hunter responded, "Either leave and look for another island, or kill you."

Looking into Dyanne's enigmatic silver eyes, Leda believed him. The Undine might like her and Mukasa, but there was no kindness in her. Acceptance and admiration, but no gentleness. She possessed the distance Leda had seen in older vampires or ancient Sidhe, removal from a world that moved on quickly while they watched.

"My people are dying," Dyanne announced.

"Because of me and the Institute?"

"Because life magic drains from the world at a rapid pace. The . . ." she said a harsh-sounding word and looked to Hunter for guidance.

"Demons," he supplied.

"Demons suck the life magic dry. A great power is at work, and as the magic is siphoned away, we sicken and die. When we felt the life magic that kept the demon from us today, we knew that a great one—an Immortal—had been sent to the island. We knew our hope had come."

"I wasn't sent here," Hunter interjected, his rough baritone a contrast to Dyanne's silken tones. "When the Calling spell grabbed me, I saw my brother Adrian with a witch—not Leda. I don't know where they were. Then something broke the spell and flung me all the way out here."

"You were sent," the Undine said with conviction. "You arrived where you were needed most."

Hunter did not look convinced. "The island is protected now by my shield. The life magic will hold."

"For how long?" Dyanne asked. "How long until the darkness eats everything in the outer world? Some of our people have already fallen ill and need healing." She turned her silver eyes full force on Hunter. "Please, Immortal. Find out what is happening. Stop it. Heal us."

Hunter glanced at Leda. She could not read what was in his eyes any more than she could Dyanne's, but she knew he struggled with something inside himself, something he would not share with her.

"You want my brother," he told the Undine. "Tain is the healer."

"I know not of this Tain," Dyanne said. "But we have you."

Hunter fingered the leather straps that held his sword in place on his back. Leda could not imagine a problem that Hunter couldn't handle, but he seemed uncertain how to answer.

"I can hunt up my brother for you. He can heal your people."

Dyanne studied him a long time, her gaze flickering as though reading something in him. "You will find him. When you do, you will be forced to choose a path. Walking either one will be painful for you, but you must choose."

He frowned at her. "What does that mean?"

"Do not linger here, Immortal. The world needs you. We need you." She turned her strange eyes full force on Leda. "You too must choose a path."

"I can't leave my animals," Leda said at once.

"They will be in good hands." Dyanne's voice faded, like a faint breeze among the rain. She turned without saying good-bye and began to glide away.

"Wait a minute," Leda called. "What choice?"

The Undine didn't answer. She disappeared under the trees, her body blending with the spray of the waterfall. One moment she was there, the next, a glimmer of sunlight shot through the water, and she was gone. Mukasa lifted his head and let out a breathy grunt.

"You said it," Hunter told him. "Water spirits are always cryptic. They enjoy it."

"She's partly right," Leda said. "Nothing happens without a reason."

Hunter flicked a green gaze to her. "You sound just like her."

"I agree with her about you being sent here. Think about it. Of all the places you could have landed, you landed in Mukasa's enclosure, shortly before Valdez's men came to try to take him back. I'd never have been able to stop them on my own."

He nodded grudgingly.

"Plus, you are probably the only being I'm likely to meet who is able to free me of the death magic. Then the Coven, who hasn't spoken to me in two years, sends Samantha here to ask for my help. Samantha asked me because she knew I'd understand. Now that my magic is no longer tainted, I *can* help her. You let Mukasa out of his compound, and he goes straight to the Undine, who needs you." She paused for breath. "You see? The universe has a pattern. It never does anything without a reason."

He studied her, eyes enigmatic. "You think so?"

"I know so. The universe—maybe the Goddess— wants us to go back to the mainland and help these people. It needs us to."

Hunter looked at the spot where Dyanne had disappeared, then back at Leda. He brushed his finger across her cheek. "I don't mind contacting Tain, if I can find him, or even locating Adrian and figuring out what's going on. But you aren't going anywhere, Leda. You aren't leaving this island until the outside world is safe."

CHAPTER SEVEN

"And who decides when the world is safe?" Leda asked heatedly. "You?"

She faced Hunter on the beach alone. The three of them and Mukasa had descended the cliff path, Leda informing Samantha about what Dyanne had told them because Hunter wouldn't speak.

At the bottom Taro met them, sniffing Leda over as though he could determine everything that had happened by scent, and perhaps he could. Bears were keen smellers and quite smart.

Taro and Mukasa returned voluntarily to their enclosures because it was late afternoon and time to be fed. Hunter helped Leda with that chore; Samantha elected to stay well out of it.

A huge freezer stood behind the house full of chunks of raw meat carefully portioned, along with nutritional supplements created specifically for each animal. Each morning Leda put the meat in its special container to thaw, and every afternoon she added the supplements and took the food out to the animals. She had enough supplies for about three weeks, which were replenished by Douglas from the Institute when she started to run low.

Leda usually threw the meat over the fence—the animals liked to run it down and then devour it—but Hunter simply walked into Mukasa's enclosure, took the meat from the bucket in his gloved hand and held it out to him.

Leda watched in shock, ready to shout at him to drop the food and run. Mukasa eyed the meat, then Hunter, then stepped a little away from Hunter in deference, a submissive gesture in a big cat.

Hunter laid down the meat. "No, thanks, my friend. It's all yours."

Without hesitation, Mukasa raked the chunk of beef toward himself with a huge paw and began to eat. Hunter came out of the enclosure and headed for the shed to get rid of the gloves and wash his hands.

Leda forced her jaw to close. "You know the best way to get attacked is to come between a lion and his food."

"If he wanted to attack me, I'd know," Hunter said absently, rinsing his hands. "He didn't want to."

"Does he think you're the pride leader?" she asked as he helped put the buckets away. "He offered you first dibs."

Hunter grinned for the first time since they'd descended from the cliffs. "He knows I'm not a lion, and neither are you. He was being polite. You just have to understand how to read them and to let them read you."

"And you're not a telepath."

"I can't read his mind, no, and I can't talk to him. But I understand him, and he understands me. I've always been able to do that with animals, for over two thousand years now. Don't ask me how."

By the time Leda and Hunter returned to the house, Samantha had started dinner, chopping greens for a salad. When Leda started to make sandwiches, Hunter revealed another of his quirks.

"No meat for me," he said.

"You're vegetarian?" Leda stared at him. So did Samantha.

"I can't eat an animal," he said, leaning against the counter and looking as delectable as ever. "What if I've met him?"

"You can't have met every chicken in the world," Leda argued.

"No, but I might have met her grandmother or cousin or aunt. Animals aren't dumb beasts to me, good only for food or labor."

"You just fed Mukasa a cow," she pointed out. "Or part of a cow."

"He has to eat meat to survive. I don't. It would be the same for me as asking you to chow down on Taro. Under certain circumstances you might have to do it for survival, but . . ." He trailed off with a shrug.

Leda looked at the ham sandwich Samantha had put together for her. "Thanks a lot, Hunter."

"Hey, don't mention it."

After their dinner of salad and bread, Hunter took his sword and went to the beach, where he began a series of exercises. Samantha volunteered to do the dishes, seeming to want to keep busy.

Leda went down to the beach to watch Hunter. He moved with grace, as lithe as Mukasa climbing the cliff path. As the sun died into the sea, it burned gold highlights in his hair and showed off the perfection of his torso. He was a beautiful man. He'd made love to her and freed her from fear; he was as wild and unpredictable as the animals she cared for, and more powerful than anyone she'd ever met.

He'd implied before they'd made love that she already knew all there was to know about him, but that wasn't true. He had told her about being an Immortal, about his brothers and their matching tattoos, that he'd lost his wife and children long ago, but she knew nothing at all about the real being called Hunter. Whatever lurked behind his emerald-green eyes was shut to her. He hadn't let her in.

Hunter finished the routine with a precise flourish and sheathed the sword, reminding Leda of samurai she'd seen in movies. He faced the sunset, put his hands together and bowed. Leda knew she should admire most his athleticism, his prowess with the sword, but what she was thinking when she went to him was that he had a great ass.

When Leda reached him, he gave her his crooked smile and leaned to kiss the corner of her mouth. "Hey, sweetheart, have you worked out the sleeping arrangements?" A hint of his wicked twinkle returned. "You and me in the bed, of course. The demon can sleep on your couch—better have her close so we can keep an eye on her."

Leda folded her arms. "I'm not Mukasa."

"Hmm?" He touched her hair. "I know you're not. Different mane, fewer whiskers."

"I wasn't trying to be funny. I meant you like to take over. But I won't step back and let you take control of my island. I make the rules here, and I decide when I come and go."

Hunter lost his teasing look, the warrior returning. "Not when bad shit is going on in the outside world."

"And who decides when the world is safe? You?"

"Yes, me. It's what I was made for."

"If bad shit is going on, the world needs me too," she argued. "I'm a strong witch, Hunter. I can't stay in a cocoon if someone's trying to drain life magic from the world. I should be out there helping."

"It isn't your fight."

"No? What about when this life-magic drain starts to affect me and my magic? I should stay here and not worry about it?"

Hunter's face clouded. "Leda, you've never fought evil, never truly faced it. I have. It can crush you like you're nothing." He snapped his fingers in demonstration.

"Exactly why I don't want to wait for it to happen. I'd rather go out fighting."

"And I'd rather not watch you go out at all," he growled. "I'll go back to the mainland, get with my brothers, find out what's going on and take care of it." He broke off, touching her cheek, his voice softening. "Then I'll come back and we can continue getting to know each other."

Tempting. His eyes went dark, and she remembered his heavy kiss on her lips when he'd lain on her after they'd made love. Tempting to sit back and say, *Go take care of that evil problem, then come home and make wild love to me.*

"How will you find your brothers?" she asked. "You said you have no idea where they are."

He shrugged, his rippling muscles distracting. "I'll look around. We're easy to spot."

"Samantha said the Coven of Light is looking for

Immortals," she reminded him. "And I know how to contact the Coven."

He held out a broad hand. "Give me a phone number and I'll know how to contact them too."

"I want to go with you, Hunter."

"I want you to stay here, Leda."

She glared at him. "And do what, needlepoint? Wait and watch the horizon to see if you come back, not knowing whether you survive?"

"I'm Immortal, I can't die."

"But you could be trapped somewhere. Demons are tricky—they could seal you someplace and keep you there forever. And I wouldn't even know where to start looking for you."

He gazed down at her, puzzled. "Why would you want to look for me?"

"Why wouldn't I? If you were stuck somewhere, trapped, hurt, of course I'd come to find you."

His green eyes were enigmatic. "But I am nothing to you."

"What are you talking about?" She looked him over, from his mussed, sun-streaked hair to his broad chest to his narrow hips, the tattoo peeking over his waistband. He was a powerful giant, and yet so gentle. "You helped me, you freed me. You made me think I could live a normal life again. If nothing else, I'm grateful. Why is that so puzzling?"

"I wasn't made to become close to anyone. I learned that lesson a long time ago. I was made to fight death-magic creatures—that is all."

"And that means I can't care about what happens to you?"

"That means you should not," he said, a stern note in his voice. "You will live and die, and I will disappear. When I lost my wife I grieved hard, but I would have lost her and my children eventually anyway. I lose everyone I care for."

Leda put her fingers on his lips. "Stop it."

"It is the way of things." He cupped her shoulders. "If I can come back, we'll have an intense time together, for a little while. If I can't come back, you won't have lost anything."

Leda wrenched away from him. "By intense, you mean sex. Is that all it will be to you? Sex?"

"That's all it can be."

She took a step back. "Dear Goddess, are your brothers as arrogant as you? You'll go and fight because *you* want to, while I stay here because *you* want me to, so you can come back and have sex with me when *you* decide to. Well, forget it. You can't always have it your way."

"It must be this way, Leda."

"Tell you what, I will give you that phone number. You go find your brothers, and I'll feel free to do as I please. Whether that means searching for a home for Mukasa or going back with Samantha and helping her—it will be none of your business."

"Why does Mukasa need a home?" he asked. "His home is here."

Leda started to walk away, then spun around. "This isn't some haven where you can keep me and your animal friends. We had our own lives before you got here, and we'll have our own lives when you leave."

She whirled again, not waiting for his response, and stamped through the sand toward the house.

Samantha looked up from drying the dishes when Leda slammed inside. She'd done them by hand even

though Leda had a dishwasher—maybe it was thera-
peutic for her. "Everything all right?" she asked.

"Immortals." Leda ground her teeth. "They should
be called Insufferables."

Hunter didn't come back to the house. Leda helped
Samantha clean up, then make up a bed for her on the
sofa. Samantha didn't ask what Leda and Hunter had
fought about, for which Leda was grateful. A young
woman who didn't pry into other people's troubles.

Reminding herself that Samantha had come for
help, she said, "Tell me what happened to your
mother. I'll need as much information as I can to do a
spell."

"Not much to it." Samantha smoothed the sheets
over the couch, not looking at Leda. "I grew up human. My mom and I were always close, though she
never liked to talk about the demon who'd sired me.
Whenever I brought it up she'd change the subject. I
was lucky, though. She could have abandoned me
when I was a baby, but she didn't, and she loves me
for myself. She's very smart and a skilled witch, and
she worked her ass off for me."

Her tone was proud and fierce. Leda acknowledged
her with a nod. "What happened the day she went
missing?"

Samantha sat down on the sofa, picking up a pillow
and holding it. "I went to my mom's on my day off
two weeks ago, and she was gone. The wards on the
house were broken, her car was still in the garage, the
place was a mess, there was blood . . ."

She stopped and swallowed. "I called it in and got
backup and we investigated, but turned up nothing.
He must have pulled her through a portal, but if so,

the portal was long gone. I'm pretty sure it was my father who took her."

"Not to doubt you, but how can you be sure? I mean, did you find evidence of it? I've been reading about a lot of demon and vampire gang activity in the papers."

"I'm aware of it," Samantha said in a hard voice. "That's exactly what my department said; they didn't take me seriously either."

Leda sat down next to her. "I do take you seriously. I'm just trying to explore all possibilities."

Samantha sighed. "I know. I apologize, I'm just getting tired of no one believing me. I was told to take a leave of absence from my job, probably because they were sick of me begging them to put more people on the case. But it was stupid of them. Things are breaking down in Los Angeles, and they need everyone they can get. The real reason they told me to go, I'm sure, is that I'm half-demon, and everyone's getting terrified of demons."

"I'm not terrified of you. I know you're a good cop. Demons are hard to pinpoint with locator spells—they can throw up all kinds of shields—but your mother is human. Likely if she's in trouble she'll be broadcasting some magic herself, whatever she can. We'll find her."

Leda tried to sound reassuring, but she was privately not optimistic. Demons were hard to track, the stronger and older, the more difficult. If the trail was already two weeks old and the paranormal police, whose job it was to hunt down demon criminals, couldn't find anything, then Leda might not be able to either.

But Samantha was scared. The young woman tried

not to show it, and she had a strong body honed from fighting and working out for her job, but her dark eyes were troubled. Samantha didn't look the type who wanted her shoulder patted, so Leda sent her a smile.

"We'll go to Los Angeles and look at the house again. I might be able to find something there that I can use to magically trace her. The Coven disapproved of what I did, but they didn't kick me out, because I was one of the strongest witches they had, and they knew it. They simply gave me a hard time until I left on my own."

"I'd be grateful." Samantha shot her a dark-eyed look. "I'm worried, but I also know that my mom's not important to most people right now. My captain made that clear."

"Some people tend to worry about the big picture," Leda said, "and forget that each person who makes up the picture has problems of their own. I might not be able to stop a horde of demons with a word of power, but I can help track your mother."

Samantha gave Leda a shrewd look, even through the tears in her eyes. "By *some people* you aren't just talking about the paranormal police. You mean the big Immortal outside with the sword."

"Maybe."

"Is he what he claims to be?"

Leda nodded. "I think so. Warriors are summoned by witches to help when things get bad. He said they haven't been summoned for centuries. I can't help thinking things are really bad if all of a sudden these guys start to turn up."

Leda's anger at Hunter faded a little as she spoke. She'd been growling at him as though he were a normal human male, when she really didn't have any idea what he was. He looked like a man—a well-shaped man—but what kind of thoughts did a person who'd lived thousands of years have?

"He did a heavy shielding spell today," Leda said. "I've never seen anything like it."

"He makes *me* nervous, anyway," Samantha said. "I'm used to people looking at me funny when they realize I'm half-demon, but I've never felt such intense power from anyone. He was ready to kill me in a heartbeat."

"I won't let him," Leda said quickly.

Samantha arched dark brows. "You're sweet, Leda, but naïve. You can't stop him from doing a damn thing."

Leda said nothing, because she knew Samantha was right. Hunter would come and go as he pleased, and she wouldn't be able to stop him.

After Samantha had bedded down on the sofa, Leda lay awake on sheets that held Hunter's scent, alone. Moonlight poured through the window, darkening as a cloud slid past.

She wondered if Hunter would return to the house and renew his interest in the sleeping arrangements. She heard him out in the dark, murmuring in a low voice to Mukasa, who made little growling noises at him. Her clock showed her it was past midnight, and still he stayed away.

So much had happened today. Hunter landing in her lion's pen at the crack of dawn, Valdez's men coming for Mukasa, Hunter revealing his immortality and his great powers. The island was still shielded— she sensed it. The only reason Samantha had been able to penetrate it and alight was because Hunter had let her.

Leda's heart softened a little when she thought of Hunter freeing her from death magic. The more she thought about it, the more she understood the gift he'd given her. Removing the death magic that had twined through the very essence of her could have hurt her unbearably. But Hunter had drawn it out slowly, masking the pain with the intense pleasure of sex.

She sat straight up in bed. He'd done that for her—well, he hadn't exactly hated the procedure, but he could have taken what he wanted from her and given her nothing in return. He'd been holding himself back, gentling himself for her and Mukasa, and even Samantha. And she'd yelled at him for being insensitive.

Leda got out of bed and quietly pulled on shorts and a T-shirt. She stuck her feet in sneakers and walked softly through the living room past the sleeping Samantha and out the door to the veranda.

Hunter stood at the edge of the breakers in the moonlight, the tide coming in, the line of foam on the beach luminous. Mukasa waited a little away from him, his face to the wind, his mane stirring.

Hunter was naked, the moon's silver orb etching sharp shadows on his perfect body. He dropped his head back, his long hair catching the wind, moonlight on his face. He was speaking softly, the words chant-like in a language she didn't know.

The sand around him began to swirl upward, flowing around his body as though he stood in the middle of a dust devil. Leda thought she saw another figure in the shimmering sand, a woman's body, her limbs outlined in fire. When Leda looked directly at the image, it faded, though it seemed sharper viewed from the corner of her eye.

The woman writhed and twisted around Hunter, and Leda thought she heard low, hissing laughter. Hunter remained in place, arms stretched overhead, eyes closed, his lips moving while the woman's ethereal figure whirled in the sand.

The woman gave off something stronger than life magic—more than the magics of life and death—the touch of a goddess. The residual magic felt exciting and terrifying at the same time, but Hunter stood motionless in the midst of it, a look of fondness on his face.

The whirling sand became denser and obscured Hunter's body a brief moment. Then suddenly the sand flowed away from him straight toward Leda. The goddess's awareness brushed her, and Leda heard a voice, a grating hiss.

"Be good to my son."

The hiss faded to a whisper. The sand streamed upward into the night and disappeared. The wind died. Hunter lowered his arms and remained staring out over the ocean.

Leda walked to him with slow steps, wondering if he would resent her intrusion. He was so beautiful in the moonlight, standing naked, unashamed, under the empty sky, a demigod not bound by human rules.

Hunter turned his head and waited for her without speaking, seeming unsurprised that she'd watched him. Moonlight kissed his body, and the tattoo on his lower abdomen stood out stark against his skin. His cock below it hung thick and long, and the memory of being his lover made her heart beat faster.

"Couldn't sleep?" he asked in a low voice when she reached him.

"I wondered where you were." She hugged her arms to her chest, the wind cool. "What was that? What were you doing?"

He gave her the ghost of a smile, green eyes bright. "Calling my mother."

CHAPTER EIGHT

Hunter liked the way Leda tried so carefully not to look at his naked body. She enjoyed looking at him and pretended she didn't. It amused him.

"Your mother?" she asked.

"Kali."

Her lovely eyes widened. "Kali is your mother? The Hindu goddess of destruction?"

"Destruction *and* creation," Hunter corrected. "And of women and childbirth. She's very caring, but don't piss her off."

"I'll remember that."

He'd summoned Kali—rather, he'd asked politely if she'd come talk to him—and asked her what was going on. Kali had come on the wind, her body surrounded by fire, not manifesting all the way so as not to scare the humans on the island to death. Kali in her pure form could do that—literally.

She'd touched him with warmth, a love beyond understanding, but at the same time it was a distant love. Hunter had spent his childhood alone with his father before being sent off to Ravenscroft to meet his brothers and begin more serious training.

Kali had been a voice in the night, a hand on his head, comfort in times of fear. While Hunter's brothers had somewhat closer relationships with their mother goddesses, Kali had always remained aloof. This time she'd spoken to him directly and actually answered his questions, in her own way.

"The world grows dark," she'd said in her hoarse whisper, using an ancient language that had not been heard in the world in eons. "You are needed."

"Who did the Calling spell?" Hunter had asked in the same language. "Why didn't it work?"

"The world needs you," she'd repeated. "The darkness grows. The evil is more than your brothers can handle. It is part of you and yet outside you."

"Something Adrian can't handle?" he'd said, trying to work through her cryptic speech. "I bet that pisses him off." His oldest brother liked to control the world around him, and took his position of leader of the Immortals too damn seriously.

"The brothers must join, or the world will be lost." Her voice had become tinged with unimaginable sadness. "Tain must be stopped before he annihilates all."

"Tain?" Hunter had blinked in surprise. "My little brother who rescues birdies fallen out of their nests? What's he got to do with it?"

"I am the destroyer of the world. If I must be called, then I cannot save even you, my son."

The sibilants of her speech hissed into the wind. Hunter listened in worried silence. Kali could unmake the world if she had to, but she had never warned him of it like this before.

"So this is more than a few Old Ones acting

up," Hunter had said. "You need us to kick some serious ass."

"Tain has found a way to unmake his pain, and he will unmake all with it. You must stop him."

Hunter pondered. Kali had to be mistaken about his youngest brother, the peacemaker, the healer, the one Hunter, closest to him in age, loved most to tease. And what pain? Hunter hadn't seen Tain or any of the others since they'd battled some Unseelies in Scotland seven hundred years ago. Hunter had gone off to slake himself after the fight with several grateful females of the village, and when he'd emerged three days later, his brothers had disappeared.

He hadn't seen them since, which was fine with him. He'd assumed they'd all gone back to Ravenscroft like good little warriors, except Kalen who probably ran back to his chosen people or whatever. Hunter had decided to remain in the world doing what he damn well pleased, trying to ease the ache that never truly left him.

Had Tain also lost someone he loved? The brief five years Hunter had stayed with Kayla and started a family had been the happiest of his existence. Their deaths had ripped away a part of him that had never healed. He dimly remembered screaming in agony for days.

If Tain had gone through something like that, then Hunter understood what his little brother felt. But Hunter hadn't wanted to unmake the world to stop his pain; he'd only wanted to lie facedown in the grass and not move.

"To stop him," Kali had continued, "you will be called to make a sacrifice."

That got his attention. "Sacrifice?" he'd asked sharply. He'd sensed Leda in the shadows of the house, watching. "Not her." A sudden sharp pain squeezed his heart. "Not Leda."

"That path is yet to come, that choice yet to be made. In the end, you must decide or die."

The Undine had said much the same thing. Two paths, one choice.

"Protect her, Kali," he'd said quickly. "I invoke your protection. Let her be safe."

"This you must do yourself." The wind whirled about him, sand stinging his bare skin. He felt her touch and a faint press of lips on his. "Be well, my son."

She'd flowed away from him, straight toward Leda, swirled once around the startled young woman, then disappeared.

Now Leda stood before him, wanting an explanation.

"She told me many things." Hunter rested his hands on Leda's shoulders. "All bad. I still don't understand everything, but it's bad."

"Hunter, I'm sorry I got mad at you earlier. I know you have a different way of looking at the world than I do, and I know you're trying to protect me, but I really can help."

"Leda." He rested his forehead against hers, finding no words. He wanted more than anything to stay here with her, in this place removed from troubles, or almost removed. He could strengthen the shield and keep her here with him, send the others away and make love to her until both of them forgot the world existed.

She rose on tiptoes and pressed a soft kiss to his lips, a kiss of apology, although she had nothing to apologize for. He groaned into it, unable to stop himself from slanting his mouth across hers.

Every part of her delighted him, the way her shoulder blades curved under his palms, the way her lips moved beneath his, the honey-cherry taste of her mouth. He liked the noise she made in her throat as the kiss deepened, and the scent of her as she became aroused for him.

Her hands grasped the back of his neck, her body lifting to his. He transferred his touch to the waistband of her shorts, sliding one finger beneath it.

She twined her foot around his calf, her eyes heavy as she broke the kiss. "We can't, not with Samantha here."

"Shh." He wanted to make love to her again, wanted the mindlessness of being inside her. Last time he'd done it to heal her; this time he just wanted to. "How about we try your boat?"

Leda started to shake her head, but Hunter scooped her against him, opening her lips for his kiss. He released her and indicated she should lead the way. He picked up his clothes, which he'd left on the sand, and tucked them under his arm as he followed her down the beach to the jetty and the sailboat that rocked there.

The cabin of the sailboat was dark and close, but Hunter didn't care. He tossed his clothes on the cushioned bench next to the door and followed Leda into the forward cabin, which was nothing but wall-to-wall bed. He'd have to be careful not to hit his head on the low ceiling, was his last thought before he undressed her.

When she lay naked under him, her body damp with perspiration, she whispered, "Do you want me to open to you again?"

He thought about the joy of joining with both her

body and her spirit, but he shook his head, too impatient. "I just want you."

She was so wet for him, he slid right in. She sank her fingers into his buttocks and pulled him deeper, sighing breathily.

"Goddess, Leda." Hunter kissed her brow and lips. "You're so damn tight."

She lifted her hips on the wide mattress and pressed up to him. "I can take all of you. I want to."

"When I can go slow. I promise, when I can go slow, you'll get it all."

"I want it now." She sounded desperate.

"No, love. I'll hurt you."

Moonlight leaked through the tiny cabin windows and glittered on the tears in her eyes. He kissed her wet lashes. "Don't cry, sweetheart. Later I'll love you slow, for hours and hours."

"There might not be a later."

"Oh, yes, there will. When I get done figuring out what's wrong, I'll come back here and love you for hours. Days. Weeks. I'll make you feel so good, I'll make it so you don't want anyone but me."

She smiled faintly in the dark. "Goddess, I thought you were arrogant before."

He grinned. "I won't be arrogant. I'll be your pleasure slave. Anything you want, chain me to your bed, whatever it takes."

Her eyes darkened. "Be careful, I might do it."

"I wouldn't mind." He moved a little inside her, another inch. "I'll taste you 'til you scream, and then I'll make love to you with my fingers and tongue." He swiped his tongue across her lower lip. "Want me to bring back some handcuffs? Or maybe Samantha has some we can borrow. She's a cop." The sudden vision of Leda standing beautiful and naked on the beach, her hands bound behind her, made his erection give a hungry throb.

She blushed in the moonlight. "Actually, when Douglas was frisking you this morning, I thought of you in them."

Hunter growled. "I was wishing it was *you* frisking me."

"Me too."

"Really?" he purred. He rocked his hips, making her gasp in delight. "I think we should explore every facet of this fantasy."

"Not now. Make love to me."

For answer he kissed her. No slow going this time, he braced his hands against the bed and rocked into her deep and fast. Her hair flowed thick and long around her, tangles of it wrapping his body as she held him close.

They made love hard, the boat swaying with it, sweat slicking their bodies. Moonlight shone on Leda's beautiful face and broke his heart.

She squeezed him tight, her hands on his back, her feet wrapped around his hips. How anyone could have given up this woman he had no idea. Her husband had to be insane, and maybe he had been.

The first time, loving Leda had been warm and sweet, riding on a wave of magic. This sex was raw and basic. Hunter bunched his fists on the bed, thrusting in and in until he was grunting with it. Not exactly elegant, but Hunter never considered himself elegant. Decadence was Adrian's forte; Hunter lived close to the bone.

His climax hit him with the force of a freight train. He groaned hard, closing his eyes and cracking his head on the low ceiling of the cabin. Ignoring the pain, he collapsed to her and held himself inside her while she writhed and screamed her own release.

She tasted damn good, and he kissed her mouth and her throat and breasts over and over. The last thing he saw before he sank beside her in oblivion was her smile, a sad smile coupled with renewed tears. He tried to tell her not to cry, but a wave of sleep swamped him, and he was gone.

When he awoke, the sun was high, and he felt the vestiges of a sleep spell slide away from him. He was alone in the bed, and Mukasa roared somewhere on the beach, Taro growling a chorus.

Hunter jerked up, swearing when he banged his head again on the ceiling. He scrambled down from the bed, pulled on his jeans and borrowed T-shirt and left the cabin, hurrying barefoot across the deck. He climbed onto the jetty, then sprang from it and sprinted around the house and to the beach.

Mukasa stood facing the empty airstrip where Samantha's plane should have been, his head thrown back, mouth open as he bellowed his lion's call. The twin-engine plane, Leda, and Samantha were gone.

Hunter strode through the house, his anger building with every step. Samantha's things had vanished, the couch pristine, blankets folded on one end. Leda had even made her own bed. In the bathroom, a few bottles of Leda's scented soap and shampoo were gone, and the room was neat and clean. They'd had plenty of time.

Leda must have crept away soon after she'd brushed Hunter with the sleep spell. He cursed himself for having missed that—she'd done it so subtly, and he'd been so far gone in the joy of the moment that it had taken hold before he'd noticed.

Hunter's shield around the island was meant to keep evil out, not people in. Besides, he'd wanted Samantha able to leave at any moment, had planned to encourage it. Just not with Leda.

Hunter slammed out of the house and made for the boat. He knew how to sail—he'd sailed around the Mediterranean on Roman vessels, then Turkish ones; had crossed oceans in tall-masted ships; had sailed pleasure craft in Greece, Brazil and North American lakes. Leda's boat was a thirty-eight-footer with a simple rigging, sturdy enough to sail in deep waters and straight back to the mainland. He rummaged through the charts and found those marked for passage to California.

The only problem was, he couldn't leave Mukasa and Taro alone. Leda had known that he wouldn't willingly abandon them. Hunter had counted on the animals keeping Leda behind when *he* left the island. His beautiful siren had turned the tables on him.

He crossed back to the house, threw food into a cardboard box—chips, packaged cookies, pretzels, candy bars. One thing about junk food, it took a long time to go bad. He found Leda's radio on the counter, snatched it up and clicked it on. He enhanced it with his magic to find the frequency to reach Samantha's plane.

"Leda!" he bellowed.

Quiet crackling answered him. He called her name a few more times, but either she wasn't answering, she was out of range, or he hadn't projected his magic right. Or she was dead—the plane could have been followed by the intense evil that stalked the island.

Hunter pushed that horrible scenario firmly out of his mind. He'd find them—he was an Immortal with incredible powers. He'd find Leda and hold on to her and not let her run off again. Those handcuffs might come in handy. He had a brief, erotic fantasy about it before he went back to readying the boat.

The animals came out of their enclosures to watch him. Mukasa did not look in the least distressed, and his body language asked, *Where are we going?* Taro, on the other hand, regarded the boat with grave suspicion.

"I can't leave you, my friend," Hunter told him. He clicked on the radio again. "Leda. You have to help me with the animals. I don't know how to feed them."

An exaggeration, but as he hoped, an appeal to the animals' welfare worked. He heard Leda's voice among the crackle. "Hunter?"

Relief flooded him, along with more anger. "Where the *hell* are you?"

"Heading to Los Angeles. I'm sorry, Hunter." A pause, like she wanted to say more but couldn't decide what. "The animals like to have one big feeding at three in the afternoon. One packet of supplements to every five pounds of food. You have to weigh it." Again, a pause. "I had to leave, I'm sorry."

"You stay put in L.A. I'm coming out there."

More crackling, then her voice. "You can't!"

"Watch me, darling."

He clicked off the radio and went on with his preparations. He would be angrier, or even amused, at her audacity if the situation weren't so dangerous. His conversation with Kali had worried him more than he liked. He needed to find his brothers, figure this thing out, then return and chain Leda to the bed.

Mukasa strolled out to the boat as Hunter carried on the last load of food and supplements (*one packet for every five pounds, got it*). The big cat stepped onto the boat's deck and peered curiously down into the cabin. Taro lumbered up and down the beach, watching them in distress.

"It won't be so bad," Hunter promised.

Taro didn't believe him. He sat on his haunches and sent up a wail of protest.

"I will care for the bear."

The voice came out of the shadows behind the house, under a stand of palm trees and thick undergrowth. The Undine stood there, stray shafts of sunlight shooting iridescent green and gold and blue through her skin and silver hair.

"You are needed in the world, Immortal," she said. She glanced at Mukasa, who was standing happily on the deck of the boat. "The lion wishes to accompany you, but I will look after the other. He is a wild creature and welcome here."

"Thank you," Hunter answered gravely. They shared a look across the space between them, one purely magical creature to another.

If life magic continued to drain, Dyanne and her kind would be the first to go—the Undines, Sidhe, Selkies, leprechauns, and other magical beings of legend. Half-human life-magic creatures would feel it next, the shifters and the Weres. Then humans, the witches first, after that the nonmagical people. The death-magic creatures would feed on the last category, people who had no defenses against them. Vampires, demons and other nasties would have a field day.

And after that? Life and death magic had to remain

in balance or the world would unmake itself. The death-magic creatures would die too, last.

Hunter stopped in the act of untying lines. Was that the demon's plan? Hunter and his brothers had been brought into the world to stop death-magic creatures from tipping the balance in their favor. Not because the death magic might win, but because the world could crumble and die if the balance shifted too far.

If an evil creature with intelligence drained the world of life magic, it would know it would only destroy itself in the end. What kind of being was that suicidal? And how could Tain be behind this—Tain, of all people?

When Hunter had lost his family, Tain had been the most sympathetic. The others had more or less implied that Hunter shouldn't have lost his heart to a human in the first place. They felt bad for him, but Adrian especially had warned him of the folly of falling in love. Love was not for Immortals.

Hunter had learned his lesson the hard way. From then on, he'd pursued women purely for fun—to give them ultimate pleasure and to enjoy himself doing it. He fought battles, made love to women, lived with intensity, and never engaged his emotions.

He did not bother to ask himself why he now cast off the sailboat and made for Los Angeles in pursuit of the beautiful witch who might be in danger, instead of figuring out how he could find his brothers and stop the death magic. That would have raised too many questions he couldn't answer.

CHAPTER NINE

"My mother lived here for twenty years," Samantha said as she and Leda looked around the living room of the house.

"I can feel the wards." Leda closed her eyes and touched a window frame, sensing the runes etched there in magic, glowing like shining silver in her mind. "Some have broken, but others are still in here. I can repair them, at least."

"She didn't go willingly." Samantha put her hands on her hips and surveyed the living room as Leda restored the broken lines of magic. "Look at this place."

It was a mess. Furniture lay scattered haphazardly; a glass had been smashed on the floor, the smell of alcohol still faint. The kitchen was likewise trashed, a smear of blood on the tile floor.

Worry pinched Samantha's eyes. "They tested the blood. It matched the DNA in a strand of hair from my mother's hairbrush. It was hers."

Leda felt a pang of sympathy. When she'd heard about her husband's illness and his doctors pronounced a death sentence, Leda had wanted to fight and scream, to do anything not to lose him. How much harder must it be for Samantha not to even know whether her mother was alive or dead?

"Wards can stop magical entries such as portals, or at least the wards give warning, like an alarm system," Leda said. "If your mother worried about this demon coming for her, she'd have strong shields against portals. It's unlikely he'd get in that way."

"Can you tell what happened at all?" Samantha asked, frustration in her voice.

"I'm afraid not, but she certainly did fight." Catching Samantha's disappointed look, Leda continued quickly, "What I can do is look at this place magically and see what shadows I can find. When something frightening happens in a place, it leaves vibrations and bad energies, which can be seen magically, kind of like taking an aura of a place. Events imprint on it. That's why people think houses are haunted when they're not—it's the residue of a terrible event, not necessarily a ghost."

Samantha nodded once. "What do you need to do the spell?"

"Incense and wind chimes. My magic is aligned with the element of air, so I do best when using air accoutrements. I brought plenty of supplies with me, so I can start right now if you want."

Samantha plopped onto the sofa, which had been dragged sideways across the room. "I'm sorry, Leda, I didn't mean to snap. I'm just worried. If you need a good night's sleep first, you should take it. I remember my mother warning that a witch shouldn't perform strong magic when she's not completely rested. She was always careful."

"The images fade as time goes on," Leda said. She retrieved her shoulder bag, which she'd dropped by the door. "Though I wouldn't mind a nap. We should stay here, if you can stand to. Even breathing the air of the house will help me reconstruct a picture."

"That's not a problem." Samantha looked around glumly. "My mother loved this house. I spent most of my childhood here."

The house was typical of old Pasadena, stucco with a Spanish-style tiled courtyard, a fountain and arched doorways. It had an airy living room that led into a kitchen, two bedrooms and a bathroom downstairs behind the kitchen, and a tiled staircase curving between smoothly plastered walls to two large bedrooms on the second floor.

The upstairs bedrooms Samantha showed her were neat and clean, with no evidence of the violence downstairs. Whoever had broken in, whatever had happened, no one had ascended the stairs.

One room belonged to Samantha's mother. "The other one was my room," Samantha said. "We fixed it up into a guest room after I left, but it's mine whenever I need to stay here. You can take it."

Leda and Samantha stood on the small landing, which held a carved Spanish-style armoire. "I'd rather stay in your mother's room if you don't mind. Every little bit will help me to get a clear picture of her."

Samantha didn't look happy, but she agreed. She followed Leda into the room and sat down on the bed. "Hunter will come after you."

"He'd never leave Mukasa and Taro alone. He cares about animals more than he does people."

Leda felt slightly guilty about tricking him, but being trapped on the island was not what she wanted.

She had no doubt he could have made a shield that wouldn't allow her to leave until he was good and ready to lift it. But after the intensity of sex, he hadn't noticed her catch air in her fingers and let a sleep spell slither into his mind. That she could spell him at all surprised her, but, granted, he'd been quite distracted.

Samantha gave her a look. "He'll find a way. Don't think that because you're sleeping with him you can trust him, that he won't hurt you. He's a killer—I saw it in his eyes."

Leda opened her bag and started sorting out her implements, spices for incense, mortar and pestle, incense bowl. "He also has an incredible gentleness in him."

Samantha did not look convinced. "How long have you known him?"

"I met him yesterday." *When he barreled into my life and took over.*

"Well, it's none of my business. But he's dangerous, far more dangerous than I could ever be. You be careful."

Leda's answer was interrupted by someone thumping on the door downstairs. Samantha rolled her eyes and left the bedroom.

Leda, more cautious, went to the window, but because of the slope of the porch roof she could see nothing directly below. No car stood in the street outside the house other than Samantha's. A concerned neighbor? An angry Hunter come to fetch her back to the island?

The warning magic of the wards suddenly went off like alarms, tingling her skin and searing inside her brain. She raced out of the room and down the stairs. "Samantha, don't—"

Samantha had already thrown open the door. The

overcast May evening had darkened, the porch light throwing a glare over the two men who stood on the doorstep. They had dark hair and sensual good looks, black eyes that tried to suck Leda to them as soon as she looked at them. *Crap.*

"Who the hell are you?" Samantha demanded.

The first man smiled, the curve of his lips sinful and seductive. But then, all demons were seductive.

"Maybe you didn't hear," he said, his voice low and velvet smooth. "This house is in our territory. You belong to us now."

Hunter docked the boat under leaden skies in an empty slip in Marina Del Rey. He'd sailed straight through the harbor and into the marina, ignoring the marked-off lanes and the shouting of people from other boats.

There were many empty slips in the marina, not too surprising, considering that the city beyond the forest of masts stank of death magic. He felt the pall of despair in a city usually vibrant; heavy clouds mixed with pollution blotted out the sunshine that many people came here to seek.

"Hey!" a man in the next boat said as Hunter tied up. "You can't pull in here. Guest slips are on the other side."

Hunter ignored him and started securing the boat. The man continued to watch until Mukasa wandered out of the cabin, looking around with interest.

"Holy shit." The man removed his baseball cap and stared, his brown eyes wide. He shoved the cap back on when Mukasa growled lightly. "That's a lion."

Hunter ignored both lion and man. He finished covering the rolled-up sail and tying up the boat, then leapt lightly to the dock, still in bare feet. Mukasa climbed after him, the fetid wind off the water stirring his mane.

Hunter unhooked the radio from his belt and flicked it on. "Leda, where are you?"

Static crackled, then nothing. He looked across the docks to the hotels that lined the shore and the teeming city beyond. Leda was out there—somewhere.

Samantha was paranormal police. They'd know where she was and how to find her, and Hunter could make them tell him. Very few people refused Hunter's requests, especially when they had his sword at their throat.

He left the boat, Mukasa following. The man in the next boat watched them go, still staring in stunned shock.

At the entrance to the marina, Hunter compelled a taxi driver to stop for him, and to allow Mukasa to ride in the backseat. He told the white-faced and terrified driver to take him to the main Los Angeles police station, and they roared out into a darkening city.

"I don't belong to anyone," Samantha declared.

She tried to slam the door in the demon's face, but it hit a magical force and sprang open again. The demon smiled. "That's better."

Leda silently began a spell that would keep her resistant to the demon's seductive magic. She tried to draw on the air to enhance her magic, but it was so tainted with death magic that she let it go immediately.

The demon's smile widened. "Everyone in this territory belongs to us. We came to see that all your needs are met."

"Go screw yourself," Samantha said. "I know demons can do that if they really want to."

The demon reached for her. "I'll enjoy teaching you obedience, I think." He touched the wards Leda had strengthened, flinched and drew his hand back.

Samantha pulled a leather card holder out of her back pocket and opened it in his face. "I'm paranormal police. You just violated about fifteen codes and three laws. Leda, why don't you call for backup?"

"Parapolice," the demon spat. "They're in our pocket, little girl. You been out of town? We own the police here." He took an automatic pistol out of his leather jacket. "Take down the wards, and maybe I won't punish you as much as I want to."

Leda's heart thumped. This was a demon out of control, no longer caring about the laws that kept his kind from sucking humans dry. The wards wouldn't stop a bullet—she couldn't make a shield like Hunter had done when Valdez's men emptied their weapons at him. If she let down the wards, she and Samantha were sitting ducks; if she didn't, they could be dead ones.

A second demon behind the first also had a pistol. He trained it on Leda and purred, "Come to papa."

Leda drew on magic deep inside her, envisioning runes in her head that sparked like fire. If she could touch the demons, she could hurt them, but not if they shot her first.

"My, my," said another voice in the growing darkness. "What have we here?"

It was not Hunter's voice, but a smooth, cultured tone that held the weight of ages, the sureness of strength, and a hell of a lot of death magic.

An Old One, Leda thought. *But not a demon.*

A man stepped into the light. He wore a well-tailored black suit, a supple leather coat and black leather gloves. His dark hair was pulled into a short ponytail, and he had a strong, handsome face with high cheekbones. He wore dark sunglasses, even though the sun had already set over the cloud-packed horizon.

Leda felt death magic roll from him, tainting the already dark air. He was powerful, whoever he was. Mortals and lesser death-magic beings wouldn't stand a chance if he let out one-tenth of the darkness she felt from him.

The first demon hissed. "Get out of here, vampire. This is our take. Everything here belongs to Eidja."

"Not anymore," the vampire answered. Leda saw several other vampires in the shadows behind him, all in black. They exuded death magic of a different kind, a lust for blood and sex that went beyond even a demon's obsession. "I killed Eidja ten minutes ago. This street is mine."

The first demon looked uneasy. The second one paled, swung around and shot the vampire in the chest.

The vampire merely turned his head and stared at the demon. He held out a gloved hand, and the pistol flew out of the demon's grip and into the vampire's. The vampire closed his fingers around the pistol, and pieces of it clattered to the tile.

The dark-magic hold on the house weakened, and Samantha had the presence of mind to slam the door and lock it. She ran for the phone while Leda traced runes over the door frame, chanting the strongest warding spell she knew. Outside she heard a crunch of bone, and both demons screamed horribly.

"Damn it!" Samantha bellowed into the phone. "What is the matter with you?"

Leda heard a distinct *click* from the other end, and then Samantha stared at the receiver in her hand. "My captain told me not to fight," she said, dazed. "He told me to do whatever the vampires said, that they're not sending squad cars out anymore." She slammed down the phone. "It's a free-for-all gang war out here."

The screaming in the courtyard died into a gurgle. After a moment's silence, there was a polite knock on the door.

"Terrific," Samantha said. "What's worse, two demons with guns or five vampires without them?"

Then came the unmistakable sound of locks clicking as the three deadbolts on Samantha's front door unlocked themselves. The door swung open on a wave of dark magic, the leather-coated vampire standing square in the doorway.

"The vermin are dead," he said smoothly. "You are under my protection now."

Leda continued to conjure wards. "Forgive me if I don't do a happy dance."

The vampire smiled faintly. "My name is Septimus. I am the acquaintance of a witch called Amber Silverthorne."

"Never heard of her," Leda said, then stopped. There had been a witch in the Coven of Light named *Susan* Silverthorne, although Leda had never met her. Susan was a powerful witch, one of the most adamant against messing with death magic. "Why would a witch make friends with a vampire?"

Again the faint smile. "Why indeed? To prevent the end of the world, perhaps."

"What are you talking about, the end of the world?" Leda demanded. "You mean the draining of life magic? Why would you care about that?"

"And why would a vampire want to work with a witch against demons?" Samantha put in.

Septimus tilted his handsome head and contemplated Leda and Samantha with his flat sunglasses. Leda realized he wore them so he wouldn't catch the women in his vampire gaze, and it interested her that he and his other vamps took the precaution. One look into the eyes of a vamp as powerful as he, and she and Samantha would be drooling blood slaves begging for his bite before they knew what happened.

"First," he said in his suave voice, "I hate demons, and I'd side with anyone and his dog against them. Second, an Immortal turned rogue has teamed up with a demon to end the world. Third, I enjoy my un-life, every brilliant facet of it. Why should I let a demon like Kehksut ruin it for me?"

Leda stared at him. "Did you say an *Immortal*? An Immortal is doing this?"

"One who's gone insane," Septimus answered. "If you think a death-magic creature run amok is bad, I assure you a life-magic creature out of control is worse. He's convinced he's on the side of good, you see. He's lost everything, and he's trying to ease his pain."

Samantha gave Leda a hard look. "You told me Hunter had lost his family. You didn't tell me it had made him this crazy."

"It can't be Hunter," Leda said quickly. "He didn't know what was going on."

Septimus's dark brows rose. "You know Hunter?"

"We've met," Leda said.

"She's his lover," Samantha said. "I'm sorry, Leda, but if Hunter's behind this—"

"It isn't Hunter," Septimus broke in calmly. "I've

had the pleasure of meeting the Immortal Hunter, once long ago. Though he is quite insane in his own way, it is his brother Tain who has teamed up with the demon. I encountered this demon, and believe me, he is as powerful as the Immortals themselves. And now he and Tain work together. You can imagine what evil deeds they could get up to."

"Hunter mentioned Tain," Leda said in surprise. "He said Tain was a healer."

"Maybe he was once. He is a force of destruction now." Septimus straightened his gloves. "You are not safe here. I will take you to my club, where you can be protected. My vampires will patrol this neighborhood, which belongs to me now, but that does not mean the demons would not attack in force."

Samantha snorted. "We'll be safe at a vampire nightclub?"

"Much safer than you will be here." He slanted his sunglasses-covered eyes at Leda. "If you, witch, are truly Hunter's lover, and he discovers I did not protect you with every power I have, he will light up his fire-sword and try to part my head from my shoulders. I fought him once. Once was enough."

"You obviously survived," Leda observed.

"Barely. He let me live after three days of constant fighting. He got bored, which is the only reason I was allowed to walk away." He made a polite gesture. "Please, ladies, my limousine is waiting to take us downtown."

"You must think we're crazy," Samantha argued.

"Wait." Leda stopped her. "Who is this witch you talked about? Amber. Is she related to Susan Silverthorne?"

"Susan was her sister's name, yes."

"Was?" Leda asked in surprise.

"Amber's sister Susan is dead. Murdered by the very demon who enslaved Tain. I assisted Amber and Adrian, the oldest Immortal brother, in trying to find out what happened to her and why."

"Dead," Leda repeated, stunned. Susan had been one of the most powerful witches in the Coven of Light.

"Slain by the demon while she was trying to find out what happened to Tain. Her sister has taken up the fight with Adrian. They and the Coven of Light invoked the Calling spell, but Kehksut interfered, and the Immortals were scattered. Adrian and Amber wait while the rest of us try to find the Immortals and gather them to stop the storm."

"Very poetic," Samantha said.

"But easy enough to verify," Leda said. "I'll need to make a call."

CHAPTER TEN

Leda expected a chilly welcome from Yvonne, one of the Coven of Light witches in Los Angeles, but the voice on the other end of the phone exuded relief. "Leda, I'm so glad to hear from you. We're having a lot of trouble."

"And you need all the help you can get?"

"Something like that. Coven of Light members, at least the ones here in L.A., are being stalked and killed—in horrible ways. You might be safe because you weren't here for . . ."

She trailed off as though wondering how much she should reveal.

"Because I didn't participate in the Calling spell?"

"How did you know about that?"

"A little vampire told me. He's trying to convince us he's legit and on our side, so tell me all about the Calling."

She listened to Yvonne's tale in growing amazement. As Septimus had claimed, the Coven had joined remotely with Amber in Seattle to form a circle to Call the Immortals. Adrian, the oldest Immortal, had declared that only the brothers together could stop Tain and his demon. Now the Coven members and Adrian's friends searched the earth for the missing Immortals and tried to stay safe.

"Septimus is on our side," Yvonne finished. "He's got most of the vampires in Los Angeles under his thumb—but not all of them, so be careful. Demon and vampire gangs are dividing the city between them, and Septimus is the only one fighting them. Everyone else has given up."

Leda hung up the phone in a daze. On her island, she'd lost track of the world, and she liked it that way. She had much pain she needed to bury. Hunter had wanted her to remain there, had wanted to stay himself. Live isolated, in relative safety, and forget about the rest of the world.

But hiding wouldn't help. If Septimus and Yvonne were right, this problem would eventually reach the corners of the earth and wipe out every living thing. Even the Undine, the strange water spirit of her island, had sensed it coming.

Yvonne had given Leda the phone number for Amber in Seattle before she'd hung up. Leda started to dial again, but Septimus moved impatiently.

"Call her in the car. We need to go. This neighborhood is unstable."

Leda insisted on fetching the magical equipment she'd left upstairs before Septimus took them out to a long black limousine with smoked-glass windows. The luxurious interior went with Septimus—leather seats, flat television screen, a stocked bar. Samantha looked around in interest mixed with distrust while

Leda punched numbers into her cell phone to call Amber Silverthorne in Seattle.

Hello, my name is Leda Stowe, and I've found an Immortal.

The city was careening toward chaos, Hunter thought as the taxi bearing him and Mukasa wound through the streets toward the Los Angeles Police Department, Paranormal Division. He saw more than one group of demons lurking in the shadows, and it was all he could do not to stop the driver so he could leap out and kill them. But he wanted to find Leda first; he could enjoy himself slaughtering demons later.

The officers at the police station confirmed his chaos theory. They didn't want to talk to him—to anyone. Hunter smelled the death magic permeating the building and realized that the first thing the demons had done was take over the law enforcement. A fearful desk sergeant did provide an address for Samantha at least.

The same taxi driver took him to Pasadena, seeming to sense that he'd be protected with Hunter. As they rode, the driver told Hunter about the demon and vampire gangs and the violence that had erupted lately, worse than the city had ever seen.

The driver stopped in front of an innocuous-looking house and got out when Hunter and Mukasa did, as though too afraid to remain in the car.

The vampire guarding the house backed away from the lion that advanced on him until he was up against the wall. Hardly less frightening was the muscle-bound warrior who held the tip of a giant serpentine sword at his throat.

"Where are they?" Hunter demanded.

The vampire babbled, "Septimus took them downtown. They're safe with him, I swear. We didn't touch them."

The vampire's eyes were wide with alarm, shining in the porch light. Hunter was one of the few beings who could look into a vamp's eyes and not be ensnared. Hunter read fear that went all the way back—fear of Hunter in front of him, fear of Septimus if he disobeyed.

Behind him, the taxi driver said, "There's a vamp called Septimus who runs a club. He's supposed to be a head honcho among vampires or something. When the gang wars started full throttle in the last couple of weeks, he staked out a large territory for himself."

The vampire's fangs gleamed. "Staked? Was that supposed to be a joke?"

"No," the driver answered, paling.

"Where is this club?" Hunter demanded.

"Hunter?"

The porch light seemed to dim, but it was Leda's voice behind him. Without moving his sword from the vampire's throat, Hunter turned.

She stood in the doorway, her blouse spreading to reveal the swell of her lovely breasts over a lace bra he could just glimpse. When she moved close to him and touched him, he knew two things: He missed Leda more than he realized he would, and this woman wasn't Leda. The taint of darkness over her was enough to make him retch. He wondered who she was and what she wanted. Only one way to find out.

"You're all right?" he asked, playing along.

Her warm fingers slid up his arm. "Yes. I'm sorry, Hunter, I didn't mean to abandon you. But they need you. Tain needs you."

She tugged at his hand, wanting him to go into the house with her. Hunter didn't want to linger, but he sensed that finding out what this demon wanted was important.

The vampire didn't look like he would run off anytime soon, and Mukasa had him pinned. Hunter said, "Be right back," and let the women lead him inside.

The vampire said nothing, but Mukasa didn't like it. The lion snarled, his eyes glowing yellow, his lips drawing back from long teeth. The door swung shut by itself behind Hunter, cutting off Mukasa's growls.

A bed stood right in the middle of the living room, swathed in black satin with a canopy of black curtains around it. The woman who looked like Leda undressed slowly, first her blouse, then the black lace bra, then her jeans and panties.

She led him to the bed and pushed him down onto the slick satin. Hunter lay back while she climbed on top of him, her knees on either side of his hips. Her long hair fell around her body in sweet ringlets.

"Hunter," she purred, her fingers on his chest. "You said you could give me a child."

"Maybe." He wondered how the hell this demon woman knew what he'd said intimately to Leda, and his rage grew with his worry. If she'd done anything to Leda, she would know pain so intense that she'd beg Hunter to simply kill her.

"I know losing your children was hard," she said silkily. "You've held back all these years so you won't be hurt again. But let me be your vessel. I want this. I'll be so good to the baby."

He heard Mukasa roar, the lion's huge paw scraping the door. She smiled down at him, seductive, beautiful, her eyes so dark they were nearly black.

He realized the demon on him had reached into his mind and pulled out what he wanted to see, what he craved most. In a thousand years he'd not again met a woman he wanted to love, to marry as the humans did, to raise a family, until he'd found Leda. He wanted the real Leda saying these things, the true Leda smiling at him and promising to be good to his children. He wanted that brief piece of happiness, even if it meant losing her in the end.

"Stop pretending to be Leda," he growled. "What did you do with her?"

She pouted. "*Hun*ter. I belong to you. I'm yours."

The lion battered at the door, his claws scraping gouges in the wood. Hunter reached out with his magic and let him in.

Leda's form vanished, to be replaced by a seductively beautiful woman with long black hair. Her hands on his chest turned to razor-sharp claws, and she plunged them into his skin.

Mukasa sprang. The demon ripped her claws from Hunter, leaving long gouges that ran with blood. She threw a stream of death magic at Mukasa, sending the big cat backward.

Hunter hit the demon with his own magic. She flew straight up to slam against the ceiling and hung there, her naked body still lush, her swath of midnight hair hanging down.

"Immortals," she hissed. "So full of yourselves."

"Get over it, darling."

"I will kill her. I will suck out her life and enjoy every screaming moment of it."

Hunter rolled out of the bed in fury. He scraped up his sword from the carpet and lunged at her, but a portal suddenly opened in the ceiling behind the demon. It sucked her into it, then closed, leaving nothing behind but her trailing laughter.

Hunter blinked once—and found himself standing outside in the quiet courtyard, fully dressed, his sword fixed on the wide-eyed vampire. The front door was closed, the wood ungouged by lion's claws, the night still. Mukasa growled softly.

"What was that?" the vampire asked nervously. "You kind of zoned out for a second or two."

Hunter pulled himself together, wondering what the hell had just happened. A vision, a dream, or some way-too-powerful magic.

"Tell me where to find this Septimus," he snarled at the vampire. "Now."

The club the vampire directed him to was in the heart of downtown Los Angeles near Little Tokyo, in an area that had once been full of chic shops and restaurants. Now most of the stores and eateries were closed, metal awnings shut tight over the windows and walls covered in graffiti. No one walked abroad on this street except vampires and those in their protection.

Mukasa leapt out of the back of the taxi when Hunter opened the door for him, his growl echoing on the quiet street. The driver gunned the engine, and Hunter smiled and slammed the door. He'd not paid his fare, but the driver didn't seem to want to wait for the money. He peeled away from the curb and roared down the street as fast as he could, happy to be quit of Hunter.

Hunter had warded the car heavily while they rode, so the driver should be the safest in town. He gave the vanishing taxi a wave and turned to enter the club.

A well-dressed vampire behind a counter in the

vestibule greeted Hunter with a flat stare. "Check your sword here. No weapons allowed."

Hunter met him stare for stare, and after a moment, the vampire began to back away uncertainly. The vampire's gaze then fell on Mukasa as the lion shouldered his way through the door, and his already pale face blanched even more.

"Where is the vamp called Septimus?" Hunter growled.

The guard swallowed hard. "In the back, in his office. He's expecting you."

"I'll find it." Hunter shouldered his sword, raised his brows at the bouncers at the door, who backed hastily away from him, then strolled into the club, followed by Mukasa.

It was a typical vampire place, decorated in black and blood-red, staccato in-your-face music, vampires dancing close and seductively with their blood slaves or one-timers who thought they wanted to be blood slaves. The dance floor was crowded with people full of bravado, believing they were safe in the citadel of a vampire lord.

Humans and vampires alike did double takes when they saw the warrior with a serpentine sword stride across the floor, followed by a lion. A path opened for him, the fearful in front pressing against the curious behind them.

The door to the back rooms was fairly obvious, because two large vampires in suits flanked it. When Hunter approached, one vampire touched an earpiece, nodded, and stepped aside to open a door for him.

Hunter found a short corridor with a door at the end, which opened of its own accord. He felt the death magic of an Old vampire, the faint tang of Samantha's death magic, but also Leda, the sharp bright aura of her, pink and orange and honey-scented.

Leda got out of a chair when he came into the room and waited uncertainly. A tall vampire in a black silk suit rose from behind the desk, but Hunter's first interest was for Leda.

"Hunter, I'm sorry," she began.

"You don't need to say that." He went to her and pulled her to him, his body relaxing into the warm feel of her. This was the real Leda, sweet and vulnerable and strong at the same time. Never minding the vampire, he brushed his lips over her mouth, wanting a taste of her.

"Hunter," she murmured, breath warm. She tried without success to push away. "You brought Mukasa to Los Angeles."

"He wanted to come. I saw no reason to stop him."

"What about Taro?" She looked alarmed. "You didn't leave him out there alone, did you?"

"The Undine is looking after him. He didn't want to go out on such a tiny boat."

Leda gave him another startled look. "Are you sure he'll be all right?"

"Very sure. Or I'd not have left him."

Leda sighed, half relieved, half resigned. "Goddess, what am I going to do with you?"

Hunter rumbled his answer into her ear. "I have some ideas."

She flushed and turned away as the tall vampire came around the desk. He wore a dark suit and sunglasses, which he removed to let Hunter see the depths of his eyes.

"Hunter, is it?" he asked. "I'm glad you've come, although our last meeting was less than convivial."

Hunter looked him up and down, smelling the death magic rolling off him. This vampire was an Old One, powerful, magical, dangerous.

"You don't remember?" the vamp asked dryly. "I remember you and that sword of yours. You did your best to kill me, about a hundred years ago."

"I fight a lot of vampires," Hunter said shortly. "I kill most of them, especially Old Ones. I must have been drunk if you're still alive."

"We went three days without a break, and then you walked away. Good thing for me; I wouldn't have lasted much longer. I tried asking for a truce, but you wouldn't listen."

"Maybe I thought I'd leave you alive, to come back and kill you another day."

"How very thoughtful of you. I'm Septimus, by the way. A colleague, shall we say, of your brother Adrian. He's looking for you."

"I heard that." Hunter seated himself in an empty chair and pulled Leda to stand next to him, his arm still firmly around her waist. "Walk me through what's been happening."

Hunter listened in disquiet while Septimus confirmed what Kali had told him. Tain wanted to end the pain of his torture by ending the world.

"The Coven of Light is searching for Kalen and Darius as we speak," Septimus finished. "Leads have turned up in Manhattan and Scotland. And now you. I'm pleased to see you, even if you're not as excited to see me. The world is going to hell fast, and I wouldn't mind if you put a stop to it."

"Why?" Hunter's eyes narrowed. "I would think you'd like the destruction."

"Not really. I like my power. I like neatness." Septi-

mus ran a fastidious gaze up and down Hunter's dusty
jeans and worn T-shirt. "And I hate demons."

"Something we can agree on."

"Adrian has a house in Malibu. With his Immortal
magic woven over it, it's more protected than anything I have. The ladies can stay there while I make
arrangements to fly you to Seattle and join Adrian. I
won't go myself. If word gets out that I've left Los Angeles, things will fall apart."

"Good ideas," Hunter agreed. "Except I go out to
the Malibu house *with* Leda. I'm not letting her travel
alone again."

"If you wish. My limousine will take you where you
want to go." He flicked a gaze to Mukasa, who was
nudging Leda with his head in the happy way of cats.
"Does he have a cage?" he asked in a pained voice. "I
fear for my leather upholstery."

"He won't hurt it," Hunter said, but Septimus
looked less than reassured.

There was plenty of room in the limousine for all of
them, as it turned out. Mukasa peered through the
smoked glass at the driver, curious.

"Easy, big fella," the vampire driver said.

Mukasa narrowed his eyes at being called *big fella*
but settled heavily onto the seat. Hunter ushered Leda
and Samantha into the car, then slid his arm around
Leda and cradled her against him as he closed the door
and the driver pulled out into the night.

CHAPTER ELEVEN

"Look at this place," Samantha said as she watched Los Angeles flowing by the darkened windows.

Leda craned to see from the circle of Hunter's arms, the heat of his body surrounding her like a cocoon. He hadn't released her hand since they left Septimus's club, his broad fingers twined firmly through her slender ones.

His breath on her neck made needy warmth move at the juncture of her legs. She'd expected Hunter to behave like an arrogant male, shouting at her for daring to put a spell on him and leave him behind. But he sat in silence, locking her in place with his strong arms. Instead of yelling at her for leaving him, he was making sure she couldn't do it again.

The solid bulk of his chest and the length of his body against hers made her realize how much she wanted him, how relieved she'd been when he'd come charging into Septimus's office after her. She wanted all of him to herself for hours, where she could show him how difficult it had been for her to leave him behind. If they'd been alone in the limousine, she would have slid open his jeans, sunk to her knees and taken him in her mouth.

She blushed in the darkness. She'd never blatantly wanted such carnality—even when she was married, sex had been nice, but she hadn't *needed* it. Now she craved Hunter like a starving woman.

As though he sensed her desire, Hunter leaned toward her and brushed a kiss to her exposed neck. His lips slid across her skin, his breath tickling and warm. She turned her head and their mouths met, his lips singeing hers.

He kissed her for a while, sliding his hand under her hair. The bulge in his jeans was suddenly under her fingers, and he made a quiet sound of longing. He seemed in no way embarrassed to kiss her like this in front of Samantha, but he was an ancient being, Leda reasoned, having lived in times and places in which sex was not always taboo.

Samantha wasn't watching them in any case. She kept her gaze out of the window, her mouth turned down. "It's already gone to hell," she went on. "I shouldn't have taken that leave of absence from my job."

"Did they give you a choice?" Leda asked her. Hunter continued to press small kisses to her neck and ear, very distracting.

Samantha shook her head. "They've let the city become a war zone. Demons and vampires have always had territories, but now they're conquering the entire metropolitan area, and the police are letting them."

"As the life magic drains, the death-magic creatures get stronger," Hunter rumbled. "When the balance is broken, there will be chaos, and then—nothing. Even the death magic will cease to exist."

"Why would a demon want that?" Leda asked. "Why should a powerful demon want everything obliterated, which I assume means himself as well?"

"I don't know." He turned his head and looked out the window, his eyes narrowing. "Something isn't right. . . ."

Suddenly he left the seat, reaching for the door handle. "Stop the car."

"This is a bad place," the driver said through the intercom. "Edge of demon territory."

Hunter opened the door anyway. The driver grated a swear word and swerved the limo to the curb. Hunter's feet touched the pavement the instant the car halted, his sword in his big hands.

Leda climbed out behind him, looking around, but she saw nothing unusual, only shut-up buildings and flickering streetlights, the occasional car rushing past as though the driver was nervous to be out.

Hunter moved away from the car and stood in the middle of the street, his feet on the painted line. His gaze took in the closed shops and boarded-up apartments above them, the dark mouths of alleys, his sword held ready.

The vampire driver hauled himself out of the car. "What are you doing? This is a bad neighborhood. I can't let something happen to the boss's car because you wanted to sightsee."

Hunter ignored him. His massive shoulders worked as he brought the sword around slowly, much like he'd done when he'd performed his precision exercises on the beach. He lowered the blade and stood poised, listening.

"We're missing something," he said softly.

"Hunter," Leda called. "He's right. We need to go."

Hunter stood still, preoccupied. He looked up one side of the street and down the other, then turned and walked back to the car, his gait unhurried. Without a word he held the door open for Leda, then climbed in behind her.

Before Hunter could even get the door shut, the driver peeled the limo out into the street. The door slammed, and Hunter fell back into the seat.

"What was that about?" Leda asked him.

He gazed out the window again, his sword at their feet, and took her hand in his protectively. "The world is . . . wrong."

"You said that before, when you first woke up in my house."

"I feel it more strongly now. Something is not right."

"The draining of life magic," Samantha suggested.

"Not just that." The limo squealed around a corner and started to climb a hill. "I can't explain. I've never felt anything like this before. Like a veil of magic is hiding what is real."

"I think I'm glad I don't know what you're talking about," Leda said.

He slanted her a glance. "You can't feel it?"

"No. Sorry."

He turned to Samantha, but she shook her head.

"Hmm." He sat back without another word, but still looked uneasy.

They completed their journey in silence, unmolested by demons or other death-magic creatures. The limousine wound up dark hills where only the richest could afford to live, gated driveways leading to hidden houses that were few and far between.

At last Septimus's chauffeur swung into a circular drive in front of a long, flat house, with large double doors and few windows. The vampire screeched the car to a halt, then revved the engine as the three in the back plus the lion climbed out. As soon as Leda slammed the door, the vampire took off fast, squealing out of the driveway and back into the street.

"What's his problem?" Leda glowered at the red taillights.

Mukasa rumbled low in his throat, and Hunter ruffled his mane. "I know, my friend."

"You know our only mode of transportation just left," Samantha pointed out.

"There will be others," Hunter said in his maddening way. Samantha rolled her eyes, but Leda didn't argue with him. Things so far had seemed to happen the way Hunter wanted them to.

Samantha rubbed her arms and shivered, though the May night was balmy. "Can't you feel it?" she asked. "This place reeks of life magic."

"I do feel it." Leda looked with her witch senses and saw ward runes glowing over the doors. She breathed the air coming off the sea and relaxed. "I like it."

Samantha shivered again. "Easy for you to say. It's shielded against death-magic creatures."

Hunter walked to the front door and opened it. Either it hadn't been locked or a deadbolt was no match for his Immortal magic. "It will let you in," he said.

He entered the house, Leda and Samantha close behind him, and Leda found and flipped on the lights. The entry opened into a wide and airy living room, the entire back wall nothing but windows that opened to the sea roaring below. Double doors on each end of the huge hall presumably opened to bedroom suites.

"Nice place," Leda commented.

"Leave it to Adrian," Hunter replied. "He always has to be decadent."

Samantha dropped her bag beside a sofa. "I could use a walk on that beach. I'll be back."

She stepped out onto the deck and started down the wooden stairs that led to the sands below. She hadn't invited Leda or Hunter to join her, which told Leda she needed some time to herself.

Hunter didn't mind. He slid his arm around Leda's waist and walked with her toward the bedroom on the east end of the house. Leda went with him willingly, exhausted from the day and the night. Hunter closed the doors.

The huge bed billowed with white sheets and pillows, the windows inviting the sea air, the kind of air that best enhanced Leda's magic. Hunter explored the room while she dropped her bag and fell backward onto the bed. Soft, clean-scented sheets caught her. She could lie here and drift . . .

"How many leather coats can one man own?" Hunter's voice came, muffled, from the closet.

"At least you'll have a change of clothes," Leda suggested around a yawn. "If you wear the same size, that is."

"Pretty damn close."

He came out, pulling up his T-shirt until it was a tight band across his shoulders, exposing rock-hard pecs and sinewy biceps. He studied Leda on the bed a moment before pulling the T-shirt all the way off and tossing it on the floor. The garment was ruined, with bloodstained bullet holes, plenty of sand, the seams parting where it hadn't quite fit his bulging shoulders.

Leda had the feeling that he went through most of his clothes this way, wore what he needed until it fell to pieces, then tossed it aside and found something new. This house had been occupied by someone who knew how to exist in the civilized world, but Hunter would be at home in a cave.

He walked into the bathroom, voice echoing on the marble walls. "Big brother lives in style. Come and see this."

Leda got off the bed and padded tiredly into the bathroom. Hunter stood in the middle of the white marble floor, hands on hips, surveying the state-of-the-art fixtures.

A large shower with clear glass doors had spigots of various shapes and sizes. The sink was black marble, contrasting with the white floor, and in the middle of it all rose a black marble round bathtub with faucets of gleaming gold. The tub was large enough for two or three. Maybe even four.

Hunter slanted Leda a look. "I know what I want to do the rest of the night."

"Sleep, I hope."

"Are you tired?" he asked, puzzled.

"Aren't you?"

"Not really." He looked fresh and rested despite the pink scars in his back from the bullets and the dark whiskers on his jaw. He might suggest they run a marathon, for all she knew.

He took a step forward and left a bloody footprint on the pristine white tile.

Leda gasped. "Hunter, your feet."

"What about them?"

"You've been running all over Los Angeles bare-foot?"

Hunter's smile returned. "Sweetheart, I've spent my entire life barefoot. Centuries of it. Your peaceful island and the streets of Los Angeles are nothing compared to the jungles of Southeast Asia or the African veldt."

"Which are full of snakes and poisonous insects to step on."

"They don't bite me."

"Right. Speaking of wild animals, will your brother be okay with a lion sleeping in the living room?"

"Mukasa has decided to sleep outside under the back deck. He doesn't like to be enclosed."

"He told you that?"

"He indicated it."

Leda shook her head. "I used to have a sane life. Now I believe an Immortal warrior when he says a lion talks to him."

"No, you didn't." Hunter moved to the bathtub and turned on the hot-water tap. "Have a sane life, I mean. If you're so concerned about my feet, you could wash them for me. . . ."

He sent her a wicked smile over his shoulder, then unzipped his pants and slid them straight from his bare hips to the floor.

Hunter sensed Leda's gaze rivet to his bare back. He liked the way she looked at him, as though she loved everything she saw. He was no stranger to women studying his body, but with Leda, her focus was like a caress, a desire that stirred his own.

He knew she watched him as he leaned to adjust the water and close the drain. For the first time in centuries, he was contemplating sleeping with a woman on a somewhat permanent basis. He never let himself stay after the first night, because he might make an emotional connection, which would lead to pain on both sides. Make love, smile, leave them with pleasant memories—that was his usual practice.

He already regretted connecting with Leda. Part of him wanted to snatch this moment of happiness and hold it tight; part of him knew he should leave her in this fortress his brother had made and go.

He closed his eyes as Leda's hands landed softly on his waist, as her lips brushed his spine. *Too late. Far too late.*

He needed her, he craved her. Her kisses touched his back near the scars Valdez's men's bullets had left. He shouldn't have frightened her, pretending to die like that, but it had been fun to see the looks on the thugs' faces when he'd stood up behind them, ready to fight. He chuckled about it even now.

"What's so funny?" Leda's breath floated across his skin.

"I was thinking about the morning we met."

He gently stepped away from her and into the tub, the hot water stinging the cuts on his feet.

"Which part?" Leda asked. She'd stepped back to watch him, arms folded across her chest, pressing her breasts slightly upward. His erection, already half aroused by her touch, began to lift in earnest.

"The best parts."

"Why did you say I didn't used to have a sane life? It was easy—take care of the animals, consult on their placement, write my reports. Very calm."

She wasn't taking off her clothes, so he reached out a wet hand and undid the first button of her blouse. "Why did you summon the demon and let it invade you?"

Pain entered her eyes. "Because there was no other way."

"Your husband was dying, wasn't he?" Hunter continued with the buttons, brushing soft skin inside her shirt.

She nodded, not asking how he'd figured that out. "He had a viral infection. He was in the hospital, dying while I watched. Healing spells on top of medicine slowed it down a little, but he had only a few days. A very powerful mage might have been able to heal him, but I couldn't find one in time. The groth demon came right away."

Her lashes were wet with tears, and Hunter pulled her close, his hands dripping water onto her open shirt. "You melded the demon's magic with yours and saved your husband," he finished for her. "You must have loved him very much."

"I did at the time." She gave him a watery smile. "But unfortunately, he didn't appreciate the sacrifice."

Hunter loved the way she smelled, all honey and roses. He kissed her forehead, reining in his anger. "You are brave, and your selfish husband didn't deserve you."

"He wasn't selfish," she said swiftly. "Anyone would have been upset by what I did."

The flicker of her eyes betrayed the lie. The man *had* been selfish. Leda might not regret saving his life, but she regretted having loved him.

Hunter kissed her smooth hair. "Where does your ex-husband live? Want me to go scare him?"

Her worried look relaxed. "No, he's gone on with his life, got married—to someone not a witch. I'm happy to never see him again."

"Everything happens for a reason," Hunter said.

She looked up at him. "I said that to you."

"I was sent to you so I could take the demon's magic out of you. That means you decided to summon the demon in the first place, so you could meet me."

She smiled, which had been his intention. "Sure, Hunter. Now we're back to you being arrogant."

The tub was mostly filled, and he seized her around the waist and pulled her down into it with him. She gasped as she fell in, still dressed, sending water over the side in a heaving wave.

"Hunter!"

He took her wet clothes off a piece at a time. The loosened T-shirt fell to the marble floor with a *splat*, followed by the strip of her bra. The jeans were more difficult, but he worked until he wriggled them off her legs and tossed them over the side. The underwear he simply ripped, breaking the bikini strings.

He gathered her close, liking her warm, bare, wet body on top of his. "The gods brought me to you. It was fated, prophesied, destined, whatever. We shouldn't fight it. Right?"

"You are so full of shit."

"I want to stay with you, and I know I can't, but I stay anyway. I could leave you here now and make it so you could never find me again, but I don't."

"You'd want me never to find you again?" she asked, her eyes quiet.

"It would be easier that way."

"Easier for who?"

"I don't know," he said.

She kissed the corner of his mouth, and he turned his head and scooped her to him, sliding his tongue between her lips. Goddess, she tasted good. She *felt* good too, warm and slick under his hands.

"Why don't you go, then?" she whispered against his lips.

"I don't seem to want to."

She slid up his body, the tight berries of her nipples slick against his chest. "It might be easier for me if you did. No more crazy Hunter to drive me insane. I can't keep up with you."

"You're the one who ditched me." He captured her bottom lip in a light nip, then released it. "Going off in the middle of the night."

"I wanted to help Samantha. She needs me. I like feeling needed."

"Be careful of her," he said in all seriousness. "She might not be what she seems."

"She's upset and confused. I know enough about demons to tell whether they're beguiling me—I've become a demon expert. Samantha is fine."

"Still, there's something not right."

Leda rested her head on his shoulder. "You said that in the car. The world was all wrong, you said."

"In some places it feels like there's a veil between what's real and what's not. That's what I felt on the street. I didn't get that on the island."

"This is real." Leda slapped the water, splashing them both. "We're real. This bathroom is real."

"Adrian's magic is all over this house," he agreed. "Mine too now. Demons can't get in except—"

A male voice interjected, "When they come in on your dreams?"

Hunter jerked his head around. A tall man with unruly red hair and eyes an impossibly deep blue stood next to the bathtub. He wore a casual black silk suit, had a pentacle tattoo on his right cheekbone, and held

Hunter's serpentine sword point downward in his black-gloved hands.

Leda didn't seem to see or hear him. She began nibbling Hunter's collarbone, oblivious.

"Tain?" Hunter breathed.

He was solid and real, not an illusion, not a dream, except that Leda had no awareness he was there or that Hunter had spoken to anyone.

"My wild brother Hunter." Tain spoke in his faint Welsh accent, the one that used to drive women crazy. He lifted the sword and rested the point on the lip of the tub, too near Leda's neck for Hunter's comfort. "You left me, too."

"Left you?" Hunter growled. "What the hell are you talking about? I haven't seen you in centuries."

"I was trapped, calling for help. But no one ever came."

Hunter looked him up and down. "Looks like you escaped."

"She set me free. My master and my lover. She thinks she has tamed me." Tain smiled.

It was a chilling smile, and his eyes held a mad light.

"I heard you're taking your pleasure with demons now," Hunter said. "I have to question your taste."

"*She* becomes whatever she needs to be, for me. It is erotic pleasure like you've never experienced."

"I don't know, I've experienced a lot."

"Not like this."

Tain leaned down, moving the sword point until it nearly touched Leda's shoulder. Hunter grasped the tip and pushed it away, and Tain twisted the blade so it cut Hunter's hand. Hunter didn't let go, and drops of crimson blood fell into the water.

"Come with me, Hunter. I'll show you." Tain scraped the sword deeper into Hunter's hand. "It is pain and pleasure all mixed together, power like you never imagined."

Hunter ignored the pain. "Now I know the vamp was right. You *have* lost it."

"The ones you loved were killed," Tain said, as though he hadn't heard him. "It hurt you so much. I remember you trying to beat the pain out of your chest. You didn't know what to do with your grief. I can help you bring them back, you know, to be with them again."

Hunter's anger surged. "How? In some nut-job illusion in my head? No way."

Tain knelt beside the bathtub, his hand still locked around the sword. He touched his fingers to Hunter's cheek. "It will be real. Come with me, and I'll show you. You can bring the witch; you can have them both. There's no taboo against that kind of thing where we would be."

Hunter felt the smooth leather of Tain's gloves, smelled the spice of Tain's breath. Tain was real and here, but only to Hunter. What kind of magic was this? It was more powerful than Immortal magic, but it didn't have the stink of death magic. It was Tain—his pure power.

Hunter scowled. "Is this master of yours—he, she, it, whatever—the same demon who pretended she was Leda yesterday? Who tried to get pregnant off me?"

"She came to you, yes. She cannot come inside here because Adrian guarded this house so well, but he never guarded against me."

"I'm thinking maybe he should have."

Tain leaned still closer, his lips brushing Hunter's

cheekbone. "I need you, Hunter. Of all my brothers, you are the closest to understanding."

"Why, because you think I'm insane, too? There's a difference between doing crazy shit because you don't care what happens, and being twisted up inside your head by a demon. Go play bondage games by yourself."

Tain's gaze flicked up so that Hunter stared straight into the blue depths of his eyes. Behind the madness he saw something that was still Tain, a desperate spark holding itself in rigid despair. It reached out to him, trying to pierce the darkness.

Help me, Hunter.

CHAPTER TWELVE

Hunter reached for the spark, but Tain closed his eyes before he could touch it, and it was gone.

"You will understand," Tain whispered. "You will come willingly—in the end."

"I thought you wanted to die in the end. Drain all the magic out of the world until it's over. Doesn't sound like a pleasure trip."

"You will understand," Tain repeated. "We will be together—you, me, Adrian, Darius, Kalen."

"One big, happy Immortal family."

"Yes." Tain smiled. "Like old times."

Hunter fought to keep from wrestling Tain to the floor and beating the madness out of him. For one thing, he didn't think it would work. For another, he realized Tain had grown incredibly strong. Hunter feared for Leda's safety should Tain decide to retaliate.

"I don't remember these old times," Hunter said. "We all had our own lives and our own things to do. We didn't sit round the hearth fire singing karaoke."

"You know what I mean. Working together, guarding each other's backs. Fighting together." Tain let out a soft sigh. "All that is gone."

Hunter didn't answer. Tain, the real Tain, was far away; this Tain was living in a fantasy world. Hunter had learned as the son of Kali the Destroyer that arguing with someone running on adrenaline and emotion was dangerous. His mother was not the most rational of goddesses, not someone to sit down and have a serious heart-to-heart with. He knew when to approach her and when to back off, and right now, with Tain, he knew it was time to back off.

Tain slowly twisted the sword again, peeling a layer of skin from Hunter's palm. Hunter refused to let go, fearing Tain would plunge the blade into Leda if he did. He had little doubt that, though Leda could not see or hear what was going on, she'd be plenty dead if Tain stabbed her.

More blood dribbled into the bathtub, tiny droplets swirling like red smoke in the water. Tain very slowly withdrew the sword, Hunter's hand burning.

"It gets better," Tain murmured. "The pain becomes exquisite. The best feeling you will ever experience."

Tain's coat and shirt gapped slightly as he moved back, and Hunter saw mottled scars not quite healed—lengthwise and disappearing under his shirt. "Son of a bitch," Hunter whispered.

Tain cast a look at Leda. "She'll die if you don't come with me. She'll be killed, or she'll die at the end. But if you bring her, you can be with her forever."

"This conversation is over," Hunter said, voice hard. He reached for the magic Adrian had woven over the house and pulled it into his body, to blend with his own power. "Get *out*."

He shoved a white-hot ripple of magic at Tain, willing his brother back through whatever hole in hell he'd sprung from. Tain laughed, the magic affecting him not at all. He stood up, dropped the sword to the marble and disappeared.

The clatter of the sword on the cold floor rang loud. Leda's voice blended with it. "Hunter? Are you all right?"

Hunter felt himself slamming back into his body, as though he'd been astral traveling. Leda touched his face, her eyes anxious. "You kind of—"

"Zoned out?" He remembered the vampire's words after the demon had wrenched him away at Samantha's mother's house. "No, I'm here, baby."

She watched him in concern. "You *stopped*. You didn't even breathe. It scared me."

"I'm sorry, sweetheart. Are you all right?"

She nodded, brows drawn. The water in the bathtub was clear and clean, no blood at all, and his palm was whole.

"Ripples in reality," he whispered.

"What does that mean exactly?"

Hunter pressed a kiss to her forehead. All he wanted was to lie in this decadent bathtub with her, hands flowing over her slick skin, exploring her. He wanted to suckle her, to teach her techniques that could only be done in a large tubful of water.

He drew her up for a long kiss, then reluctantly unwrapped himself from her. "I need to make a phone call."

Leda got out of the bath with him, delectable and naked. Wrapping herself in a snowy towel, she followed him back to the bedroom and dug out the phone number Septimus had given her for Amber in Seattle. Not bothering with a towel, Hunter dialed with damp fingers and waited until the sweet-voiced woman who answered put his older brother on the line.

"Adrian?" he said when he heard the deep voice for the first time in centuries. "What the *fuck* is going on?"

Hunter talked to Adrian a long time, but he would not tell Leda right away what he said. Hunter made love to her instead.

He made love like his life depended on it. His hair, still wet from the bathtub, dripped water to her skin, and the damp of his sweat and the bath coated her body. His arms corded with muscle as he rode her until she ached, and still she lifted her hips to him, wanting more.

No slow sensuality of opening her chakras or becoming one with him. He took her in need, as he had on the boat, his jaw hard, green eyes intense.

He sucked the hard point of her nipple into his mouth, his teeth and tongue winding her to a frenzy. When he got to his knees and lifted her onto him, she screamed, her mind going numb to everything but the feel of him widening her, making her slick and hot.

The one thought that slid through her mind was Hunter's claim that he could give her a child or not as she chose. One door her divorce had closed was her chance to have children. Her husband had wanted to wait at first—until they were truly ready, he'd said. When they divorced, he'd said it was a mercy they'd waited because it would have been hard on the children. Leda had been left bereft and wondering if she'd have the chance for a family again.

She could ask Hunter. When all this was over, she could ask him to leave her with a child. She almost did it on the moment, but Hunter closed his eyes and climaxed in a rush, his semen flowing into her hot and hard.

Leda's own coming masked her disappointment. She cried his name and held him close, wanting it and never wanting it to end.

Hunter kissed the curve of her neck and stroked her hair across his mouth. "I need you, Leda," he said, voice hoarse. "I need you so much."

She held him while they wound down, her body still hungry even though she'd just had one hell of an orgasm. She wanted him to stay inside her, to love her again, to go even deeper.

His green eyes clouded with longing that went beyond a human's understanding of it. He was still hard, nowhere near satiation, and he stroked the pad of her lip, gaze intent on her. To his unspoken question, she nodded, and he made a raw sound of anticipation.

He slid himself almost out of her, then back in again, her slick heat sliding him right in. It did not take as long this time for her to press her hips against him, begging for him to take her hard, harder.

Hunter shook his head, the ends of his hair brushing her face. "I don't want to hurt you, love."

"I don't care." She sank her fingers into his arms, her teeth grazing his neck. "I don't want anything but you."

Her orgasm lasted longer this time, her body pulsing against his as his weight pressed her back into the bed. A lovely feeling, to ride the wave of her orgasm with his warmth covering her, the pillows at her back. Another wave came at her, this one of sleep, dark and soothing. It picked her up and rolled her over, her eyes closing on Hunter kissing her damp skin.

When she opened her eyes again, it was daylight and she lay in bed alone, her stiff body punishing her for the frenzy she'd encouraged it to enjoy. She smelled eggs frying and heard water rushing in the shower, Hunter's voice singing over it in a faulty baritone.

She relaxed in relief. He hadn't gone off looking for demons or his brothers, hadn't trapped her here with his magic, claiming it was for her protection. That didn't mean he *wouldn't* rush off without her, just that he hadn't yet.

Leda swung her legs out of bed and suppressed a groan as her muscles protested. She really should learn not to have wild sex with an Immortal man twice her strength, especially not three times in two days. Her job looking after wild animals required physical stamina, but it couldn't keep up with Hunter.

That reminded her she needed to contact the Institute and get some food shipped over here for Mukasa, or else buy up every steak in the local grocery store. She hoped Hunter had brought the supplements, though the Institute could provide those as well.

She pulled clean underwear and clothes out of her bag and slid into them. She needed to shower, but the cooking breakfast smelled so good, she wanted it inside her quickly. She'd clean up later.

Hunter strolled out of the bathroom before she could go, a white towel draped around his neck. This gave her a nice view of his long body, tight pectorals and abs, strong legs, red-gold hair at his groin, and the perfection of his dark, firm cock.

He sent her a half smile as he entered the walk-in closet and started plucking clothes off shelves. He pulled on a sleeveless T-shirt first, leaving the rest of his body exposed a few moments before he slid leather motorcycle pants on over nothing.

Leda closed her gaping mouth. Goddess, he looked good. "Won't those chafe?" she asked in a faint voice.

Hunter sat on the bed next to her, a clean soapy scent blending with the leather of the motorcycle pants. "I still haven't got used to underwear. It was only invented a hundred or so years ago." His thigh touched hers, the sag of the bed pressing her against him.

"What did Adrian say last night on the phone?" she asked, trying to pull herself together. "We were—distracted—before you could tell me."

Hunter smiled at her choice of word. "In a nutshell, he said Tain's crazy and for me to get my ass to Seattle."

"I guessed that part of it. We'll go presumably as soon as Septimus has his plane ready?"

"Yes, but I hate to rely on a vamp."

"We don't have much choice. We could use my boat, but it would take days to sail up there. With a plane it's only a couple hours."

"You could persuade Samantha to lend me hers," Hunter suggested.

"She rented it." Leda looked at him in alarm. "And who would fly it anyway? You?"

"You'd be amazed at my skills, sweetheart. I'm not just good in bed."

"Don't try to make me laugh, this is serious." She paused. "I know you don't want me to go with you, but I can help. I know spells, and I know a bit about how demons think."

"What I want is for you to be safe." He pressed a kiss to her hair. "But I've changed my mind. I do want you to come with me. This house is protected, but you'll be more protected if you're with both Adrian and me. Double protection, even if we have to fight."

"And if your other brothers are there, then four times as much protection."

"If Adrian can find my brothers," Hunter mused. "Kalen doesn't exactly come when called, and I don't know what happened to Darius after we fought together in Scotland. Darius was a good drinking buddy; Kalen, too full of himself. Adrian and Tain were close. This must break Adrian's heart."

"Has Tain gotten that bad?"

"I saw him last night," Hunter said. "When you said I zoned out, I had a vision of Tain. Except I don't think it was entirely a vision. He messed with reality, or my perception of it. He cut my hand with my own sword."

Leda touched his hand, but Hunter's skin was whole and unblemished. He shook his head. "When I came out of it, the blood was gone. But I saw Tain, the real Tain. His mind is twisted all to hell. He's the love slave of some demon and tried to persuade me it was perfectly wonderful. That I should join him."

Leda traced lines across his palm. "Demons do try to make it wonderful. They promise the most intense pleasure you'll ever have."

"Sure, while they're sucking out your life force. Like a drug that makes a person crave the euphoria at the same time as it's melting his brain."

"That's why demons are evil." Leda paused, looking for a way to ask her next question. "Hunter, I know that at the end of this you'll leave. No." She pressed her hand to his lips as he started to speak. "Hear me out. If we win this, if you rescue Tain and kill the demon, I'd like you to give me a child. I want children, Hunter—and something to remember you by."

He went still, all traces of humor and playfulness gone. Hunter liked to act crazy or oblivious sometimes, but the intelligence in his green eyes was vast and ran deep. He'd seen so much in his two millennia of existence and had experienced profound grief.

"It would be a mistake," he said quietly.

"I'm not asking this on a whim. I truly mean it. Why not?"

"I can think of a thousand reasons why not."

"I can think of a thousand reasons why," she countered.

He looked at her sharply. "I know better than most that things don't last. Things, lives, people."

"No kidding," Leda interrupted. "I know life is short and goes by fast. So I grab on to what I have and enjoy the hell out of it while I can."

Hunter's expression was bleak. "That's what I do."

"No, you don't. You don't connect at all. You play the bad boy and pretend you don't care, so you can walk away at the end and say *Didn't we have fun?* I know that when you're finished with me, you'll leave and won't give me a choice. So forgive me if I want some part of you to cherish after you're gone."

Her chest rose and fell with her agitated breath, her fingers curling into fists.

"Leda." He didn't touch her, but his eyes held her in place. "I'm not a man. I'm an Immortal warrior created by goddesses to right wrongs. I can't give you what you want."

She stood up and walked away from him. Her stomach recoiled now at the smell of cooking food, but she knew that if she stayed in the room with Hunter she'd want to knock him back across the bed.

He got between her and the door faster than she thought he could move. "Leda."

"What?" she demanded. "Are you not finished telling me what I can and can't feel?"

"Another woman loved me," he said in a harsh voice. "She died for that love. She wanted my children, and *they* died for it."

"Are you saying it was her fault?"

"No. It was mine. If I had walked away, she would have lived a normal life to its full extent."

"That was a thousand years ago, right?" Leda asked. "Where Hungary is now, you said. I'm betting her lifespan wouldn't have been very long anyway, and you probably gave her incredible joy while she had time. You're only a demigod, Hunter. You don't get to decide who we fall in love with and who we die for."

He gave her a fierce glare. "Do you know how it feels to have someone die for you? Not good. It tears you to pieces. You spend the rest of your life wondering whether you could have prevented it—if you had done something else a minute sooner would it have happened at all?"

Leda put her hands on his shoulders and pushed, but she couldn't move him any more than she could have moved a twenty-ton boulder. "Guess what, Hunter. It's not all about you. Now get out of my way so I can have breakfast. I'm hungry."

He remained in place, watching her with eyes that gave nothing away. She sensed vast hurting in him and anger he hid under his usual banter. Maybe for Immortals, time didn't ease pain as it could do with humans. He'd lived so long and seen so much—maybe it all stayed with him and never went away.

She watched as he slowly tucked his emotions away again, the harsh glow of his eyes softening. He sniffed and frowned. "Someone's frying bacon."

"Don't worry, I'm sure they can make yours vegetarian."

She slid around him, and he let her go this time. She heard him come behind her, but his silence told her the conversation was over. She hid her hurt and pasted on a cheerful expression, vowing not to give up just yet.

The living room was empty, but in the spacious kitchen overlooking a deck she found Samantha with a long-legged blond woman, and a dark-haired man cooking up a storm at the stove.

Samantha greeted her neutrally. She looked more rested, though her face was still pale with worry. "This is Kelly," she said, indicating the blond woman. "She lives next door and has a chauffeur, and says we can use him and her car. So we have transportation again."

Leda gazed blankly at the beautiful young woman in a linen dress and sandals who seemed very much at home in Adrian's kitchen. "You look familiar."

"Kelly O'Byrne," Hunter rumbled behind her. "The actress. She was in that movie *Last Summer*."

Leda placed her. "I really liked that one."

Hunter went on. "And *What's New, The Twenty-one Brigade*, and *Total Shutdown*.

Kelly looked at him in surprise and respect. "Not many know I was in *Total Shutdown*. You must have been talking to Adrian."

Hunter shrugged and peered over the counter at the chef. "I go to the movies a lot. What's that?"

"Don't worry," Samantha said. "I told him about your interesting aversion to meat."

Hunter ignored her. "When did you pick up the vampire lover?" he said over his shoulder to Kelly.

She started, her face whitening. "How did you know?"

"You try to hide the bite marks, but I know what to look for."

Kelly put her hand self-consciously to the silk scarf she'd tied around her neck. "It's Septimus, if you must know. He called last night and told me you were coming, so I brought my cook over for you."

"Septimus is doing a lot for us," Samantha observed dryly.

"He doesn't like what's happening. And he's loyal to Adrian, and is willing to help him."

"Or Adrian will kick his undead ass?" Hunter asked, still watching the cook.

"Something like that."

Further conversation was interrupted by a phone call from Septimus himself. Hunter talked to him for a while in the living room, then returned as Leda scooped a heavenly concoction of eggs, spices, tomatoes and cheese into her mouth.

"He wants to see me," Hunter announced. "He's sending his car. Why they hell are vampires awake in the daytime?"

"He doesn't need much sleep," Kelly supplied. "Septimus is an Old One."

"I know that. Where's the coffee?"

Manny the chef had ground fresh beans and brewed coffee, and Hunter downed three cups of it, not speaking, while the other three ate in silence too. By the time they finished breakfast, Septimus's car, driven by a human this time, pulled up in front of the house.

Hunter got into it alone, telling them to stay put until he got back. He spoke generally, saying nothing directly to Leda. Leda pretended it didn't hurt that the only one he addressed by name was Mukasa.

"Stay here and guard them," he told the lion. "Take care of her for me."

Mukasa seemed to understand. He sat on his haunches as the car glided away, then he turned and walked slowly down the path that led to the beach.

"So what do *we* do?" Samantha demanded. "Twiddle our thumbs until he comes back?"

"No, we do magic," Leda said, reentering the house. "I want to try that locator spell on your mother. I'd prefer to do it at her house, but that's not an option anymore."

"Do you think it will work?" Samantha asked, less than hopefully.

Leda began opening the windows that led to the deck overlooking the sea. "This is where my magic is strongest, where air flows unimpeded. On top of mountains, by the sea, in the middle of the desert. Plus, this place is powerfully magical. If a locator spell will work, it will work best here."

CHAPTER THIRTEEN

The limousine with Hunter in it hadn't made it to the end of the street before the driver jammed it to a halt. Hunter wrapped his hands around his sword hilt, alert, when someone flung the door open. Leda scrambled inside, breathless, and waved the driver to go on.

She cuddled up to Hunter, oblivious of the sword, and said, "I wanted to come with you."

The driver, thinking everything was fine, sped down the hill with a squeal of rubber. At the bottom he turned into a busier street, traffic flowing thick and heavy. Even demons and vampires dividing up the metropolis couldn't thin Los Angeles traffic very much.

"What do you want?" Hunter growled. "Stop trying to look like Leda."

"Oh, darling, you're no fun."

The demon flickered, for a moment becoming the lush black-haired woman he'd seen at Samantha's house, before she took on Leda's lovely features again. She slipped one long leg over Hunter's thighs and slid onto his lap.

Hunter let go of his sword and fastened his hands around the demon's throat. "My favorite method of killing demons is ripping their heads off."

She laughed, a throaty purr. "You won't kill me, Immortal. I'm not your garden-variety demon. I'll find one for you if you like, a lesser breed. You can pull his head off if you want."

"But it would be more fun to rip off yours."

He knew even as he spoke that she was right. This demon possessed more power than anything he'd ever felt. She was the demon who'd sent the death-magic storm to the island, and she could destroy this car, the driver, and a twenty-mile radius of the freeway with the flick of a finger. An Old One who'd grown more powerful than any he'd ever fought.

"Which demon are you?" he asked.

She leaned into him, breasts in a tight satin shirt pressing his chest. "Why do you want to know? So you can bind me with my name?"

"You'd never tell me your true name, any more than I'd tell you mine."

"But I know your name, Immortal. Or I will. I have Tain as my pet, and he'll tell me."

Hunter gave her a fierce smile. "Ah, then he hasn't told you yet."

Annoyance crossed her features. "A matter of time. You can call me Kehksut if you want. Or Amadja. Or Culsu. Whatever you please."

"How about Get-off-me-you-bitch?"

She ran clawed fingers down his chest, tearing the fabric of his T-shirt and drawing blood, as she'd done the day before. "Now, Hunter, honey, that's no way to talk. I want you. I have your brother, but I want you too. What a sweet threesome we'd make."

"I only do threesomes with women, and *not* demons."

She smiled. "It doesn't matter. I will have you in the end. I seduced him, and I will seduce you. And then the others. I'm already working to get Darius and Kalen, and their witch bitches won't stop me." She looked momentarily frustrated, and Hunter wondered if Kalen and Darius had found themselves women as sweet and strong as Leda. She smoothed her features again. "I'll soon have a nice collection."

He wondered also why this demon wanted—or needed—a collection of Immortals. Tain talked about draining the world of magic so he could die, but Hunter couldn't imagine this powerful demon sacrificing herself to ease Tain's pain, particularly when she'd caused that pain in the first place.

So why did she want them? To make sure all the Immortals died together? Or for some other purpose?

Hunter tried to throw her off his lap, but she clung to him in a stranglehold, her death magic wrapping him like chains. She licked his neck. "Come with me, sweetheart. I'll take you to a beautiful place."

"Sorry, there's somewhere I have to be."

"A meeting with Septimus? He'll get over it."

Hunter focused on her perfect face. "Why don't you want me to see him? Will he tell me something that will help me kill you?"

Her lip curled. "The vampire knows nothing, as much as he tries to oppose me. I am saving his death to savor as a treat. Right now, you will come with me."

A portal opened behind her. Dark wind blew out of it, rank and evil. Beyond it was only blackness. Hunter called forth every ounce of magic he could, white-hot fires he'd learned from Kali. The car rippled with his white light, entwined with the dark magic of a demon who'd fed on millions of deaths. He and the demon grappled silently, Hunter's sword falling unheeded to the floor of the limousine.

The portal expanded, widening to enclose the demon, then Hunter. The sword spun once like a weather vane, pointing to the place where he'd sat. Then the portal closed and the light winked out.

The driver, oblivious, pulled the car to a halt in front of Septimus's club, which was quiet for the day. He looked around nervously, not quite trusting Septimus's influence to keep demons away, and opened the back door for the weird being Septimus called an Immortal.

The driver gasped, then swore. The backseat was empty except for a steel serpentine sword lying by itself on the black carpet.

Kelly and Samantha watched with interest as Leda dragged her bag out from the bedroom and began to unpack. Leda hung wind chimes on a hook on the deck, letting the sea air shimmer through them, a sweet, bright sound.

She brought out her mortar and pestle to grind incense and oils, and set yellow pillar candles around the living room. She prepared a mixture of frankincense, sandalwood and patchouli and sprinkled it into a small bowl she used as a brazier.

"Do you mind if I stay?" Kelly asked. "I find this so fascinating."

"I don't mind."

Despite Kelly's relationship with a vampire, her aura was clean and strong, which would lend itself to Leda's spell. Samantha too had a powerful aura, and in this case her death magic might help, since her mother had been brushed with it.

"You wouldn't happen to have a map, would you?" Leda asked Kelly after searching drawers all over the house. Adrian had a paucity of personal possessions and no maps at all. A man who always knew where he was going, perhaps.

"I'll check." Kelly lifted her cell phone in slender, manicured fingers and called her housekeeper. Within half an hour, her housekeeper had delivered five maps—of Los Angeles, Southern California, the state, the western U.S. and the entire country. Manny provided sea salt and a bowl from the kitchen, and matches to light the incense.

It had been a while since Leda had cast a circle. She used to regularly cast one every other day to do devotions or work a little magic on the island. But with the increase in death magic making her circles a little scary—the darkness tapping into the death magic she'd possessed—and then Hunter springing into her life, she'd been too busy.

She regretted it now, because she was out of practice. It was difficult to empty her mind and think only of the circle and its magic, but touching the energy now that Hunter had taken the dark magic from her felt good.

Leda felt the ley line weaving under Adrian's house and opened her mind to it, at the same time as she reached out for the fresh air that poured over the ocean. The wind filled her, swirling power through her like colored light.

She relaxed into the magic, knowing it worked best when she let the element flow through her, and asked the Goddess to enter here. It felt so good to do this again, washed clean of death magic, her powers once more at full strength.

She began centering herself and looking for the magic in the spaces around her. On her right she felt the drag of Samantha's death magic, a small black tint in the otherwise bright white magic of Adrian's home.

Hunter's power swirled through the house like golden fire where he'd reinforced Adrian's wards. Kelly was neutral, her aura touched by neither kind of magic. Septimus hadn't marked her or made her a blood slave. Interesting.

Leda had spread a map of Greater Los Angeles on the table, and over this she suspended a crystal pendulum on a thin chain.

"By Luna and the gods of the air, reveal your sister." Leda closed her eyes, holding the pendulum still. She waited for it to move, to pull firmly in one direction or the other, to give her a starting point at least.

"It isn't working," Samantha said after about five minutes. The darkness of her aura stirred, answering her despair.

"Give it a moment. Magic isn't all flash and show, you know?" Leda said.

"It feels good, though," Kelly breathed. "Like a great meditation session."

"That's what you think," Samantha growled.

Leda stilled herself again, trying to quiet her emotions and feel the nuances of the pendulum, but her argument with Hunter about children had left her restless and hurt. She knew that what she felt for him would only cause her more pain in the long run, and that he was probably right—they should have fun and end it with a clean break.

I don't want a clean break, her treacherous thoughts ran. *I want you, Hunter. All of you, from your crooked smile to your beautiful body, to the way you growl before you come inside me. I want to have that for the rest of my life.*

The pendulum jumped under her fingers. With effort, Leda pulled her concentration back to the crystal. Just when she thought she'd imagined the move, the pendulum swung in a hard arc north. The incense she'd sprinkled on the map moved with it, tracing a trail that led north beyond the Santa Monica Mountains, then it kept going, right off the map.

Leda smiled in excitement. "We'll have to get a bigger map, but it's working . . ."

She broke off and stared in horror. The black powder began to swirl in circles, faster and faster, making the pendulum twist in her hand until the chain broke.

The map exploded. Candles, brazier and pendulum flew across the room, Leda barely letting go of the chain before it ripped her skin raw. The powder drove itself into a point and surged to the ceiling, turning solid, dirty black. Then the incense burst apart like sand in a ferocious storm and slashed through the room.

Kelly screamed. Leda shielded her face with her arms, the powder cutting and burning, and then suddenly everything went still. The incense hung in midair for a moment in silence, then rained abruptly to the floor.

Kelly lowered her arms, smeared with blood, and stared wide-eyed at the pile of ash that had been the map.

Samantha, breathing hard, wiped a trickle of blood from her mouth, hand shaking. "What the hell was that?"

"Demon," Leda said, feeling just as shaky.

"My father?" Samantha gasped. "And he has my mother hidden?"

"I don't know." Leda stared at the ash, loath to touch it. "That was a very strong counterspell, a hell of a shield. Is your father that powerful?"

Samantha slowly shook her head. "I wouldn't have thought so, but I don't really know. We never exactly had many father-daughter talks."

"You might have your chance now," Kelly said from the front window. She'd left the table as soon as everything had quieted, snatching up paper towels to dab off her skin. She stood in the living room, gazing out at something with interest.

Leda heard Mukasa's rumbling before she reached Kelly's side. The lion stood at the end of the driveway, his bulk squarely in front of a man with long black hair. He was too far away for Leda to make out his features, but his dark aura clashed with the life magic around the house.

Beside her, Samantha said a foul word. "That's him all right. The demon who calls himself my father."

"Then it couldn't have been him doing the counterspell," Leda said. "If he was strong enough to get through the shield of two Immortals to counterspell me, he wouldn't be stuck at the end of the driveway hoping Mukasa isn't hungry."

Samantha gave her an incredulous look. "You think he didn't take her? I think you're wrong."

She slammed out of the house and started down the drive at a run. Leda went after her. The shield only extended to the end of the drive, and after that Samantha would be vulnerable. Leda didn't think this demon was the one who'd stopped the spell—that magic had been incredible, more like what had been thrown at her island before Hunter shielded it.

Samantha stopped at the very end of the driveway, staying inside the shield of life magic. Leda reached her the next moment and studied the demon who'd come to call.

He had a handsome face, like all demons, and wore tight clothes that showed a muscular body under a duster coat. He eyed Mukasa warily—demons were hard to kill, but a lion eating one would probably do the trick.

"Where is she?" he and Samantha yelled at each other.

"What are you talking about?" Samantha broke in first. "What the hell did you do with her?"

The demon regarded her in fury, but the look in his eyes was almost worried. "I didn't do anything with her. Where did you hide her? I went to the house, I saw her blood."

"You think *I* did that?"

"I think you never forgave your mother for falling in love with a demon."

"In love?" Samantha spat. "That's a joke—"

"Stop!" Leda held up her hands. They both turned to glare at her. "If neither of you know where she is, don't you think we'd better figure it out?"

"He's lying. Of course he took her!"

Leda studied the demon. "No, I don't think he did."

For one thing, that look of worry. He had typical demon good looks, darkly handsome, silky hair, eyes that made you want to promise him your soul. Though he had a daughter in her late twenties, he looked to be only about thirty himself—an illusion, but a good one.

"I would never hurt your mother," he said, tight-lipped.

"You've got to be kidding me. You enslaved her," Samantha said.

"That was different."

Leda held up her hands again. "All right, both of you be quiet or I'll let Mukasa sort this out. You obviously need to talk—with me as referee."

"I'm not talking to *him,* Leda. You have no idea—"

"You're right, I don't. But it's more important right now to find your mother."

"Joanne," the demon said.

"What?"

"She has a name. It's Joanne."

"Fine," Leda snapped. "The idea is to find her. Like it or not, Samantha, we need to know what he knows. So we talk."

The demon glanced impatiently upward. "Would you lower this shield? I can't move past it."

Leda folded her arms. "We can talk right here, and if I don't like what I hear, I'll either pull you in to let the life magic eat your brain, or I'll let my lion use you as a chew toy."

Samantha smirked.

"And *you.*" Leda pointed at her. "Let him talk. I don't care about your family problems, I care about finding a woman who might be hurt. All right?"

Samantha glowered, but nodded. "All right."

"Thank you." Leda blew out her breath. The tension shimmered between them, but at least they'd let her mediate. "Now start talking."

Samantha's father called himself Fulton. Not his demon name, which would be unpronounceable, or his true name, which would be a deep secret, because whoever wielded a demon's true name controlled him. That was why witches who used death magic drew circles and used amulets and spells of protection when they summoned demons. The demon would answer a summons, but unless the witch knew his true name, he would be in control, not the witch.

Fulton was a lesser demon. He would still be seductive, with the power to suck out a human's life essence and make the human consider it a glorious experience. But he lacked the overwhelming death magic that Old demons possessed, and he looked genuinely concerned about Samantha's mother.

Once Leda got both him and Samantha calmed to a simmer, she asked Fulton to tell everything he knew about Joanne's disappearance.

He didn't know much. They'd planned to meet at a club downtown. She never came, and Joanne was never late. Fulton went to the house to see what happened, and when he got there, he found the furniture overturned and blood in the kitchen.

"Did you call the police?" Leda asked him.

"No, I called friends. The police would've probably just arrested me instead. By the time I rounded up a few demons who could help me investigate, Samantha showed up and did call the police, and I had to lie low. Then Samantha didn't come back, and a demon gang moved into the neighborhood. I couldn't get inside the house again. I saw you yesterday and followed you here. But the damned life magic around this place, not to mention the lion, kept me out."

Samantha folded her arms. "I see a lot of flaws in your story. First, how could you get in the house at all? My mother warded it."

"Not against me. And yes, the doors were locked, before you ask. I have a key."

Samantha whitened. "You have to be lying. She hated you."

Fulton gave her a withering glance. "There's a lot you don't know about your mother. She knew her relationship with me upset you, so we met in secret."

"Relationship? You coercing her down to demon clubs where you could seduce her? She was terrified of you."

"She was at first. But it grew into something. I can't help it that you don't approve. It was between your mother and me. If you hadn't been so disgusted at having a demon for a father, we might have been a family."

Samantha rolled her eyes. "Listen to yourself. A family."

"You know nothing about it," Fulton snapped.

Leda waved for quiet again. "When you're all together you can have a huge three-way fight. Let's find her first."

Both of them scowled at Leda, then gave grudging nods.

Fulton's lack of knowledge depressed Leda a little. She'd hoped the demon would have some insight on how Samantha's mother had been magicked away. They had nothing to go on except that Joanne had fought and had been overwhelmed by someone who could enter the house through locked doors and strong witch wards.

That narrowed the possibilities to something like a powerful demon, but there was no clue why one would want Samantha's mother. At the house, Leda had felt nowhere near the strength of the demon that had attacked her island, but the counterspell had been fierce. No garden-variety demon had done that.

She wished Hunter hadn't run off so quickly, because he could tell her whether her idea had merit, and share his expertise. But he'd jumped at the chance to leave the house because Leda had twitted him about not wanting a long-term relationship.

She got mad at herself. She was berating Samantha and her father for letting their emotional hang-ups get in the way of solving the immediate problem, yet she'd done the same thing with Hunter. No wonder he'd hurried out to the limo and got himself the hell out of there. He was an Immortal demigod; a human woman berating him for not doing what she wanted must grate on his nerves.

"Let me call Hunter," she made herself say. "Whatever could do this, he'd know. And if it's our big bad demon, we need to know that, too."

Fulton gave her a nod. "Why don't you run along and do that? I'll stay here—not that I have a choice."

"With Mukasa." Leda smiled sweetly. "We'll be right back."

She went back up the drive, with Samantha following in silence.

Kelly, still waiting at the window, agreed to call Septimus for Leda. She dialed his direct number, greeting her lover with a silken voice. Then she lost her smile, looked quickly at Leda and held out the phone.

"What?" Leda asked, heart thumping hard. She pressed the phone to her ear. "Septimus?"

"Hunter is gone," the vampire said crisply. "He vanished somewhere between Adrian's house and here. My driver swears by his blood that Hunter never got out, and that he never stopped the car. Adrian tells me Hunter can't create a portal, so someone must have come in and got him."

CHAPTER FOURTEEN

"This is the lamest dungeon I've ever seen," Hunter called out to no one.

He stood against a stone wall that could only be called *dank,* his hands pinned behind him by rope that he could break, and a spell, which he could not.

He knew this wasn't a real dungeon but an illusion. It looked and felt real, from the slime-coated stone walls to the clammy air, to the filthy straw, to the empty manacles on the walls, to the cage suspended by a heavy chain. It also smelled like a dungeon.

"You've been watching too many movies," he shouted.

Apart from himself, the room was empty. He'd blacked out in the portal to awaken here, bound and annoyed. With his magic, he reached across the room and ripped the cage from the ceiling and broke it on the floor. He twisted the empty manacle cuffs around until they shattered, but try as he might he couldn't unbind himself.

He had no clue where he was. This could be an ordinary building in Los Angeles that the demon had made over into her personal dungeon, or he could be somewhere in the Antarctic, or he could be in a dimension hidden behind the ripple of reality he kept sensing. Wherever it was, he could only destroy the details, not the place itself.

"I'm getting bored," he said in a loud voice.

He wanted to see the demon front and center, because if the demon was with him she couldn't be out hurting or killing Leda. Leda had grown angry when Hunter told her not to die for him, but she'd misunderstood. He should have said, "Don't die *because* of me."

His wife, a fighter, had taken up a sword to defend him, and the Old demon they'd fought had mowed her down. Then he'd turned around and killed Hunter's babies just to prove he could.

Hunter had fought like a madman until the demon had escaped into some hell dimension. In his grief and frustration, Hunter had wiped out the other attacking demons without remorse. They never knew what hit them.

Grief had been a new sensation for him. Sadness he knew, sorrow for other people's loss. But as Tain reminded him, Hunter had clawed at his chest, trying to get the intense pain out; then he'd lain in a stupor for days, not wanting to live and knowing he couldn't die.

He'd been saved not by his brothers or the goddesses, but by a mother terrified for a child who'd been stolen by efreets, creatures who haunted the mountains and lived on blood—similar to vampires but without any memory of their humanity.

Hunter had taken up his sword and searched for the child, going seven days and seven nights without sleep or food before finding him with the efreets in a remote valley in the Transylvanian mountains. He'd destroyed the enclave of creatures with a blast of white magic, then carried the half-dead child back down the mountains to his mother, keeping the boy warm and alive throughout the journey.

The child's innocent trust in Hunter and the mother's stunned gratitude had given him back his reason to live. *Never again,* he'd ground out to himself. *This will never happen again.*

Hunter knew damn well that he couldn't police the entire world all the time, that plenty of women and children would die undefended. But none would when he was there. He'd be their champion and defend them until their enemies were all dead. He took reckless risks, and people called him crazy, but he'd never let anyone down who needed him.

He wouldn't let Leda down now.

He enjoyed himself destroying bits of the dungeon, pulling the dangling manacles out of the walls, ripping the grate and various pieces of stone from the floor. By the time his arms and legs began cramping from remaining still so long, he heard a grating of a key in a lock and the screech of an unoiled door.

He rolled his eyes at the theatrical touch as the demoness strolled into the room dressed in full dominatrix gear—shiny black vinyl corset, thigh-high boots, full-length gloves, whip. She still looked like Leda, her honey-gold hair curling around her shoulders, except for her eyes, which were completely black. She sidled across the room, the door closing of its own accord.

"Most men climax when they see me come in and know what I'm about to do," she said.

"Most men obviously need more to do."

"But I fulfill their darkest fantasies. You'd give anything to see your witch like this, wouldn't you? Or perhaps submitting to you?"

She lowered her head and peeped up at him from the corners of her eyes, holding the whip stretched between both hands and offering it to him. Goddess, she looked like Leda, smiling shyly but with excited anticipation, imagining what games he might like to play.

"You suck at reading fantasies," Hunter said calmly.

The demon lifted her head and gave him a wide smile. "You lie to me and yourself. You want her, any and every way you can have her. You will kill her with your wanting because she's human, so she can never sate you."

The demoness couldn't even begin to understand what Hunter longed for with Leda, and Hunter wasn't about to enlighten her. "This is why demons are stupid. Everything is about sex to you."

"I have watched you over the years, Immortal. You and your brothers, but especially you. You are so protective of the weak humans and your animals, but when you choose a bed mate, you use her, then walk away. You think you're being kind, not wearing her out before you discard her. This one you want more than the others, but you will hurt her if you keep at her." She stepped close to him, the smell of perfume and vinyl cloying. "Use me instead. I will look like her for you, and you can have her all you want. I never get tired, and I can match you hour for hour. We can go on for centuries."

"Even stupider," Hunter said softly.

She put her lips to his jaw. "I will have you, Hunter. I am trying to make it nice for you."

"And here I thought you were trying to make me sick."

Her smile became fixed. "You like to banter. I find that adorable in Immortals. Tain used to like it too. I think I've finally broken him of the habit."

Hunter thought of his vision of Tain last night, looking into Tain's crazed eyes and seeing the spark of sanity trying to pierce his madness. His anger rose. "I'm really looking forward to killing you."

"And I am looking forward to you screaming. It will stop that snotty tone of yours."

"I thought you liked my banter."

She licked the line of his jaw. "I like screaming better. Either that or you begging me to hurt you."

Hunter hid his revulsion at the wet heat of her tongue. "You don't know anything about why people want sex."

"I know everything about it. Desires hidden in shame, the human need to master one another, the struggle with their need to submit."

"Back to bondage, are you? You're obsessed with it."

She drew back, smiling Leda's smile. "It's all *you* can think of. Leda kneeling to you, wanting you to master her. You want it but you are afraid to admit it. With me, you can live the fantasy." She knelt before him, once again raising the whip in offering. "Do to me what you secretly want to do to her. You can have her the way you want her, for eternity if you want. I'll be your Leda-slave."

Hunter's rage surged. This demon sparked an anger he kept buried deep inside, the kind that came forth rarely, the anger that had once slain a hundred efreets in a flash. Kehksut could torture Hunter all she wanted, but she wouldn't use Leda to do it.

Hunter could not break his spelled restraints, but he could reach out with his magic and rip the illusion of Leda from the demon's form. The demon shimmered, blurring between male and female before settling down into female again. She still wore the corset and boots, but her hair was straight and black, her face narrow, no longer Leda's.

She pouted. "You're no fun."

"You can't read minds worth shit."

Hunter hadn't been dreaming of Leda as his absolute slave. Playing bed games with her, yes, but what he wanted with Leda went far beyond that. Such as her face lighting up when she saw him, as it had when he'd walked into Septimus's office to find her there. She hadn't known she looked happy to see him, but she had.

And her sleeping next to him, her breathing deep and even, as she'd done last night. He'd spent an hour watching her sleep, never getting tired of it. Leda glaring at him over the breakfast table about some argument they'd had. And her carrying his child.

The demon couldn't know what Hunter really wanted, because she didn't understand the concept of love. Lust, greed, envy, demented desires, yes. Love and comfort, no.

The demon woman leaned forward and licked his areola, the movement tight and practiced. His muscles jerked in reaction.

"I'm tired of this," he said. "Tell me why you want to play bondage games with Immortals."

"Go with it, Hunter." Tain's voice rolled out of the darkness, and Tain himself walked into the circle of light a moment later. It made Hunter wonder what was in the shadows—the backs of flats like on a theater set?

"You'll enjoy it," Tain went on.

Hunter turned his head and tried to look straight into Tain's eyes, but Tain kept his gaze averted.

"Right," Hunter drawled. "The crazy man tells me I'll like the torture."

"It hurts at first." Tain moved to Hunter's side, leaning against the wall next to him. He wore medieval dress now, a chain-mail shirt covered with a surcoat, his broad shoulders stretching the tiny linked rings. His red hair spilled down his back unbound, the pentacle tattoo on his cheek sharp on his tanned skin.

The demoness lifted her fingers to caress Tain's face, but Hunter noticed she very carefully didn't touch the tattoo. Tain turned his head and kissed her palm. His eyes closed, but not before Hunter saw again the spark of loathing.

"Tain," Hunter said. He sent a tendril of white magic toward him.

The demon snapped the tendril as soon as it touched Tain, and Tain frowned. The whip in the demon's hand shimmered and turned into a long, hooked knife. Tain's eyes began to glow.

"Not for you, my pet," the demon said. She turned to Hunter. "He needs to learn."

Hunter thought of the scarring he'd glimpsed on Tain's body the night before. Tain's hands and face were unblemished, but Hunter wondered how much of his torso the demon had cut.

"Let her teach you," Tain whispered.

"I made a mistake with Adrian," the demon said conversationally. "I tried to break him too fast, and his damned witch ruined everything. I should have tamed him slowly, like I did my beloved."

She smiled as Tain trailed his fingers down Hunter's torso, tracing a line. Marking the first cut?

Tain's fingertips stopped an inch below Hunter's navel, brushing the edges of the tattoo. Sudden pain stung the entire circle and pentacle on his lower abdomen. Tain flinched and pulled back, putting his hand to his cheek. The brief sanity flashed in his eyes, then vanished.

The demon noticed nothing. She had the tip of the blade on Hunter's neck, staring at it hungrily. Hunter felt the bite of the knife, a trickle of blood, which the demon leaned forward and licked.

"I thought only vampires liked blood," Hunter said, keeping his voice steady.

"There are many things about demons you don't know," she smiled. "But I will let you find out. I can't wait to teach you—everything."

She cut. Hunter gritted his teeth. *Not that bad,* he told himself. *I've been hurt much worse than this.*

The next cut was not that bad either, or the next, but putting them all together smarted like hell. He found his head banging against the wall, his teeth clenching against crying out. His hair stung his raw flesh, as did the tears that leaked unheeded from his eyes.

"It is a beginning," the demon said. She licked the knife with a long tongue, her shiny corset spattered with blood. She turned a smile on Tain. "Do you want me, my love?"

"Yes." Tain said the word with longing, his face lit with desire.

"Oh, please don't," Hunter grated through his

teeth. "Skinning me is one thing, but making me watch you—that's just cruel."

Tain was so far gone he never heard his brother. He swept the demoness up in his arms and headed for the shadows. After a moment, he heard the sound of a door slamming, and Hunter found himself alone.

The pain was nauseating, even if his Immortal body immediately tried to heal him. Hunter closed his eyes tight against the agony, and to keep himself from screaming, he started to sing.

Leda recruited Fulton, who had an SUV waiting halfway down the road, to drive them to Septimus's club. Kelly followed in her sedate limo.

The vampire club looked lifeless when they pulled in front of it, the black-painted doors closed, a metal grate pulled over them. The rest of the tall building was bare brick with no windows—vampires lived there. The street lay empty, scattered trash moving in the breeze.

Leda got out of the car, Mukasa jumping out of the back as soon as Fulton released the latch. The black eye of a camera above the door trained on them; then the grates began to roll back.

Kelly emerged from her own car as gracefully as a socialite arriving at a soiree. She pushed open the club's door with the ease of one accustomed to entering this place anytime she wanted and walked inside.

"Septimus?" she called.

The club looked much different than it did when open, chairs stacked on tables, dim fluorescent bulbs throwing a chill light over the place. Everything was tidy, the floor polished, looking more like an ordinary restaurant with a meticulous owner than a club where people came to indulge themselves with vampires.

Septimus stepped out of the shadows to Kelly and took her hands, pressing a brief kiss on her upturned lips. He glanced at the others, raising brows when he saw Fulton.

"Samantha's father," Leda explained. "Long story."

Septimus's elegant brows rose another notch, but he led them all back to his office.

The human driver waited there, his face as white as any vampire's. He had two red puncture wounds on his neck, though he was still alive and radiating fear.

"Tell us what happened," Leda said to the driver before Septimus could speak. She tried to sound reassuring, but the man paled further.

"He doesn't know," Septimus said in disgust. "He swears he picked up Hunter and drove straight here, making no stops. Hunter never got out of the car, he claims, and no one got in."

"If the door opens, the dash lights up," the driver stammered. "And there's a buzzer. Has to be, for the safety of the passengers. Some people like to party in Septimus's limos, hang out of the car or try to jump out. So I control the doors from the front."

Septimus listened with strained patience. "We found Hunter's sword and nothing else." He gestured to the thick, wavy blade that rested on a table by itself. "I know it's his. It radiates so much magic I don't want to touch it."

Leda moved numbly to the table. She hadn't seen the sword far from Hunter's side since he'd first dropped onto her island. She touched the black hilt, worn from centuries of use.

"He wouldn't have left it behind if he could have helped it," she said.

"I never saw him go," the driver bleated. "Never saw anyone in the back with him, never saw a portal."

"He's telling the truth," Septimus said in a dry voice. "I tasted it on him, but that doesn't mean he wasn't spelled."

"Could a demon do that?" Leda asked Fulton. "Come in and take Hunter through a portal without anyone seeing or hearing or sensing death magic being done?"

Fulton nodded. "A very powerful demon, yes."

Leda brushed her fingertip over the sword, her heart sinking. "This demon, the one you call Kehksut, must have taken him. I can't imagine Hunter not being able to get away from anyone else." She looked at Fulton. "If you could examine the limo, could you tell where the portal went?"

"Not if the demon was very powerful, and not after an hour or so has passed. I possibly could if I'd been there when he used the portal, but not now." Fulton stopped. "That's why I couldn't tell where whoever it was took my wife." He glanced at Septimus. "My daughter told me your vampires were guarding her house."

"For now," Septimus answered coolly, gazing at Fulton with a vampire's antipathy for demons. "But if I have to pull guards out of that neighborhood to help search for Hunter, I will."

"Then another vampire gang or a demon gang will take it," Fulton growled.

"Perhaps. But finding the Immortal is a little bit more important right now."

"Not to me," Fulton flared.

"Or me." Samantha stepped next to him.

Septimus's face set. "Then you can explain to Adrian why I'm not putting every vampire and human I own out to find his brother. I haven't reported Hunter's disappearance yet; I'd hoped to restore him before Adrian had to know he was gone. But if you want to call him and explain why I should try to find a demonwhore witch instead of his brother, you go right ahead."

Fulton snarled. "Bloodsuckers. This is my *wife* you're talking about."

Leda whirled on them. "Stop arguing! Just . . . stop."

She walked blindly past them and out of the office, unable to listen to squabbling between vampire and demon while Hunter was gone, stolen. She knew what Fulton and Samantha felt, because she felt the same way—someone she cared about had been snatched away to Goddess-knew-where, and no one was able to help.

She heard a heavy tread behind her; then Mukasa shoved his broad head under her hand. The wiry warmth of his mane comforted her as she stroked it. *Hunter is like him,* she thought. *A wild animal gentling himself to offer solace.*

"You might be able to sense where he went," she said to Mukasa, then laughed a little ruefully. "But I wouldn't understand what you were trying to tell me."

Mukasa gave her a look from his great, golden eyes and rumbled an answer. The rumble seemed to expand from his chest to vibrate the floor, then across the club, rattling the chairs on the tables, making the glasses ring over the bar. Leda started for the main entrance, Mukasa at her heels, and the others hurried out behind her.

CHAPTER FIFTEEN

Hunter understood why Tain had gone insane. His body itched as it healed—slowly—and any brush against the wall behind him hurt like hell, and the pain didn't go away.

The demon had done him twice now, the second time digging a little deeper with the knife. Tain had endured being flayed thousands of times, he said, every three days for seven hundred years. It had become routine to Tain, a routine he now welcomed. His face had been white and strained when he said it, but Hunter understood. Tain's choices had been to turn into screaming, mewling mush or let the insanity make him believe he enjoyed it.

One curious point: the demon had avoided Hunter's tattoo, even with the knife. That gave him an idea. The world pretty much thought Hunter was crazy, a viewpoint that came in handy sometimes. It would come in handy now.

When the demon returned, clad in a gold satin sarong this time, Hunter gave her a wide smile. Tain, behind her, regarded Hunter uncertainly.

"Come here, baby," Hunter said.

He kept the feral smile on his face while the demon sashayed toward him, triumph and distrust warring in her dark eyes. Despite his body screaming in pain, Hunter reached out with his foot and hooked it around her hips.

"Have you come to do it again?" he purred.

The demon eyed him in suspicion. It must have taken her years to break down Tain; she'd never believe she could do it to Hunter in two hours.

"Come on," he said. "And this time stay with me after. Don't go off with my brother like the last time. I was jealous."

The demon's look turned sly. "Perhaps it could be all of us together."

"Mmm, maybe." Hunter caressed her thigh with his foot, hoping he was ruining her satin with his blood.

"How about if I look like your witch again?" The demon morphed as she spoke, changing into the lithe form of Leda, looking at him from Leda's eyes.

Hunter held his fury in check. He would play along now and make the demon pay—big time—later. "Sure, sweetheart. How did you know I was into pain? The real kind, not the pretend, dress-up-in-leather kind."

She laughed Leda's lovely, silver laugh. "I suspected."

Hunter leaned his head back. "Do it," he groaned. "Do it now."

He knew he'd be more convincing if he could get his cock to rise, but no way could he accomplish that short of a glam spell, and both Tain and the demon would see through that.

Hunter closed his eyes as she started with the knife

again at his throat. It hurt, it hurt like holy hell, but he held himself still as she drew the knife down his torso and to his belly. At the last minute, he jerked his body so the knife tip slid inside the pentacle shape of his tattoo.

A jolt of white magic surged up through the knife like electricity and threw the demon ten feet backward. Tain shouted and caught her in his arms.

Hunter laughed. "Thought so. Come on, honey, let's do that again."

Tain set the demon on her feet, strode to Hunter and punched him full in the face. Hunter's head rocked back and cracked on the stone wall.

He managed to right himself and catch Tain in his glare. "The goddesses knew what they were doing when they made us, bro. It wasn't to be pleasure slaves to a demon."

"You know nothing," Tain said.

"Go on, make her touch your cheek. You don't belong to her, and you never will. You belong to Cerridwen, and her mark is on you. Remember when you got that tattoo at your coming-of-age party? Cerridwen infused it with goddess magic, like Kali did mine. And then we all got drunk on mead that would corrode bronze? Remember?"

Tain's lips drew back in fury. He grabbed the demon by the wrist and slapped her palm to his cheek, right over the pentacle.

The demon screamed, her eyes widening into pools of white and black. The Leda disguise fell away, and the demon's beautiful black-haired beauty blurred into something foul and hideous.

Tain shoved her aside. "Get him out of here," he roared at her. "Get him out before he kills you."

"Kill *her*, Tain, and leave with me," Hunter said. "We'll find Cerridwen and she'll heal you. She'll find you in there under all that mess."

"Cerridwen abandoned me. You all abandoned me. My greatest joy when I die is that my brothers will die with me."

"Resist her, Tain. She can't have all of you."

Tain whirled on him, palm out, white fire shooting from his hand. "Get *out!*"

Tain's magic whipped around Hunter like a sandstorm, searing his already raw body. The bonds broke, but Tain's greater power held Hunter fast. Hunter felt the demon's death magic slide through Tain's, blackness against intense white.

The dungeon shattered and fell away, and Hunter found himself floating high above the street outside Septimus's club. He saw Leda in the doorway, Mukasa behind her. The ground was shaking, Leda staring upward in surprise and horror.

Tain had disappeared, his white magic with him. Wrapped in tendrils of the demon's death magic, Hunter hung over the street, the pain in his body absolute. He saw Leda trace runes in the air, heard her chanting. He wanted to scream at her to run, to get away, but nothing came from his throat.

The earthquake intensified. A fissure opened the length of the street, asphalt crumbling and spewing upward. Darkness waited below—no subways, no walls, nothing but dense earth.

The demoness laughed and threw Hunter straight down into the crack. He fell a long way, ten feet, twenty, thirty, forty. He landed with a crunch of bone and flesh on solid rock and lay still.

Above him, the crack began to close, the earth and

rock pressing together. Dirt and pebbles rained on him in an increasing shower, driving the breath from his lungs. It pounded him and choked him, the weight crushing him.

Then suddenly the crack sealed with a snap, and all light vanished. Hunter lay broken and alone, the darkness absolute.

Leda screamed as the crack in the street sealed itself. She ran into the street and fell to her knees, Mukasa roaring behind her. The demon woman stood with her feet on either side of the crack, laughing, her tight satin dress bloodstained.

Septimus hovered inside the shadows of the club doorway, shouting at human thugs who fanned out to point weapons at the demon woman. She drew back a dainty hand and launched a thick stream of death magic at Septimus's men. They dropped to the pavement—unconscious or dead, Leda couldn't tell.

The demon floated to Leda and stood in front of her, black leather stiletto heels making her bare legs shapely.

"He was good, little witch," she said in a silken voice. "Very, very good. I can see why you like him."

Leda glared, and the demon woman kicked her, catching her in the side with a razor-sharp heel. Mukasa sprang at the woman with a snarl, and she tossed him aside.

Leda scrambled to her feet and ran to where Mukasa lay unmoving in the street. "Bitch!" she cried over her shoulder.

Septimus shot the demon from the doorway. A dart embedded itself halfway into her side before she grabbed it and pulled it out.

Leda sensed her death magic dim slightly, not

enough to weaken her, but enough to make her take a step back. The demon threw the dart at Septimus, spat a foul word and vanished with a bang. The breeze stirred the litter on the street and Mukasa's mane, but other than that, all was silent.

"Interesting weapon," Leda heard Fulton say nervously to Septimus. "What is it?"

"An air gun. After the last time this Old One insinuated herself into my club, I had some darts made that are spelled against demons, even though they can only slow her down a little. Very helpful against lesser demons who occasionally gain entrance to the club and cause trouble."

Samantha impatiently pushed past the two men and hurried to Leda. Leda stroked Mukasa's mane, tears rolling down her face.

"Oh, no," Samantha said mournfully. "Leda, is he . . ."

Under Leda's hand, Mukasa suddenly heaved himself upright, opening his eyes and blinking in the afternoon light. He yawned, gums drawing back from his huge red mouth.

Samantha put her hand over her nose. "Lion breath. Great."

"You're all right," Leda said to the lion in surprise.

Mukasa climbed to his feet and shook himself. He lumbered to where the fissure had closed over Hunter and began to paw at it.

"I think he was playing dead," Samantha said, watching him. "I didn't know lions could do that."

Leda's knowledge of lion behavior was the last thing on her mind. She studied the inch-wide crack in the pavement, the only thing left of the huge crevice into which the demon had thrown Hunter.

He was Immortal. He wouldn't die buried by tons of earth, rock and concrete, but he could be trapped, and he could suffer.

"Septimus!" she called. "We need to dig. Get equipment."

"You need to drag my men in here first," Septimus answered in a tight voice. "I can't come out in the light to help them."

"I'll do it," Samantha said.

She grabbed one of the men under the arms in a professional grip, her slight body strong, and began dragging him back to the club. Fulton came out to help her without speaking.

Two of the men were dead, but the others would recover. Septimus commanded the dead ones to be brought inside first, quickly. Leda had the feeling there would be two more vampires working for Septimus tonight.

While Samantha and Fulton worked, Leda drew runes along either side of the crack in the asphalt. She tried to still her mind, to reach for the air that poured over the ocean not far from the center of the city, but calming and centering herself right now was out of the question.

She had to reach Hunter fast, and she needed help, powerful help. She thought of the whirl of sand that had touched her body after Hunter had spoken to Kali. She'd felt the immense power of the goddess, but also the caring, the admonition for Leda to be good to her son.

Leda didn't remember the symbols for Kali, and she didn't have salt or chalk with which to draw them in any case. She would have to pour out her heart and hope the goddess would respond.

She knelt on the pavement and drew a pentacle with her finger—air, earth, fire, water, Akasha—and surrounded it with a circle. The mark of the goddesses, of magic, of the gods. The same symbol imprinted on the Immortals.

The symbol began to glow with magic, blue on the black pavement. "Kali," Leda whispered. "Help him."

Faint wind stirred her face, the polluted air of a huge city that not even an entire ocean's wind could wash away. Here among the huge buildings and the clogged streets, the sea and beaches might belong to another world.

The ground began to rumble again, and then to rock. The pentacle she'd drawn cracked in half, and Leda sprang to her feet. The asphalt splintered, the gap widening, pebbles and rocks spewing skyward.

Leda sprinted for the open door of the club, Mukasa behind her. Samantha and Fulton, having gotten the men inside, grabbed Leda and dragged her into the vestibule. Mukasa squeezed between them, making for the space behind the counter.

"You know it's bad when a lion is afraid," Fulton said.

"I think he's just taking cover," Septimus answered.

"Does that mean we all should?" Fulton asked nervously.

His words were drowned out by an explosion of sound. Wind roared down the street, gathering up the random trash and flinging it against the walls in tornadolike fury. The whirlwind's vortex covered the entire street, the air turning black as night.

The wind whipped through the club behind them, ripping down curtains and toppling chairs. Over the noise, the earth continued to shake and tremble.

A finger of fire stabbed downward from the clouds, and the pavement exploded. Leda covered her face with her arms as tiny pebbles showered over them, cutting skin. Septimus tried to slam the door, but the wind held it in place like a powerful force.

The rumble grew, the walls of the club shaking so much that Leda and Samantha clung to each other. The street buckled and heaved apart. Then a single shaft of white light burst from the widening gap and shot skyward.

Leda heard Hunter's voice, a warrior's cry that swelled and roared over the wind. His body shot from the chasm in a blaze of light. He hovered in midair. Hunter the wickedly sensual, good-humored man was gone. In his place was a warrior, his body wreathed in white fire, his eyes blazing green.

The green light from his eyes sliced through the darkness of the street, lighting it like a strobe. He cried a single word and held out his hand.

A clattering came from inside the club, then men shouting and Kelly's scream. Septimus turned to go to her, then swore and flattened himself against the wall. Fulton slammed Samantha and Leda out of the way as Hunter's sword whirled past them, flying on a streak of magic unerringly to Hunter's hand.

Hunter floated to the ground and landed on his feet. He seemed taller, bigger, his clothes gone, his body shrouded with light.

Leda stepped cautiously out of the club. Hunter turned, the green light from his eyes streaking across her. The light felt like a blanket of warmth, but she sensed he could cut her in half with it if he wanted to.

"I will cleanse this place," he announced, his voice booming. "I smell death magic here."

"Hunter," Leda said.

He shifted his gaze to her, the green of it prickling her skin. "You are a witch," he said. "Life magic and air. Are you a demonwhore?"

"I'm Leda."

No flicker of recognition. "Do I know you?"

She held her breath as he looked her up and down. Then a flicker of Hunter's usual tone entered his voice. "I would like to know you if I don't. You must run, witch Leda, lest I kill you with the others. Perhaps I can meet you later."

"You can't kill them. They're friends. They're helping us."

He looked past her, the glare swerving into the club. She heard Septimus swear again.

"I smell vampire and demon." He tilted his head. "But the innocent beast hiding there may go free."

"He is your friend too."

"The son of the Destroyer does not have friends. You will move, or I will obliterate you as one of them."

Samantha suddenly ran out of the club, followed by Mukasa. "Leda, get out of here. He's too strong to fight, and he doesn't know you."

"You don't deserve to die," Leda told her stubbornly. "And Septimus is the only one holding Los Angeles together right now."

"Not if Hunter goes on a rampage. Get out of his way. You can't reason with him, Leda. Kehksut obviously did something to him."

"Kehksut?" Hunter asked, his brow furrowing. "My brother drove him away long ago. Why do you speak of him?"

Leda pointed at the ripped-apart concrete. "He is the one who trapped you underground."

"I remember this not," Hunter said, untroubled. "Now I wish to begin the cleansing."

He started to move around Leda, and she caught his arm. His energy surged through her, a spike of white-hot power that lifted her off her feet.

"Do not touch me," he warned.

"Hunter, I love you."

His brows knit again, and he tilted his head to study her curiously. "Why do you say this?"

She gave a self-deprecating laugh. "I have to wonder. Because you're you, I guess."

"I am not a god. You do not need to worship me."

"I don't. It's not the same thing."

He shot a glance at Samantha. "You are willing to die for her, witch Leda? For a demon?"

"I am willing to hope you trust me. To believe me when I say we need them to keep the death-magic balance right."

"To trust you because you love me?"

"Yes." She held on to him, even though the magic firing through her hurt her like nothing ever had.

"I fight," Hunter said. "I do not love."

"Yes, you do. You had a wife and two children, a long time ago. You loved them."

"I remember this not." He sounded a little more uncertain.

"And you have brothers. Four of them. You love them, even though you pretend not to."

"The other Immortals?" He frowned. "I love them? This seems unlikely."

"Well, you do. I see it when you talk about them. You're worried about Tain."

"Tain." The white light dimmed a little. Behind it, Leda sensed vast pain that Hunter's magic was shutting away from him. "Tain is lost."

"He was captured by a demon and tortured until he went crazy. You and your brothers are trying to find him."

"I don't . . . know this."

"That's why we need those vampires in there. To help rescue Tain, to keep death magic in balance until you do. Your brother Adrian needs you. Please remember."

The light dimmed a little more. Leda realized the arm she held was wet with blood.

She jerked back in horror. "Goddess. What did he do to you?"

"Don't let the pain come back," he whispered. "There's too much. It will break my mind."

"Shut it out." Leda stepped back from him, eyes wide. "Do what you have to do to shut it out, but let them live."

"I don't want to forget about you, Leda."

"It doesn't matter. Be the warrior. Shut out the pain. Do it!"

He gave her the ghost of his crooked smile. "Maybe if I forget you, I'll get to meet you all over again."

She made herself smile, tears on her cheeks. "I'm looking forward to it."

Hunter briefly closed his eyes, and when he opened them, the green light flashed out again. He drew white magic around him like a cloak, his skin again appearing whole and strong.

"If they are here tomorrow, they will be dead," he declared.

He turned away and soared down the street on a wave of magic, vanishing into the bright afternoon light. Residual magic sparkled like live wires in his wake, then died. Mukasa sat down to watch the empty corner around which Hunter had disappeared, and gave a forlorn growl.

CHAPTER SIXTEEN

Leda waited at Adrian's house high above the water for two more days, but Hunter never reappeared. Mukasa wandered the circumference of the house, eating little, sleeping little, his step heavy.

Septimus paid a visit on the evening of the second day, dressed in Armani suit and expensive sunglasses, looking every inch a modern vampire and successful businessman.

"I've heard from Adrian," he said after Leda lowered the wards to let him in the house. "Actually, I called him myself and confessed my failure in keeping track of Hunter. To say Adrian was not happy with me is an understatement."

"It wasn't your fault," Leda said with a stir of indignation.

She'd grown used to Hunter's casual approach to life—imbibe coffee, kill the bad guys, make love—and she wondered if the other Immortals would be less straightforward and more frightening. If Adrian were angry at Septimus, how much angrier would he be at

Leda, who'd caused Hunter to chase her to Los Angeles and get caught by the demon? The fact that neither Amber Silverthorne nor Adrian had called her directly but contacted Septimus did not bode well.

"Don't worry about me," Septimus said, fastidiously adjusting his gloves. "My pilot will fly you to Seattle, and I will continue to search for Hunter, although I don't anticipate much success. When Immortals don't want to be found, they are vastly difficult to track down."

"I can't leave," Leda argued. "What if Hunter comes back here? He might be drawn to the magic around this house, and the ley lines."

"I will keep watch on the house, and so will Kelly. I'll position my men and vampires here to inform me if they see him."

"Why does Adrian want me anyway? It's Hunter they need."

"You're a strong witch, so there will be need for you. I'm certain Adrian has his reasons for everything."

"And you obey Adrian."

Septimus looked pained. "Let's just say we have a business agreement."

Samantha, who'd been listening, snorted. "In other words, you do what he says so he'll let you live."

"Something like that. You will make it easier all around if you go," he said to Leda.

She only agreed in the end because she reasoned that if anyone would have a chance of finding Hunter, it would be his brother Adrian. Septimus insisted she pack and leave then and there, and she resigned herself to obeying.

It was an easy task to throw her things into her bags

again, including her magical accoutrements. She toyed with the idea of sending Mukasa back to the island, courtesy of Septimus, but the lion made it clear he was coming with Leda. He stuck by her side when they left the house and forced his way into the limousine.

Samantha stayed behind. While she did not trust her father, she had common cause with him to find her mother. Leda felt guilty that she hadn't been able to assist Samantha much, but Samantha claimed that Leda had helped simply by believing Samantha's story and caring.

"I'll stay in touch," Samantha promised, then closed the door for her.

The journey to Seattle was uneventful, which gave Leda too much time to think. She amused herself watching the uneasiness of Septimus's vampires as Mukasa boarded the plane and settled himself at the rear.

The plane landed at a small airfield in Seattle after the few hours' flight, and Leda descended alone to the pavement, waiting for Mukasa to lumber down the plane's steps. She studied the roiling clouds in the night sky, sensing much the same darkness from this city as she had from Los Angeles. The clouds were denser here than in California, the Washington coast having a rainy climate, but the oiliness of the darkness made Leda's skin crawl.

Just outside the terminal Leda found a young woman with a mane of blond hair who radiated life magic, a powerful dose of it. She was Were, with the golden gaze of a predator. That gaze took in Leda and Mukasa behind her, and her eyes widened.

"No one said anything about a lion."

"He insisted on coming," Leda said.

Amber had sent a message her werewolf friend Sabina would meet Leda at the airfield. Sabina smiled wide—werewolves liked to show their teeth—and led Leda out to the parking lot. A large man, handsome and blond with very blue eyes, leaned against a black convertible Mustang not far from the entrance. He reeked of life magic, but Leda did not feel the over-whelming flood of magic she'd sensed when she'd first met Hunter. He was not Adrian, not an Immortal.

He stood up as they approached and opened a car door with a flourish. "Valerian's taxi service," he said in a rumbling baritone.

Not a witch, Leda thought as he took her nylon bags and tossed them into the trunk. He didn't do magic, he *was* magic. A shifter perhaps, but not a werewolf.

"This is my boyfriend," Sabina said. "His name's Valerian. Are you afraid of lizards?"

"Very funny." Valerian slid sunglasses on despite the gloom outside. "How am I supposed to fit a lion in a Mustang?"

"Put the top down?" Sabina suggested.

Mukasa nosed around Valerian's legs as he leaned inside to flip the controls to lower the convertible's roof. The lion seemed to approve of Valerian, much as he approved of Hunter, and Valerian looked in no way worried that he was being investigated by a lion. Once the top was down, Valerian folded back the seat and gestured Mukasa inside. "There, how's that?"

Leda squeezed herself into the seat next to Mukasa and waited while Sabina and Valerian got into the front.

"Just hope it doesn't rain," Valerian muttered,

glowering at the sky as he raced the car out of the parking lot. He swerved into traffic outside, waving at drivers who leaned on their horns and screamed obscenities at him.

"Afraid of lizards?" Leda repeated Sabina's words.

"Not lizard," Valerian growled. "I'm a dragon."

Leda peered at him curiously over the seat. Dragon-shifters were very rare creatures; possibly only a dozen existed in the entire world. Valerian didn't look particularly dragonish. He had unruly blond hair, blue eyes with irises wider than a normal human's, and brawny muscles stretching his clothes. His aura was intensely magical, golden yellow with streaks of red and blue.

"Adrian told me to look after you," he went on as he careened the car through the near-deserted streets. "Dragon baby-sitter service, that's me."

"Just get us there in one piece," Sabina said, clutching the dashboard in front of her.

"Everyone's a critic," Valerian muttered. "I'm a tropical dragon, sweetheart. Born to sit on my ass in the sun."

He drove swiftly through deserted streets, ending up at a large house set on a rise above the street. "Home sweet home," he said, stopping the car. "At least for now."

Leda stared into the dark abyss of Adrian's eyes and knew he was a stronger, even more intensely magical, Immortal than Hunter.

He resembled Hunter in physique, possessing the same tall, broad-shouldered body and square face, his long black hair pulled into ponytail bound at his nape and again halfway down his back. He wore a sleeveless shirt, with a silver armband in the shape of a cobra around his biceps.

The witch called Amber stood next to him, a slim young woman with dark hair and tawny eyes, a Celtic tattoo on her upper arm. The closeness to Adrian in which she stood plus the way she looked at him told Leda they were a couple. Another witch who couldn't resist an Immortal.

"You're Leda Stowe?" Amber asked, her look welcoming. "Of the Coven of Light?"

"Formerly of the Coven of Light."

Amber's gaze turned curious, but she didn't ask, to Leda's relief. Adrian's obsidian eyes flicked over her, and she sensed that he knew everything about her, including how she felt about Hunter. The pair hadn't heard from him, which Adrian growled was typical, but she could tell he was worried.

Amber let Leda refresh herself in a large bedroom at the top of the stairs with an attached bathroom, then Leda descended again to meet everyone. Mukasa had wandered behind the house to the green grass in the back, seeming content there.

Leda couldn't help but admire Amber's house, an old-fashioned place layered with generations of witch wards, and over those, the sharp, hot magic of an Immortal. The spacious living room was filled with homey photographs, the kitchen large and airy.

Adrian entered as Amber dispensed coffee for all and tea for herself. He dominated the room without saying a word, much the way Hunter did, but with a difference. Where Hunter pretended to be nonchalant, Adrian simply took over. He stood next to Amber as she prepared supper, cradling the coffee cup she handed him, and bade Leda tell him the entire story.

Leda hadn't wanted to talk much, but something about Adrian compelled her to spill the whole tale, from the moment she'd awakened to find Hunter in her lion's enclosure to the moment she'd boarded the plane to come here.

Amber studied her over the steam of her tea, no doubt guessing Leda had left out some parts—Leda dabbling in death magic and Hunter taking it from her in an intense sexual moment. Amber must know that Leda hadn't been able to resist Hunter; all evidence pointed to the fact that Amber was now Adrian's lover.

Adrian drank his coffee, oblivious of glances Amber and Leda exchanged, and told Leda things she didn't know. They'd heard from Darius, who was in Manhattan, having run-ins with nasty demons there. A witch called Christine had contacted them to say she was on Kalen's trail in Scotland, but they hadn't heard from her since.

Over supper, Amber outlined her adventures with Adrian, with input from Valerian and Sabina. She told of their search for Tain, and the discovery that the demon held him captive. Comparing notes, she and Leda decided that the demon who'd attacked the island must have been Kehksut, drawn to Hunter when he used a word of power, and that it was Kehksut who'd stolen away Hunter and tried to bury him. The discussion was less than happy.

After supper, Leda wandered to the back porch for a few moments to herself. The Exotic Species Institute had a branch here, and she'd contact them in the morning for food for Mukasa, though Adrian had already told her he would go and fetch the food himself, not liking anyone to leave the protection of the house. For tonight, he sent Valerian to buy meat at the nearest grocery store, and Mukasa waited patiently for his return.

Leda had only a few minutes alone before the back door opened and Adrian joined her. He closed the door, then the screen door, and leaned on the rail next to her, looking over the green strip of land that wound behind the houses.

"This is a magical place," Leda observed. Magic sparkled and shimmered in the air, although something felt not quite right.

"We did the Calling there." Adrian pointed to a circle of green near tall trees. "It produced—the best word is a *pocket*—of unreality. A ripple with hell waiting behind it. I've been finding them all over the city now."

Leda nodded, her heart heavy. "I think Hunter sensed the same thing. In Los Angeles, he said they were hiding what was real."

"It's like ripples on the surface of the ocean," he told her. "You know there's a whole world under those ripples, but you can't see it until you dive into it. I believe the ripples will grow until they open up and swallow all life in the world." He nodded toward the grove. "The strong life magic here keeps this one in, but one day it will break."

Leda hadn't been able to sense the pockets as Hunter had in Los Angeles, but this one she could almost see, like viewing the grove through slightly wavy glass.

"The Calling must have been a powerful spell," she murmured. "I can still feel the residue."

"The backlash was just as powerful. It killed Amber."

Leda looked up at him in surprise. Amber had left

this particular fact out of her stories. "*Killed* her? What do you mean?"

"She died when the demon broke the spell. I took Amber to Ravenscroft and begged for her life. Isis gave it back to her. I tell you this so you know what happens when you become involved with an Immortal."

She gave a rueful laugh. "It's too late for that. I'm already involved. And I can't help thinking that Hunter, not to mention the other Immortals, would get found faster if you went out and helped look."

Adrian turned his gaze to her, white sparks swimming in his eyes. He was a dangerous man, older and more powerful even than Hunter. He could kill her easily, with one burst of his magic, and she wouldn't stand a chance.

"I made a bargain with Isis," he said quietly. "I stay here and let my brothers come to me. I can't look for them, even though Hunter might be lost, Darius in trouble, and Kalen . . . Goddess only knows. If you don't think it doesn't hurt for me to stand here while they're missing, while Tain is in the power of Kehksut, you're wrong. I want to tear the world apart to find Kehksut and make him pay for every hurt he's caused Tain and me and my brothers."

He broke off, his mouth set in a grim line, and trained his gaze back to the grove. White sparks played a little in the darkness, his power barely contained.

"I'm worried about Hunter, too," Leda said softly.

"I was so close to helping Tain. If I'd just held on to him before the demon took him away . . . but I was too slow, too weakened." His hands closed on the rail, the wood creaking beneath his fingers.

"You're doing it for Amber, aren't you?"

He nodded once, not looking at her. "That was my

bargain with Isis. She gave Amber back her life, I stay here and let my brothers play their parts."

"It's hard for me, too," Leda said, understanding. "Hunter has done a lot for me—more than anyone ever has. And when he was hurt, I couldn't help him."

"You're not an Immortal."

"I know that, but I'm a pretty damn good witch, and I should have been able to do *something*."

Adrian gave her a conceding look. "You can do something. When it's time, you can help kick that demon's ass, and you can help Amber stay safe. Avenge Hunter, like I plan to avenge Tain."

She was pleased that he didn't tell her to stay behind the lines and hide while the others fought. He knew how she felt—angry and guilty and scared for Hunter all at the same time. *Avenge him.* She could do that.

She nodded, and Adrian returned a fierce smile. They understood one another.

Leda stayed with Amber a week before they heard news of anyone. During that time she helped Amber research Kehksut and spells to stop him, as well as spells that might find the brothers. She heard from Samantha, who said she and Fulton were still searching for her mother, and she was not yet ready to give up hope.

At the end of the week, Lexi, the werewolf who'd had a lead on Darius, reported that things were heating up in Manhattan and that Darius wanted to stay and figure out what was going on. They heard nothing at all from Scotland but did get word that Coven of Light witches there had been murdered, which threw a coldness over the house.

The night the moon was at its darkest point, Leda

lay awake in her bedroom, staring at the ceiling. She missed Hunter. She ached with it. He'd invaded her life, and now she felt nothing but emptiness. She missed his lazy smile and rumbling voice, the sexy growl he made before he kissed her. She missed his gentleness with the animals, and his absolute courage in the face of his enemies. He knew he should be afraid; he simply refused to be.

Hot tears streamed down her cheeks. She remembered him in front of Septimus's club, cloaked in white light, staring at her without recognition. He hadn't known her, and that had hurt the worst of all.

Dimly she heard Mukasa growling in the darkness. Then he gave a warning roar that was cut off abruptly. Leda was out of bed shoving her feet into a pair of shoes before her mind completely registered what she was doing. She tore down the stairs in her nightshirt, joined by Adrian, Valerian, Sabina and Amber.

Adrian tried to stop Leda before she could open the back door, but her fear for her lion overrode her caution. She unbolted the door and flung it open.

Hunter lay on the back porch, his naked body folded into a fetal position. His skin had regenerated, pink and raw, his cheeks pockmarked where the dirt had crushed him, his nose broken. The only unblemished place on his body was the pentacle tattoo on his abdomen, which was whole and uncut.

Mukasa stood over him, licking his face, though he moved when Leda flung herself to her knees beside Hunter's body. Adrian knelt on his other side, hand gentle on his brother's shoulder.

"Want me to call an ambulance?" Valerian offered.

"He's past the worst," Adrian said, his voice subdued. He touched the lengthwise scars on Hunter's back, knowing what they meant, that the demon had tortured him, had cut him deeply. "His body will heal on its own."

Leda lifted Hunter's head into her lap and smoothed his hair, which was matted and filthy. His face was rough with beard, his body streaked with dirt.

Leda didn't care at this point if he never remembered who she was. She leaned down and kissed his lips, feeling them rough and chapped beneath hers.

As she lifted her head, Hunter's eyelids fluttered. After a moment, a slit of green appeared; then his eyes opened all the way, clear and focused. A smile cracked his lips, a ghost of his usual wickedness behind the exhaustion.

"Hey, baby," he rasped, his voice broken. "Miss me?"

CHAPTER SEVENTEEN

Hunter convalesced in the bedroom Amber had given Leda, propped up against the pillows like an old-fashioned rajah. Mukasa had pushed his way into the house and positioned himself beside the bed, refusing to move.

Leda spent most of her time in the bedroom as well, sitting or lying at Hunter's side. She didn't like to leave him for long stretches, and he seemed content to hold her hand as much as possible.

At first she thought Hunter was reluctant to tell them what had happened to him, but she soon realized that he didn't remember much about it. Bits and pieces came back to him as he lay healing, and they got a disjointed account over the next few days.

"How could she do that to you?" Leda demanded when he described how the demon had cut and skinned him.

Hunter shrugged. "She's evil."

"But Tain isn't evil, or he shouldn't be. How could he stand by and let his own brother be tortured?"

Adrian answered from where he lounged in the corner. "Kehksut has broken him."

Hunter agreed. "I thought maybe she'd trapped him and he wanted rescue, but when I practically handed him a way out, he wouldn't take it. I think the technical term for our brother is *wacko*."

Adrian flinched but didn't dispute him.

"I'm sorry," Leda said, heartfelt.

"Not your fault, sweetheart. He did it to himself."

"I mean I'm sorry for you and Adrian. To lose him like this."

Hunter peered at her, his eyes clear and green. "You know, for a kick-ass witch, you're really sweet."

"Kick-ass?"

He splayed a large hand over her thigh. "Kick-ass and sexy."

"I can tell you're feeling better."

He dragged her down to him. "Want to see how much better?"

She pushed at his bandaged ribs, and he grunted in pain. "Ow! Damn witch." He glanced at Adrian. "Give me some sympathy here."

Adrian shook his head, some amusement in his dark eyes. "Even Immortals need to heal before they do any strenuous activity."

"I heal fast," Hunter told Leda with a wicked glint. "I consider it my Immortal duty to give pleasure as soon after battle as possible."

"Oh, sure," she returned. "So self-sacrificing."

"Hey, we aim to please."

Leda kissed him on the mouth. "You are so full of bullshit."

He tried to continue with the kissing, despite Adrian in the room, but Leda pushed herself away, still curious. "When you came out of the fissure, you didn't know me. What exactly happened down there? And what did Kali do?"

His eyes darkened. "The demon broke every bone in my body and stripped my psyche down to its core. Kali lent me her strength. She infused me with her god-powers to help with the healing. Or else I'd be worse off than I am now." He paused. "Kind of like a mom bandaging a skinned knee."

Leda smiled faintly. "Not really."

"Maybe not. When I blasted my way out, wrapped in her magic, I was a little out of it."

"Hunter, the master of understatement."

"It keeps me from looking things full in the face." His eyes dimmed, a haunted look entering them. "Sometimes it's best not to."

Leda rested light fingers on the pentacle tattoo that showed just over the blankets. "The demon never touched this."

"She couldn't, for some reason. There's goddess magic in it that the demon didn't like."

"Could be useful," Adrian commented.

"That's what I thought. We have to have something on our side to thwart her plan."

"What plan?" Leda asked.

Hunter loosely clasped her fingers. "Something involving all the Immortals. She wants the five of us in one place, she let that much slip."

"Maybe she wanted it to slip," Valerian rumbled. He'd paused from wherever he was heading upstairs and leaned on the door frame to listen. "So you'd think that."

"It was pretty clear she wants us all together."

Valerian cocked his head. "Why do you keep calling

Kehksut *she*? When Adrian and I fought Kehksut—
once at the club and once at the Calling—he was defi-
nitely male."

"I think Kehksut has reasons for appearing in one
form or another," Hunter answered. "Besides, she
tried to sexually assault me, so it's less disturbing to
think of her as *she*. Demons are *its*, no matter what
they project."

"Samantha's father doesn't seem to be an *it*," Leda
pointed out.

"He's a lesser demon. They choose one or the other
early on and stick to it. But the more powerful the demon, the more subtle and manipulative. They change
forms, or appear to different people in different
guises, for their own reasons."

"That's true," Adrian agreed. "You'll see an Old
One pop up again and again throughout history—
different name, different guise, same demon."

"This one is very ancient," Hunter said somberly.
"Powerful enough to keep me bound and do whatever
she wanted with me. Stronger than any of us individu-
ally." His gaze flicked to Adrian. "You decided we
should gather against Kehksut, but I think that's just
what she wants."

"Then why would she break the Calling spell in the
first place?" Leda asked. "Why not let you get together and then capture you?"

"She wasn't strong enough then, maybe," Hunter
offered. "Maybe she needs to collect us one at a
time, build her strength from breaking each one of
us."

"Not a good thought," Valerian said.

"That's why we keep looking for Kalen and Darius," Adrian said, rising. "You concentrate on getting

healed, I'll keep trying to pry our other two damn brothers out of hiding."

Adrian and Valerian left them alone then. As soon as the door closed, Hunter rolled over onto Leda, his body warm and strong, smelling of soap.

"Hunter," she began, pressing her hands to his shoulders.

"Talk later," he growled. "I need to reassure myself that you're here—with me. That I really do have you, and you're not an illusion."

She touched his face, which bore lines that hadn't been there a week ago. "I'm not the one most likely to be an illusion, Immortal man."

"That's why I like you. You're solid and real and you ground me."

"Sweet-talker. Most women want to be told they're amazingly beautiful."

He gazed down at her, all banter gone. "You are amazingly beautiful."

"With an incredible personality."

He grinned again. "That's my darling. I missed you."

She slid her fingers behind his neck. "I missed you too."

"It wasn't Adrian's magic that lured me here, you know." He nuzzled her neck, breath warm, sending shivers along her spine. "It was yours."

"Mine?"

"Your beautiful golden magic waiting for me here. That, and Septimus told me where you were."

She gave a startled laugh. "You found him?"

"He found me. Stretched out on the beach behind Adrian's house. He took good care of me, probably because he's worried Adrian or I will kill him for letting me get captured." He brushed his hand through her hair. "But Septimus really is trying to help, so he's safe. A long time ago, I might have killed him simply because he was a death-magic being, but I can't get into death for the sake of it anymore."

Leda's expression softened. "Good. That means the demon didn't break you."

"She made me realize that being a cold-blooded warrior has a price. And how much I need you to keep me from becoming that."

She arched her brows. "That's a lot to ask."

"Not really. You don't need to do anything except be you."

"Goddess, you know how to make a woman feel special."

His sinful smile returned, and dark desires stirred inside her.

"I know many ways to make a woman feel special. Want to see?"

"Just kiss me, Hunter."

He chuckled and slanted his mouth across hers, the desires flaring into full-blown fire.

A week later, just when Hunter's body had restored itself to normal, a strange, squat woman appeared at the house, asking for Adrian. Several tiny man-shaped creatures peered out from around her legs, dark eyes shining.

"Me name's Pearl," she said in a gruff voice when Adrian came to see what she wanted. "I worked for Kalen. Now I work for you."

Valerian gazed down at the small beings with her. "Brownies. Don't let them in, Adrian. They're little troublemakers."

One stuck his tongue out at Valerian.

"See what I mean?" Valerian growled.

Pearl curled her lip. "A dragon. Humph." She pushed past the people in the hall and made her way unerringly to the kitchen. Within ten minutes she had an apron around her plump form and started creating astonishing food.

Pearl reassured them somewhat about Kalen—he was alive and well, and the witch Christine Lachlan was with him. At least, last she'd seen. Kalen had gone to battle the demon Culsu, and no, Pearl didn't know the outcome.

Two days later their tension eased when Christine herself called. She and Kalen were on their way to New York, where they'd change planes, and she let them know their arrival time in Seattle.

"You won't believe this," Christine said in her soft voice. "But my Immortal is afraid to fly. In planes, I mean. He can open portals, but he's being nice and not using them because they make me nauseous."

"Kalen is being *nice*?" Adrian asked incredulously when Leda related the conversation. "It can't be him, then."

Hunter laughed out loud. He'd healed almost completely, and on the surface was back to his good-natured ways, but he slept poorly at night, tossing and turning or leaving the bed altogether.

"She said she's bringing someone else powerful who can help," Leda continued. "She wouldn't say much more than that. She told us to not judge him by what he looked like."

"Sounds promising," Hunter said.

"They should arrive this evening. Not that flights have been running on time lately. Who's for picking them up?"

Leda grew a little excited as she spoke. They had two Immortals together, and a third, the elusive and enigmatic Kalen, was about to join them.

Hunter took Leda with him to Sea-Tac airport to pick up Kalen, Christine and whatever friend they brought.

The monitors showed the flight from JFK delayed, which didn't surprise Leda too much. She settled herself in the uncomfortable airport seating to wait.

"I smell coffee," Hunter said. He closed his eyes and inhaled. "Mmmm. Want some?"

"I'm fine," Leda said.

"Be right back, then." He made for the nearest coffee stand, while Leda enjoyed watching the way his jeans cupped his backside.

This last week had been both idyllic and frustrating. Idyllic because Hunter had put aside his worries about the future and concentrated on making intense love to her. Not only had the sex been spectacular, they'd lain side by side and talked far into the night, or into the day, depending on when Hunter went out with Adrian to help keep Seattle safe.

The intimacy had been wonderful, with the feel of his long body stretched beside her, his arm folded behind his head as he made her laugh with his outrageous humor. But then when they drifted off to sleep, he'd dream, muttering to himself or coming awake abruptly with a gasp. He'd tell Leda he was fine when she asked, but would either lie awake while she drifted back to sleep, or get up to sit by himself on the porch.

She worried about him, but knew there was little she could do. She couldn't imagine what he'd been through, what it had been like to see that his brother had gone completely crazy, to come across an opponent he couldn't best. She sensed that Adrian understood Hunter's feelings, but otherwise Hunter buried it deep.

When she at last peeled her gaze away from admiring Hunter's backside, she realized that the flight-information board had changed. Kalen's flight was listed as "At Gate."

Leda grabbed her purse and hurried over to Hunter, at the same time punching her cell phone to leave Amber the message, "They're here."

Passengers poured down the hall to exit the terminal. Thirty minutes passed, and they saw no sign of a tall Immortal striding down the passageway, a witch by his side. Leda felt a faint life-magic force, though, somewhere down there, one glowing and flitting and . . . worried?

Hunter took three strides forward, earning a warning look from a security guard, and closed his hands around the shoulders of a kid with long blond hair who looked about sixteen. He carried a duffel bag and had a guitar case strapped to his back, earphone wires around his neck, and a bluish tattoo on his cheek. The kid gave Hunter a startled look with intense green eyes, but didn't try to pull away.

Once they got clear of the crowd, the young man gasped, "Are you Adrian? Or Darius? Or Hunter?" His accent was pure northern Scotland.

"Hunter," he replied tersely. "Who the hell are you?"

"*What* are you?" Leda put in.

Hunter unceremoniously yanked back a lock of the kid's hair and studied his ear, which looked normal to Leda. "Half-Sidhe," he growled. "Troublemakers."

"He's something more than that," Leda said. "Can't you feel his aura?"

"Tell me who you are, and how you knew I was one of the brothers."

"The name's Mac. I know Kalen. I left Scotland with him."

Hunter's grip tightened. "So where is he now?"

"That's the thing, mate. They're gone. One second they're sitting beside me, then next, poof, gone. I couldn't sense where, and I couldn't do anything about it. I figured I'd better land with the plane and let you know."

CHAPTER EIGHTEEN

"You'd better not be lying to me, half-Sidhe," Hunter said.

A flare of life magic crackled, and Hunter jerked his hand from Mac's shoulder. Hunter glared at him, but Mac adjusted his guitar case and said quietly, "I'm not."

"Is that why the flight was delayed?" Leda asked him.

"No, the flight was delayed because of bad weather. Funny thing, no one seemed to notice them gone. Two empty seats appear when we were over the American Midwest and no one said a thing. The hostess didn't even remember they'd ordered drinks. She brought mine and kind of wandered away."

"Kalen can teleport," Hunter said. "Maybe he teleported himself and his witch someplace they could have some privacy. Kalen's big on privacy."

Mac shook his head. "It wasn't any portal, and Kalen didn't do it. I saw the surprised look on his face before he disappeared. And other people would have noticed. It was more"—he made an undulating motion with his hand—"they just bloody winked out."

Hunter swore. Before Leda or Mac could stop him, he started running back up the concourse, shoving people out of the way. He dove the wrong way through the security exit, and the inevitable happened. Alarms rang, men shouted, people screamed. Hunter moved unhampered through the crowd, people parting like water from a ship's prow to let him pass.

"Come on, love," Mac said, grabbing Leda's hand.

He dragged her after him, some magic propelling her along with his rapid, youthful pace. He ran as though nothing impeded him, not the heavy bag over his shoulder, not pulling Leda along behind him. She felt the sparks of his magic dancing over her skin; he was a powerfully magical being too agitated to hide it.

They caught up to Hunter at the gate where the long airplane was now boarding tired-looking people who wanted out of this city. Hunter slammed past the hostesses, threw off the security guards and charged into the plane. Mac and Leda hurried after him, and no one tried to stop them.

Hunter searched every row as though he expected to find his large Immortal brother hiding under a seat. "Which one?" he snapped at Mac.

"Um, this one I think." Mac pointed at row 22 on the right side of the plane.

Hunter thumped down into the middle seat. "I don't feel anything. I don't feel a damned thing."

"I didn't either. I told you, one second they were there, the next, they'd gone."

Hunter put his hands in the air in front of him, not touching anything but moving as though groping for something unseen. Mac and Leda watched him, both curious, both not wanting to interrupt whatever it was he did.

Hunter dropped his hands and hauled himself out of the seat in disgust. "Nothing."

Mac refrained from speaking, his man-boy face puckered with worry. Hunter moved down the aisle, people pressing themselves out of the way for him.

Leda took his hand as they stepped into the terminal again. "Hunter, there are about sixty people out here waiting to arrest you."

"What for?" he growled.

"Breaking every security law known to man," Mac drawled, then he laughed. "It's tough being a magical being in a mundane world, but I like it."

How Hunter talked himself out of being hauled off to jail, Leda never knew, but he did it. They were allowed to pick up Kalen's checked bags—including a long spear with a crystal tip; then the three of them were escorted to Leda's car and told not to come back.

Leda drove back to Amber's house very carefully. Mac sat in the back, face stricken, Kalen's spear across his lap. He shoved earbuds from an MP3 player in his ears, cranking up music that crackled and whined. "Helps me think," he explained.

Hunter had retrieved his sword from the trunk and sat in the small car with its hilt sticking up between his knees. He was first out of the car when Leda pulled into the driveway, leaving Leda to extract Mac from the tiny backseat.

"Where is he?" Adrian asked from the dark of the porch.

Leda hadn't had the nerve to call and confess that Kalen had vanished. Hunter told Adrian what had happened in a few short sentences, and Adrian came down the porch steps, the snake on his arm slithering to his hand before morphing into a sword. Adrian brought the point around and set it against young Mac's throat.

"Easy now," Mac said, raising his hands.

"You're magical," Adrian said. "Where's my brother?"

"You must be Adrian." Mac looked him up and down, his green eyes almost amused. "Kalen told me about you, bloke."

Hunter stood behind Adrian, broad arms folded across his chest. "He's Sidhe-get."

"Watch what you say about me mum. She's got a temper. And like as not, she'll be ringing me anytime now. Had a respite on the plane—mobiles off."

"Tell me who you are and what you have to do with Kalen," Adrian repeated.

The young man took a step back and bowed slightly, keeping his eye on the sword. "My name is Manannán mac Lir. Niniane, Queen of the Sidhe, is my loving mother. Lir, God of the Sea, my da."

Adrian lowered the sword but kept it in his firm grip. Behind him Hunter huffed. "Just what we need. Another bloody demigod."

"No," Leda said, grinning at Mac. "Another demigod is exactly what we need."

Leda woke abruptly that night when Hunter rolled out of bed and ran out of the room. After a few moments, she heard the back door slam, then a whisper of wind chimes shimmering on the night. For a few moments she toyed with the idea of leaving him alone to wrestle with his dreams, but then she decided she'd left him on his own enough.

She pulled on jeans under her nightshirt and moved silently down the stairs and out onto the quiet back porch. Hunter leaned on the rail staring out across the green, his jeans his only protection against the cool wind. Moonlight revealed the white and pink scars on his back, vicious lines running through his brown skin. He'd healed almost completely, but the scars would be with him for centuries.

Mukasa lay below him on the grass, so still in the starlight that he might have been carved from marble, except for his glittering eyes.

Leda closed the door carefully and moved to Hunter's side. "Everything all right?"

He glanced at her. "Dream. Didn't mean to wake you."

"About the demon?"

He pushed off the rail and sat heavily on the porch swing, which creaked as he moved it. The house behind them remained quiet and dark, no one coming to investigate.

"A dream about a ton of dirt falling on me." The brawny hand that rested on the back of the swing shook. "One of the worst things that ever happened to me."

"Seeing it happen was pretty much the worst thing for me."

"I knew I wouldn't die," he said, his voice inflectionless. "I knew I'd lie down there forever with no light and no air." He looked up at her. "And the very worst of it was, I'd never see you again."

She sat down next to him and looked straight into his eyes. "I was prepared to get you out any way possible; I wouldn't have left you there. Even Mukasa was ready to dig through the concrete with his paws. And then Kali came for you. You aren't alone anymore, Hunter."

"But I might be alone in the end." His face was bleak, no longer Hunter the teasing, playful Immortal but a warrior who'd lived with loneliness. "Maybe that's what Kali and the Undine meant when they said I'd have to make a choice. The choice to be alone."

Leda took his face between her hands. "You don't know that. The big sacrifice they're talking about might be you giving up coffee."

He gave her a very faint grin which did not meet his eyes. "No way will that ever happen."

Leda got off the swing and slid herself between his long legs. "You're not alone, Hunter. You have me and Mukasa, and you're with your brother and all his friends. You're safe here."

"I know."

She straddled his lap, placing her knees on either side of his thighs. "You can sleep now without fear. No demon will reach you here."

"You're beautiful when you go all protective." He slid his hands up her arms. "Not to mention when you sleep. Have I said how much I like watching you sleep?"

"With my face smashed against the pillow?"

"With your hair tangled around you and your eyes closed. You look so peaceful." He smoothed his hand through her hair. "I want to remember you like that."

"Don't talk like you're going to disappear again."

"Not yet." His voice gentled to a whisper. "Not tonight."

His lips were warm in the cold air. He pulled her

down to him and slid his hands under the hem of her nightshirt. His warm, callused palms moved across her bare abdomen and up to cup her breasts.

They kissed for a long time while the wind tickled her with cold that Leda barely felt. His night's growth of whiskers abraded her cheek, his breath hot on her skin. He flicked broad thumbs over her nipples, raising them to hot, tight points, making her crave him.

She leaned her forehead against his, loving the warmth of him against her. She wanted to tell him she wished things could be different, but she knew he didn't want to hear that. Hunter, the man who would exist forever, wanted to live for now, to take comfort against the emptiness he faced.

He resisted connecting with anyone even when he needed most to connect. He was right about one thing: If his wife and children hadn't been killed that faraway day, they would have died a natural death sooner or later. A thousand years had passed, and still he grieved; to him, the loss was as fresh as though it had happened yesterday.

Such loneliness would drive a normal human crazy. Leda knew she could never have handled all that he'd been through since the day Kali gave birth to him and handed him over to a barbarian slave to raise. That man, his human father, had died long ago too.

Leda couldn't imagine such aloneness. Even though Hunter had four brothers who shared the same kind of existence, they weren't exactly coming together every day for a group hug. Likely they too were trying to get through the loneliness in their own way.

Leda slid her hands down Hunter's hard chest and the long, white scars the demon had left. She traced the outline of the tattoo that showed over his waist-band, and tugged open the button of his jeans.

"What are you doing?" he asked in a warm voice.

"Giving you something else to remember me by."

She unzipped the jeans, and he made no move to stop her. She knew countless other women had done this—how could they resist him? She also knew he could eas-ily have seduced her, made fantastic love to her, and left her with a wave and his cheerful grin over his shoulder.

He'd decided to stay, protect her island and Mukasa, and send her to Adrian to make sure she was safe. Leda had said a few foolish things to him like *I love you*, which, fortunately, he didn't seem to re-member. She had a horror of being whiny or clingy, and she was determined to make sure he had the best damn time with her that he would never forget.

She unzipped his jeans all the way and scooted them down his hips. He helped her, rising a little and sitting his naked butt back on the swing. She pulled the jeans down his legs so they wadded at his ankles, then sank to her knees and licked his very interested erection from base to tip.

"Goddess," he breathed. Leda swirled her tongue around his velvety flange and sucked his tip into her mouth. She felt his hands in her hair, heard his heart-felt groan. "You wonderful witch."

She slanted a smile at him. "You think this is witchcraft?"

"I don't care what you call it, just keep doing it."

She pulled him into her mouth again, working him, licking him, nibbling his tip. She hadn't had much ex-perience at this kind of pleasuring, but Hunter didn't seem to mind.

His erection grew harder and longer, filling her

mouth. He rocked back so she could reach more of him, swallowing another groan. He tasted warm and salty, his skin hot and stretched.

Leda felt his climax build, balls tightening under her fingers, his shaft smooth and tight. Just when she thought he'd come, he wrenched her up by the shoulders and pressed a hard kiss to her mouth.

"No," she said in disappointment.

"I want to be in you," he said hoarsely. "I want to feel your whole body."

She started to say they should go upstairs, but Hunter had no intention of leaving the porch. He skimmed her nightshirt from her body, then undid her jeans with frantic hands, nearly tearing them and her underwear from her.

She found herself on the board floor of the porch, cradled by his strong arms, his naked body on top of hers. He kicked his jeans away and, without readying her, entered her in a swift stroke.

She was never quite sure what happened after that. White magic swirled around her, and the house and pungent-smelling pines and sky and stars seemed to disappear. All that existed was Hunter and herself. She felt his weight on her and him stretching her open wide, his lips on her face, his hands on her body.

He needed this coupling. It was more than desire, more than physical longing—he needed *her*. She suddenly saw through his mind's eye the terror and pain he'd tried to forget, what he was using this frenzied sex to forget.

She screamed, and the sensations shut off as if he'd thrown a switch. The white light vanished, and she was on the wooden floor, her nightshirt cushioning her back, while a demigod made love to her like a wild thing.

He threw back his head when he came, his hair falling across his back, and an instant later, dark climax jerked through her. She felt an ache where they joined, felt the heat of his seed and her own moisture. Then he was kissing her, mouth, throat, breasts, his lips closing over the points of her nipples.

She pressed him closer. "How can you stand it? Feeling that way? How can you take it?"

"I have you," he whispered against her cheek. "I have you, love."

"I can't possibly protect you."

"I don't expect you to, sweetheart."

She balled her fists. "I won't let that demon bitch torture you again."

He chuckled and nuzzled her cheek. "My fierce little witch."

"I'm not joking."

"I know, love." He kissed her, mouth heavy on hers. "You're sweet, but you're not going anywhere near her."

He stopped further comment by kissing her slowly, his mouth a warm point in the cold darkness. She could lie here underneath him all night, savoring the weight of his body, the wonderful way he felt inside her.

He slid out of her suddenly, still slick and erect, and pulled her onto the swing with him. He positioned her on his lap, legs wrapped around him while he sat on the edge of the swing.

"Want a ride?" he murmured.

"What if someone sees us?"

His smile was positively sinful. "Their own fault for spying."

He was inside her, hard and wanting, and he moved

his hips so that the swing moved forward. Back and forth, back and forth they swayed, Hunter making slow, sweet love to her.

She held on to him and kissed him, feeling his huge erection pressing into her, and she dimly wondered if she could take him only because of his magic. His hair was rough silk under her fingers, his lips hot and hard.

"So wet for me," he whispered. "You feel good."

"You make me feel good."

"I'd like to think you're always wet for me. I can't get enough of you."

She leaned her head back, pleasure making her incoherent. She'd like to think he wanted her too, as much as she wanted him.

He slid his hand between them, as tight as they were, and brushed his thumb over the hard berry of her clit. Leda screamed, and Hunter caught the scream in his mouth. "Shhhh, love."

"I can't help it."

His laughter was low and sultry, the sound of a man who had a woman right where he wanted her. "But the others will hear." She stifled a moan, writhing against him, unable to feel anything but him inside her, his hand between her legs and the cool night air on her bare skin.

"You're mine, Leda. No one else gets to have you but me."

She barely focused on what he was saying. Her orgasm went on and on, her skin hot to the touch, his cock so *hard* inside her. His fingers continued to stroke her, taking her to heights she'd never achieved, not even with him, while he cradled her backside with his other hand.

"My Leda. My witch." His mouth turned frenzied, kissing her with madness while his seed shot high into her. She felt his teeth on her neck while he moaned his climax. Then he gently licked where he'd bitten.

Slowly Leda realized she was sitting on Amber's back porch, stark naked, making love to Hunter on the swing. But just for this moment, she didn't care. He protected her with his body and his Immortal magic, and instead of simply easing his fears by taking her, he'd given her plenty of pleasure in return.

She loved him for that, and she knew that, whatever the outcome of this battle with the demon, it would hurt in ways she'd never experienced in her life.

In the small hours of the morning, Hunter walked again onto the back porch, having taken Leda upstairs to bed. Adrian was there to watch the sunrise, leaning on the rail. Hunter joined him, both gazing across the green barely visible in the dawn light to a grove of trees to the glasslike ripple in reality. Hunter's mood had lightened. Making love to Leda had restored not only his strength but his sanity.

"Have you reached Darius yet?" Hunter asked Adrian in a low voice.

Adrian shook his head. He'd been trying to call Darius all week, redoubling the effort now that they knew Kalen had disappeared. "Haven't heard a word."

"What about this witch who's following him?"

"Her either. They're not answering. If Kalen were here he could portal himself to Manhattan and find out what's going on, but . . ."

"You want to consider Darius MIA too?" Hunter asked.

"I don't want to." Adrian said heavily, moonlight glittering on his cobra arm band. "But he might be."

They stood in silence awhile, two men who'd known each other so long they didn't have to keep up a conversation. Adrian looked almost exactly the same as he had when they'd fought the Unseelies back in Scotland around 1300, except for a slight softening around his eyes. Hunter put that down to Amber's influence.

"Tain's gone, Adrian."

Adrian turned his head, black eyes glittering. "He's a captive, and his mind has been messed with."

"I talked to him. There's still some sanity in there, but I couldn't reach it."

"We get rid of the demon, we find Tain again."

"It might not be that easy."

Adrian rested his hip on the rail, folding his arms. "This from Hunter, the kill-it-and-move-on warrior?"

"Tain's pretty far under the spell or whatever—the demon hasn't had to use magic on him in years, I'm willing to bet."

Adrian looked away. "The others—Valerian and even Amber—believe we'll have to kill Tain in the long run. They think I don't know, but that's what they want to do."

"Maybe they're right. Maybe it's the only way we can help him. I got a look in his eyes, big brother. He's screaming to get out, and if he never can, I for one am happy to help take away his life any way we can. He can't stand much more of it."

"And I refuse to give up on him," Adrian said.

Hunter made an impatient noise. "I never said I was giving up. I have some ideas on how to reach him if we can. But I agree that we need to get rid of the de-

mon. I'm sick of her." He paused, remembering the il-
lusionary dungeon. "The big bad demon of annoying
clichés."

"That's how he struck you?"

Hunter flung him a glance. "What do you mean?"

"To me he was a suave smooth-talker who became
the woman you likely saw only when she brainwashed
Tain. Darius sees him as a demon called Amadja, and
he's building up a demon following in Manhattan. He
was playing a different game with you."

"A stupid game. She kept trying to take Leda's
shape, like I'd go all drooly because I could have a
Leda look-alike do anything I wanted." Hunter shook
his head. "What she didn't understand was I'd rather
have ten minutes with the real Leda than a lifetime
with a substitute. That's why she couldn't break me,
or imprison me."

Adrian's face was in shadow, so Hunter couldn't see
his expression. "That's how she tried to snare you?"

"Yep. Like I said, it didn't work. Clever Immortal,
see through ploy."

"With me, he threatened to torture Amber. Made
me choose between him torturing Tain or her."
Adrian shrugged. "I figured Tain was used to it, so I
had to choose him. That surprised the demon—he
thought I'd agonize over the choice and beat myself
up about it. But I knew he was going to hurt Tain
anyway, no matter what I decided, so I chose to save
Amber."

"Seems like the demon doesn't know much about
relationships."

"Seems like," Adrian agreed. "I'm trying to figure
out how to use that against him."

"She keeps making mistakes like that, she'll never trap us."

Adrian turned his head again, black hair sliding across his shoulders. "If we can band against him, Kehksut will be one dead demon. He must know that."

"Exactly. So why does she want us to be so strong?" Hunter asked. "That's what's been rolling through my mind with no answer. What does she want to do that needs five Immortals to do it?"

"We can always ask her when we confront her," Adrian said. "Side by side."

"Four sane Immortals and one who's loony. I don't like those odds."

Adrian gazed across the green again, studying the thick ripple. "You think Kalen is behind a ripple in reality like that one. That the demon has trapped him there, and possibly Darius as well."

Hunter nodded. "Tain's demon wants four Immortals together, so I say we give her four Immortals. If you want to save Tain, this is the way."

"If we can extract Tain—"

"Adrian," Hunter said patiently. "Tain's gone around the bend while the choo-choo's still in the station. I know you two were close, but you have to get your mind around this. We scrag the demon, we pull Tain back to the sane side of life."

"And your plan is what?"

Hunter clapped him on the shoulder. "I have a few ideas, but mostly I'll leave the planning to you, big brother. I fight, I drink, I get the girl. That's Hunter."

"From the noises I heard last night, I'd say you did the last thing first."

"Why not? She's the best thing that's happened to me in a long time. I know I have to lose her, but I'm grabbing on to what I've got while I've got it. I notice you can't look away from Amber, so you have no room to talk."

"Isis made it so we can be together," Adrian said. "I have time to love her. You be careful."

Hunter lost his smile. "I learned all about grief and a broken heart a long time ago. I know the lay of the land."

Adrian regarded him for a long time, then looked at the dark windows behind him. "You're talking about leaving Amber and Leda alone."

Hunter laced his fingers loosely together. "Not something I want to do, believe me. But if it helps us kill the demon, we can return to them that much faster."

"You know it might not work," Adrian said. "We might never be able to come back, if you're thinking of searching for the demon and Tain the way I'm thinking."

"I know."

Adrian's hard gaze softened, and Hunter knew he was thinking of Amber. Hunter pictured again Leda's body beneath him, her soft laughter, red lips and beautiful smile. His heart stung, and his selfish inner being cried out, *Don't let her go.*

On the other side of the trees, the sun rose. They heard light, female voices in the kitchen as Amber and Leda entered it with Pearl to start breakfast. Hunter and Adrian turned as one and bumped into each other on the way to the door.

Adrian looked annoyed, and Hunter laughed. "Aw,

we're pathetic." He opened the door and gestured Adrian through. "After you."

Adrian shouldered his way into the kitchen, throwing his brother an irritated glance. The smile that blossomed on Leda's face when she saw Hunter more than made up for it.

CHAPTER NINETEEN

"We're going with you," Amber said at once.

From the expressions on the two Immortals' faces, they hadn't anticipated this argument. Shortsighted of them, Leda thought in anger. Did they really think she and Amber would sit quietly at home while they went out and hunted the demon?

"You can't," Adrian said. "We might have to journey to Ravenscroft, and mortals can't join us there."

"I went to Ravenscroft," Amber pointed out. "After the Calling spell."

"That was different. You were dead."

"Only briefly." Her tawny eyes held challenge.

"After that, you were there with the permission of Isis."

"So ask her permission again."

The two faced off in the middle of the kitchen, small witch against tall warrior. Mac folded his arms and leaned against a counter, not bothering to hide his grin. Hunter noisily made coffee, paying absolutely no attention to anyone else in the room.

Adrian's gaze slid sideways to her. "Leda."

"Don't expect me to take your side," Leda said. "Amber's right. Christine is presumably where Kalen is, we hope. She'll need our help."

Hunter thumped a mug onto the counter and poured a thick stream of coffee into it. No one else would drink his coffee, which he made like mud, so he usually had a pot to himself. He rested his backside against the counter and slurped down half the cup.

"There's nothing to argue about," he said when he'd finished drinking. "Adrian and I go. You stay. There's no other way."

He drained the cup, dropped it back to the counter and stalked out of the room.

Leda caught up to him at the top of the stairs. He glanced down at her, eyes bleak, but kept moving to the bedroom they shared.

"We keep having this discussion," Leda said. She closed the door behind her and leaned against it. "Amber and I can help you find Kalen. So can Mac."

Hunter pulled off his shirt, the sight of his hard body never failing to stir warmth in her veins. "You can't go where we're going."

She took a step forward. "I don't pretend to have the same powers you do. But doesn't it make sense to have as many people at your back as you can? Kehksut already captured you and hurt you, Adrian too. And now she has Kalen. Strength in numbers, Hunter. We can distract her, if nothing else."

Hunter swung around, white-hot magic blazing out of him like lava from a volcano. The wave jerked Leda from her feet and slammed her hard against a wall. She couldn't speak, couldn't think, couldn't draw enough energy to counteract him with her own magic.

Hunter looked up at her, once more bathed in light as he had been when Kali had broken him free of the street. Green light from his eyes sliced across her.

"Can you fight me?" he demanded. "Can you break free?"

Leda couldn't answer. She couldn't even shake her head.

"I could kill you in the blink of an eye," Hunter said, his voice hard. "There would be nothing left of you, like you never existed. It would be so easy for me."

Leda hung helpless, her back pressed into the pretty wallpaper of Amber's guest bedroom. She knew he spoke the truth. Affable Hunter with his good-natured grin hid the demigod who could rip the life out of anything he wanted to. The only thing stopping him from destroying everything he touched was himself.

Tain, once upon a time, must have been very much like him. A gentle, godlike being, raising his sword to save others. But beneath lurked a warrior, a killer, and that killer had taken over.

Hunter's voice rolled like thunder. "This is what you face. This and more, because even as strong as I am, I can't defeat Kehksut alone. She would play with you a long time, decades maybe, keeping you alive in agony before she got bored and finally let you die."

Leda struggled for breath. "I know," she gasped out.

Hunter abruptly lowered his arm, and Leda floated to the floor, still wrapped in the white cocoon of light.

"I can't let that happen to you," he said. "I can't let her anywhere near you."

Leda still couldn't speak. She could only stand and watch him.

The white light began to recede. Hunter rested his arms at his sides, standing much like she'd first seen him, bare torso, blue jeans riding low on his hips. He closed his eyes briefly, the emerald light vanishing.

"Are you all right, love?" he asked softly. "Did I hurt you?"

"I'll be fine." Her voice wavered. She put her hand on the wall to steady herself. "You made your point." She moved to him on shaking legs. "But why do I have the feeling that if I let you go off to find Kalen with Adrian, I'll never see you again?"

"Because you might not."

She stopped, her heart squeezing. "How do you know? Do you think Kehksut will kill you? Wait, you're Immortal, you can't die. Trap you, then, like she did before?"

He cupped her shoulders as he liked to do when he talked to her, his voice quiet. "I don't know if we can open that ripple in reality in the grove, and I don't know what we'll find behind it. We might be able to find a way to Ravenscroft or back here—we might not. All I know is that we can't leave Kalen—or Tain—to her mercy." His fingers bit into her shoulders, not to hurt her, but as though he didn't want to let her go.

Her throat tightened. "Can't you find another way to look for him?"

"I can't think of one."

"Were you going to tell me good-bye?"

"That's why I came up here."

Leda's eyes filled. "I can't exactly tell you to not

to look for your brothers because I'd be lonely without you."

Hunter touched the tear that trickled down her cheek. "Kali said I'd have to make a choice, follow a path. I didn't know it would be so damn hard."

"You think this is what she meant?"

"I don't know. You can never tell with goddesses."

Leda slid her hands around his waist, leaning into the warm firmness of his skin. "Do something for me before you go."

"What's that, love?"

"Give me a child."

He stopped, eyes going enigmatic. "Why?"

"You told me you could give me a child if you chose. I don't want you to walk out of my life and leave me with nothing."

His eyes grew bleaker still. "We had this argument before. You want me not only to abandon you but my child too?"

"You said you would do your best to come back. This will give you more incentive."

She saw the swallow that moved down his throat, his indecision plain. "I'd give anything to be a father again," he whispered. "You don't know how much I want that."

Leda's pulse quickened. "Then will you give me this gift?"

For answer he kissed her slowly. "Pick out a good name. Nothing that will embarrass him in front of the other kids."

"How do you know it will be a boy?"

"I can make sure of that too."

He drew his tongue along her lips in a long, warm

stroke. Need fluttered in her, and she drew him down to her, fingers finding his waistband.

Hunter unzipped and pushed off his jeans, letting her hands wander to his backside, firm, naked skin. She liked the feel of him bare against her clothed body, a wicked, naughty feeling, as though he were hers to do with as she pleased.

His kiss told her he was happy for her to do whatever she wanted. She drew her fingers to his thighs, dipping between to cup his sac, which lifted and tightened under her palm. From there she ran her hand all the way up his shaft to the tip, rubbing her thumb lightly over the top.

She explored his body, tracing the tawny points of his nipples, running hands down his ridged abdomen, skimming the outline of his pentacle tattoo before moving again to his lovely cock. He gathered her against him, nuzzling her hair, making low noises of appreciation.

He pulled off her shirt and caught the globes of her breasts in his hands, thumbs stroking her already tingling nipples to hard points. He leaned down and suckled one, his long hair brushing her skin.

When they finally made it to the bed, they lay on their sides, facing each other for a long time while they touched and kissed and caressed. Hunter said very little, no banter, no teasing, no seduction. He simply touched her, his brow puckered in a little frown.

Leda drew her foot up the strong muscles of his leg, twining it around his thigh. She cupped his face, looking into his green eyes, memorizing every nuance of them—how they sparkled green in the light, how they could cloud with sadness and brighten in laughter a moment later.

"I'll never forget you," she whispered.

Hunter pushed her down into the bed, rolling on top of her. He kissed her hard as he pushed his tip inside her needy opening, making a soft noise in his throat.

He began to love her slowly, giving all of himself, opening her wide. She pressed her fingers into his back and pulled him into her, watching his eyes as he rocked his hips against hers.

In the mirror above the dresser she watched his buttocks rise and fall, a bronze-skinned warrior making love to her on white sheets. The idea of never seeing him again broke her heart, but forcing him to stay, to not search for his missing brother, would leave her guilt-ridden and unfulfilled. He would come to resent her if she coerced him to stay. She'd rather have him go and remember her with fondness if he remembered her at all.

He splayed his large hand across her cheek, making her look up at him. His green eyes were dark, holding so many secrets. "Do you truly want this?" he whispered. "You want my child?"

"Please."

"You could marry. Have someone else. A real family."

She kissed the side of his mouth. "I want *your* child."

He lowered his head, pressing fists into the mattress. His coming was quiet, a soft groan as he drove himself into her. Her own climax happened simultaneously, also quiet. She held him tightly while the dark waves of it took her, his seed hot and raw inside her.

Then he passed his fingers over her eyes, whispered one word of a sleep spell, and she succumbed. *I did it to him on the island*, was her last coherent thought. *Tit for tat.*

She was still half asleep in the gray dawn light when Hunter rose from the bed. She watched groggily as Hunter pulled on jeans and shirt, located his leather-sheathed sword and strapped it to his back. He came to her and pressed a kiss to her temple.

"Sleep well, love," he said, and she felt another frisson of his magic.

Hunter stood over the bed watching Leda sleep for a long time. He hated taking the risk that he'd never see her again, but he didn't feel he had a choice. He leaned over and kissed her again, but his sleep spell was strong and she didn't stir.

He loved the scent of her, everything about her, in fact. He traced his fingers down her face and chest and rested them briefly over her abdomen. He'd done what she wanted, given her his child, a child he'd possibly never see.

One of the hardest things he ever did in his life was turn away from the bed and walk out into the hall.

He didn't have to go. He could take Leda far away from here and make love to her every day while Adrian sorted out this problem. Adrian liked complications and long battles, while Hunter preferred to get the killing over with quickly so he could get back to the sex.

Adrian met him at the bottom of the stairs, carrying Kalen's crystal-tipped spear, his expression grave. He'd taken his leave of Amber, and Hunter sensed that his big brother hadn't liked it any better than

Hunter had liked saying good-bye to Leda. These witches had done something to them.

Mukasa came around to the back of the house as Adrian and Hunter stepped off the porch. The lion butted his head against Hunter's thigh, and Hunter absently petted him.

"You can't come with us, old friend." Hunter ruffled his mane. "Take care of Leda for me."

Mukasa grumbled a little but let them walk away without him to the center of the grove. The ripple here was pronounced, thick and heavy like a sluggish stream. Adrian stopped in a little circle near trees. The branches were hung with pink and purple ribbons.

Adrian pushed at the ripple, and Hunter saw his fingers sink in like it was colorless gelatin. "During the Beltane ritual, Amber and I were pulled into an alternate reality," he said in a thoughtful voice. "The god and goddess did it. But I have a feeling the reality behind this ripple is different now." He held up Kalen's spear. "If I'm right, this will be drawn to Kalen, as Ferrin is drawn to me, your sword to you. Our weapons don't like to be far from our hands."

Hunter grinned. "Mine likes to be in Leda's hands."

"Very funny. The sooner we go, the better. The demon's strength is building in logarithmic increments."

"Logga-whats?"

"In a big way, very fast."

Hunter stared in mock outrage. "Hey, your father was a high priest; mine was a slave who didn't use big words."

He turned as he sensed someone approaching, a woman whose aura was slightly tinged with death magic. Right on time.

Samantha approached, looking uneasy. "Leda won't be happy about this."

"She's already pissed at me," Hunter said. "I'm getting used to it. Was I right?"

Samantha nodded. "She was there where you said she'd be. I wanted to stay, but Septimus told me you insisted I come up here."

Adrian frowned, puzzled. "What's going on?"

"This is Samantha Taylor," Hunter explained, feeling gleeful. "A half-demon who happens to be paranormal police. Her mother disappeared, and I figured out after a while that she must have gotten trapped in one of these ripples. I sensed it when I was in the house, when Kehksut first tried to snare me, without realizing I sensed it. If demon gangs broke into her house, and she fought with magic, the residue might have created one. It trapped her and she couldn't get out. I told Samantha and Fulton, her demon father, that they could pierce the ripple and find her. Death magic created it; death magic can break it."

He stopped, pleased with himself that he'd been right. Leda had told him how her locator spell had backfired, in a big way. Kehksut, she'd assumed, but she'd been trying to penetrate the ripple, which blasted back at her strong life magic.

Adrian merely nodded, as if the deduction should have been simple. "And you asked her to come up here because she's a half-demon and can help us open it now."

"You could sound more impressed with your baby brother. I called Septimus and had him send her up."

"Right away," Samantha said in a hard voice. "I haven't slept tonight, let alone hugged my mother."

"You'll have another chance if this goes right," Hunter told her.

Samantha frowned at him, her dark demon eyes troubled. "Forgive me if I don't dance with joy. But I owe you for helping me find her. What do you want me to do?"

Hunter took the spear from Adrian and pressed it into Samantha's hands. She blanched at the intense life magic flowing from it, but held it steadily.

"We need your death magic," Hunter said. "Just point the spear and go. Then Pearl will make you breakfast."

"Who's Pearl?"

"Half a halfling and half a gnome," Hunter answered. "Crabby as hell but a wonderful cook. She used to work for Kalen."

"That's it?" Samantha broke in. "That's all you want me to do?"

"Yes." Hunter nodded and drew his sword. "And then we're even. Leda was right about you. You're not bad, for a demon."

"Gee, thanks."

Adrian broke in impatiently. "Can we do this?"

Hunter gestured with his sword. "After you, big brother."

Adrian's silver armband morphed into his cobra Ferrin and slithered down his outstretched arm to wrap himself around Adrian's wrist. Looking skeptical, Samantha dipped the tip of the spear through the ripple in reality.

"Find Kalen," Hunter said.

Mukasa, standing at the base of the porch steps, smelled a sharp tang of magic. The air shimmered like heat wave on the Serengeti, and when it calmed, Adrian, Hunter and Samantha were gone. Mukasa stared at the spot for a long time, then lay down with a little moan and rested his great head on his paws.

CHAPTER TWENTY

Leda went downstairs after she'd showered and mastered her tears, to find Amber in the kitchen making tea, her eyes as red as Leda's.

"Our own fault," Leda said shakily. "For falling in love with Immortals."

Sabina was reading a newspaper at the table, Mac next to her playing something in his earphones at an amazing level, Pearl at the stove. Valerian hadn't returned from his night patrolling the city.

Sabina glanced up at Leda in sympathy. "Don't be too hard on yourselves. They're gorgeous and magical. You didn't stand a chance."

Leda slid into the chair opposite her, coffee in hand. "Did Samantha arrive?"

"Not this morning, as far as I know," Sabina answered.

Leda sighed and turned her cup in her hands. She wondered if she'd ever drink coffee without remembering Hunter's sensual delight in it. "I just wonder why Hunter was so adamant about her coming up here. And then he and Adrian left before she could get here."

Mac had cut off his music and listened with interest. "She's paranormal police, right? Mebbe Hunter wants her to arrest the demon. Or mebbe she's bait."

Leda arched her brows. "Bait? How do you mean?

"She's a half-demon, you told me. Tain might be attracted to her death magic and forget about his obsession with the other demon."

Leda thought about it, wondering what demigod thoughts spun behind the youth's innocuous smile. "I don't think that's likely."

Mac shrugged and stuffed his earbud back into his ear. "Just an idea."

Leda felt her treacherous tears returning as her thoughts turned to Hunter's last searing kiss and his suspicion he might never make it back. She had no way of knowing whether Hunter had fulfilled her last request to give her a child. Only time would tell.

Sabina gave her a sympathetic look and started to speak. She broke off when Leda gasped.

A wave of magic swamped the house, rattling the foundations like an earthquake. It jolted through Leda's head, pounding with migraine intensity. Amber put her hand to her forehead, and Mac sucked in his breath.

"What the hell was that?" Amber said. "I felt it, and I know you did."

"Outside," Mac said.

He pushed away from the table and dashed down the hall to the front door and flung it open, Leda right behind him. At the bottom of the porch steps, right on the fringe of the magic shield over the house, lay a young woman. She had long black hair, a slim body and a tattoo on her shoulder bared by her tank top.

Mac gave a cry of surprise and anguish, and dropped to his knees beside her. "Christine!"

Leda reached them just as the young woman fluttered open her eyes. "Mac?"

Leda crouched next to them. "Are you Christine Lachlan?"

"Yes. Who are you?" Christine's eyes cleared, and she sat up and looked around wildly. "Where's Kalen?"

Mac's face went somber. "Gone, love. Taken by the enemy."

Christine looked stricken. "Culsu trapped him. I need to talk to Adrian."

Mac and Leda exchanged a glance, then looked up as Amber and Sabina reached them.

"What?" Christine asked. "He's here, isn't he? He'd better be, or we're all in trouble."

Leda put her hand under the young woman's arm. "Come on. We need to go in the house where it's safe—relatively. Then you need to tell us exactly what happened."

Adrian and Hunter did not end up where Hunter thought they would. He assumed they'd still be in the grove but in an unreal one. Instead he found himself back in the stupid dungeon. Not only that—the ripple had sucked Samantha in as well.

"What am I doing here?" she demanded. "I thought I got to have breakfast."

Neither Immortal could answer her. The slime-covered walls looked even faker than before. The room receded into shadows that the three of them never quite reached, as though the floor moved when they did.

"Screw this," Hunter said after ten minutes of nothing.

"Wait a minute," Adrian said behind him. "Look at the spear."

The crystal tip was alive with white magic. Ferrin the snake sat up on Adrian's arm and hissed.

Adrian grabbed the spear from Samantha and held it in front of him. "This way," Adrian said.

He walked off to the left, and Hunter and Samantha followed. As before, the room moved them so they never reached the shadows, but suddenly they came upon a man standing in a circle of light.

Hunter hadn't seen Kalen in seven hundred years. He looked the same, from his unruly dark hair to his charcoal-gray eyes, only now he was naked, the tattoo on his thigh stark in the eerie light. He stood stiffly upright, hands behind him, his head thrown back, his face turned up to the light. Of the witch Christine there was no sign.

"Kalen," Hunter called softly. He touched Kalen's shoulder, but though the big man rocked under Hunter's hand, he didn't snap out of whatever spell held him.

Adrian brought the spear around and touched Kalen with the tip of it. The magic in the crystal flared white, then suddenly died into a dull, gray-yellow glow. Kalen never moved.

"That can't be good," Hunter said.

His palms began to sweat, remembering the pain the demon had inflicted on him, remembering even more vividly his fall into the narrow chasm in the

street. His plan had been to find Kalen in this unreality and try to get him to Ravenscroft, where they
could regroup and look for Tain. Even better if Tain
were here and could be pulled along with them.

"Let's grab him and go," Hunter said.

"What about Samantha?"

Samantha folded her slim arms, her eyes defiant but
liquid with fear. "Yes, what about me? Are you going
to leave me in here?"

Half-demon or no, the young woman was terrified.
Hunter laid a gentle hand on her shoulder. "No. We'll
find some way to send you back to Amber's."

She didn't look reassured as Adrian grasped one of
Kalen's arms and Hunter took the other. About that
time, Ferrin slipped from Adrian's wrist and fell to the
floor with a sickening *plop*.

"Shit." Adrian let go of Kalen and crouched to
scoop up Ferrin's limp body.

"Is he dead?" Hunter asked.

"No. But out of it."

Hunter had a thought. He unsheathed his sword
and held it up, willing it to burst into flame. Nothing
happened. "Shit," he echoed.

Adrian cradled Ferrin in his hand. "I can't open a
portal to Ravenscroft without my weapon. Kalen
might be able to, but he's down for the count."

"How about we go back to the grove then? If we
can," Hunter said.

"No," Adrian said.

Samantha's eyes widened. "What? Why not?"

Adrian rapped Kalen's spear once on the floor. "I
want to get Kehksut. If we've walked into his little
cage, fine. I couldn't go after him when Amber freed
me from her tower room because I needed to help her.

I couldn't do it at the Calling for the same reason." His eyes burned with fanatic fire. "I'm not letting this chance go."

"He's crazy," Samantha said to Hunter. "I thought *you* were crazy, but he's even worse."

Adrian's dark eyes swam with sparks. He turned an angry glance on Samantha, and she shrank back into Hunter.

"Three Immortals are better odds than two," Hunter said to Adrian. "We take Kalen back to Amber's, wake him up, then go hunting."

"Oh, don't go," came Kehksut's voice. "That would be a shame."

The demon walked toward them in her female form, dressed in a red body-hugging dress and impossibly high heels. Adrian gripped the spear, ready to fight, as the demon stopped in front of Hunter and Samantha.

"Did you bring me a present?" She drew one scarlet fingernail across Samantha's cheek. "A half-demon. Less than a lesser demon, and meat and drink to me." She drew her tongue across her lower lip.

Hunter extended his magic over Samantha, protecting her. The demon sneered at him. "Your pet, is she?"

"Don't you get tired of those stupid dominatrix outfits?" Hunter asked her in a disgusted tone.

"You don't like me like this?" Kehksut purred. "Maybe you want to remember me a different way."

The red dress fell away, the she-creature morphing into a tall, muscular male. He had long black hair and a sensuous face, and his clothes became the leather armor Hunter had last seen people wearing on the plains of what was now Hungary. He'd seen this demon with a bloody sword in his hand, right after having driven the blade through Hunter's wife.

The red rage that welled up inside him terrified him at the same time as it exhilarated him. So *this* was the demon—the same Old One who had destroyed Hunter's wife and children and made his life a living hell. The same demon who had laughed when Hunter launched into berserker rage.

The demon laughed now. Hunter lunged, his sword coming down in an arc to cut off the demon's head. He heard Adrian shouting words from ancient Egypt, a war cry that would have terrified any mortal to death. But before the sword and the spear could make contact, everything went black.

Tain walked out of the shadows in his chain-mail vest and surcoat, surveying the three warriors in the middle of the room. They stood back to back in a pool of white light, blank faces turned upward. Ferrin was stretched out in front of Adrian, Hunter's sword lying at his feet, Kalen's spear on the floor in front of him.

Three Immortals. Three brothers. Almost complete.

And a young woman who hovered in the shadows, terrified. Her aura was unusual, tainted with death magic that warred with her life magic.

"Who is this?" Tain asked curiously.

"A treat," Kehksut-Culsu-Amadja answered. "Your brothers brought her for us."

Tain reached his fingers toward her but didn't touch her. "An innocent."

Kehksut snorted. "No human is completely innocent. I'll save her for a snack."

Tain looked the young woman up and down, but the

presence of his brothers, so close to him after so long, distracted him. He turned away. "You sent the witch Christine back to the others?" he asked Kehksut.

"I did as you wished."

Tain walked a slow circle around the three Immortals, a lock of red hair tickling his cheek over his tattoo. Kalen and Adrian were dark-haired like demons; Hunter's hair was a shade lighter.

"It's just like my brothers to strike first and think later," he remarked.

"So it seems," Kehksut agreed.

"Three down, one to go." Tain walked around them again, feeling a strange pang of regret and longing. "And then it will be over. I am so very tired of this."

"I know, love." The demon morphed back into her beautiful form and touched his cheek, not the side of his face with the tattoo. "Shall we celebrate?"

She wet her lips with a bright red tongue. Tain frowned at her. *Demons*. They thought about sex and little else.

"Not right now," he said in a stern voice. "I want to think a little. Alone."

The demon opened her mouth to argue, then simpered and nodded. "As you wish, love. You know you have but to call me."

She touched her fingers to Tain's lips, then turned around and sauntered away, moving her hips to catch Tain's attention.

Later. Tain would sate himself again on her beautiful body, but right now he wanted to look at his brothers standing here so quietly, so peacefully, and remember. . . .

The dark human woman lowered herself to the floor and wrapped her arms around her knees.

* * *

Christine related her story from the moment she scryed for Kalen in Rome to the moment they'd been riding in the connecting flight from New York and had been pulled out of the plane.

"I don't remember much after that." Wrapped in a blanket, her dark hair straggling around her face, Christine cradled a mug of coffee and shivered. "I remember seeing Tain again, and Culsu. Then Kalen was trying to hang on to me, and something was dragging me from him. I screamed that it was tearing me apart, and Kalen let go. I landed here."

"Did you know where you were?" Amber asked Christine.

She shook her head. "I have no idea. Everything was a blur. I only saw faces."

Leda exchanged a glance with Amber, her fear echoed in Amber's eyes. "Hunter and Adrian have gone after Kalen," Leda said.

Christine shot them a worried look. "What about Darius? That was the name of the other Immortal, right?"

"We haven't heard from him in a while," Amber answered.

"We could try the Calling spell again," Leda suggested. "If it has the power to Call the Immortals, it might yank them out of wherever they are."

Amber didn't look hopeful. "The first attempt was so easily thwarted by the demon. And look what happened—we had to scour the world to find them all. We don't have time to do that again."

Mac had taken his earbuds out of his ears to listen. "I don't like the idea of an Immortal-less world. But that's about what we've got."

"You know, I never knew they existed before this," Leda said. "I never realized how much we needed them. And now it scares me very much to not have them around." Plus she missed Hunter like crazy. Waking up to the empty bed, knowing he was gone, had taken the heart out of her.

"So what do we do?" Sabina demanded. "Sit around and wonder? You are three magic-ass witches—do spells or something." She vaguely waved her hands, then lowered them as they stared at her. "Sorry. It's the wolf in me, I guess."

"She's right," Christine said. "We need to strike."

Leda put in, "Hunter left me here with the understanding that I'd sit tight and wait for him and Adrian to solve all the problems." She grinned. "They don't know us very well, do they?"

Mac gave a short laugh. "You're right there, love. They have no idea what they've gotten themselves into, falling for you lot. I'm enjoying this."

"So do you have any big ideas, Mr. Half-god Sidhe?" Leda asked him.

"Magic," Mac said promptly. "The three of you have magic that, put together, would be mighty powerful. This will be solved by pooling talents, not by going off in different directions. Me, I'm getting a cool new song out of it." He picked up his black Ovation guitar and started moving his fingers up and down the neck in swift and complex patterns. Eyes closed, he drifted off into his world of music, a beatific expression on his face.

The three witches looked at each other. "You heard him," Amber said quietly. "Let's go save the Immortals."

* * *

They spent every hour of the next several days looking up spells and inventing new ones, trying to puzzle out how to open the ripples in reality, using scrying, cards, runes and other spells to try to figure out what to do. As when Leda had tried the location spell to find Samantha's mother, the minute any magic touched the ripples, the backlash was terrible and painful.

Leda hadn't heard from Samantha at all. Septimus swore he'd put her on his plane and sent her up there, and his vampires had promised they'd dropped her off in front of Amber's house the morning Hunter and Adrian had disappeared. The only conclusion to draw was that she'd disappeared with Adrian and Hunter.

If Leda hadn't been so anxious for Hunter and Samantha and the other Immortals, she would have found the work exhilarating. It had been a long time since she was able to pool ideas and magic workings with witches who were on the same level as she was.

Amber had incredible magic based in stones and the bones of the earth. She could easily tap into any ley line where Leda had to search for them. Christine had water magic. She was almost blind without touching water, but once she did, she could do amazing things.

Christine loved salty foods and sent Pearl's brownies out every day to get chips, pretzels and popcorn. With consecrated water, Christine could work stronger magic than Leda could imagine. She could also reach into a person and use the water in him either against him or in his favor, to destroy or heal. She had trouble with demons, she confessed, because they had no water in them.

Leda, on the other hand, worked well against demons because her magic was of the air. She fed on the power of the wind and of instruments made to catch wind—

chimes, flutes, even the rustle of wind in leaves. She had been able to tap into the magic of demons because she could touch their air magic and bend it to her will. But that price was too high, she remembered with a shudder. If not for Hunter . . .

Such thoughts would remind her of Hunter lying with her in her bed on the island, teaching her to open herself to him, pleasuring her while he drew the dark magic out of her. She thought of how he'd smiled when he held the dark magic between his fingers and so easily crushed it out of existence.

Then tears would fill her eyes, her worry would return, and whatever spell she tried to work would fizzle and die. Safer to not think of Hunter at all.

She knew that Hunter and Adrian hadn't been successful in finding the demon and destroying him, because the world didn't get any better. It grew worse—darker, grittier, fouler. Leaving the house was dangerous, and Valerian would not let them out without his protection.

Only Mac seemed oblivious, plucking at his guitar and tapping notes on Amber's piano, head bent, humming under his breath. Leda had listened to his music and found it amazing. Beautiful and harsh at the same time, it mixed ancient Celtic tunes and electric grunge into something entirely new. If they prevailed against the demon, the Seattle scene would love him.

In the kitchen, Pearl cooked, her gnarled form moving quickly between refrigerator, stove and ovens. Valerian had learned to tolerate the brownies because he loved Pearl's cooking. But he too worried, and was hard on himself because he could do so little.

At nightfall of the day that marked two weeks since Hunter, Adrian and Kalen had disappeared, Mac lifted his head and swiveled around so he could stare at the front hall. The witches had learned to trust his instincts, and Leda rose warily before someone started banging on the door.

"Let us in, quick," came a rumbling voice. For a moment Leda froze, thinking it was Hunter. She saw Christine and Amber hesitate too, then they all raced into the hall.

Valerian came out of the back and reached the door first. "You ladies get behind me. I'm supposed to be protecting you."

Leda saw the wisdom of letting him open the door for them, but it was difficult to hold back. She sensed death magic out there, the wards singing with it, but life magic as well. A powerful dose of life magic.

Valerian cracked the door open. His back stiffened. "Vampire," he announced.

"And nymph," said a light, almost musical voice with a touch of the sultry. "And a werewolf-witch, and a . . . whatever Darius is."

CHAPTER TWENTY-ONE

"Darius?" Leda ducked under Valerian's thick arm to see a tall warrior standing on the porch in a black leather sleeveless duster.

Now that she was familiar with Immortals, everything about him screamed it—the broad-shouldered build, the square face, the intense eyes, the magic that crackled just below the surface. The huge sword he held was also a clue.

He brushed the hair from his eyes with one sinewy hand and peered at her sharply. "Are you Amber Silverthorne?"

"No, that would be me." Amber craned to see him around Valerian, who wasn't moving an inch.

"He's with a vampire," Valerian rumbled.

"This is Ricco," said a tall woman with long blue-black hair and light gray eyes. Her eyes flickered from normal human's to a wolf's and back so fast Leda almost missed it. "He's decided to join the good guys for a while."

"Like Septimus," Amber said.

Valerian rumbled in his throat. "I don't like Septimus either."

"What about me?" asked the woman with her hand on the vampire's arm. It had been her voice they'd heard through the door. "I'm Mai, cute and harmless."

The werewolf woman snorted. "Sure."

Valerian's gaze rested on Mai appreciatively. "You seem fine."

The werewolf woman suddenly looked beyond Valerian, her eyes changing again, her stance wary. Sabina had come in from the back door, and now she stared at the other werewolf in muted hostility. Wolves were very territorial.

"I'm Lexi Corbin," the woman with Darius said. "Of the Oak Moon pack in New York. I'm just visiting."

"Sabina Brown of the Bright Angel pack. We live three doors down." She looked Lexi over, her gaze straying to Darius. "Well met and welcome."

Lexi relaxed a bit as though she'd passed a test. Leda did not know much about werewolves, but she sensed that Sabina had just signaled that Lexi would be accepted on Sabina's pack's territory—temporarily.

"May we come in, please?" Darius asked tightly. "There's a shitload of death magic behind us. We barely made it to the porch in time."

Inky darkness hovered outside the bubble of protection around the house, hanging there as though waiting to swallow anyone who came out.

"Where's Mukasa?" Leda asked in alarm. The lion had taken to spending most of his time in the grove, gazing mournfully at the ripple in reality there. *Waiting for Hunter,* Leda knew. *Like the rest of us.*

"He's on the back porch," Sabina answered. "I just saw him. He's fine."

"Mukasa?" Darius asked as Valerian finally stepped back so they could enter. "Is he a witch?"

"Hunter's pet lion," Valerian answered him.

Mai blanched and held tighter to Ricco. The vampire was handsome, dark-haired and blue-eyed, and like Septimus, carried vast death magic, though not quite as all-powerful as Septimus's. An Old One, but not quite as old.

"Hunter's here?" Darius demanded.

"Not exactly."

Darius strode into the house, brushing his fingers along the door frame as he went. Leda sensed his magic flow into the walls, fusing with what his brothers had already marked.

When he entered the living room, he lifted his sword and slid it point downward behind the collar of his duster, where it suddenly disappeared. Leda stared, then realized his arms were covered with colorful tattoos, daggers, knives and throwing stars. When his duster swung open, she saw even more tattoos on his chest.

"What do you mean, not exactly?" Darius asked her.

Lexi came in behind him. "You know we could introduce ourselves first. Get acquainted. Have drinks."

Leda shook her head. "This is too important."

She filled Darius in, his scowl growing fiercer by the minute. The others drifted in to join them, Lexi remaining close to Darius.

They're a couple too, Leda realized. *We've all fallen for our Immortals.*

She wondered how many women had done that through the ages, witches who'd Called the Immortals to help them, then fallen in love with the big, sexy warriors with dangerous eyes.

It's either a significant event that we each paired off with one, or we're just four witches in a long line of fools.

She finished telling the story of Kalen's disappearance, and how Adrian and Hunter had gone after him, with side comments from Mac, Christine, Amber, Sabina, Valerian and Pearl—who'd come out to see how many more dishes she'd have to lay out for supper.

"I won't be dining," Ricco told her. The vampire looked uncomfortable in the house bursting with life magic, though Amber had given him a special invitation to enter through the wards.

Pearl shot him a belligerent look and an even greater one at Mai. Ricco seemed to like Mai's attention, and surreptitiously slid his hand to the small of her back. The sun was completely down, and he'd be strengthening for the night.

When Leda finished, Darius said, "Well, they didn't come to Ravenscroft. I was there for a while. Probably why I didn't get snatched when the demon was busy plucking up Immortals."

"Then you think the demon did take them?" Leda asked. "All of them?"

Darius scrubbed his hand through his hair. He wore it shorter than the others did, the dark locks falling to skim his shoulders. "I think they would have checked back by now, or one of them at least would have passed through Ravenscroft. What was Hunter going on about—a ripple in reality? He's always been a little nuts."

"Maybe, but this time he's right," Leda said. "Hunter implied that whatever imprisoned Kalen would be hard to reach, even for them."

"Where did Adrian and Hunter go? We can start looking there at least."

"Probably the green behind the house," Leda said. "There's a powerful magical field out there, and Mukasa walks up and down looking mournful, as though he's waiting for Hunter to pop back out from somewhere. But we've done all kinds of locating and tracking spells back there without any luck."

"Hmm," Darius said. He wandered to the windows that looked out over the lawn sloping down to the grove. It was dark outside and lightly raining, the moon hidden.

"Do you want to take a look?" Lexi asked him. "See if you sense anything?"

"No."

Lexi looked at him in surprise. "Why not?"

Darius continued to stare out into the darkness. "Go to the exact spot two other Immortals disappeared and see if I disappear too? Good plan."

"We could put a tracking device on you," Valerian suggested. "So when you disappear you can send back signals, magical or otherwise."

Darius looked him up and down. "What are you, my friend? Very magical, that's for sure."

Valerian pointed to the tattoo spread across Darius's pectorals. "Is that a dragon on your chest or are you just happy to see me?"

Darius looked down at himself, touching the outline of the tattoo. "This is Fury. He's not a dragon; he's a Bocca demon."

"Really?" Leda asked in interest. She leaned forward to get a better look at the precise picture of the winged demon. "I thought they were extinct."

"All but Fury. I'll tell you the story sometime. We're friends, and he helps me out now and then."

"Thought maybe he was a long-lost cousin or something," Valerian said.

"Ah." Darius nodded. "You're one of the Great Dragons."

"Don't tell him that." Sabina folded her arms and leaned back against Valerian's solid body. "He's insufferable as it is. Valerian is a swamp dragon."

"*Tropical* dragon," he corrected her. "There's a big difference."

"Right, honey," Sabina said with a straight face.

"We don't know that Hunter and Adrian are trapped," Christine broke in. "But we do know that Kalen is. I saw him taken myself, before I was thrown out of wherever it was."

"I still don't understand why the demon let you go," Amber said. "Why come back and warn us?"

"Probably so Adrian and Hunter would search for him," Darius said. "We need to think about this. We need—"

"Ye need to sit yourselves down to the supper I've been slaving over," came Pearl's gruff and thickly accented voice. "It's in the dining room, and I put another leaf in the table."

"Who is she?" Darius asked Leda quietly. "*What* is she?"

"Her name is Pearl, and she's wonderful," Christine broke in. "She's looked after Kalen for over a century."

"Aye, that I have," Pearl said, her ugly face softening. "The brownies have set everything up all nice, so don't hurt their feelings."

"Brownies," Valerian muttered as they trickled through the hall to the vast dining room. One of the creatures scurried in front of the big man, causing him to trip, then scuttled away, laughing. Valerian caught himself on the door frame. "Little vermin."

Leda dreamed. She sat up in her bed, knowing she was still asleep, and gazed at the white-curtained window. She sensed the others in the house around her—Ricco pulsing strongly of dark magic while he made phone calls downstairs, the white-hot power of Darius in the front guest room, Lexi's witch and werewolf power mingling with it. Lexi had fire magic which went with her personality, hot and sharp, nothing you wanted to mess with.

Amber had a blue aura, the earth as her strength; Christine, in the same room with her, had water magic. And then Mac, sparking like a firework as he wandered the house, Mai a lesser glow near Ricco. Mai was a wood nymph, which explained her slim lightness, her beauty, her laughter, her blatant liking for sex. "Just call me a nymph-omaniac," she joked.

The window beckoned to Leda in her dream. Softly she went to it and pushed back the curtain.

The darkness beyond was complete, thick and black. In it she saw shadows, then suddenly Hunter's face. When his gaze met hers, his green eyes lit up. "Hey, sweetheart."

Leda reached for him, heart aching, but he vanished abruptly, and a handsome demon filled the void. "He's here with me," the male form of Kehksut said, his voice sultry and low. "Why don't you come get him?"

Leda balled her fist. "Why do you want them? What are you going to do to them?"

"*To* them? Nothing." He smiled. "They will help me. But I need all five with me. Five. Remember that."

"Why? And why should you give me hints?"

His form blurred and fire sprang from the darkness, divine fire. A woman's face came at Leda wreathed in flames, her hands held in the elegant but contorted positions of an Oriental statue.

"Five is a magical number," the woman hissed, her tongue a flame of light.

"Kali?" Leda breathed. The goddess herself? Or a trick of the demon's?

"Five Immortals," the woman went on. "Five goddesses, five elements, five points of the pentacle. Five witches. Know."

Kali's visage vanished, and a powerfully beautiful woman with red hair appeared. "Save my son," she said, her Welsh accent vibrant. "Let the world end, I care nothing for it, but save my son."

The vision changed again, and a woman with a stern but beautiful face and fiery eyes frowned at Leda. "Things have gotten out of hand," she growled. "Listen to Darius. He's learned a thing or two from that werewolf-witch."

Again a change, to a powerful, dark-haired woman in a linen tunic like those worn in ancient Rome. "Kalen has both wisdom and power. He will survive, but only with your help."

The next and last woman had jet-black hair and slender horns rising from her head. "Help them all, Leda. You are wise without knowing it. Search inside yourself—what can you do, what have you survived that the others have not? In that survival lies your strength. So many others would have succumbed."

Leda listened without understanding. The moon played over the window like ripples of silver, the night breeze touching her skin. Isis dissolved, and Hunter sat on her windowsill again, in low-slung jeans with bare feet. He pulled one knee to his chest, hooking his muscled arms around it.

"Have the goddesses been driving you crazy? Let me guess, they're being cryptic and telling you to figure it out for yourself?"

"Something like that." Leda felt her lips move, but no sound came from her mouth.

Hunter rose and came to her. She loved the way he looked, straight and tall, his muscled torso rising from the waistband of his jeans. The pentacle tattoo on his abdomen seemed to pulse with light.

"Are you real?" Leda whispered, reaching for him.

"Sort of. But I'm Hunter, and no demon."

Leda found his skin firm and warm. She ran her hands up his torso, tracing across his collarbone, feeling the powerful muscles of his shoulders. He stood still, green eyes dark, letting her explore him to her satisfaction.

He began kissing her, and suddenly she found herself in bed with him, their clothes gone. He loved her gently first, then with a wildness that left her breathless. His mouth was warm in the darkness, his body heavy and comforting.

"I love you," Leda murmured.

"I love you too, baby."

He began to fade, and Leda clutched him. "Don't go."

"I have to, sweetheart. I can't stay." His face was profoundly sad as he kissed her. "You come find me. Do what the goddesses said."

"But I don't understand what the goddesses said."

"You will. You're my witch, you'll do it."

"Hunter."

Another kiss, and he was gone. Leda slid back into sleep and spent the rest of the night in oblivion.

Tain watched his brothers. He loved to come here and walk around them, gazing at the men he'd at one time looked up to, and even loved. Theirs had been a turbulent relationship; brothers who were at once competitive and supportive.

Tain had been close to Adrian, the oldest brother guiding and protecting the youngest. Hunter and Darius had a friendship that sometimes segued into rivalry, but always came back to banter and joking in the end. Kalen had been a man apart, interested in his own special people, to whom he played god.

Tain gazed at Kalen, a dark-haired, gray-eyed warrior with arrogance etched into every line of his face. He was naked—they all were—his head tilted back to rest against Adrian's and Hunter's.

Adrian next, Tain's beloved older brother, black hair tumbling down his back, dark eyes open and unseeing. What was going on behind that enigmatic gaze? The demon's and Tain's combined magic held them in stasis, but these were Immortals, and their minds were closed to him. Behind the blank stares he sensed spinning thoughts and dreams.

Hunter seemed to be having a good dream. His eyes were half closed, green light glowing from them. His organ was not erect, but from the flush on his skin, the sparkle in his eyes, what he dreamed of was sexual.

Tain couldn't do anything about that. Let Hunter enjoy his last illusion. The demon would take it all away soon.

Hunter's tattoo stood out stark blue-black against his abdomen, Adrian's on his left hip, Kalen's high on his thigh. Tain's fingers moved involuntarily to his cheek, remembering how Hunter had taunted him into making Tain's demon lover touch it. He remembered how she'd cringed away, eyes alight with pain.

But Hunter was wrong. The demon couldn't be killed with the magic in the tattoo. Tain had tried that eons ago, when the demon had first enslaved him. He'd tried to use his Immortal magic, and the demon had only sucked it into herself, bolstering her own power.

Something seemed to have changed. Bringing the Immortals together perhaps? The air was infused with magic here, crackling with it.

Tain frowned. The demon had insisted on bringing them together, saying that things would drain more swiftly and easily once they were trapped, but Tain wasn't a fool. Immortals together were dangerous. They'd try to stop Tain from doing what was necessary, and the demon must know this.

Hunter, even in his immobility, managed to close his eyes and made a little noise of satisfaction. Tain watched him with a pang of envy.

The demon gave Tain deep sexual satisfaction, but he knew it wasn't the same as being with a flesh-and-blood woman. Hunter had that—Adrian and Kalen too. Tain missed the joy of having a woman look up at him with fondness in her eyes, caress his cheek, smile a little smile. He could never have that simple pleasure again.

He growled in pain and frustration, swung on his heel and disappeared into the shadows.

Samantha watched him go, still folded in on herself. Tain hadn't looked at her, seeming fascinated by the Immortals standing fixed and rigid in the middle of the light.

She unclenched her hands, palms sweaty. The Immortals were dangerous, but she sensed that Tain was the most dangerous of all. He was crazed and unpredictable, and if he had turned his head and noticed her there in the darkness, there was no telling what he would have done to her.

"Immortals," she whispered. "And I thought demons were bad."

CHAPTER TWENTY-TWO

Leda woke and stared at the ceiling for a long time. It was raining outside, as usual these days, the window gray. She heard noises downstairs of a full house awakening, but she lay still, her gaze on the ceiling, feeling flushed and tired.

She remembered Hunter's last words to her in her dream, the touch of his fingers on her lips. She laid her hand over her abdomen, wondering whether she felt a flutter of magic there that meant Hunter's child, but she had no way of knowing, except to wait and see.

Leda threw back the covers and crawled out of bed, limbs stiff. Dream lover or no, having Hunter in her bed took its toll.

Downstairs Pearl whipped up a breakfast for an army and growled at anyone who got in her way. Leda had heard Amber's shower running when she'd passed her door, but nothing from Mai's or Mac's rooms. Ricco had mentioned he'd check things out in the city during the night, and either he'd returned silently or had gone to ground somewhere out in the city to hide from the daylight.

"Darius," Leda said as she entered the kitchen. Valerian reached around Pearl to grab a mug from the cupboard, earning a blistering glare. He poured Leda coffee and shoved it at her, while Darius flicked a dark gaze over her.

"You look awful," Darius observed.

"Very diplomatic, Dar," Lexi told him.

"I meant she looks like she's been in a fight."

"I didn't sleep much," Leda admitted. "I had many dreams, and I can't explain them all now. Darius, you have to go after your brothers. You have to be with them. There must be five of you together."

Darius's brows rose a fraction. Leda had grown used to that Immortal stare, green and piercing from Hunter, dark and closed from Adrian. Eyes that told her that behind the "I'm-just-a-brawny-warrior" facade lurked an ancient being who had learned incredible things while watching the centuries roll by.

"Five," he repeated.

"Five warriors, five points of the star. No, don't ask me what it means. I have no idea." Leda glanced at Lexi and frowned. "She was wrong, though. She said five witches, and there are only four of us."

"She?" Lexi asked. Her gaze said she considered Leda as nuts as Darius did. "She who?"

"Kali."

"Kali visited you in the night?" Darius asked. His entire interest and focus was on her, magic flickering through his body. It was, to say the least, unnerving. "What did she say?"

"All the goddesses came. They said different things." Leda closed her eyes, trying to sort out the fuzzy images. It didn't help that her brain kept flooding with memories of Hunter, his hands and lips burning her.

"It's hard to explain," she said. "Very clear in the dream, not clear now. But you need to go to them."

"And how do you propose I do that?" Darius demanded. "Wave my arms around and say *Hey, demon, over here. Take me*"?

Leda shook her head. "I don't know. They didn't exactly give me directions."

"Goddesses never do," he growled. "Or if they do, they won't tell you the reason behind it."

Lexi laid her hand on Darius's strong shoulder, the gesture both affectionate and protective. "And if Darius disappears, what makes you think we'll ever see him again?"

"I have some ideas," Leda answered. She tried to sound mysterious and cryptic like the goddesses, but her voice came out an unconvincing croak.

"Hmm." Darius drank coffee, set the mug thoughtfully on the counter and without a word walked out the back door.

Lexi blinked, her lips parted. Then she ran after him. Leda watched out the window as Darius strode down to the grove where the streamers from Beltane still fluttered. Lexi, almost as long-legged as Darius, caught up to him quickly.

Valerian joined Leda at the window. Together they watched the witch and the warrior face each other, he tall and bulked with muscle, she lithe and lean, her werewolf's strength evident in every line.

They argued. Lexi planted her hands on her hips, and Darius folded his arms and stood with feet slightly apart, his leather duster moving in the wind and rain. After a few moments of this, Darius caught her in his arms and drew her against him. Lexi rose on her toes, and Darius leaned down to give her a long, passionate kiss.

"We shouldn't watch," Valerian murmured.

"I know."

They didn't move as Darius's hands slid down Lexi's body to cup her buttocks and scoop her closer. Leda became aware that Pearl had stopped stirring whatever she had in the pot and craned her head to look. Two of the brownies climbed up on the windowsill and made little "aw" noises. Mukasa wandered down the porch steps and sat down, tail stretched out on the grass.

Darius kissed Lexi for a long time, then deliberately set her away from him. Lexi took one step toward him, then mastered herself, wiping her eyes.

Darius removed his duster and handed it to her. Leda looked curiously at the tattoos covering his back and chest, amazed at the variety of weapons one man could have on his body. Lexi folded the duster over her arm and backed away as he placed his palms over his pectorals and came away with his hands full of winged demon.

For one moment, Fury remained small; then his head grew to the size of Mukasa's, and the rest of his body followed. Darius pointed to the air in front of him, toward the grove. Fury swooped once around him, then flamed.

There was a red flash as the air rent. Darius shouted something, then a darkness engulfed him, the earth shook, and a light nearly blinded them all. Lexi threw her arm over her eyes, and Mukasa flinched.

Just as quickly, the light disappeared, and with it, Darius. Lexi lowered her arm and stared at the spot from which he'd vanished. Fury flew in circles like a whirlwind, then settled on the grass, becoming a leathery, smallish, dragonlike demon, wings drooping.

Amber and Christine ran into the kitchen. "What just happened?" Christine demanded.

Leda hurried out the back door without speaking, Christine and Amber following, along with Valerian. Lexi waited for them at the grove, tears on her face.

The werewolf woman swung on Leda, her gray eyes full. "He's gone," she snapped at Leda. "Are you happy now?"

"No," Leda said, perfectly serious. "But now we have a chance."

Four warriors. Kehksut gloated as he glided around them as a wisp of darkness.

Kalen, Hunter, Adrian, Darius. Naked and back to back, each one facing a point of the compass. Kalen with his scowl stood facing south, backing on Darius with his tattoos, with Adrian and Hunter facing east and west.

One warrior—Tain—to help drain the life magic from the world. Four more to hold enough life magic to keep the world in place, with Kehksut as its god. Enough magic at his disposal to challenge the goddesses. They could find another plane of existence to rule—this one would be his.

He'd taught Tain well and enjoyed every minute of it. Tain and his brothers would live here for eternity, shut in this space, keeping the world from being *entirely* drained of life magic. They were so powerful that enough life magic would remain to keep the death magic from destroying the world completely. It would be his world, the world of Kehksut.

He'd have four warriors exactly like Tain to torture, and for his female form to ravish. How lovely.

Tain himself came in from the shadows, from wherever he'd retreated to brood. Even Kehksut couldn't entirely reach him in his madness anymore, and he had no idea where Tain disappeared to, lately more than ever.

Tain had dressed in his mail again, and his blue surcoat with the pentacle embroidered on it. He liked it, even though the last time he'd worn it in reality, the pentacles had been torn and bloody.

Tain regarded his brothers with calm blue eyes, looking over each one as he would statues in a collection. Kehksut morphed into her female self, feeling excitement rise in her blood.

"They're all here, darling." She went to him and put her hands on his chest. She loved his hard, beautiful body, couldn't get enough of it. "Now you can die."

Tain kissed her, stirring her lusts to full life. "Yes," he whispered. "At last I will be free of you."

"Almost." She touched his red hair, liking the fiery color, the feel of rough silk. "Let me take you one more time, darling. For the last time, let me have you inside me."

Tain gazed down at her with unblinking eyes. A shudder of desire with a touch of uncertainty went through Kehksut's frame. She and her masculine self had done their job a little too well, she thought. Tain was far gone in insanity.

Without expression, Tain pushed her away with a strong hand. "Get away from me, you filth," he said calmly. He turned and walked back into the darkness.

Kehksut stared after him in astonishment. She morphed back into a man. Something was wrong. He looked at the four Immortals bathed in light, noticed their tattoos glowing like dark blue fire, and snarled.

He searched for the half-demon woman, to kill her, to tear her apart to avenge his feelings, but he was unable to sense her in the dark. Tain must be shielding her, and that thought made him explode into rage.

He threw his magic at the Immortals, but the white light held, and gradually Kehksut calmed himself. He needed them. Soon they'd be in eternal torment, and that would be vengeance enough.

"And now you're going to rescue them all by yourself?" Lexi demanded. She sat belligerently on the porch swing, refusing to go back into the house.

"Not by myself," Leda said. "All us witches together." She made herself not flinch from the glare of the werewolf bounty hunter. Lexi must scare the daylights out of the skips she hunted down, with those eyes and that fierce stare.

Leda had asked the other witches to gather with her and Lexi for a council of war. The others, of their own accord, stayed away, although Leda guessed that Mac was holding his own council in the kitchen with Valerian, Mai, Sabina and Pearl. She doubted the half-god Sidhe would merely sit in the living room playing with his music—although, truth to tell, she couldn't predict what he'd do.

"Look," Leda began, sitting forward on the porch chair. "Hunter knew what was going on, but he wouldn't, or couldn't, explain. At first the demon didn't want the Immortals together. He stole Tain and hid him for centuries. When it was time to start putting the pieces in place, Kehksut revealed Tain to Amber's sister. But he still wasn't ready for all the

Immortals to be together, so he broke the Calling spell. Then the demon kept Kalen, Darius and Hunter busy until the time was right."

"Right for what?" Lexi demanded. She stretched out her long legs, her restless energy palpable.

Christine, quieter and thoughtful, nodded. "Time to gather the final pieces for his spell. A spell he needs the Immortals to complete."

Amber fingered the tattoo on her bare arm. "And now we've gone and given him his four Immortals."

"Five," Leda said. "Kali said it had to be five. With them all together, things can happen."

"I suppose that's true," Amber conceded. "Even with Tain crazy, the five of them together will be formidable."

Leda continued, "Five warriors. Five elements. Five witches. I'm air, Lexi is fire, Amber earth, and Christine water."

"That's only four," Amber said. "Where is witch number five? Who gets to represent Akasha?"

"Samantha," Leda said.

The other three stared at her, Amber's tawny gaze, Christine's blue one, and Lexi's silver-gray trained on her.

Lexi was the one who answered. "Samantha, the half-demon who's disappeared."

"Hunter wanted her for a reason," Leda said softly. "I wouldn't be a bit surprised if they took her with them behind the ripple."

"But why?" Lexi snapped. "Mac and Pearl and Ricco, and even Mai, are more powerful than a half-demon, half-witch without many powers."

"I don't claim to understand everything that goes on

in Hunter's head, but I'm sure he knew what he was doing."

Lexi scowled, her wolf's eyes flickering. "I think you're as crazy as Hunter is."

"Maybe." Leda spread her hands. "But the goddesses didn't send me the dreams until Darius arrived, until all four Immortals could be together. There's something each of them—and each of us—must do."

"I agree with her," Amber said.

Christine nodded, her face glum. "Can it be a coincidence that each of us fell in love with an Immortal round about the same time?"

Lexi's stern look relaxed into a smile. "I don't think that was coincidence. I think it's just them."

"I had the same thought," Leda said.

Amber smiled as though remembering something fondly. "Who can resist a gorgeous warrior racing to your rescue? We didn't stand a chance."

The others nodded in silent agreement, expressions thoughtful.

"And now we have to rescue them," Lexi said, losing her smile. "We pool our talents and go after them. How do you propose we do it, Leda? Have you worked that out as well?"

"Easy," Leda replied, but her heart beat fast and hard. "We conjure a demon and use his death magic to open the ripple."

Another argument ensued in the grove that night after Leda had finished her preparations. This time the whole household joined in, including Ricco, up again for another night.

Ricco had spent half the previous night checking

out what was going on with vamps in Seattle. He reported, in disgust, that it was much as in Manhattan—vampires dividing themselves into those for Kehksut and those against. Nightly battles ensued, the vampires for Kehksut slowly but surely defeating those who wanted the demon to lose.

Valerian snorted when Ricco had finished. "You know it's bad when I'm hoping *vampires* kick some ass. I hate vampires."

"I know," Ricco said coolly. "You have a reputation downtown as the Destroyer."

Valerian's face lit. "Yeah? The Destroyer? Maybe I should get some T-shirts made up."

"You're cute, sweetie," Sabina told him.

In the grove, at the apex of the moon, Leda drew her circle while the others grouped outside it and continued the argument.

"Practicing death magic killed my sister," Amber said, face set.

Leda straightened up, marking the boundaries with her long wand. "I won't be practicing death magic—not exactly. But this barrier between realities, the 'rippling,' Hunter called it, can most easily be pierced by demons. We've spent two weeks chanting spells and throwing life magic at it to no avail. Samantha's father opened the small bubble of it to release her mother. I'm betting Hunter used Samantha's demon magic to open the way for them. Fury, a Bocca demon, opened it for Darius, and Fury has been sick as a—demon—since, probably because he has absorbed so much of Darius's life magic over the years. Ricco has death magic, but I have the feeling we need the demon brand of it, or Hunter would have just asked Septimus or one of his vampires to help him open the bubble." She drew a breath. "We need a demon to stop a demon, ladies."

Leda didn't feel as glib as her words. When she'd used demon magic before, she'd felt sick and violated, a feeling that had lasted until Hunter had removed the residual death magic from her. There was a chance, she knew, that Hunter would not be available to cure her this time.

But Leda had figured out what Isis meant when she'd said in the dream that Leda had the courage and strength to do what must be done. Leda had survived using death magic because of her strength. She would survive again, at least long enough to save the world. What happened to her after that didn't really matter.

Before anyone had the chance to stop her, she closed her circle, raising a sphere of power around her, a bubble of blue light that blocked the others out. She heard Mukasa grumble low in his throat.

Leda lifted her hands, and with an inward apology to the Goddess and the God, she chanted several lines of a demon language. She was glad she didn't need to speak the words in English, because she would gag on them.

Roughly translated, they meant: *Come to me, come to me, I need your wisdom, glorious one. Take of me what you will, my body, my soul, for my need is great.* She chanted the lines three times, then lowered her arms, heart beating swiftly.

She did not have long to wait. Not ten seconds after the echo of her words died, she felt a black surge in her mind and the ground trembled. A rush of displaced air blasted her face, its smell foul, and with an audible *pop* the groth demon she'd summoned to save her husband arrived.

He looked at Leda, gazed at the grove, the house in the background, and the crowd of life-magic users behind them, and let out a sigh of relief.

"Thank the dark ones you summoned me!" he exclaimed, his handsome face twisting. "I was getting so *bored*."

CHAPTER TWENTY-THREE

"Isn't that a groth demon?" Ricco asked.

The demon bowed, very carefully not touching the sides of Leda's circle. "That's me. Thanks for doing the circle, Leda, and protecting me. There are some mean-looking critters out there, like the dragon and the half-Sidhe teenager. Ew." He shuddered.

"Watch it, demon," Valerian growled. Mukasa had come up beside him and growled as well.

"Kitty, kitty," the demon said brightly. If a lion could look disgusted, Mukasa did.

"I need you to open a portal for me," Leda said sternly. She was in control of the groth demon for now, but she knew the moment she let her guard down, he would slip in and take full advantage.

"Love to, darling. How big and to where?"

"Large enough for all of us to enter . . . somewhere here."

He looked to where she gestured, and his eyes widened. "You don't want much, do you? Open a hole in reality and let us slide into the dark dimensions?"

"Can you do it?"

"I can *maybe* do it. But it will cost you, sweetheart. I was cheated out of my price before—I felt my compulsion spell on you crumble and die—so this will be double." He smiled at Mai, who gave him a disgusted look in return. "I'll take you plus that cutie over there."

"That cutie's boyfriend is a vampire," Leda told him while Ricco glowered dangerously. "We'll discuss the price when you've opened the portal and we've gone in and returned safely."

"You mean when *you've* gone in. I'm not going anywhere. Do you have digital cable here? Better still, a wireless connection? I'll wait for you inside."

Leda shrugged. "Fair enough. I'll lower the wards for you to enter the house once, but only once. If you leave, you can't return." If everything went as planned, she thought, it wouldn't matter.

The demon put his hands on his narrow hips, his body honed and beautiful. "I should be suspicious of your so easy consent. But I'll enjoy thinking about my payment." He wet his lips.

Leda strove not to shudder. "Let's get it over with."

"Gladly, my dear."

He came to stand behind her. As he slid his arms around her, his human-looking arms began to shrivel and blacken, morphing into leathery, wrinkled demon skin as he changed to his real form, and his breath on her neck burned like acid.

"I'm ready," he said in seductive tones.

"Hunter is *so* not going to like this," Mac muttered.

He wouldn't, no more than Leda's husband had liked that she'd used demon magic to save his life. But saving Hunter—and his brothers—was more important.

The groth demon's death magic seeped into her like black and foul vines. Her powerful life magic kept the demon from taking her over fully, but the darkness of it squeezed her heart and burned along her nerves. Her body tried to rebel, not wanting to let the darkness back in when it had been so wonderfully taken away.

Tamping down the urge to scream and fight, she concentrated the dark energy deep inside her, building it up. The coupling of her magic with the demon's sickened her, but it was necessary. She raised her hands, the force within her crackling and swirling.

Hunter, I love you, she thought, then she pointed her fingers at the ripple in the air and let the magic fly.

A huge gap tore through the rippling air, and foul blackness rushed out of it at them. Behind Leda the demon said, "Oh, shit," and yanked his hands from around her waist.

The hole widened and widened until the darkness encompassed the entire grove, the green, the houses beyond, and still it grew. In Leda's little bubble of magic, nothing touched her or the groth demon, who hunkered behind her trying to become as small as possible, but it rushed at the others, exposed and vulnerable.

They defended themselves as best they could—Lexi and Sabina hurriedly shucking clothes as their bodies morphed into wolves. Valerian's clothes splintered off him as he became sixty feet of dragon, and Ricco's lips pulled back into a vampire snarl, his fangs gleaming.

Christine and Amber were busy doing a circle of their own. They pulled Lexi and Mai and Mukasa into it, closing them in a glowing sphere of protection.

Mac sparkled with magic. Leda thought she heard him mutter—"Och, Mum's going to *kill* me"—as he plucked from nowhere, of all things, his guitar.

Then darkness swallowed them, blotting out the grove, the house, the street, and flowing swift and deadly to cover the rest of Seattle. Someone came running out of the darkness, her eyes wide with terror, her hair hanging in black hanks. It was Samantha, her face white, her demon eyes huge.

She fell, but rolled to her feet, her police training helping her to not collapse. She made for Mac, instinctively honing in on the immense strength of the demigod. Lexi snarled at her, but Leda shouted that Samantha needed to be protected. Mac, after his first startled look, said, "Right," and shoved Samantha behind him.

Leda turned as a painfully bright light appeared in the center of the darkness. Inside the light, she saw four men standing back to back, heads tilted upward, eyes open, bodies unmoving. Her jaw dropped. Kalen, Darius, Hunter and Adrian, their weapons at their feet, Darius's tattoos gone.

Another warrior, dressed in chain mail and surcoat, his unruly red hair pulled into a ponytail, came around the four Immortals and faced Leda through her protective screen.

"You are too late," he said softly. He had a slight lilt to his voice, a faint Welsh accent. "I have gathered my brothers to me, and now you will watch us die."

"No!" Leda screamed.

She threw the demon magic that entwined hers at Tain. Tain's eyes blazed like Hunter's had when he'd been infused with Kali's magic, swaths of blue cutting the darkness. White Immortal magic poured from him, grown stronger and more powerful than Hunter's over the centuries.

"Hunter!" she shouted as Tain's magic lifted her,

breaking her sphere as though it were a soap bubble. "Hunter, wake up, damn it."

Tain continued to lift her, his eyes beautiful and burning with magic. "I don't want to hurt you, little witch. But you must understand. The world is a horrible place, and it needs to cease. Let us die and find our peace."

"She's brainwashed you," Leda cried. She hung in midair, high enough that if Tain let her go, the landing would break her bones and possibly kill her. "Don't listen to her. Let them go. Let them help you."

Tain smiled sadly, though his power, if anything, grew. "You can't understand what it is like to be an Immortal. The centuries, the loneliness, the emptiness of it all. Being used again and again, then left to while away the time until someone wants you again. Never able to get close to anyone because time will take them away. An Immortal's greatest enemy, time. Now we will have it no more."

"Did you ask them first whether they wanted to die?" Leda jabbed her finger at the motionless Immortals. "They might enjoy what life they have. Did you think of that?"

"Hunter loved a woman once upon a time," Tain said. "And I saw what losing her did to him. He wanted to die, and he couldn't. Immortals suffer differently from humans, you see. Nothing erases our grief."

"Then the good times can't be erased either, right?" she argued desperately. On the ground, the groth demon had pressed himself flat, whimpering and quavering.

Tain continued as though he didn't hear either of them. "Kalen was punished in oblivion for killing

the last of the people he meant to protect. Then
when he was finally released, he whiled away his
time with art and women. Was he happy? Or was
Darius happy, held to Ravenscroft by the selfishness
of his mother-goddess? Or Adrian, drowning his
troubles in decadence? They have nothing. Why
should they not die?"

"Because we love them," Leda said. "Christine and
Amber and Lexi and I all love them. Give us a chance
to prove that, and to take away their hurts."

Tain's brow furrowed, and he lowered her the
slightest bit. "It is not for Immortals to fall in love."

"This isn't about *them* falling in love. It's about us
caring for them. Please, Tain."

"You are wrong, little witch," he said. "When you
watch them die, you will understand that my way is
better."

Samantha's voice came ringing out of the darkness.
"Or you might let them wake up and decide for themselves. It's not all about what you want."

Leda felt herself lowered another foot as Tain
peered past her at the woman who stepped out of the
darkness. "You let them in," he said as though troubled by a niggling thought. "You hid from me in the
darkness, and I let you because you were innocent.
Who are you to challenge me now, when you are even
weaker?"

"Her name is Samantha," Leda said, her jaw
clenched.

Tain studied Samantha, head tilted. "Her aura is
strange. Dark. She is . . ."

"Half-demon." Samantha snapped. "I'm getting
tired of that Immortal look, like I'm something they
stepped in."

Tain continued to study her, Leda floating down farther as his attention shifted. "You are not angry," he said to Samantha. "You are afraid."

"You bet I am. Scared shitless. But I have demon blood in me. That means I can live a good long time and will probably endure a lot of loss. But you know what? I still want to do it. Maybe your brothers do too."

Tain shook his head. "They came here voluntarily. They understand now."

"They didn't!" Leda shouted at him. "Kalen was taken by the demon against his will. The other three were trying to rescue him."

Tain glanced at the Immortals, his blue gaze bathing them in a strange, cold glow. "Why would my love lie to me?"

"Because he's a demon," Samantha said. "Hell-o?"

Tain's glare swept Samantha, lifting her from her feet while he set Leda down almost gently. "Why do you say these things, half-demon? I could kill you so easily."

Samantha's face set, her demon looks beautiful despite her terror and her weeks spent behind the ripple. "I prefer to go out kicking and screaming. And my name is Samantha."

"You are defiant. You do not chatter on and on about love."

Even dangling from his magic, Samantha managed to fold her arms and look annoyed. "Love never really did much for me. I want my life."

"Your half-demon, half-human existence? Neither one thing nor the other?"

Samantha scowled. "I'm me. I've learned to be me with everything I can. I'm a cop. I solve crimes and arrest people who hurt other people. I like it."

"It is small and petty, this life of yours."

"Yeah, well, not everyone can be a big, bad warrior."

Unnoticed, Leda slipped around Tain and stopped next to the glowing white that encased the Immortals. They stood quietly, oblivious to what went on outside the circle surrounding them.

Leda blessed Samantha for distracting Tain, though it was in vain. Leda couldn't even touch the light barrier—her hand stopped a foot away from it as though some unseen force blocked her way.

She continued, "You fight, you win, you make women want to dive into bed with you. Don't pretend you hated that existence."

Samantha made a show of looking at him up and down. "At the moment you're a homicidal maniac, but maybe back when you had all your marbles, you were good-looking. I bet women went for you."

"This is naught but flattery. You say these things to keep me from my purpose, but you will *not*."

He let go of Samantha, and she plummeted downward. At the last moment he broke her fall and let her land hard on her feet. He turned and made for his four brothers.

With a crash and a swirl of darkness, Kehksut-Amadja-Culsu made a dramatic entrance, no longer the seductive man or the beautiful black-haired woman, but a full-scale demon, an Old One in his true guise. The demon grew to fantastic height, his body easily as large as that of Valerian's, huge wings unfolding from his back.

"It is time to die, Tain" Kehksut said, his voice rumbling through the darkness-stained grove.

Tain faced him without fear—an Old One who predated the Immortals themselves, who had hidden himself from them until he was strong enough to defeat them, and Tain looked him in the face without flinching.

Maybe Kehksut did his job too well, Leda thought, even as another wave of the demon's dark magic sent her to the ground. She tasted mud as foul slime entered her mouth. Above her, Tain raised his hand.

"They want my brothers free to choose," he said. "So they shall be."

Leda expected the demon to slap aside the white magic that flowed from Tain's hand to explode the glow surrounding the Immortals. But Kehksut stepped back, wings folding.

"It doesn't matter," he boomed. "I like a challenge."

The light around the Immortals splintered like shards of glass. The four brothers sprang apart and looked at each other in amazement. Hunter's green gaze took in Leda on the ground, Kehksut towering over them all, and Tain glowing like a god.

"Well, hell," Hunter said. "The party started without us."

He wanted to shout with the burst of magic that surged through him. The demon had finally showed his true face, not the dark-haired bondage woman or the gloating man who'd killed Hunter's wife a thousand years before, but his true, ugly, son-of-a-bitch self.

Hunter swept up his sword and felt a pull of satisfaction when it burst instantly into flame. With a roar of rage, he launched himself at the demon. Kalen, at his side, snatched up his weapon and joined him, white light glowing from the tip of his spear.

They were stopped by one downward blow of a

short bronze Roman sword, infused by so much magic that it sent both men stumbling back. Tain stood in front of them, tall and straight, his eyes blazing blue fire.

"No," he said clearly.

"Why the hell not?" Hunter demanded. "Get out of the way. It's time for revenge."

"No, my brother. It is time to die."

Tain swept his sword in a large arc. Darius tried to dive beneath his reach and bowl him to the ground, but Tain easily sidestepped him. *Little brother Tain has grown strong indeed,* Hunter thought as he tried to smack Tain aside with his sword, only to be thwarted again.

He was dimly aware of Valerian in his dragon form swooping in from above, two werewolves flanking him, a bubble of magic with witches and Mukasa inside, and Leda crumpled on the ground like a paper doll, a groth demon cowering next to her. He tasted the faint tang of death magic on Leda's aura and realized she'd bonded with the demon's magic to open the ripple to try to get him out.

That sacrifice must have cost her much. She'd been free of the death magic, clear of the demon, and yet she'd done it to break the barrier and come after him.

Hunter raised his sword again, screaming in rage, and thrust Tain out of the way. Behind him, Kehksut seemed to grow taller, his winged form blotting out all light. He stretched out his hand, palm up, and the life magic began to recede from the world in a rush.

The blue magic surrounding the witches dissolved, exposing them to the blackness. A pretty, petite girl—*wood nymph,* Hunter registered—spun around like a leaf in the wind, then crumpled and lay still. The vampire who ran to her, his darkness increasing as the life magic vanished, let out a stream of death magic at the demon, but the demon barely noticed.

Valerian fell from about a hundred feet up with a rumbling crash. He was not a human, he was a creature of magic, his magic allowing him to take human form when he wished. Now his dragon magic had suddenly died, and Valerian likely was dead too.

Sabina ran to him, her howl enough to break anyone's heart. Hunter heard echoing howls up and down the green, Sabina's werewolf family coming to join the fight. Another black wolf rushed to Darius's side, snarling, but she flickered in and out of her wolf shape, unable to hold it.

And Leda . . .

Leda tried to rise, her body weakening as her magic left her, the demon magic that twined her not enough to keep her alive. On the other side of her, Samantha rolled to her feet, face pale, her death magic strong enough to keep her standing.

Amber and Christine hung on to each other, trying to chant life-magic spells. Even the half-Sidhe, Mac, was weakening. He looked less like a teenage kid and more like what he was, a seven-hundred-year-old demigod. A dying one.

Hunter raised his sword again, its flames pale against the darkness. "Let me do this!" he shouted at Tain. "He killed my wife, my children. Don't you get it? He was after us even then."

"It doesn't matter," Tain said in front of him.

"It does matter," Adrian said, his cobra-sword glinting in his hand. "Join us, and we'll defeat him. It won't take but one swat from all of us to kill this fly."

Tain easily held all his brothers back. He was so

damn powerful, having the strength of all of them, their little brother whom they'd tried to protect when he was little.

"So you've said," Tain answered. "But I do not want you to kill him. I want you to die with me."

"Screw that!" Darius shouted.

Tain sent a bolt of magic at Darius that swept him off his feet. The black wolf loped to him, morphing into a tall human woman along the way.

Kehksut rumbled like a small earthquake. "They have no choice. One way or the other, all will die here. It has begun."

He moved his fingers, and a rent appeared in the air. More darkness poured through it, and with it, demons. Stoked on death magic, they swooped through and fell on Leda's little army as did the hounds of hell that streaked toward the werewolves.

Hunter ran to Leda and turned to fight. Leda lay helpless in the mud, her magic dying. Hunter stood over her, hacking and slashing at demons, enjoying when his sword went cleanly through one of them.

His rage wound higher and higher. Tain protected Kehksut like a dog guarding his master, but Hunter would take the Old One out if it was the last thing he did. If he had to slice Tain into pieces to do it, so be it.

"Hunter."

Leda's voice was weak, her touch feather-light on his bare ankle. He dropped to one knee beside her, breathing hard, his sword going slack in his grip. He brushed her hair from her face, his heart full.

"Leda, sweet baby, I'm sorry."

She tried to push herself up, her tone urgent.

"Don't worry about me. Get your brothers. The key is five—Kali told me. Five warriors, five witches . . ." Her voice trailed off. "Five points of the star . . ."

Hunter gathered her against him, his sword point-down in the mud. "Don't leave me yet, Leda. I want to sail around the world with you in your boat; you and me and the sun and sea." His laugh came out hoarse. "Mukasa will want to come with us."

Leda tried to push him away. "Go. Do it, Hunter."

"Let me get you safe first."

"Hunter, *go!* There's not enough time."

He sensed a shadow above him and looked up to see Kehksut towering over them. The demon gazed down on them with eyes as black as the depths of a well, death magic in the abyss.

Not enough time. The words pounded through Hunter's head. Just as with Kayla, there wasn't enough *time.* He got to his feet, a berserker yell leaving his throat, his sword on fire, and launched himself at Kehksut.

"Hunter, no!"

It was Adrian screaming at him, Adrian trying to hold him back. Kehksut reached out a giant hand, ready to crush Hunter's bones.

"Come on!" Hunter raged at the demon. "Come and get me, you son of a bitch."

Adrian and Kalen both grabbed him by the arms and yanked him out of the way. Hunter cursed and screamed. Kehksut laughed—a loud, ringing sound—and floated back to watch his demons and hellhounds wreak havoc.

"Let me go!" Hunter screamed. "Let me stop him."

Adrian shook him. "Listen to me. Darius told me

about Leda's dream. I understand now. I know what we have to do."

"So do I. Kill that damn demon."

"No. We save Tain."

Hunter jerked free. "You're fucking crazy, you know that? Demon dies, world is saved, end of problem. If Tain's sucked away, it's his own damn fault."

"Shut up and stand still for once," Kalen said, voice harsh. "We join together, all five of us, or we're screwed. It's the only way."

"Five," Hunter said, hesitating.

"Five," Darius repeated. "That's what Leda told us. The goddesses came to her, even Cerridwen. We have to do it."

A demon swooped out of the darkness. It saw Leda lying helpless, and with a delighted cry, it sprang on her. Hunter launched himself after it—stopped by his three brothers.

"Let me go. It'll kill her."

"We join," Adrian snapped. "We have to. You have to choose, Hunter. If you run over and fight with her now, we might not have another chance."

You will have to choose a path, the Undine on the island had said. *Walking either one will be painful for you, but you must choose.*

Hunter had assumed the choice was between staying with Leda or leaving her to find Kalen. That hadn't been as difficult a choice as this, because then there'd been a chance he could return and be with her.

But this was the real choice. He could save Tain, but Leda might die.

"Adrian, I can't."

"You have to," Adrian ground out, his dark eyes haunted. "We all have to make the choice. Me and

Kalen and Darius and you. We've found our mates, and now we have to let them fight alone."

Hunter swallowed a sob that threatened to cut off his breath. He said to Adrian, "You'd better fucking be right."

"I am," Adrian said.

CHAPTER TWENTY-FOUR

Leda fought hard, dimly seeing Hunter charging toward her. *No,* she wanted to cry. *Do what the goddesses told me.*

She saw him being pulled back by his brothers, saw them gather into a circle of four. Relief. The only way to stop everything was to have Hunter and his brothers come together, to fuse their magic. That was what the goddesses meant.

She chanted a spell, trying to find a breath of clean air to help her. Blue magic crackled in her hands, pushing the demon who attacked her back a little. He was a lesser demon, like the groth demon, still strong but not as intensely magical as an Old One.

The demon was lifted off her suddenly, a knife ripping through his heart. Ricco the vampire, his Armani suit stained with blood, lifted her easily to her feet. His strength had grown, Leda could tell, and she thanked the goddesses he was on their side.

She glanced to where the four Immortals had gathered in the heart of the grove, in the center of that sacred space. White light glowed around them again, as it had when they'd been suspended and unmoving, but this light was different. It pulsed with life magic, repelling darkness. She heard their voices as they argued about something; then the light grew opaque, obscuring them from view.

Kehksut merely watched, as though curious about what they'd do. Leda sensed he was in no way worried.

"Terrific," she muttered.

Ricco pulled her out of the path of another attacking demon. "Come on, witch. Time to fight. We keep Amadja away from Darius and his brothers and we might live to see another day. Another night, in my case."

Be good to my son, Kali had said.

Leda drew a breath. She clung to Ricco's hand, letting the darkness that the groth demon had given her swirl and grow inside her. If darkness was winning, she'd use it to give the Old One a taste of his own medicine before she went out.

Ricco grinned, fangs sharp. "Atta girl. Now you know how good it can feel. Let's rock and roll."

Adrian drew his brothers together to form a circle. They needed powerful magic, the most powerful the Immortals had ever done. He understood Hunter's anguish, because Adrian felt it too—had felt it the night of the Calling spell when Amber had lain dead at his feet. He also knew that if they did not complete this spell, Amber would die again, this time forever.

The tears on Hunter's face struck Adrian through the heart, but he firmed his resolve. "Let's do this," he said.

Hunter threw him a baleful look. "Darius, stand

next to me. No way am I putting my hand on Adrian's ass."

"When are you going to grow up?" Kalen growled at him.

"What for?"

"That's fine," Darius said, sliding in on Hunter's right. "Hunter's tattoo is too close to his cock for my comfort."

"Hey, the ladies like it."

Darius shot back, "If you want to compete on who can woo the ladies with the best tattoos, I win."

"You and the macho Bocca demon on your chest."

"Can I *pay* you two to shut up?" Kalen snarled.

Looking disgusted at the two younger Immortals, Kalen stepped next to Adrian and placed his palm on the tattoo on Adrian's hip. Darius closed in on his left and covered the tattoo on Kalen's thigh, while Hunter slid his hand under Darius's hair and found the pentacle on the back of his brother's neck.

"We're good to go," Hunter said. "All we need is baby brother."

White magic began to move through Adrian, Immortal magic building stronger and harder, and they hadn't even closed the circle. Hunter reached out with a tendril of that pulsing magic and wrapped it around Tain's wrist.

Tain whirled around from Kehksut's side, his blue eyes searing with power. "No."

"Yes."

Tain looked to Kehksut for help, but the demon still had his hand upthrust, focusing all his energy on draining the life magic.

Adrian stopped being Mr. Nice Guy. He tightened the tendril on Tain unmercifully and yanked his brother to the circle. Adrian slapped his hand to Tain's cheek, and Hunter hauled Tain's hand around and forced it to touch the tattoo on Hunter's lower abdomen. Something clicked in Adrian's body, the circle closing.

Complete.

Tain started to scream, and then Hunter, then Darius, then Kalen, all the way around the circle.

Hunter nearly doubled over with the sensations pouring through him. The outline of the pentacle Tain's hand covered burned and seared like hellfire. He began to feel every hurt, every fear, every cut the demon had made on Tain—seven hundred years of agony. Hunter experienced Tain's fear, the hollowness of his despair, the lingering hopes that were snuffed out one by one.

No wonder Tain had gone completely insane. No one could experience this and not go crazy, not even an Immortal. The pain and insanity tore through Hunter until he screamed with it too.

The demon continued to suck out the life magic, letting death magic flow thick and fast. Hunter thought grimly that Kehksut didn't have to do anything—the Immortals were ripping themselves apart inside out for him.

Pain flowed from his hand into Darius's pentacle tattoo, across Darius's body to be emptied into Kalen. Darius screamed in anguish, his eyes shut tight, cords standing out on his neck.

And then Kalen threw his head back, his cry cutting the night. Adrian groaned in pain, but he had the presence of mind to collect the life magic as it flowed through all of them, and fed it back into Tain.

Around and around it went. Tain's darkness flashed

through them, divided and absorbed by each brother, and then their own life magic fed back into him. Hunter knew he could easily escape the agony; all he had to do was rip Tain's hand away from him and dive out of the circle. He could break free and not have to live Tain's suffering.

But he did not. He kept his grip firmly around Tain's wrist, though his own hands were slick with sweat, keeping Tain's palm against his tattoo. Just as firmly, he pressed Darius's neck, and Darius in turn held his ground, keeping hold of Kalen.

They each stayed put, screaming in pain and loneliness and despair, drawing it out of Tain, sharing it among them. *Five Immortals,* Leda had said. *Five goddesses.* A beginning.

Hunter suddenly found himself on the ground on his knees, but still he did not let go of either Tain or Darius. Kalen was swearing hard, Darius writhing in pain and trying to catch his breath.

"I can't . . ." Darius panted.

"You can if I can," Hunter gasped. "Don't let me one-up you."

"Never," Darius ground out. "Never, never."

Tain was kneeling next to him, face gray, his voice hoarse. "Damn you all," he whispered.

He sounded moderately sane. Hunter knew better than to relax, to believe the worst was over and let go. He held on to Tain until he felt the life magic at last begin to cut through the pain, through the dark madness that wrapped them in chains of fire.

For a few moments he wasn't sure that the pain had lessened. Then he began to hope, and then to fear that the hope would be false. This was what Tain had gone through, he realized, every day for seven hundred years.

After a longer time, he realized the pain really had receded, the Immortal life magic trickling through to soothe him. He also realized that it would never completely go away. Tain had been so ruined inside and out that the scars would remain in all of them.

At long last, Hunter found himself no longer screaming. He lay on his side, body contorted, as he held Tain's hand to him and his own to Darius. Darius was a tangle of tattooed limbs, but he never lost his hold of Kalen, nor Kalen of Adrian, and so on around the circle.

Tain opened his eyes, the terrible blue light gone. He raised his head and looked at Hunter the same way he'd done on mornings a thousand years ago when he and Hunter had awakened with hell-pounding hangovers.

"Hell," he croaked.

Hunter gave him a faint smile that hurt his mouth. "Hey, little brother. Welcome back."

Kehksut honed in on them with attention as sharp as a knife, bathing them in darkness, the white light around them wavering and dimming. But Kehksut didn't pounce—perhaps the demon didn't believe Tain could ever break free of his hold, Hunter thought, or—a more worrying idea—perhaps Kehksut didn't care. Which meant Kehksut didn't believe they could prevail, even all five together—which meant they were in deep shit.

Hunter eased his fingers from Tain's wrist, his hands cramped and aching. Darius and Kalen lay on their sides, both struggling to catch their breath. Adrian was on his hands and knees, his long hair cascading around him, eyes empty and tired.

Tain's surcoat had reverted from whole and pristine

to the bloodstained and torn garment he'd worn on the battlefield with the Unseelies seven hundred years ago. He'd been wearing it when Hunter and Darius had watched him stride back to the castle like he had somewhere important to go.

Tain looked down at the surcoat in disgust and ripped it from his body, then the linked mail and the stained tunic beneath it. He stood up, his body whole, the scars the demon had left faded to pink and white lines.

"You might want to keep the chain mail," Hunter said. "We're in the middle of a battle, if you hadn't noticed."

Tain snarled. "I can't stand it touching me. Not ever again." He studied Hunter at his feet. "You know, you look like crap."

Hunter started to laugh. The laughter hurt, grating him from inside out. Beside him, Darius climbed shakily to his feet and put his arm around Tain. "Welcome back, runt."

Adrian hauled himself up beside Tain, unashamedly gathering his brother into his arms. "It's all right, kid," he said.

Kalen rested his arm across Hunter's shoulder, leaning on him. His face was creased with pain, but for once his eyes looked almost light.

"We'll let you make it up to us," Kalen said to Tain, and Hunter and Darius laughed.

"Don't listen to them, they're assholes," Adrian said. He buried his face in Tain's hair and held him tight.

Leda sensed the change even as she swiped the knife Ricco had given her against another demon who had pinned her to the ground. The white light receded from the five Immortals, revealing Darius, Hunter and Kalen trying to hold each other up, and Tain weeping on Adrian's shoulder.

Despite Kehksut's attention on them, Leda's heart lightened, knowing that whatever spell the Immortals had worked had been successful. They'd rescued Tain. There were five of them again.

But they were still up against a huge, ancient demon with more power in his little finger than she'd ever seen and an army of minions at his back. The battle was not over.

Kehksut opened his mouth and roared out another wave of death magic. It struck the werewolves and Valerian and Mac, weakening the already weak life-magic creatures. The maw of the death magic began to suck the life magic from the world even faster. The Immortals were weak and disoriented, and the demon knew he had to finish before they regained their strength.

Aside from the Immortals, Valerian and Mac were the most powerful fighters. Leda plunged her knife through the demon who held her down and shoved him aside. On hands and knees she began to crawl toward Valerian, chanting protective spells as she went. She desperately tried to raise a shield around herself, but the drain of life magic made it too difficult to conjure much more than a weak blue light.

Valerian, in dragon shape, lay on his side, helpless, with Sabina as a wolf nudging him with her nose. Mukasa was with her, also trying to rouse the dragon.

"Christine," Leda called.

Christine, looking haggard and exhausted, staggered to Leda.

"Help me with Valerian," Leda said when Christine reached her. "I think we can keep him from dying if we help him change back to human form and get him inside where it's shielded."

Christine pushed her hair from her face. "Are you kidding? I couldn't help a butterfly right now."

"We can do it if we pool our magic. What about Lexi? She might help us create a morphing field."

Christine scanned the grounds for the black wolf. "I think she's lost the ability to do any magic."

"It's worth a try. Get her, and Amber too. And Mac. We need him."

Christine gave her a dark look but limped away, making for Lexi. Kehksut seemed more interested in the Immortals, who were still weak and disoriented, ignoring the witches. Leda found Amber first and helped her over to Valerian. Amber had blood on her face and arms, her shirt torn, but her eyes blazed anger. Mac fought on, but he saw them waving him over and redoubled his effort to break free of the two demons and a hellhound fighting him.

Christine rounded up the black wolf that was Lexi. Amber and Leda began casting a circle to encompass the dragon, Sabina and Mukasa, who would not move. Mac finished off the demons and hellhound and came loping over, grinning like he was having a good time. He dove inside the circle just before they closed it.

"Hang on, love." He again produced his guitar out of thin air, the strings crackling and humming with sparkles of magic. "I've been working on something."

"Are you going to serenade us?" Christine asked, a little testily.

Mac laughed, a golden sound in all the darkness. "Not quite."

Leda clung to Amber's and Christine's hands, and they threw their magic into the middle of the circle. The pool of life magic didn't amount to much more than any of them could raise on their own at normal times, and Leda worried that it wouldn't be enough.

She reached heavenward with her senses, past the dense blackness of death magic, and found the merest breath of fresh air. She pulled it down to waft through the clearing, sending the wind chimes on Amber's porch dancing. At the same time, silver tones spilled from Mac's guitar, chords and melodic runs that wound through her magic like white-hot fire. It was beautiful and heady and peaceful and exiting.

She gazed at him in astonishment, and Mac the teenager grinned at her, overlaid with the power of Mac the demigod.

He winked. "Been working on it a while. One big, powerful musical spell. Take whatever you need from it."

Leda shot him a grateful smile, then gathered the white magic to her and let it flow into the circle. The other two witches did the same, building power that felt damn good.

Outside the circle, the demons fought on with the werewolves and humans who had come out of their houses to fight. Ricco or Septimus must have sent out a contingent of vampires, because they joined the fray, fighting hard against the demons, keeping them away from the witches.

Leda raised her hands. "Mother Goddess, restore your children," she cried, and the others repeated the plea.

She felt Lexi's magic mixing with theirs, her witch self drawing her fire magic and morph magic from deep within to share among them. The morph field strengthened, and Lexi grew suddenly from her wolf shape into a tall, naked woman with gray wolf's eyes.

"Oh, nice, love," Mac said appreciatively, earning a growl from Lexi's throat.

The morph field touched Sabina, who shifted into her blond, tawny-eyed human self and blinked at them tiredly from where she lay next to Valerian. Then Valerian finally shimmered and became a broad-shouldered man. He put his hand to his head and groaned.

The morphing magic of both Sabina and Valerian had strengthened the field, mixing with Mac's music to be intensely powerful. Before Leda could withdraw the magic, it touched Mukasa. The lion's eyes widened in surprise as his body began to stretch, his tail shrinking to nothing, his ears growing smaller and moving downward on his now-human head.

After a few seconds, a large man with shaggy golden hair, body tight like a wrestler's, glared at them with tawny eyes.

"Owwww . . . thhhhisssss . . . hurrttss."

"Oops," Christine said.

"Mukasa?" Leda blinked.

He worked his jaw as though unused to the sounds coming out of it. "My naaaame is Muuuuukasssa." He scanned the clearing. "Where issss my friend?"

His golden gaze alighted on the five Immortals still unable to hold themselves up, while Kehksut watched them, building himself into something terrible. Mukasa gave a snarl of distress and he started off in their direction.

"Wait, Mukasa, don't break the circle—"

The lion-man loped away, stumbling a little until he

got the hang of running on two legs. The circle shimmered and the blue field dissolved. Mac took his fingers off the guitar strings, and the magic flowed swiftly back into the instrument.

So fixed was Mukasa on the gathering of Immortals that the death magic Kehksut shot at him caught him in the side. He went down at once and lay unmoving.

"Hey!" Hunter shouted. "You're paying for that."

Leda shoved Sabina and Valerian in the opposite direction, toward the house, which had been swallowed by the ripple. "Get him into the house to recoup. He's our best fighter; we need him well. Mac, go with him."

"Can't do it, love," Mac said, looking even more tired than before. "You need me and my sweet music here."

Leda conceded, and Sabina and Valerian limped toward the house together, met halfway by Pearl, who'd dodged demons to bring them blankets.

Hunter had his sword out, standing over the fallen Mukasa, still in man form. Whether the lion-man was dead or alive, Leda couldn't tell, but Hunter was in no shape to stand up to Kehksut now.

"Five witches!" Leda shouted. "We need Samantha!"

The half-demon was fighting hard, standing back to back with Ricco. The body of the groth demon lay at their feet.

Mac raced to help them, holding his guitar carefully by its neck, and pushed Samantha toward Leda. "Go," he cried.

Without words, the four witches joined hands and ran toward Hunter and Mukasa. Leda grabbed Samantha in passing, dragging her along. Hunter touched Mukasa's shoulder, and Leda relaxed in relief when Mukasa twitched in response. Not dead—yet.

"Five witches!" Leda yelled at Hunter, reaching him.

Hunter looked up at her, his face haggard. "What about them?"

"I don't know! I thought you'd figured it all out by now."

"I thought when Tain was restored to us, everything would be better." He glared at Adrian.

"It is better," Leda said. "I'm still alive, and so are you."

"Good point." He snaked one arm around her and pulled her against him for a kiss. Nothing much wrong with his physical strength.

"I think I know," Tain said behind Hunter.

The red-haired warrior stood the same height as Hunter, a little broader of shoulder. Now that the madness had left him, Leda could see that he was probably the most handsome of the Immortals, his face not as hard as the others', with eyes blue as a clear lake. A faint curve to his lips made him look like he could turn a devastating smile on a lucky woman at any time.

"My," Samantha muttered appreciatively. "He cleans up nice."

"We need the five goddesses," Tain said.

"They're not here," Samantha answered, glancing around at the attacking demons and the valiant life-magic fighters who were losing little by little. "In case you haven't noticed, not much goddess action in this grove."

Tain's lips twitched. "You are still defiant."

"You remember that, do you?"

"I remember everything."

The two shared a look, Samantha's dark gaze fixed on him.

"The witches will represent the goddesses," Tain continued. "Five Immortals, five witches, five goddesses. You will understand."

He turned away abruptly. Mukasa started to come around, golden eyes blinking in the harsh light. "Hunterrrr."

"Rest easy, my friend." Hunter touched Mukasa's shoulder, trickling some of his life magic into him. "You'll be back in your right form in no time."

Mukasa gave him an anguished look. "This body is . . . *ugly*."

Hunter laughed, a wonderful sound in the hell whirling around them. He hauled Leda to him, arm firmly around her waist, and took her with him to where his brothers and the other witches waited.

CHAPTER TWENTY-FIVE

Kehksut knew he'd lost Tain. He'd suspected he would, if the other Immortals discovered the secret to helping him heal. But it didn't matter. He'd sucked Tain dry, and now Kehksut was stronger than the strongest Immortal.

What the little witches did in their rituals couldn't touch him. Now that the Immortals had weakened themselves saving their brother, they'd be easier to trap, a fact they did not yet understand. Kehksut knew the truth: Love meant weakness, not strength. The life magic was almost gone. He needed to pull a little bit more, than he could kill the witches and trap the Immortals for eternity.

The brothers stood in a circle again, reaching to the middle to pile their right hands together. Each Immortal stretched out his left palm and clasped the hand of a witch: Adrian to Amber, Darius to Lexi, Kalen to Christine, Hunter to Leda, Tain to Samantha.

"So what do we do now?" Hunter yelled above the din of the battle. "The hokeypokey?"

"What's the hokeypokey?" Darius shouted back. "A spell?"

"Something like that," Lexi answered.

"We focus," Leda admonished. "We concentrate on the star, like you did to save Tain."

Kehksut felt the concentration of life magic flowing through the Immortals, but it was nothing compared to the death magic that rushed in to fill the void life magic left. The world was dying, almost dead. The Immortals and their witches struggled to raise a white sphere over them, a thick concentration of pure life magic.

Almost. Kehksut smiled. There was a flaw, a chink—two chinks. Samantha, with her half-demon self, opened the way for him, as did the death magic Leda had merged with. The two small flaws gave him his chance. *Poor fools.*

Kehksut let fly a blast of death magic that slid in through Samantha and Leda and exploded the nice star-circle they'd created. He laughed in pure enjoyment as witches screamed and bodies flew everywhere. He twined one tendril around Samantha, easiest to hold as she was the darkest, and whisked her high into the air.

Samantha gasped for breath and beat at the rope of magic, and he enjoyed crushing her, slowly, her life essence dying in a wash of death magic and pain.

"*No!*"

The cry ripped from Tain's throat. What turned toward Kehksut was a warrior wrapped in a blaze of white, his bronze sword gleaming like fire. Tain sliced the rope of death magic holding Samantha, and she fell, to be caught by Kalen and Christine.

Then Tain came after Kehksut. Hunter and Darius

started to follow him, but Adrian, their damned leader, halted them with a word.

Idiots. Kehksut blasted Tain with death magic. Tain fell, but climbed quickly to his feet, wiping blood from his face.

"Do you understand nothing?" he shouted up at Kehksut. "You have lost."

"I have won," Kehksut proclaimed. "The life magic is almost gone. I have five Immortals in my power who will hold enough life magic in the world to ensure death magic can still exist. I never meant for you to die, Tain, my sweet, but instead for you to suffer for eternity. With your brothers."

Tain lunged, but Kehksut easily spun him away. "It's your own fault, you know," Kehksut purred. "We used to walk tall and proud, our race ancient and strong. Then Immortals came, and we were treated like second-class citizens, tolerated only because the world needs enough death magic to hold everything in check. We once controlled the world."

Tain held his sword ready, breathing hard. "You can't hold against the goddesses and the Immortals. That's why most of the Old demons are dead."

"The goddesses are not here," Kehksut pointed out. "They don't like to interfere, silly girls."

Tain gave him a fierce look. "They *are* here. In the witches my brothers love."

"Love," Kehksut spat. "You of all of them should have learned that love only makes you weak, blind and stupid."

Tain nodded sagely. "Yes, if you are weak, blind and stupid to begin with. My brothers have discovered love, and through their love, the goddesses manifest."

Kehksut glimpsed movement out of the corner of

his eye. The witch called Amber, who had so cleverly rescued Adrian from the tower room, floated across the dead grass to him, her form glowing.

"The goddess Isis has lent me her powers of earth," Amber said.

"I bring water, infused with the power of Uni," Christine Lachlan said. "Mother goddess of the Etruscan peoples."

Next, the hated werewolf with the gray eyes. "I bring Fire, enhanced by the goddess Sehkmet." She blinked once, and grinned. "This feels cool, and you know, she's really pissed."

The last witch's form—Leda—glimmered toward him, surrounded by fire. "And I have air magic, infused by the mother goddess Kali. And that means—destruction."

She let out a shrill, primitive cry, like one heard only once before, at the dawn of time when Kali and her lover Shiva danced the world into being.

Leda sent a tornadolike wind at Kehksut's head, followed by a stream of fire from Lexi. The earth undulated and opened at his feet when Amber pointed to it, dirt climbing his gigantic legs and sucking him downward. Clouds built into intense proportions above, and rain came down in torrents, infused with powerful water magic.

And the fifth goddess? Kehksut, fighting to regain control, barely saw the half-demon girl rise, her broken body propelled by another force.

"You used my son," she breathed, and fire came from her mouth. "You tortured him until he was lost to me, and he kept crying out. The fifth element is infused in me, Akasha, all and one, with the power of the universe. Death magic, life magic, all is the same to me."

She sent her power at him, the fire-sharp power of Cerridwen, goddess of the darkening moon, made even stronger by the death magic residing in this demon-child. The other four witch-goddesses smote him again, and then came the combined power of the Immortals warriors, their life magic hitting him at the same time.

They confronted him, all five Immortals standing shoulder to shoulder—Adrian, Darius, Kalen, Hunter, Tain—each raising his weapon with a whirl of sound, eyes narrowed in grim concentration. The flame-sword, the cobra, the spear, the blood-bronze sword, Darius with knives and the Bocca demon he called Fury, infused with Darius's magic once more.

Over that came the sudden roar of a mighty dragon, his incandescent fire washing over Kehksut's hide.

"Just *die* already, will you?" Valerian snarled as he swooped past.

Kehksut began to feel a twinge of fear, something he hadn't experienced in a long, long time. Not since fighting his first Immortal, Adrian, long ago in the searing heat of the Egyptian desert. From that day to this he'd determined the Immortals would pay for making him vulnerable.

Tain loved him, Tain would help him. Kehksut had made Tain his slave, treated him as son, as a lover. He'd trained him, made him strong and able to take massive amounts of pain. Pain made one strong, not love.

Kehksut deflated from his true demon form into the shape of a woman, the one Tain liked best. Her hair fell over her lush breasts, but her body was still scaled like a serpent's, Kehksut's magic depleted too much to be able to hold the shape she wanted.

"Tain, honey," she pouted, but her voice was gravelly and wrong. "Don't hurt me. You love me. We'll go somewhere, just the two of us, and we'll be together like before."

She reached out a hand, alarmed to find it a claw. She dragged the hooked nails down Tain's chest, trailing a line of blood, and with the other hand blasted Samantha with another wave of death magic. The light left Samantha's eyes, and she crashed to the ground.

"You know you like it rough," Kehksut said, at last able to insert the sultry note into her voice.

Tain roared and lunged. Kehksut looked down in surprise at the gleaming bronze sword stuck between her breasts, the blade penetrating her black heart.

"Tain, honey . . ." And then there was nothing.

"Get down!" Adrian shouted.

The body of the dead woman morphed back into Kehksut's true form, the huge, ancient demon of the kind that walked the land when Egypt and Mesopotamia were struggling to eke out an existence, humans putting forth their first tendrils of civilization.

Hunter hit the ground, pulling Leda beneath him as the death magic Kehksut had unleashed suddenly imploded. Everything that Kehksut's magic had created—the horde of demons, the pockets of nonreality, the wash of darkness—suddenly tore back into the body of the demon.

Blackness poured into the demon with terrible intensity, the force destroying everything in its path.

Trees uprooted and fell, the ground opened, the wind grew to hurricane strength.

Hunter tried to protect Leda the best he could, shielding her from the worst with his body. He tried to use his magic, but the dense concentration of death magic wouldn't let a flicker through. He couldn't lift his head to see what happened to everyone else, but he felt a warm weight land on his back and a frustrated sound of a man trying to growl—Mukasa, dragging himself over to protect Hunter.

"I love you," Hunter thought he heard Leda say through the noise.

"I love you too, baby."

There was a sharp explosion of sound, complete darkness, and then a pall of utter silence.

Hunter opened his eyes to quiet sunlight. He lay facedown in dappled shade, a cooling breeze wafting across his back. Wind chimes shimmered in the distance, and he was alone. He tried to raise his head, but pain exploded through his skull, and he groaned and fell back to the mud.

After another few minutes he heard footsteps, and then a pair of ugly, old-fashioned hobnailed boots stopped in front of his face. He looked up past stumpy legs and a coarse gray skirt to a formidable bosom over which the ugly countenance of Pearl glared at him.

She had a pair of blue jeans in her hands, which she shook out in front of his face. "You'll be wanting to put these on. I washed and pressed them. And these." She held up a pair of boxer shorts studded with large red flowers.

"You've got to be kidding," he croaked.

"Only thing left in your size at the corner store. Breakfast is ready, and you're not coming into my kitchen in your altogether."

She lay the jeans and gaudy shorts on a clean patch of grass, then turned around and marched back to the house.

Hunter finally turned his head—worth the pain to not have to see those godawful boxers. He saw Leda sitting not ten feet from him, clad in jeans and tank top, her knees drawn up to her chin. Mukasa lay next to her, returned somehow to his lion form, watching Hunter with accusing eyes.

Leda's smile was like the sun breaking through a cloudy day. The most beautiful thing he'd seen in his life.

He pressed his hand to the back of his neck. "Hey, darling. What hit me?"

"A tree."

He tried to laugh, and broke off with a groan. "I believe it."

She came to him and helped him sit up. While he waited for the world to stop spinning, he thought it a very good idea to put his arms around her and rest his head on her shoulder. "Mukasa is a lion again, I see," he murmured.

"Adrian did that. He reversed the spell. The poor guy was miserable as a human."

Hunter snorted, remembering the anguish in the man-lion's golden eyes when he realized he was a lion no more. Mukasa rumbled slightly under his breath, his nose wrinkling.

Hunter's amusement deserted him as he thought over the dark battle they'd just fought. "Kehksut is really dead, isn't he?" he asked. "I think I remember Tain killing him."

"You do." Leda's smile dimmed. "Scary stuff."

"And you flying around, letting loose destructo-magic. Very sexy."

"A gift from your mom."

"Well, she knew you already had a DVD player."

The smile returned. "Stop it."

He slanted her a wicked grin—as much as he could through the pain in his head. "Where is every-one?"

"In the house. Or the hospital. Depending on how bad things were. Pearl said you'd be fine and we shouldn't try to move you." She paused. "All right, what she really said was that she didn't fancy lugging your carcass over her shoulder, and she was the only one strong enough to do any lugging. So she left you to sleep it off."

"What a sweetheart. Where does Kalen find these people?"

"She's devoted to him."

"Figures. I am *not* wearing those shorts."

"I bet you'd be cute in them."

He sent her an evil look and reached for the jeans. It took him several tries to stand up, and Leda had to assist him to his feet. With her arms around him, her sweet body pressed to his, he wanted to forget all about the stupid shorts, and the jeans, and the people waiting inside for them, and the demon. He just wanted her.

Leda gently broke the embrace and waited while he slid the jeans over his bare buttocks. He worked the zipper up and struggled to close the button that had been loose before.

"Washed and pressed," he grumbled. "Is this Kalen's idea of a joke?"

He started to put his arm around her to walk back to the house, but she stepped in front of him, her eyes grave.

"What?" he asked. "You have bad news, don't you? Give it to me straight."

Leda rested her hands on his biceps, the pads of her thumbs stroking his skin. "Tain got a huge dose of death magic when he killed Kehksut. At first he seemed fine and helped heal some of us, but then he collapsed. Adrian's with him."

Hunter turned abruptly, catching her hand in his, and strode back toward the house. Behind them on the green, the red and white boxer shorts rippled faintly on the breeze.

Inside the house they found chaos. Leda and Hunter moved through a kitchen filled with brownies washing and stacking dishes, Pearl cooking like a madwoman, Valerian trying to get around the brownies to get himself coffee. A refreshed-looking Mac with his arm in a sling dug into a stack of very American pancakes and syrup.

"Good grub," he said around a sticky mouthful. "I see you made it, Hunter."

"Where's Tain?"

Mac pointed to the ceiling with his fork. "Upstairs in Amber's bedroom. Your brothers are with him."

"He's in a bad way," Pearl said, thumping a bowl to the counter. "But he's Immortal, inn't he?"

Even so, Pearl looked worried. So did Mac and Valerian. Hunter left the kitchen in long strides, and

Leda after him. They went up to a large, sunny bedroom now crowded with Immortals and witches.

They had dressed, Darius with his duster wrapped around him, Kalen large and handsome in a tartan kilt, Adrian in sleeveless shirt and jeans. Amber, Lexi and Christine each stayed close to her Immortal, but Samantha was notably absent.

Tain lay on the bed, covered in blankets, eyes closed in a waxen face. His body shivered, but he was clearly unconscious. Hunter crossed to him and touched his forehead.

"He's out cold," Darius said. "He seemed fine, then suddenly went down."

"He tried to help us all," Leda said softly. "He spent so much of his magic healing everyone that he didn't have anything left for himself."

Hunter brushed his fingers over Tain's tattoo, stark and blue-black on his cheek. "Did you try pooling your magic?"

Adrian nodded. "He's too far gone. Kehksut dosed him good."

"One last thing to remember him by, I guess," Hunter muttered, rubbing the back of his aching neck. "Damn demons."

"I'm not going to lose him now," Adrian said stubbornly. "Not after all I went through to find him."

"Ravenscroft," Darius said. "That's the only place that will heal him."

Hunter swung around, his face clouded. "So why is he still here?"

Kalen broke in, his voice deep and rumbling. "We were waiting for you."

"For what? To draw straws over who gets to take him?"

Adrian shook his head. "We all have to go." Leda saw Amber quietly reach for Adrian's hand.

"Why?" Hunter demanded.

"The goddesses want us," Adrian said. "Isis came to me and told me we all had to go. Just us."

Hunter folded his arms, muscles playing. "Screw that. We'll answer their summons, and they'll have some new, earth-shattering task they want us to do. Too bad that we have our own lives." He glanced at Leda. "I plan to keep busy for a long, long time."

"Then Tain stays like this." Adrian gestured to the bed.

"We can open the way and shove him through," Hunter growled.

Leda broke in. "Do we get a say? Or have you decided for us?"

The Immortals exchanged uncomfortable glances. Amber smiled at Leda. "Oh, we argued about it already."

"And?" Leda asked her.

"They're going." She exchanged looks with Lexi and Christine, who both nodded.

Hunter scowled. "Let the goddesses do their own dirty work. They haven't exactly always been there when we need them."

Leda threaded her fingers through his and rubbed the inside of his wrist. She liked touching him, the strong warrior who'd been through so much. The scars on his skin reminded her what he'd suffered, lines of pain.

"Go, Hunter."

Hunter looked down at her, his green eyes hard. "And if they contrive it so we can't come back?"

She swallowed, hating to think of that. "I had a pretty uneventful life before you came into it," she said, giving him a faint smile. "It was quiet, even. Maybe I could learn to live with that again."

Hunter's gaze on her was intense, for her and her alone. "I need you, Leda. *I* don't want to go back to what it was like before I met you."

"Then find out what the goddesses want and insist on returning," Leda said. "I'll wait."

Hunter growled something under his breath, like a predator rumbling annoyance. He swept his brothers a glance. "All right. I'll go with you. But first I say good-bye to Leda."

Adrian nodded, clasping Amber's fingers tightly. "I didn't think you'd have it any other way."

Chapter Twenty-six

Hunter didn't bother trying to find the right room. He pulled Leda into the nearest bedroom and went down on the mattress, Leda beneath him.

He'd survived death magic and darkness and pain and torture, and he wanted to forget, to bury himself in her and revel in the taste and scent of her. He skimmed her shirt from her body and took the hot point of his nipple into his mouth. Her breast tasted salty and warm, and she moved underneath him, wriggling against his rock-hard erection.

He sensed the death magic in her again, cloying and tainting her beautiful aura. She'd been willing to expose herself to it, knowing what it would do to her. She'd made the sacrifice to find and save him, and now she was willing for him to go find out what the goddesses wanted, even with the chance that they'd never be together again.

She was a sweet, wonderful woman, and he blessed whatever magic or luck had dropped him at her feet. He opened her mouth with his kisses while he unbuttoned her jeans and dipped his fingers inside to find her warm wetness.

"Are you ready for me?" he whispered.

"I've been ready." She traced his shoulders and the curve of his spine. "Why do you think I was sitting there waiting for you to wake up?"

"I'll have to take the death magic out of you again." He wagged a playful finger in her face. "Promise me you won't go dabbling again. I might not be here to fix it next time."

She nipped at his fingertip. "I promise."

She looked so contrite, her lashes coyly shielding the blue of her eyes, that his erection stiffened even more.

"You are so going to pay for being so cute," he growled.

"Being cute is a crime?"

"It is after I was terrified I'd lose you. Come here." He wrapped his arms around her and kissed her for a long time.

They undressed each other, pushing their jeans to the floor, Leda's bra and shirt landing beside them. Hunter splayed his hand across her thighs, opening her, and slid his aching tip inside her.

"An Immortal cock," Leda murmured. "It goes on forever."

"Smart-ass." He pressed inside her, deeper, deeper, loving how her tight sheath squeezed closed on him. She was so damn wet and tight, the curls around her opening tickling him, an erotic stimulus.

He'd never get enough of her. He would only be able to have her for a short time, a human life span, but he would love her as much as he possibly could. He'd do as she asked and listen to the goddesses, but they could find other flunkies to save the world this time. Hunter would spend the next crisis buried inside Leda.

He slid partway out and back in, rocking his hips against hers, enjoying the half moan of pleasure she made. Her eyes were half closed, gleaming slits of blue. Her golden hair curled across her body, and he wrapped the silken strands around his hand.

"Now," he said. "About that pesky death magic."

She lifted her hips, ready to align herself with him before he even instructed her to. Lights formed down their bodies, from white to scarlet, the chakras opening and aligning. He felt the last, red and hot where they joined, and he lost himself in the pleasure of it.

The death magic was easier to pull out of her than before, perhaps because she trusted him now. The first time they'd made love, she'd been hesitant, uncertain, but now she twined her legs around him and gave him her entire body, letting him reach down into her soul.

She moaned and lifted to him, her pleasure deep and intense. Hunter kissed her hot mouth; then the darkness came away from her, sticky and foul, to dissolve in Hunter's hands like nightmares fleeing the dawn.

Just after sundown, Hunter joined his brothers in the room where Tain lay. The evening felt peaceful and cool, no longer containing the horrors of the growing dark. He heard laughter downstairs as Mai joked with Mac, and the deep tones of Ricco, who was just waking.

The Immortals had brought their weapons, necessary if they wanted to open the way to Ravenscroft themselves. Hunter had made love to Leda twice more after removing the death magic from her; the last time, the two of them crashed to the bed in exhaustion, to drowse in the afternoon heat.

When he'd risen to find his brothers again, Leda had put her arms around him and given him a sleepy kiss, but she hadn't clung, hadn't begged him not to go.

His brothers' ladies hadn't come to see them off either. Each brother looked grim and unhappy as he took a position around Tain's bed.

The one person who did walk in the door before they left was Samantha. She had bandages on one arm and angry red contusions on her face.

"Amber told me what you were going to do," she said, studying each Immortal in turn. "Will this save him?"

"It's his best chance," Adrian said.

Samantha's gaze flicked to Tain and rested there for a time. "I was dying after that battle," she said in a quiet voice. "His magic kept me from slipping away altogether. When he wakes up"—she broke off as though groping for words—"tell him thanks."

Adrian gave her a nod. She looked back at them a moment longer, knowing they didn't like the fact that she was demon-get, then turned and went quickly out of the room.

"Brave girl," Hunter commented. "If more demons were like her, they wouldn't be so bad."

"Can we get on with this?" Darius said, impatience in every part of him.

Hunter raised his sword, which burst into fierce flame. "Right away. Wouldn't want to keep you from Sekhmet's lectures too long."

"You were more fun when you were unconscious," Darius shot back.

Kalen lifted his spear, whose tip began to glow. "Now I remember why I avoid you all."

"Because he likes to play with his great big spear all by himself," Hunter suggested.

Adrian brought his sword up, giving the other three a withering glance. Then they brought their weapons together. A crackling white light appeared at the points of them, the air burst open, and they fell with Tain into the fragrant green fields of Ravenscroft.

"What can we do?" Lexi asked, pacing the kitchen. "I feel so ineffectual here just *waiting.*"

Leda understood. It had been two days since the Immortals disappeared back to Ravenscroft, and Lexi in particular had found the interval jarring. Christine had filled the time with her painting, but by the way she scowled at the canvas, Leda suspected it wasn't going well.

"You can stay out of my kitchen, for one thing," Pearl growled. "How I can fix a meal with four moping women underfoot is beyond my ken."

They all exchanged a glance, then trooped out the back door and down the short hill to the grove. Mukasa was sleeping in the shade, liking the place now that it had gone back to normal. Magic did linger there, a crackle of life magic every once in a while that made a bough flourish, or a strain of music ripple— probably left over from Mac's spell.

The four of them decided to do a circle, to calm their nerves if nothing else. Amber traced a circle in the earth, and Lexi sent flickers of flame into the air at the four corners of the circle, calling the element of fire.

Leda loved working with other witches who not only had great gifts of magic but also true spirituality. Life magic filled the circle subtly and softly, not the overwhelming fire-heat of Immortals' magic but the soothing and bolstering calm of connection with the Goddess.

The four witches knelt, each at their point of the compass, Amber taking earth and north, Leda east for air, Lexi south for fire, and Christine west for water. They each spoke a prayer to the Goddess, and then said one together.

Nothing dramatic happened, but Leda felt the comfort of the Goddess in the magic of the circle. The cradling strength in the circle was incredible, love and magic and caring all wrapped together.

Residue from the spell that the Immortals had woven to save Tain lingered in the grove as well. In her meditation, Leda could feel Hunter's love for his brothers embedded here, and the love he'd extended to her.

It was difficult for him to love, she'd come to understand. He'd lost too much and suffered too much loneliness to give love easily, and yet he helped everyone he met. A giving man who wouldn't believe her if she told him how giving he was.

The quietness of the grove bound the witches together—Amber and her no-nonsense connection to earth. Christine and the amazing depth of her water magic, an artistry that made her aura a splendid blue. Lexi, her aura fiery and sparkling, like her personality. Leda sensed the threads of Amber's magic next, golden and white, serene in the knowledge of Adrian's love.

A silver light, the witches' magic joined, flowed around them. It wove around Leda's body, a loving caress. It made a sound like shimmering wind chimes and was gone.

The witches opened their eyes and exhaled. "Did you feel that?" Amber asked. "It was wonderful."

Mukasa, who had been dozing, suddenly came alert. He raised his head, then climbed to his feet, facing the center of the grove, growling. The silver light arced to the middle of the clearing and exploded into blue and white, throwing the witches backward. Only Mukasa remained on his feet, his golden eyes animated.

Four warriors burst out of the light, Adrian, Darius, Kalen and Hunter, weapons aloft, demigod magic swirling around them like a whirlwind. The air crackled and hummed, dancing snakes of electricity sizzling around the clearing. Hunter's sword flamed as he brought it down, white light glowing around him, his eyes flashing green as they had when Kali had infused him with power.

That power snaked around Leda and yanked her to him. She landed against his side, white light engulfing her, and his strong, muscular arms drew her in. She began laughing and crying, incoherent in her joy to see him again. He held her close, the flame of his sword dying off, and laid his cheek against her hair.

"Told you I wouldn't leave you forever."

She hugged him hard, dimly aware of the other couples doing the same. "Thank you for coming back," she whispered. She clung to him a little while longer, then raised her head. "Where's Tain? Did he stay? Was he healed?"

"One thing at a time—" Hunter began; then his words were cut off by another explosion of sound and light. Tain walked through the slit, his sword in front of him, upright and striding, his face grim.

Once he stood with his feet firmly on the earth, the

crack closed, and the light dissolved. Snakes of power wound through the clearing, sparkling and hissing, and then died in tiny pops.

"He's fine," Hunter said, grabbing Leda's hand. The glow around him had vanished, his eyes returning to normal. "We're leaving. Pack some bags—or don't bother. We'll get what we need on the way."

She stared at him, mystified. "Why? Where are we going?"

"Anywhere, darling. Anywhere we want."

"What does that mean?"

Hunter caught her in his arms and swung her around, squeezing her tight, tight. "No more Calling spell, no more doing the goddesses' bidding, just hanging out with my girl."

Leda tried to catch her breath and looked at Adrian for enlightenment. He had his arm around Amber, his dark eyes holding a mixture of mirth and hope. "The goddesses have released us from our duty," he said. "After centuries righting the world's wrongs we, in essence, get to take a vacation."

Kalen broke in, his warm voice smooth but animated. "To have our own lives, with family."

Hunter grinned down at Leda. "To carry on the race of Immortals, which means no more being loners." He kissed her. "So I figure you and I can go back to your island and spend some time in the sun. The sea and the sand, not much in the way of clothes."

Leda looked past him at Tain, who remained a little apart from the others, the sun dappling his red hair. "Tain as well?"

Tain heard her. "I've been released from my obligations, but I won't be doing any settling down soon, I think."

"You're always welcome here," Adrian said. "Any-where I am. I looked for you for a long time, I don't want to lose you again."

"I appreciate it." Tain's smile was sad, his voice a rich timbre with a faint Welsh lilt. "But there is much I need to do, much I need to make up for."

Adrian gave him a grave look. "What Kehksut made you become, that wasn't your fault."

Tain shook his head. "It was, somewhat. Kehksut wove a spell around me, and I couldn't break it. After a while I didn't want to. It was easier to give in." His gaze went dark with memories. "I shouldn't have given in."

Hunter's eyes flickered, and Leda knew he was re-membering his own pain at Kehksut's hands. "I for one don't blame you," Hunter told him. "Easier to take something that awful if you make believe you like it."

Tain looked away, across the green, sun-drenched grove. "I don't understand a lot of what happened to me, but I know I caused so much destruction. I did it, not Kehksut, not the demons. *Me.*"

The brothers glanced at each other but said nothing, men happier with silence than declarations.

"So I'll be going." Tain smiled, his handsome face for just a moment taking on the devastating Immortal sinfulness with which he must have dazzled women for centuries. He gave Amber a graceful, courtly bow. "Thank you for your hospitality."

"Our home is open to you anytime," Amber said.

"Ours too," Darius put in. "Wherever it might be."

Kalen made a conceding gesture. "My castle is yours," he said.

All eyes turned expectantly to Hunter.

"What?" Hunter asked. "I want to be alone with my lady while I can, without the lot of you interrupting. Besides, Tain is right. He doesn't need his concerned older brothers constantly watching him, waiting for him to become a demon-obsessed slave again. He needs time, not mother hens."

Tain laughed, sounding like his normal self from centuries past. "It's all right, Hunter. I won't bother you."

"Well," Hunter said, "if you need a place to crash, the island's nice and isolated. That is, except for the Undines. And Leda's animals. And that assistant of hers who likes to come blundering in."

"Sounds like paradise," Tain said dryly. "Thank you. But I need to go my own way for a while. I want to get reacquainted with myself, find out what happened in the world all those years I was imprisoned. Starting now."

Before the others could say another word, he turned on his heel, his sword sheathed on his back, and strode across the yard. His dark jeans and black coat blended into the shadows a moment, a beam of sunshine shone on his impossibly red hair, and then he was gone.

Adrian took a step after him, then stopped, resigned.

"Let him go," Hunter said. "He'll be all right."

"Maybe he will."

Hunter grinned. "Of course. He's an Immortal. And maybe he'll find himself a good witch and settle down too." He pulled Leda close and pressed a kiss to the top of her head. "We can't have gotten all the luck."

CHAPTER TWENTY-SEVEN

"It's sad to say good-bye," Leda said a week later. "I was just getting to know everyone."

"Sad?" Hunter answered. They were in Los Angeles packing the boat, readying it and Mukasa to return to Leda's island. Despite Hunter's wish to run off as soon as he'd returned from Ravenscroft, Leda had persuaded him that they needed to take their time, pack, provision themselves and take leave of the others.

Hunter continued, "To go back to your tropical island, with the sun and sand and you, and no one bothering us? Can't say that I'm sad."

Leda paused to watch Hunter's body in action as he planted his strong bare feet on the deck and worked to untie the sails.

"How long will we—will you—stay on the island?"

He sent her a grin, but his eyes were unreadable. "Until you vote me off."

He turned his back and leaned over to grab something on the deck, giving her a nice view of his very fine buttocks. Hunter was a master at turning on

the charm, distracting her with sexiness. Kali and
the other goddesses had given him respite to be
with Leda, but they'd said nothing about forever,
nothing about Leda having nothing but her mortal
life span.

Hunter and Leda had said their good-byes to the
others before boarding a plane for L.A. and the marina. Septimus had flown up on his private jet not long
after Kehksut had been defeated, bringing Kelly with
him. He and Ricco had instantly gone into "executive-
meeting mode," sitting in Amber's kitchen all night
talking plans and takeovers and conducting cell-phone
conversations with who-knew-who.

Now that the big bad undead was gone, Ricco had
said, the vampires would reorganize. Septimus had
decided who he wanted to be at the top of this
organization—himself—and he and Ricco had formed
a loose partnership.

Kelly and Mai had compared notes and discovered
that they both loved vampires, fine clothes, and shoes,
and both wanted to write a movie, so they'd decided
to write one together.

"We need something to keep us busy while these
two sleep during the day and plot for vampire domi-
nation at night," Mai had said.

Pearl only just tolerated vampires in the kitchen—as
long as they were gone when she came in to make
breakfast in the morning. Adrian said Septimus would
control vampires better than anyone, but Pearl said
that didn't make her like them in her kitchen any more
than necessary.

Pearl had decided to stay on with Amber and
Adrian until they were settled. Adrian had moved in
permanently, and as soon as Septimus could arrange

it, he'd make a legal identity for Adrian to please paper-pushers, and he and Amber would marry.

"I like the idea," Kalen had said, and revealed his and Christine's plans to marry too.

Kalen and Christine were leaving for Scotland to begin restoring artwork, safe now, to museums and collections from which Kalen had liberated them for protection. Christine had been painting almost every minute since the fall of Kehksut, and she presented Leda and Hunter, Amber and Adrian, and Lexi and Darius lovely watercolors before she and Kalen departed to catch their flight.

Leda had expressed delight—the painting flowed with vibrant colors and a magic of its own. Kalen, she could see, admired and was proud of Christine's ability. He said not a word, but his eyes spoke volumes.

Lexi and Darius too were departing, not for a specific destination—though Manhattan first—but to see the world. "There will be someone out there who needs protecting," Darius had said. He'd slid his hand to Lexi's abdomen, a loving move. "Including our own."

Amber had congratulated Lexi with warm hugs and confessed, with a blush, her own pregnancy. Christine had announced hers as well, although Leda, still not sure, had kept her silence.

"Just what the world needs," Valerian had said with a booming laugh. "More pesky Immortals."

"I think it's exactly what we need," Amber had said, leaning back into Adrian's embrace.

Valerian had gone with Sabina to her family's house, helping them regroup after the battle. The shape-shifter pair were firmly a couple now, bantering with each other, both giving as good as they got.

Mac had decided not to travel back to Scotland

with Kalen and Christine, although he would eventually return to his studio in London to record another collection.

"Need to wander a bit," he'd said. "Hitch my way around the country, collect some more tunes. Don't want Manannán getting stale."

"Can't have anything to do with avoiding your mum, could it?" Christine had asked teasingly.

Mac's face darkened. "Mebbe."

He'd dispensed kisses, hugs and firm handshakes all around and departed on foot, the guitar on his back, earbuds in his ears. Leda had heard his cell phone go off as he reached the bottom of the driveway, and his irritated Scottish voice as he answered. *"What is it naaow?"*

Samantha had flown back to Los Angeles with Leda and Hunter and Mukasa, eager to see her mother again, even if she knew she'd have to include her father in the reunion. She seemed more accepting now than she had before.

Samantha had remained strangely subdued when Leda had told her that Tain had gone off alone to make his peace with the world. She'd nodded, face strained. "I'd hoped he'd at least say good-bye."

Leda could think of no response. She remembered the sparks she'd sensed between Samantha and Tain during the battle, but perhaps Tain wasn't ready to pursue sparks yet.

"Stay in touch," Leda had said when they parted, and hugged her.

Samantha had managed a tired smile. "I will. I might need to come sunbathe on your island after all this."

"You're always welcome," Leda had said.

"By you, maybe," Samantha had said. "Not necessarily by Immortals."

"We'll work on that."

Samantha had not looked convinced.

Now as Leda's sailboat pulled away from the marina in Los Angeles, Leda at the wheel, she was both sad and excited. Sad to leave her new friends, but excited at the prospect of sailing across the ocean, just herself and Hunter, with Mukasa lolling on the upper deck.

She steered while Hunter worked the lines and the sails, guiding the boat through the bay and out to open sea. Mukasa sat up, ready to go, earning startled looks from passing boats. The sun was high, the wind brisk, the darkness gone. People were coming out to enjoy life again, as it should be.

The journey to the island was fairly uneventful, except for Leda getting a mild sunburn. Taro greeted them enthusiastically, the little bear as robust and happy as he'd ever been. Not many days later, Japanese wildlife specialists arrived in their ship to transport Taro to his new home in Hokkaido. Leda bade him a tearful farewell, but the bear seemed to know he was going back where he belonged and was looking forward to it.

Hunter scratched behind Taro's ears and said, "Be well, my friend."

Taro rumbled softly at him, then scampered into the pen, startling the wildlife researchers who'd come armed with tranquilizer darts and slings for transporting hesitant creatures. Leda waved good-bye until the boat disappeared into the mist, Mukasa beside her.

Hunter was quiet and scarce the rest of the day, and before they had dinner, Leda glimpsed him at the base of the cliff path speaking to the Undine.

Leda hurried outside, hoping to talk to the water

spirit herself. She had been looking for Dyanne since returning to the island, but never had been able to catch a glimpse of her or any of her people. Even now, as she approached them, Dyanne glided back into the shadows, vanishing into a pocket of mist.

Leda expressed her disappointment when Hunter reached her. "I'd hope to speak to her, to thank her and her people for taking care of Taro."

Hunter twined his fingers through hers as they walked back to the house. "Their kind is shy with humans, only contacting them when the need is great. I don't count, I'm not human."

He grinned when he said it, but he looked after the Undine as though not wanting to meet Leda's eyes.

"Hunter," she said. "We need to talk."

He slid his arm around her waist. "You know, when a woman says that, she strikes fear into a man's heart." He pulled her to a halt and pressed a kiss to her hair. "It's a beautiful night. I'd rather do something besides talk."

"Hunter."

Leda stopped. Hunter circled in front of her, his large hands on her waist. "Talking changes nothing."

"I have to know," she said. "How long do we get this free-for-all? You are immortal, and perhaps our children will be, but I'm not and you know we can't have forever. Will you walk out of my life one day? I know how you think, Hunter—you'll consider it better that you simply disappear."

His eyes were bleak. "Won't it be?"

"I don't think so. And I certainly don't want to live day to day wondering when you'll decide the time is up." She drew a breath that hurt her. "So maybe you should go now and get it over with."

His hands stilled. "No."

"Why not? We might as well break our hearts now as later. Later we will have so much more to lose."

He growled. "I want—I *need*—time with you. You are the only one, after all these years, who I can heal with. The only one. I'm not going to throw that away."

Her eyes filled. "I heal you, and then what?"

He slid his hands to her hips, thumbs moving in little circles on her hipbones. "Leda, I can't ever explain what you mean to me. I'm not the Immortal who can pour out his soul into art or heal with his touch. I think I have the affinity to animals because they don't talk, not in words anyway. This is the part I'm bad at."

"You don't have to make speeches. That's not what I want."

"Then what do you want? I can't explain—"

She closed the space between them, putting his hard body against her shaking one. "I just want you, Hunter. I want you in my life—for always."

He skimmed back a lock of her hair. "Leda, my love, you are going to break my heart in the worst way."

Leda opened her mouth to answer, but suddenly Hunter pulled her to him and held her tight, burying his face in the curve of her neck. Leda hugged him back, marveling that she'd made this amazingly strong man cry.

They made love in her bed in the airy white room, moonlight and tropical breezes pouring through the windows. Hunter was uncharacteristically silent, loving her with a tenderness that surpassed all he'd done before. Later he lay beside her, touching her with light fingers, tracing her breasts, resting his warm hand across her abdomen.

"I love you," he whispered.

She turned her head, taking in his troubled expression, the line between his brows. She touched the crease in his forehead. "Is that so bad?"

"I never thought I'd love anyone again. It hurt so much the first time."

"The same thing happened to me. But I'm willing to try."

"I'll try if you will." He cupped her face. "Only for you, Leda."

She kissed him for answer. Their lovemaking after that was more intense and left her exhausted. She slid easily into sleep and dreamed that the goddess Kali danced on her beach in the wind for the joy of it, her hair writhing around her like flames.

Kali whirled and whirled and suddenly snaked around Leda where she stood motionless. The moonlight was so bright everything stood out in stark black and silver, sharp-edged and clear.

"You love my son," Kali declared in her hissing whisper.

"I do." Leda felt love flood her body. "I do."

"Then I will give you a gift."

Kali brushed long fingers across Leda's abdomen, and Leda flinched at the searing trail of her touch.

"When your child is born," Kali said, "go to Ravenscroft and live there a year and a day of your time. Then you and your son will be Immortal, and you will be the mate of Hunter until the world dies and the Immortals are needed no more."

"Thank you," Leda said, heartfelt. "Why didn't

you . . . With Hunter's first wife, why didn't you make her immortal? Or her children? You could have spared him that grief."

Flames sprang around Kali's face, reminding Leda that this was the goddess of destruction.

"It was not written," Kali hissed. "He needed to join with Tain and destroy the evil. If he had not met you, he would not have joined with them, and all would have been lost."

The sibilants in her voice rang out across the sea.

"Oh," Leda said. "I think I would have fallen in love with him regardless, whether the world needed saving or not."

"Obviously." Kali made another strange hissing noise that Leda realized was laughter. "Take care of my son. And grandson."

She whirled again, stirring up a choking dust devil of sand, and was gone. Leda coughed, then awoke in her bedroom alone, the moon still high.

Leda threw back the sheets, climbed out of bed and went to the window. Outside, all was still but for the wind sighing in the palms and the soothing rush of the ocean. The beach was lit almost as brightly as it had been in her dream, the pale light touching Mukasa as he lay, statuelike, and watched Hunter.

Hunter, clad only in his jeans, stood above the line of wet sand on the beach, going through his sword exercises. The long blade of his serpentine sword whistled, his muscles working in precision as he silently and deliberately went through his routine.

A beautiful man, son of the wild goddess Kali and a barbarian slave, from whom Hunter must have come by his good-natured grin, the twinkle in his eyes, the gentleness beneath his power. A demigod, lonely and vulnerable, yet magical beyond anything the world had seen.

Leda pulled on shorts and tank top and walked out of the house barefoot. She stopped near Mukasa to watch Hunter continue with his exercises, loving the perfection of his body, the lithe grace with which he moved.

Hunter finished the routine with a quiet flourish. He slid the sword into the scabbard he picked up from the sand, bowed once to the sea, then turned around. He spied Leda watching, and the serious warrior god gave place to the mischievous lover.

"I didn't mean to wake you," he said as she came to him. He took her hand and pressed her palm to the bulge waiting behind his zipper. "But I'm starting to be glad I did."

"You didn't wake me. I had a dream."

She told him about Kali's visit. She knew it had been a true visit and not a dream, as the goddesses' visit to her in Amber's house hadn't been a real dream but a necessary message.

The story stunned him. "She offered you that?"

"I have to stay in Ravenscroft a year and a day after our son is born. I think she added that caveat so I could have time to think about it, so I'd understand what being an Immortal really means."

Hunter shook his head in amazement. "She really likes you."

"She knows you need me. That we need each other."

"No, I mean she really likes you. She told me."

Leda raised her brows, skeptical. "When was this?"

"She came to me when I walked out here to practice. She said, *Good choice, Hunter. I like that Leda.*"

"Just like that? No cryptic message?"

"Just like that." He grinned. "Helps to have her on your side. I wouldn't want Kali as a mother-in-law."

"Thanks, Hunter, don't scare me."

He laid his sword on the sand and gathered her against him. "I'm looking forward to the family reunions. My Immortal brothers, their wives, their children, the goddesses cooing at their grandchildren. Beats centuries of being alone."

"You aren't alone anymore."

"I know. I love it." He kissed her. "I love you."

Leda kissed him back, savoring his magic, his warmth, the essence of Hunter. The kiss turned suggestive, reminding her he had enough stamina to make love to her all night. Every night.

She felt Mukasa's dry nose thrust under her palm, and she broke away, laughing.

"We'll take him to Ravenscroft too," Hunter said. "There are beaches where he can run for miles and miles—no cages, no chains, no tranquilizer guns. Think he'd like that?"

Mukasa growled in pleasure and butted his head against Hunter, nearly knocking him over. Hunter ran his hands through Mukasa's mane, rubbing hard, and the lion rumbled in delight.

"Besides," Hunter said to Leda, a roguish twinkle in his green eyes. "Our little Immortal son will need a friend."